Gillian White is a former journalist who comes from Liverpool and now lives in Devon, with her husband and two dogs. She has written sixteen novels, several of which have been successfully adapted for television, and *The Sleeper* has recently been shown on BBC television with an all-star cast.

www.**booksattransworld**.co.uk

Veil of Darkness

'Compelling novel of suspense' *Good Housekeeping*
'Simply spine-tingling' *Woman & Home*

The Witch's Cradle

'Ten out of ten for topicality . . . strong narrative keeps the pages turning to the end where the reader is left guiltily wondering about TV intrusion and the viewer's complicity in it' *Home and Country*

'This fast-paced tale explores the lengths to which people go to be loved, as well as the ruthlessness of the media when transforming real life into drama'
Good Housekeeping

'A gripping read which will make you think twice about the influence and motives of TV media'
Shine

Night Visitor

'A sinister thriller' *Express*

'*Marrying The Mistress* meets *Misery*' *Mirror*

REFUGE

Gillian White

CORGI BOOKS

REFUGE ·
A CORGI BOOK : 0 552 14886 5

Originally published in Great Britain by Bantam Press,
a division of Transworld Publishers

PRINTING HISTORY
Bantam Press edition published 2002
Corgi edition published 2003

1 3 5 7 9 10 8 6 4 2

Set in 11/12pt Times by
Falcon Oast Graphic Art Ltd.

Corgi Books are published by Transworld Publishers,
61–63 Uxbridge Road, London W5 5SA,
a division of The Random House Group Ltd,
in Australia by Random House Australia (Pty) Ltd,
20 Alfred Street, Milsons Point, Sydney, NSW 2061, Australia,
in New Zealand by Random House New Zealand Ltd,
18 Poland Road, Glenfield, Auckland 10, New Zealand
and in South Africa by Random House (Pty) Ltd,
Endulini, 5a Jubilee Road, Parktown 2193, South Africa.

Printed and bound in Great Britain by
Cox & Wyman Ltd, Reading, Berkshire.

For Sam Bamforth and Molly May White –
a welcome to the world
to two extraordinarily special people

ONE

Immediately she knew who had burned the baby. Eight weeks old. A newborn baby. She knew this with her eyes closed. She had no need to stare at the fuzzy image created by the surveillance cameras two shops along from Clinton Cards, at the group of boys who tore off down the High Street darting in between the buses, the only vehicles allowed in this pedestrianized precinct.

You know what it's like when you're swimming in the sea and a huge wave crashes over you and drags you onto the shingle and you have time to think this is it – you're dying? Well, that's what Shelley felt when she saw her son on the news. And while the knowledge came drowning her she still had a moment to wonder at the way one's mind goes on silly trips at life-changing moments like this – her brain, like a vulture picking at offal, kept beating round the question: where the hell has that bloody kid left his blue jacket this time?

Shelley slammed her mind shut to the rest of the story. Just one or two words leaped out like wolves, words like paraffin, intensive care and a silver Zippo with a lion engraving which was found at the scene by a passer-by and handed in to the law. Motionless now in her state of shock, she drew on her cigarette for company and comfort. From upstairs she heard her own baby cry. Joey shared a room with Julie. He'd most likely wake up in a minute and come down bleary-eyed, ruffled with sleep, a child-killer and all innocence.

Later Shelley had time to consider whether she was the only mother whose second most terrible fear – after the threat of her child being hurt – was that one day he might hurt someone else. It wasn't because he was naturally savage; she just couldn't help her imagination taking her down that road. Joey had the background all right. His qualifications were impressive. In spite of Shelley's love for him, which ranged from the despairing to the proudest of all life's moments, the poor little sod had negative equity where life expectations were concerned. Too many dads, too many homes, too many schools, too many failures. The normal, the well-adjusted, don't go round burning babies to death.

Burning babies to death.

Burning babies just eight weeks old.

Shelley banged her mind closed to that. There was no scream loud enough for release so she pulled up the drawbridge instead; she called up her defences.

And if Shelley knew who'd committed the crime, how long before the law came to her door? How long before his teachers caught on, the neighbours or the others involved? And then they would take away her boy and expose him to the communal rage reserved for paedophiles and serial rapists. The film was blurred. Outlines only. She'd known it was Joey because of his walk. They hadn't filmed the deed itself, the pavement outside Clinton Cards wasn't covered by the cameras; no, they'd only got pictures of the gang before the burning and afterwards.

She stood up, crossed the room and moved the curtain. Outside was quite dark. No-one there. Not yet.

But the baby. The baby is dead. The baby died of shock.

They had called her names when she was little; she'd worn specs to correct a squint and their name-calling had broken her heart. It had ruined her childhood. '*Specky Four-Eyes. Specky Four-Eyes.*' Now Shelley's thoughts were of killing crowds, rocking police vans and courtroom sieges. The bullies who taunted her as a child were pussy cats compared with an outraged public.

Women with prams.

Thugs with studs.

Lonely grannies with tongues sharp as knitting needles.

She had no intention of giving her eldest child up to all that. If he lied she would back him with all the power in her wiry body but she knew in her heart that kids of that age don't keep their gobs shut for long. They said they thought there were five involved. Five . . . she knew they'd all be under twelve. One of the lads would squeal and confessions would spread like some childhood infection and by then the press would be on the trail. Dawn raids. Cameras and crowds. Dear God, please make this a nightmare. Let me wake up from this hell in a minute, go upstairs to check the kids, see Joey asleep like an angel and smile and go down again, make a coffee, watch telly and tell someone about the dream first thing in the morning and shudder.

For the love of God, how could her Joey, eleven years old, come home, have his pizza, watch *A Question of Sport* with the others and then go to bed and sleep? *How the hell could Joey do that knowing what he had done?* Had the six o'clock news led with the story while her son was knocking a ball around outside, maybe with his fellow culprits, while she fussed about in the kitchen smacking Jason for filching Wotsits?

They said it had happened that afternoon. Shelley dug round for reliable memories. She must get it right because of the pigs but that meant she'd have to square it with Joey. He had probably skived off school again with Marcus and Shane Lessing and crew. He'd demanded two quid to have a school dinner and Shelley had nagged on about making bloody sure he did; she'd check up on him, she warned him again, but he knew pretty well that she wouldn't. Just lately Shelley had taken to dragging the kids down the road to the new family centre where at least there were cups of tea and coffee and a few sane women to talk to. The three boys too young for school could spend the morning playing with fresh toys. It took some of the pressure off her; at least she'd only the baby to cope with. Joey was in his last year at primary. Kez, at six, came next, leaving Saul, then Jason, then Casey, then Julie still at home with mum. Six kids. No man. No money to speak of and her not yet thirty, for God's sake.

This was never how Shelley had imagined her life was going to be.

In spite of her mother's dire warnings.

Man-mad, Mum used to say. You'll learn. But she hadn't. She trusted too easily, that was her problem, and she had something to prove. *'Specky Four-Eyes. Specky Four-Eyes.'* She got shot of her glasses when she was twelve and then they stopped calling her names. All at once she was pretty; Shelley Tremayne was normal.

Mum was Cornish, born and bred, and so was Dad although he was Chinese. He worked on the ferry as a steward. He called himself a sailor but his uniform was disappointing – he looked more like a snooker player in those maroon trousers and matching waistcoat. He disappeared when Shelley was six; he never sailed back from Santander. From that day on, Iris, his wife, broke off with his family and she never remarried.

And now, alone again without a man, this time with the world collapsing around her, there was no-one in whom Shelley could confide. But however close to someone you were, would you ever confide over something as horrific as this? Wouldn't you be more likely to sit side by side with your own thoughts, careful not to communicate your worst fears to anyone? Because what if your partner decided on a different course of

13

action to yours? What if your partner was all for the law running its merciless course, sod the consequences? Shelley didn't think she'd ever had anyone she could be really certain would be absolutely on her side. Certainly nobody else in the world loved her children as much as she did.

She would die for any one of them.

God, if only she could share this with someone.

The first thing they'd say would be, 'What kind of mother would bring up a child from hell like that?'

She had asked that same question herself, back when life was normal.

Shelley stared at the phone as a drowning man might spy a raft far off on a choppy horizon. The Samaritans? Don't be a fool. The first thing the law would do would be to check who she'd rung. And why would she call the Samaritans when she'd never called them before? No, she must do nothing unusual. They could even be watching the house already. She must put out the milk bottles, go to bed at her normal time, turn out the light – and then she noticed how hard she was trembling and her lip was bleeding where she'd torn off skin, unaware what she did with her fingers.

'Mum,' he whined. 'Julie's crying.'

And there he stood.

Joey.

Firstborn.

Skinny in his underpants.

Skeletal legs bruised from ankle to knee, scabs half off, mucky fluff between his toes. Hair thick and black, almost oriental, and eyes as dark as eyes ever get. Shelley's hair was blue-black like that until the dyes, the highlights and the perms stripped the heaviness from it.

'*Muuuuuum*,' Joey moaned. 'Are you coming?'

This was it. Grasping the nettle. Shelley turned away. Her fists were tight when she asked him so simply, 'Why weren't you wearing your jacket today?'

'Darren wanted to borrow it. Why? What's your problem?'

She whirled round to face him, a wisp herself but still so much larger than the little boy lost on the stairs. '*D'you know how I knew you weren't wearing your jacket?*'

'Wha-at?' Joey drawled out sleepily. He was confused, he showed no signs of defence whatever. And why should he? She was no threat. Never had been. Too soft? Too tired more like. Now look.

Shelley drew closer. She spat in a whisper, 'I know you weren't wearing your sodding jacket, Joey, *because I saw you without it tonight on the telly*.'

'Wha'd'y'mean?' But his eyes grew sharper.

'You know bloody well what I mean.'

'*Muuum?*' A wheedle.

'You were there, Joey, weren't you? You were there when they threw that fucking stuff at that baby?'

'Naw—'

She slapped his face hard. He fell back, alarmed. 'Don't you dare lie to me, not this time,

15

not now.' She grabbed her son's skinny arm and dragged him to the sofa. He was shivering, most probably cold; it was going on eleven o'clock and the heating went off at ten. Shelley hadn't noticed.

'Tell me,' she said, hard-voiced. 'Believe me, you've just got to tell me.'

'I don't know what—'

She slapped him again and he attempted to curl up into a ball. 'How could you? Jesus, how could you? Whatever the others were doing, how could you?' She was pleading like a beggar. Oh dear Jesus, let this not be happening. 'You've got Julie there upstairs, only a baby herself. You've seen the others grow up. You've helped me, you've loved them, you've played with them and wheeled them about . . .'

Shelley retched but nothing came up. She screwed up a tissue in front of her mouth. '*Dear God, Joey.*' She was shaking so hard the words wouldn't come. She was like this, in shock, last time she gave birth but then they gave her the pethidine. 'Did you not think . . .? *Were you mad?* The pain . . . the little innocent mite and you great fool with your bloody mates, mindless, twisted bastards, anything for a dare, for a laugh. What the fuck did you think you were doing?' This time she was sick, but only bile came out on the tissue and she turned when she felt the sofa shaking.

Joey stared out of a storm of tears. Suddenly his age fell off him and he was a sticky-thumbed baby again, scared stiff and defenceless. 'We never meant . . .' was all he could manage. His shoulders were thin, like a much younger child's. At one time

16

the clinic had suggested that he was malnourished.

Shelley, speechless, shook her head before it dropped to her chest, too heavy for the knowledge inside it.

'W-w-what's going to h-h—?'

'What's going to happen? You tell me.'

'H-h-how did y-y—'

'You stupid little sod. The camera caught it all. Yeah, all five of you ... mucking about, nicking fags, kicking that bloody ball, pains in the arses. How come you had petrol anyway?'

'It weren't petrol.'

She sniffed hard, looking anywhere but at him. 'Don't give me that.'

'It weren't petrol. It were paraffin.'

'So how come you had the stuff then, dammit?'

Tears continued to slide down his face. 'It were Marcus and Shane. They nicked it from B&Q. Their mum's doing up her hall and landing...'

Shelley's voice went high, touching hysteria. 'So where did the baby come into this?'

'That was Darren Long. He was mucking about. That's what I thought, he was mucking about.'

'So Darren got hold of this bottle of paraffin and threw it over a pram? Is that it? Just out of the blue like that? Without you others knowing?'

'That's how it was, Mum. I swear. *I swear.*'

She couldn't believe this conversation. She just couldn't come to terms with the fact that this was happening between her and her son. 'And then? What then? I have to know, Joey. If you want my help you have to say, and it has to be the truth.'

17

'We'd all started to run away when suddenly Connor Mason turned round and threw this lighter he'd nicked into the pram.' Joey glanced at his mother's face. She was pale, drawn and all twisted. 'We never knew a baby was in it. We never knew. It had this hood with teddy bears on. We thought it was empty. We thought the mum had it in the shop.'

'*The pram caught fire*,' whispered Shelley. '*That baby was two months old*.'

Joey hung his head as if he'd been caught throwing stones, that was all.

'They didn't get her to hospital.' Shelley didn't know she'd taken so much in. She must have registered the details somewhere in her subconscious. 'That little one died in the ambulance. Her mum's out of her mind. Drugged. Can't speak.' Her teeth almost gnawed through her lip.

Joey continued to stare at his feet. They were filthy. His toenails badly needed cutting. It seemed he had nothing else to say.

'They'll come for you,' she said. 'You must know that.'

This time he shook his head. 'No, I didn't.'

She repeated, 'They've got you on film.'

He said nothing.

'I knew who you were at once. And two of the others.'

'Yep.'

'You've killed somebody. You're eleven years old and you've done a murder.'

'No, no, no, not like that.'

'Yes, Joey, it is like that.'

'*Not a murder.*'

She was in no state to argue. 'So you skived off
chool . . . You must've done to be in the precinct
t that time.'

There was no point in denying any more. 'It
were Tanner for art, and he hates me.'

What could Shelley say, faced with that? 'And
he two quid I gave you for dinner?'

'We went to McDonald's.'

Her sense of despair became overwhelming. 'Ah
es. Yes.'

'I didn't do any of it, Mum. Not the really bad
tuff.'

Did her son believe he was innocent? Did he
hink he would get away with this? Did he expect
a smack round the head, a detention, a week's
exclusion? Where did he live, in some wonderland
where eleven-year-olds could do what they liked,
piss people off, throw dogshit down on pensioners'
heads outside the bookie's, run people down with
heir wretched scooters, scream obscenities, break
windows, torment and bully the frightened public
and nobody gave a damn? Maybe it was this lack
of restrictions that led them to this terrible crime,
to push the boundaries, to test themselves . . .
Shelley just didn't know. There seemed no answer.
There is never an answer. *To kill a baby for
kicks* . . .

They'd say she had given birth to a monster.

And had she? Might she have done? There must
be some severe behavioural disorder; if not, Joey
must be psychotic. They would go through his
past reports, establish all sorts of signs which

19

should have been picked up on earlier – and wh
ought to have spotted the signs? *His mother, c
course*. Who else but his mother?

When Shelley spoke next, Joey sobbing besid
her, it was to say, 'We're going to have to stick t
a story.'

'What story?'

'We're going to have to say you were here, a
home, nowhere near the precinct. You've got
blue jacket, there was no sign of a blue jacket o
those video films, so how could it have been you?

'But I lent it—'

She was firm. 'No-one can prove that.'

'The others'll tell . . .'

'They can say what they like.'

'The people, the crowds, somebody might have
seen me. They might do an identity parade. Anc
I'm always going around with those mates.'

'Not this afternoon you weren't.' Shelley turnec
and grabbed Joey's wrists. She squeezed then
hard while she rammed her words home. 'You fel
sick. You came home lunchtime. I was already
back from the centre and I let you in. The kids
had cheese biscuits and an apple cut into five, but
you had nothing. You went to bed with a pain
You stayed in bed. You never left it.'

'People saw me playing footy, they saw me
teatime, in the road.'

'OK.' Shelley drew herself up. 'OK, so you felt
better. You went out for a while around teatime.
You felt rough again so you came back in and
went to bed. What matters is – you never went
near that precinct this afternoon. Right?'

With black smudges down his face Joey nodded, chewing his lip.

'Whatever they say, however they try to trick you, whatever stories they might make up – and they might make you cry – you stick to that, you understand?'

He struggled to free his wrists; she was hurting. Dementedly, Shelley hung on. 'Otherwise . . .' and she shook her head. '*Otherwise . . .*'

'What?' Joey's jaw had dropped open now. Could it be he just hadn't considered the consequences of what he'd done?

'They'll take you away. They'll lock you up. Probably for most of your life.' She paused. She released him. 'And there's no point you shaking your head like that, looking daft, as if you don't know.' She shook a cigarette from the packet sitting on the coffee table. Her hand was still shaking as she lit up, but the first rush of nicotine calmed her. 'You're cold. Here . . .' and she threw him the fluffy blanket she used on the top of Julie's pushchair. She walked swiftly towards the window, pulled back the curtain and searched the street with dread.

The television droned on in the background. Shelley daren't turn it off in case there was more news. Maybe a report on the progress the police were making. They had been known to interrupt programmes over issues particularly dreadful and no doubt this event would count as dreadful. A baby, for God's sake. *A baby burning.* How sick, they would ask, was society becoming? They asked that each time, they kept on asking. And up until now she'd asked that too

'Mum.' Joey, uneasy, was driven to say, 'Mum Julie's crying.'

'What?'

'*Julie's crying.*'

Shelley sagged. She could hardly stand. She'd stopped listening to the row from upstairs. All distractions had ceased to exist. Now she jumped. faced with reality. Normality, she'd kill to find it. 'Be a good boy and bring her down, will you?'

He gave his sweetest, cutest smile. 'Any chance of a cup of tea?'

'You bring Julie down and I'll see,' she said.

Just like any ordinary evening.

TWO

The three-bedroomed boxes, like toddlers' blocks, were stacked on a hillside overlooking the city. Long straight roads led through the estate, acting as an assembly line; occasionally a standard cherry or a box hedge recklessly broke the symmetry. But lately, with unemployment running at 20 per cent and rising, broken cars had started to sprout their own brambly protest from neglected tarmac, and supermarket trolleys, prams and one badly stained mattress had been dumped on the Tremaynes' windy street corner.

Standards were slipping.

This morning Shelley gripped Joey and brought her face a threatening few inches from his. 'You go to school, you register, you use that two quid for dinner, you keep right away from you know who. You don't put a foot wrong, you hear me? And if I hear different I'll kill you.'

'*What if the pigs . . . ?*' Joey cast a covert glance over his mother's shoulder to the kitchen, where Kez had his face in a piece of toast but would be alert to the morning's tension. Kez had no heavy boulder weighing down his heart and making it ache. He wished to God he was Kez. He wished to God he could take time back. His mother's use of that word 'murder' had struck terror in his heart, but today's unease was caused by this sense of collusion between himself and an adult. It put him squarely on the adults' side and that situation was foreign to Joey. He was eager to go but he couldn't leave for school until Kez was ready. He had to make sure Kez reached St Martin's Primary safe and with his packed lunch-box intact. But Joey was desperate to be gone. His mum might have made him swear not to go near his mates, but shit, he had to know how the land lay, didn't he?

'You know what to say. I've told you what to say. You stick to that and you keep your mouth shut.'

'But the others . . .'

'What happens to the others is none of your bloody business.'

She started hassling Kez to get a move on; he was snot-nosed already after his wash. After they'd left for school Shelley would make a coffee and sit with a fag to calm her nerves before the trek to the family centre with four-year-old Saul trailing, wailing, behind, and Casey and Jason, both still in nappies, hanging on to the pushchair with Julie squalling inside.

Her worst fears had been confirmed when she'd picked up the *Mirror* first thing, folded it and tucked it under the pile of bills waiting in the kitchen drawer. It would do Joey no good to see how frenziedly the press had jumped on the case.

It did Shelley no good either. To see the name 'Holly' across the front page, the little bonneted face in the centre and the word 'monsters', charcoal black, daubed along the bottom.

The minute the boys were out of the door Shelley rushed to the drawer. Ignoring the mayhem of morning around her she spread the paper across the dross and pounced on the words like a ravenous dog. Across the inside pages was an enlarged and 'enhanced' frame from the news video of last night. Only the backs of the boys were visible, thank God. She skimmed the headlines and moved to the text. Her hands were shaking so hard she could barely read the leaping print. The police were appealing for witnesses. Already they were assuming that families and friends of the group would know who the culprits were. They feared a cover-up, they said, but the Voice of the *Mirror* questioned quite clearly what scum would stoop so low. They were concentrating on schools today; they didn't specify junior or senior.

Although there were no recorded images of the actual attack on Holly, numerous witnesses had already come forward. 'It just happened too fast,' said one of them. Catherine Pole from Plympton, still in shock from the experience, was offered immediate counselling. 'There was nothing anyone could do. I saw the boys approach one moment, the next there were flames ... A man beside me threw his coat across the pram. Another man dived for the baby and burned his hands badly. It was then that poor Mrs Coates came out . . . That scream will haunt me for ever.'

'Her heart just stopped,' said a paramedic. 'It wasn't the burns as such that killed her. It was the shock to her tiny system.'

It seemed that the local population were outraged that such a tragedy should occur, not in Liverpool, Birmingham or Manchester but in the peaceful, law-abiding South West.

A post-mortem would take place today.

Oh my God. Shelley blinked back stinging tears. She had to concentrate to keep breathing and recognized this as a panic attack. She hadn't had one of these since school, during the gruelling spells of bullying. It took some minutes for the gasping to stop and this entailed pacing the kitchen, clutching the fridge, the sink, grabbing each object as she passed else she would drown in this void of terror. Her kids watched her round-eyed and silent. It would have been worse, she convinced herself, drawing in breath with less urgency, if that poor little soul had survived the burns and had to lie in intensive care for months of agony. At least it was quick . . . And then she stopped, incredulous. She realized how she was thinking: she was actually attempting to justify the demonic behaviour of her eleven-year-old son.

The *Mirror* was right in its leader. What scum would stoop so low as to protect any one of these little bastards?

But if those boys were caught and tried for this they would be hunted for the rest of their lives, not just by the press but by an enraged public and a mother and father with nothing else to live for.

Oh no, not him again.

'I'm on my way out,' she said to Kenny ten minutes later, as if he was blind to her struggles. He had this habit of turning up with no warning, no proper reason. This morning Joey's feckless father was the last person she wanted to see.

'I've got your fags,' he said shiftily. 'Two fifty a packet. Not bad.'

She had to concentrate to connect with her old life. 'How many?'

'Six packs of twenty. But it's getting harder. Customs and Excise are having a ball. I'll walk along with you.'

'Shove that lot inside first,' Shelley said. 'I can't pay you now. I'll pay you Monday.' She shrugged. 'You're on shore leave then?' If he must come with her he must. Kez and Saul were also his, each one a result of some sad reunion after she'd chucked him out of the house. Each time she saw Kenny her amazement grew. How could she ever have felt anything for this? She looked at him now and was tempted to tell him that his eldest son was in big trouble, but her motives would be wrong. If she gave him the news it would be to shake him, to see some expression cross that dopey face. Yet once she had swooned at the sight of him, at the shaven head, the strong-muscled arms with the string of tattoos, the laughing eyes and the navy uniform. Jesus. She was loyal for the months he spent at sea and prepared like a whore for his return, waxing her legs, plucking her nipples, tinting her hair, bathing in the essence of roses. Always clean sheets

– she ironed them too – and babysitters on tap for those boozy nights down the Union Street clubs.

But Shelley was glad to have Kenny beside her when they wheeled their way past Connor Mason's house. It gave her something to concentrate on instead of the figure behind the porch. Connor's mum, Dot, appeared to be lurking: was she waiting for Shelley to pass and did she pull back in when she saw she had company? Did Dot Mason share this loathsome secret? How about the mother of Marcus and Shane Lessing, and what about Hayley Long? Did they know, like she did, that their young sons were killers? How she wished she knew the answer so she would have someone to talk to.

'Bloody awful,' said Kenny, as usual assuming she knew what he meant.

Shelley turned to him, irritated. He ought to fall back and give Casey a carry, he could see the toddler was tiring. 'What's awful?' It was time he got rid of those stupid sleepers. At thirty-five he was far too old.

'Local, they reckon.'

Shelley leaped to attention. Of course. What else would anyone round here be talking about this morning? 'That baby?'

'Yep.' He paused to roll a fag and repeated more loudly, 'Bloody awful.'

'They'll catch 'em,' said Shelley.

'They bloody will. They'll throw the book at the bastards too.'

'They were kids,' said Shelley with a sideways glance.

'They're never kids, they're born old. They're born evil, arseholes like that.'

'They should hang 'em,' said Shelley.

'Too good,' muttered Kenny, at last hoisting Casey, protesting, onto his shoulders.

The last hill was steep and her boots were hurting and she had forgotten Julie's bottle. Sod it. She'd not last all morning without a drink, but how could Shelley be expected to organize stuff like that when loaded with this burden of horror? She felt the tears and fought them back. Kenny needed only one sign of weakness and he'd be all over her, groping, sex mad. He was still unable to grasp the fact that Shelley couldn't give a toss about him, or any man come to that. Her thoughts were all with Joey this morning.

Would the pigs be at the school taking statements from those they suspected?

Was there other evidence apart from the witnesses' descriptions, the video, the Zippo, the bottle of paraffin? They'd have fingerprints already for sure. But not Joey's fingerprints – he'd sworn to her that he'd not touched anything. Would Joey be strong enough to resist the kind of pressure they might put on him? And were they allowed, by law, to do that? Could they interview him without his mum?

'Coming in?' she asked Kenny as they reached the centre, knowing that he would not.

'Nah,' he said, slouched by the wall. Boredom, that was his problem. Shore leave and nowhere to go except to his mum's, and she was far from a bag of laughs. He'd never found another woman after Shelley last told him to sling his hook.

'How long have you got?' she asked. 'Want to see Joey?'

'I could come round one evening,' said Kenny.

'I wasn't thinking of that,' she said firmly. 'You could take him out, get him out of my hair. Do something – skating, swimming, bowling . . .'

'I could, I'spose.' He scratched his head and some flakes came off. Disgusted, Shelley looked away and said, 'Well then? I'm sure Kez'd like to come too.'

Saul was already inside, aiming straight for the plastic digger. You would never think Kenny was his dad, such little notice Kenny took. His kids were never excited to see him and who could wonder at it?

'Maybe I will,' said Kenny. 'Some time.'

Shelley turned and went inside, heaving the pushchair over the step and into a room startling with primary colours. The family centre was run by a charity set up to forge some sense of community, a challenge when faced with the straggly estate, the lack of funds, the residents' apathy. Crime statistics were rising in Eastwood, mostly car crimes, theft and vandalism, and to tackle these problems it was thought that the kids of Eastwood must be caught early. Hence the Play-Doh and the finger paints for expression, hence the bosomy Jean for comfort. Mrs Cresswell, as she would rather be known, was a trained nursery-school teacher, trained in the days of happy clapping, trained in times of rusks and juice, trained all of thirty years ago when children stayed children, and mothers stayed mothers.

What kind of mother . . . ?

And so her greetings were bright and cheery in a high-pitched voice that unnerved the kids. Her helpers were young trainees from the tech. With great relief Shelley unloaded her pram and carried Julie towards the group of mothers who stood with their fags lit, clustered round the door where on the floor grew a pillar of dog-ends. Because of the way their eyes were sliding it was obvious there was some gossip afoot and it wasn't to do with the no-smoking rule or the price of a mug of coffee.

The young mum with the acne nodded to Shelley. 'She was there, she saw it.' She shrugged towards her infamous friend. 'Val'll be haunted by it for ever. Well you are, something like that.'

Shelley froze as the star witness spoke. 'I didn't know them, but I would, I've told them I would if I saw them again.'

'Wrong age group for her, see,' said the mum with acne. 'These kids were well old enough to know what they did.'

'I told the law they were all about twelve. And that poor sod who burned his hands, he got a better look than anyone.'

The girl with the sleeping baby spoke next. 'There were so many people around you'd think someone'd recognize one of them. Get one of the buggers, you've got them all.'

'They say the parents must know.'

'Well, you would know,' said the acned mum, a

31

greasy fringe tapping her eyelids. 'You're not telling me you wouldn't know if one of them bleeders was yours.'

'All they need ask is who skipped school.'

'Oh yeah?' came the answer. 'Easier to count who was there, I reckon.'

'Well, without knowing anything at all and I wouldn't want to be quoted,' said Pam, the fat one with the flesh-coloured leggings, 'I'd bet my last quid those Lessings were there.'

Shelley felt her legs weakening. Marcus and Shane, she'd recognized them, too. It was the swagger, the aggro.

'And I say that,' Pam went on, 'because I'm the poor bleeder who lives next door but one, and I know for a fact Mrs Turner next door has put her name down for a transfer. It's not that poor old git who ought to be moved, it's that whole sodding family. They're evil.' She grimaced.

'Have you been to the law? You should tell them.'

'The law? They know too well, don't you worry.'

'You've got a kid around that age – how old's your lad, the eldest? He must know those bloody Lessings.' The mum with acne sprung this on her so quickly that Shelley imagined she stepped back a pace. It was the same as being smacked in the gob.

'He knows what he'd get if he went near that lot,' she answered quickly, on automatic.

'*Any little ones over there for juice?*'

Mrs Cresswell's bird-like trill provided an escape route. Maybe there would be a spare

32

bottle, or was it time to get Julie using a cup? Saul, Jason and Casey were already seated on miniature chairs around a miniature table. They passed a warm flannel round the group, one kid using it to blow his nose.

'Mum, I want crisps,' called Saul. 'I don't like this biscuit.' He held it out. Shelley took the damp digestive.

'There aren't any crisps,' she said firmly. 'You know they don't give you crisps here. Look, have a drink,' she encouraged him.

'Ugh,' said Saul with a screwed-up nose. Shelley took a sip. The juice was so weak it tasted like water and her kids had been weaned on Coke and Tango.

'Just leave it and don't make a fuss,' she said.

'The police called in this morning with a poster.' Mrs Cresswell bounced towards the group of mothers. She dipped her pudgy hand in her apron and unfolded the picture of baby Holly, the one that had been in the *Mirror*. Shelley's throat went dry. She struggled to clear it, tried to swallow. 'I didn't consider that this was the place,' Mrs Cresswell went on. 'Inappropriate to say the least. And I told them so. I told them I'd rather not. Not in a place where young children gather. Who knows what effect such a sight might have, and we know how susceptible they can be to atmosphere.'

She refolded the poster and replaced it. 'As if anyone here with information would not have come forward already. The very idea is ridiculous,' she said, striding off. 'We're all mothers here after all.'

Sing along, children – here we go . . .

Oh the mummies on the bus go chatter chatter
chatter,
Chatter chatter chatter
Chatter chatter chatter,
The mummies on the bus go chatter chatter chatter
All day long.

There was no other topic of conversation, and even if there had been Shelley could not have followed it. She turned down coffee and concentrated on her children instead, following them round the nursery, helping them with their cutouts and stickings, but whatever she did, however she tried, Holly's tiny wrinkled face was imprinted on her mind.

There would be a funeral, a pathetic little white coffin too small to be believable, a couple of broken-hearted parents being helped through the church doors to nowhere. The trial would be world news: it sometimes seemed that countries competed for the child-killer challenge cup, there were so many these days. Kids with guns who slaughtered whole classes, gangs with machetes running riot in cafés, sick little loners with collections of weapons – the tale of woe went on and on.

And now her son. Joseph Tremayne. Eleven. His name linked for ever with Crippen and Hindley.

Maybe she could send him away to some

country where he couldn't be touched? Then, some time, they could join him; she could raise the money and they would all be together. What country? Where? Didn't most criminals flee to Spain? It seemed hard to believe in this day and age that Spain had no agreement with Britain. After all, we were in Europe now.

No, no. Not Spain. It would have to be some place far more obscure, maybe Mauritius or Peru, or what about Cuba?

Stop this, stop this right now!

Shelley's brain was storming, rioting. If she kept her cool the situation would never come to that. If Joey kept his mouth shut. If nobody could identify him. If his prints were not on the evidence. If he could deny with confidence the accusations his mates might make. If they could both be strong and withstand all pressures from the law.

She glanced at her watch.

Midday.

She would drag the children home.

She would put Julie down for a sleep.

She would give the little ones some lunch and try to force something down herself.

Whatever happened, she must not crack up and she had so nearly done just now.

No hysterics.

No dramas.

By the time she reached home, Shelley was exhausted. All she wanted to do was sleep; she craved that white oblivion. Fat chance. But as she came to the crest of the hill, as she passed the mattress on the corner and saw yet another trolley parked beside the broken pram, all her strived-for courage evaporated when she saw the police car outside her door, two uniformed coppers on her step, the man ringing the bell that never worked, the woman scanning the road.

Shelley lifted her hand.

She waved.

As you would to a couple of friends. Unexpected.

THREE

For the first few weeks after Shelley moved in she could pick out her house only from the colour on the front door – poppy red. And now that colour, shadowed by the uniforms, shouted not welcome home but danger.

Had Joey blabbed?

Were they picking her up?

Who the hell would mind her kids if they whisked her away without warning?

'Mrs Tremayne? Shelley Tremayne?'

'I'm Shelley Tremayne.' Routine saved her from collapse although she flushed and her lip trembled. She squeaked the pushchair to a halt, tucked Julie under her arm from habit, folded the pushchair with a kick of expertise and shepherded her little ones up the front steps before she looked up and asked, 'What's up?'

'Nothing, I hope,' said the cop with the boyish face, following Shelley and the kids inside while his eyes were still intent on his notebook. 'Just a routine visit.' Tall and thin, he ducked at the kitchen door. He looked up and gave her a tentative smile. 'You just carry on,' he said, eyeing the fretting children.

Guilt and fear slowed Shelley down, heavier than a lead weight. Someone had filled their nappy. It stank. But she wasn't about to change it, not with that woman's contemptuous attitude.

The woman PC who had showed her identity card had a sharp little face and a nose that turned white at the end. It took Shelley just seconds to realize that this was the more dangerous one of the two. She was at the sink when the woman said, 'WPC Juliet Hollis, and this is PC Michael Frey.'

'I'll just get their drinks and I'll be right with you,' said Shelley, now warming Julie's bottle. 'What's this about anyway? What have you come for? What's wrong?'

The kitchen was in its mad morning mess and at any other time Shelley might have wished she'd cleared up before she left for the centre. No such thought now crossed her mind – it was too full to take in any more – but she did move a huge pub ashtray which was spilling over with old dog-ends.

Kenny's maintenance paid half the mortgage plus the interest on this three-bedroomed former council house, and the DHS paid the rest. When they split for the last time she was forced to go for maintenance or face the threat of benefit cuts. He tried to deny that the kids were his, but when faced with DNA tests he'd had no alternative but to cough up. The navy deducted the money from his wages at source so Shelley never had to worry about him scarpering like her own dad did. He showed no signs of wanting to.

'Go through.' She gestured towards the lounge. 'It's a bit of a tip . . .'

'That's fine,' said Frey, long and spiderish on the sofa and crossing his large bony legs.

The dramatic presence of the two coppers had magically shut the kids up. They were happy to sit and watch, open-mouthed, although Shelley switched the telly on low and dragged out the Lego box. She drew back the curtains she had peered through last night and then sat in the spare armchair to feed Julie.

'So what . . . ?' she began.

'Shelley. You've heard of the death of the little girl at the High Street precinct yesterday?'

Oh Jesus . . . for one moment she had prayed for a miracle, that this visit would be for some other purpose. Surely her heart's frantic thudding was bound to betray her? 'Of course,' she said warily, 'who hasn't?'

'Well, this morning we are acting on help received from the general public and we have been informed that your son, Joey, often skives off school.'

'Who told you that?'

'It doesn't matter who told us. Is it true?'

'Oh I see,' sneered Shelley, 'it's like that, is it? Some crumblies round here will say anything to get kids in trouble.' Shelley immediately suspected Mrs Rowe and that old crony of hers, Phyllis Baker. So this was a visit based on malicious rumours, the worst kind of gossip, no more than that. 'Some folks round here live in a time warp and expect kids to doff their caps and go to bed at six. It's crazy.' She added with small defiance, 'Joey's never been in real trouble. He's never been down the nick. He's never had any warnings. He's kept himself out of court. He's a kid, for God's sake, he has to play somewhere.'

'Well, we realize that,' said the sharp-nosed Hollis. 'But several residents of this estate have named Joey as no respecter of property or person – a pain in the arse is how most of them put it. Out of parental control. Running wild.'

'But they've never reported him before. You've never picked him up. OK, he might be overactive and he does tend to shoot his mouth off but he means well. I'm his mum, I know his heart is in the right place. But anyway, what's this got to do with that baby? Just because Joey's a little sod you can't go accusing him of doing such a sick thing as that.'

'Where was Joey yesterday afternoon?' asked WPC Hollis, ignoring four-year-old Saul who'd approached her shyly with a Lego bus.

They must have already found out about school. 'Joey was sick. He was home. With me.'

'Is there anyone else who could confirm that?'

'Unless Mrs twitch-curtain Rowe or her hairy-chinned crony just happened to see him come in at lunchtime, I doubt that very much,' said Shelley. 'You'll have to ask him yourself. He won't lie.'

'Oh, we intend to,' said Hollis matter-of-factly. 'And Joey's particular friends. We are interested in them, too,' she continued, now actively pushing off little Saul's attentions. What a hard-faced bitch she was. 'The Lessing brothers, I believe, are particular mates of his.' She got out her notebook and read, 'Darren Long, Connor Mason . . .'

'Have you been round their houses?'

'We will, we will.'

'And what d'you think the street will be thinking now that you've pitched up like this on my doorstep?' said Shelley, disliking the neat WPC Hollis so much she wanted to smack her face. 'They'll all suspect Joey's up to his neck in all this. Naturally they will. So how do we deal with that when you're gone, when it's found that Joey had nothing to do with it? I'd be bloody grateful if you'd tell me that!'

'There's no need for hysteria, Shelley.'

'Mrs Tremayne, if you don't mind.'

'We didn't think you were married,' said Frey, who'd been leaving the attack to his small, waspish friend. At least, give him his due, he leaned forward and pretended to admire Jason's picture done in heavy black crayon.

'What's in a name?' said Shelley. 'I can call myself what I bloody well like.'

'You live here alone with the kids, is that it?' asked Frey.

'I've lived here alone since last year when Julie's dad got himself locked up.' But they'd have known that before they came. She might as well admit it and get that out of the way.

'And before him?' the mean cow Hollis persisted.

'Before him, let's see . . .' Shelley leaned back and made out she was counting on her fingers. 'They're attracted by the house, see. It's a cosy

41

set-up for a man alone if he can stick the kids. Well, for what it's got to do with you, first there was Kenny, then Keith, then Malc, and last but not least Julie's dad, Dave.'

'Burglary, wasn't it?'

'He got five years,' said Shelley.

'Do you still see him?'

'I don't bother,' said Shelley. Her voice was tight and her knuckles were white against Julie's yellowy bottle.

'Would you call yourself a good mother?' asked Hollis of a startled Shelley. There was a small sneer on the policewoman's lips. They were thin, like her eyebrows, and a pulse in her forehead beat unpleasantly.

'Would *you*?' she snapped back.

'I don't have children.'

'That figures,' said Shelley, putting Julie on the floor and lighting herself a fag. 'I'm not making tea if that's what you're wanting.'

Frey flipped his notepad back a page. 'So you were here at home with Joey yesterday afternoon when the incident occurred?'

'Yep.'

'And at no time did Joey leave the house?'

'That's right.'

'And you would be happy to swear to that?'

'Yep. No problem.'

'We'll see what the neighbours have to say,' said Hollis, rising and brushing her skirt as if she'd picked up some infection from the crumbs and smears on Shelley's sofa. Her flat would be immaculate, probably mostly stainless steel. And she'd sleep on one of those rigid futons. Her hair was hard. She smelt of lacquer.

'Well, you do that,' said Shelley.

Frey turned at the door and adopted a softly-softly approach. 'Joey must be a difficult child, bearing in mind his age, his past experiences, his changes of school, his missing dad. You must find it hard to cope with him sometimes, all alone with this little lot.'

'Joey's an open, easy child,' Shelley lied without batting an eyelid. 'I dunno what I'd do without him.'

'No doubt, Mrs Tremayne, we will see you again,' was Hollis's last loaded remark as she strutted purposefully down the steps and headed round towards next door.

'Shit,' whispered Shelley. And she stood at the open door and noted how many lingerers were hovering around to see just what exactly was going on inside the house with the poppy-red door. She closed it with a slam. All she could do now was try to go on breathing while counting the hours till Joey got home.

How to pass the time?

The local radio station blared.

Every hour there was more news but nothing that told her much more than she knew. They knew the killers were local kids. They had several witnesses to the crime. Holly's mother was heavily sedated. Her dad and her uncles were now determined to spend the rest of their lives seeking revenge. Nothing was too

43

bad for the perpetrators of such an attack.

Shelley changed all the bedding.

She shoved the sheets in the washing machine.

She paused each time she crossed the room, checking for updates on the telly. *But Joey had only been there, for God's sake*, he had not committed a crime.

Money was tight for Shelley but she was better off than most others round here. She got her family credit of course, Kenny's mortgage contribution, child allowance and odd bits of help from the social services (the washer/dryer came from them). Her house was not dirty, just a permanent mess; she had been brought up in a spotless flat and had not rebelled against the sterility. She had a good eye for decent clothes and got most of them from charity shops. Amazing what you could find if you were careful. The younger kids had a bath every night and clean clothes every morning, and the same with Joey and Kez if she could, if they didn't protest too much.

She and Kenny had moved to Eastwood just before Saul was born. Kenny put down a deposit. Shelley thought she'd arrived. They'd stuck together, off and on, for seven years until the sight of his stupid face drove her crazy and she realized they had nothing in common, not even sex. She'd hated every moment of that, wham bam thank you mam and off with his adenoidal snoring.

Before Eastwood it had been rented accommodation, mostly in grotty areas. They were always just about to get married, and that would have given them a Forces' house, but somehow they never got round to it. When she chucked him out Kenny said that she'd planned it, all those years of moving around with not a stick of furniture their own. Then came the house, carpets and curtains and out Kenny went just like that, the proverbial cat.

But Shelley hadn't planned it, she wasn't remotely like that. It was just that when he was due home from sea she found herself dreading the long boring evenings, sport on TV with the curtains drawn even if it was sunny outside, the Abba he insisted on playing, the meat and two veg, the structured mealtimes. He was no longer able to make her laugh and his uniform did nothing for her.

But he was the father of three of her children. He was constantly hanging around. Thank God, she suddenly thought, that Joey didn't belong to Dave. With Dave's crime record, the shrinks would say it was in his genes. At least they wouldn't be able to say that Joey was a criminal's son.

When Shelley was upstairs wiping down the surfaces in the bedrooms she caught a glimpse of a group on the street – lads mainly, not from round here. Some rumour must have got about; they were staring at her house . . . How bad was this going to get? For now the little crowd was just curious but how long would it be before their emotions changed to something far more lethal?

Life-threatening?

She stayed well away from the windows.

It wasn't just her and Joey involved, it was the other kids too who would face the music if this mess got any worse. *'Specky Four-Eyes.'* The phrase seemed almost gentle now, over the distance of so many years. There was even something endearing about it and the thought of the little wounded girl who had taken it all so seriously. Kids calling out names, not knowing what they did. What sort of names would they start calling Joey?

With relief she saw that the police car had gone. The neighbours had done their worst, she supposed.

Joey was a naturally naughty kid.

Some kids are born that way.

He'd been troublesome from the beginning – colic, sleep problems, terrible tantrums that lasted for hours, slow to toilet train and certainly over-active. He had been her only child for five years, time enough for spoiling, and with Kenny away at sea they had spent so much of their time alone, mother and son against the world. There were no nursery schools in those days, certainly none for those who were constantly on the move from winter lets to B.&B.s, from condemned flats to hostels. She had her name down for a council house but each time she went to enquire she was further down the list than before; she didn't have the points. To get them she should make herself homeless.

Sod that.

'Go and live with your mother,' they said. Or 'What's Joey's father doing with his money? He should be paying your rent.' Oh yeah, he went to sea and came home with nothing, nothing for her and Joey. It wasn't until she got pregnant with Kez that Kenny began to grow up and take on his responsibilities. And that was only because he'd been hauled up before his commander.

Joey detested school, right from year one in the infants'. For months she was forced to leave him screaming, beating against the door, throwing toys, while the other mums gave Shelley sad looks. He was the last one of his group to settle. The word autism was mentioned but they decided that wasn't the case, thank God. Shelley was broken-hearted every time she left him, but the one thing she was firm about was that he shouldn't let himself be bullied.

'You fight back,' she used to say. 'Bullies are cowards really. Once they know you're going to fight back they'll soon turn on somebody else. You'll see.' And she used to tell him about the girls who had made her own childhood a misery. 'And that was just because I wore glasses,' she said. 'So silly, over something like that. They made me feel so ugly. They took away all my confidence.'

'But you're beautiful, Mummy,' said Joey, stroking her silky jet-black hair.

'He's a bit of a bully, isn't he,' said Mrs Potts nicely when Shelley went to the open day at Joey's first junior school. 'Always got his little hand in somebody else's lunch-box. He's a leader, that's for sure. And such a bundle of mischief. If there's trouble I always know who'll be there in the middle of it all.'

47

And both women smiled, a kind of sympathy.

At three forty-five Shelley heard the back door open to Joey's kick as usual. She hurried downstairs and accosted him before he'd managed to take off his jacket.

'Well?' she demanded. '*What happened?*'

He looked tired and paler than usual. She could see that he had been shaken by the enormous impact the burning had had on the whole school. And the quiet horror that had invaded every classroom and corridor. 'We had a talk in the hall,' said Joey, moving towards the biscuit tin before Kez could reach it.

'*And . . . ?*'

'Jennings talked for a while and then handed over to the coppers. Some of the girls were crying, specially when they showed the picture.'

'Did they question anyone separately?'

'No, but the teachers went into the secretary's room one by one.'

'And did you keep away from the others like I said?'

'Yep,' said Joey, but she guessed he was lying. The fool, *the stupid fool*. He was too young and ignorant to know that somebody would have been watching that group's every move.

'*So come on then, what did they say?*' She was almost hysterical, following her son round the kitchen while he took a Coke from the fridge, a banana from the basket, switched channels obsessively on the telly in the lounge. She knew him so well, she knew these were nervous

48

reactions to something so utterly horrendous he couldn't face up to the truth. She wanted to grab him and shake out some answers.

'That Connor's saying he never did it.'

Dear God. '*What?*'

'He's saying he never touched the lighter, and Darren Long says it was me threw the paraffin.'

This was outrageous, beyond belief. 'But you saw them both, Joey, you told me you saw them, so the Lessings must have seen them too.' My God – those deranged monsters who burned that child, who threw the paraffin and the lighter knowing full well what was going to happen, would be treated a thousand times more severely than the brainless group who merely stood by. From what Shelley had gleaned from Joey's version, they had all been gobsmacked by Connor's lighter attack. Certainly there had been no collusion, no premeditation either.

That thundering wave of chaos caught her and crashed her down helplessly onto the shingle.

FOUR

After four gruelling hours questioning Joey, pacing the floor and pacifying the kids before getting them bathed and into bed, the first item on the ten o'clock news sent Shelley flying from her house, knowing at heart that it was a mistake, the wrong move to make, but what else was there?

The police were now saying they had pulled in two boys for questioning about the killing of baby Holly Coates. The boys were too young to be named, and no, at this stage they would not be charged. The authorities were still appealing for information from the general public. Shelley was tormented by the stories Joey brought back from school – Darren and Connor were both denying they played any part in the horror and it appeared that together they had concocted a story they were determined to stick to.

So everything now depended on those gits, Marcus and Shane.

This wasn't the first time that Shelley had left her house with eleven-year-old Joey in charge. With babysitters in short supply and with so few chances to get out, she had risked prosecution on many occasions to pop round the corner to the Painted Lady, the only pub within walking distance. During Malc's and Dave's brief residences with her she had relied on Joey more often. Every weekend they had left the kids safe in a younger Joey's care. She had relied on her eldest son, believing in his common sense, and was shattered when eventually informed by a neighbour that ten minutes after she left home Joey crept out to join his cronies. The tyke.

But this night it was different. He swore on little Julie's life that he'd stay indoors out of trouble, and anyway *Gladiators* was on. Shelley threatened him with the direst warnings – 'They're just out there waiting, probably watching, and the first step out of line from you and they'll pounce and have you in there, in a cell on your own for God knows how long. So for Jesus' sake, stay put.'

He was reluctant to let her go. 'What if they come for me while you're out?'

'They won't be allowed to take you without me knowing where you are,' she told him uncertainly. More than likely social services would be able to do exactly what they bloody well liked with six little kids left alone in a house. She told Joey where she was going, looked up the number and left a note where even he would manage to see it, right next to the remote control.

Based on the fact that the square-jawed police spokesman had not mentioned the word brothers, Shelley reckoned the lads they'd pulled in were probably Darren and Connor. When she passed

Connor Mason's house she crossed to the other side of the road and noted that the lights were off and the curtains firmly drawn.

No sign of life.

No car outside and so far no frenzied crowds.

She drew the strings of her hood tightly round her head. Her pace quickened. She huddled along. Joey had told her the Lessing brothers had been absent from school today. She had to find out if Marcus and Shane were part of the conspiracy to nail Joey for the crime; there was no way she could sleep tonight without knowing the worst.

The Lessings' garden was a right tip under the one working street light. The shed was daubed with graffiti, broken toys littered the lawn and the rusted gate hung off its hinges. Aged dried dog turds looked large enough to be human. The minute Shelley rang the bell a deep bark echoed from inside the house and was joined by a clamour of ugly shouts.

Although it was nearly 10.30 p.m., the door was slowly opened by a child no older than three. A bull terrier with a spiked collar snarled quietly behind him, its red eyes focused on Shelley.

'Is your mum in?' Shelley asked, instantly recognizing the smell that hit her from the small hall . . . unwashed bodies, animals, old washing.

'Who is it?' a woman's voice called above the TV crackle of guns. Motors roared from the screen as Mrs Lessing, manlike and mean, strode towards the interruption.

'Get back in there,' she ordered the child. She clutched the dog's collar and gave him a kick that sent him sloping off out of sight, but his growls still sounded too close for comfort. She turned to Shelley. 'Well? What is it?'

'I'm Shelley Tremayne,' Shelley said quietly, as if afraid the neighbours might hear and know already what she wanted.

'Joey's mum?'

Shelley nodded.

Mrs Lessing folded her beefy arms. She stood firmly stuck to her mat. 'You've got some nerve to come round here. I'm forever shouting at my bloody lads to stay away from your kid and now there's the kind of fucking trouble I always said would happen.'

'Have you heard the news?'

'Of course I've heard the fucking news . . .'

For God's sake. Shelley couldn't stay out on this step any longer. Sooner or later she would attract attention. Who knew who was watching the house? 'Would it be OK if I came in?' Mrs Lessing's face clouded. 'Just for a second? Please, I need to talk.'

'There's too much bloody talking gone on and not enough action,' said the large woman in working-man's jeans and a bold football T-shirt which made her look larger. 'Come on then. As you're here.'

She shoved the bull terrier into the kitchen and closed the door behind it. The lounge was dominated by newspapers, some damp with yellowing stains. 'That's Bob.' Mrs Lessing nodded towards the unshaven man in the armchair while she threw herself down in the matching one nearest the gas fire. In the room the stink of sweat was intense. There was no shade over the centre bulb. On the sofa lolled the brothers Marcus and Shane, sharing the space with a large mongrel bitch with teats like cow's udders. Three cats dangled, sleeping, on the sofa back; not one opened its eyes to view the late visitor.

How to begin?

This had worried Shelley all the way here. She didn't even know if the Lessings had recognized their kids on the film, or spoken to them about the murder, or were happily unaware of their involvement. No wonder the two boys scowled, the image of their flop-bellied father. A bundle of greasy chip paper lay scrunched beside his horny bare feet.

'Gerrup to bed, you two, now,' he growled, and without a murmur the three-year-old who had opened the door and his slightly older sister got up from the carpet and its box of puppies – clearly the newly born litter of the tatty bitch on the sofa – and went upstairs. They were both dressed in nappies and T-shirts.

'Have you just the four?' Shelley asked from politeness.

'Two older daughters. They come home late.'

'I had the police round today,' Shelley began, choosing to sit on a leather stool perched on a stack of old *Daily Mirror*s. 'People round here had been complaining about my Joey so they came round to ask where he was ... when it happened.'

'What's that got to do with us?' asked Mrs Lessing aggressively.

Shelley went on with more meaning, '. . . when that baby was killed in the precinct.'

'I know what happened yesterday,' Mrs Lessing said, while her husband turned up the sound. There was no clear skin showing all the way down his arm to his hand. Every inch was covered in bruise-blue tattoos. 'And that's why I'm asking again, what the hell's that got to do with us?' said his wife.

'Well, I only heard this evening when Joey got home from school,' said Shelley, 'that the two boys who admit they were there are saying that your Marcus and Shane were with them and that my Joey caused the accident.'

'We never,' said Shane from the sofa. 'We never.'

'Shuddup,' growled Bob Lessing. There was a drifting violence about him; it was in his hair, in his clothes, in his stare.

'You say you weren't there either?' Shelley asked them directly.

They just looked dumb and turned to their mother. 'What's she trying to make out?'

'Yeah, what are you trying to make out, coming here like this?' Mrs Lessing demanded.

'I've come here because of my Joey,' she told them. 'Because I'm so scared they're trying to pin the blame on someone who wasn't even there and that he's going to cop it . . .'

''Bout bloody time,' said Mrs Lessing, lighting up. She paused and puffed out angry smoke.

''Bout bloody time that little scrote got some of his just rewards.'

'I haven't come here to cause a fight.' Shelley refused to be drawn. For Joey's sake she couldn't afford to lose her temper tonight. 'I came here to find out if you knew that Darren Long and Connor Mason were shouting their mouths off to the pigs about your boys. And mine.'

'What those little wankers are saying means not a toss to me. My boys weren't there,' stated Mrs Lessing, her large face turning brutal and her nostrils steaming, bull-like. 'They went to their gran's that afternoon and the cops haven't come round here. What I would do if I were you is go back to that little sod of yours and beat the living daylights out of him till he tells you the truth. I wouldn't bat an eyelid if they proved it was your Joey who set fire to that pram.'

Was this family lying, using a concocted alibi just as she and Joey were, or did the parents genuinely believe that Marcus and Shane had gone to their gran's? Surely they'd seen their sons on the video? Whatever, they weren't going to budge. There was nothing for it but to leave none the wiser than when she'd arrived.

It was good to breathe fresh air once again. But she should never have come. She knew that now. She should have stopped home and kept her mouth shut.

Joey was up, the film just ending as Shelley let herself into her house.

'They say they weren't there.'

'*But they were,*' argued Joey.

'The cops haven't been round to them yet.'

'That's not fair,' said Joey, as if fairness still mattered, for God's sake. She took off her jacket and stared at her son. He shifted his gaze.

'Cup of tea?' she asked, and then, '*You didn't do it, did you, Joey?*' She hated to say it, but she had to.

He screamed loud enough to wake the others. 'I've fucking well told you. How many times . . .?' His face screwed up, he kicked at the fridge, his teeth clamped together in rage. 'You never believe me.' He continued to shout: 'What is it with you? *You're my mum . . .*'

Shelley stepped forward and slapped his face hard.

He swung at her with a tight-balled fist, catching the side of her arm.

'*Don't you ever . . .*' she spat at him, grabbing his wrist. He was strong, he writhed, he kicked for his freedom. With her free hand she slapped his head again, and again, and a fourth time. The pain on her shins where his trainers made contact seemed like the least of her worries.

All at once he gave up the struggle and sank to the kitchen floor in tears. Breathless, Shelley drooped on a chair.

'Don't you get it, Joey? *I have to know.* I have to know what really happened.'

'Sod off,' he said brokenly through his tears. And then, 'You know what happened.'

After he'd gone, still tearful, to bed, Shelley

kicked off her shoes and lay on the sofa in the darkened room with her hands behind her head.

She felt so shagged out and defeated, it was hard to examine her motives; her thoughts were too confused for her to be able to make much sense of them. Any mother would stick by her child whatever that child might have done, wouldn't she? She knew Joey could be a pain to other residents of the estate but kids his age go through these phases, and many of Joey's problems were caused by the mates he chose to hang out with.

OK, he was cheeky, he had a temper, he'd been excluded from school once or twice and she'd been hauled up in front of the head on several awkward occasions. But people ought to recognize that Joey's life had not been easy. He'd resented the men she'd had in her life, he found it hard to settle to new surroundings, new schools, and he had behaviour problems.

What was she supposed to do?

What would her own mother have done if faced with this sort of situation?

Being an only child made a difference. Shelley's mum, Iris, was the old-fashioned kind, having been brought up in a hamlet on Bodmin Moor and being hauled into the present only when she met and married Liu Qi and moved into Plymouth. She never got over the pace and the wickedness of that nautical city. Her family never forgave her for marrying somebody from north of the Tamar, and worse than that, 'a slit-eyed Chink'.

Awed by authority all her life, Iris failed to do what any modern mother would do when faced with her daughter's unhappiness. Instead of going up to the school to complain and put a stop to the bullying, Iris used clichés to comfort her child: 'They'll give up when they see you don't care,' and 'These burdens you are carrying now will make you stronger when you're older,' and 'Turn the other cheek.'

Iris, dead now (a heart attack at fifty-five), had reverted to her maiden name after Liu Qi sodded off to Santander but stuck with her deep religious beliefs and much of the culture she had picked up during her Cornish childhood. There were few grey areas in her Methodism; right was right and wrong was wrong. *'Jesus bids us shine with a pure clear light.'* There was little forgiveness in this village religion, so there was no doubt about it: if Shelley had sinned as grievously as they were saying Joey had sinned, Iris would have marched her daughter to the nearest cop shop, no messing.

The one thought that Shelley pushed from her mind was the dreadful possibility that Joey might be guilty. She'd accept his word to the bitter end no matter how anyone tried to persuade her. That he was there on the scene was bad enough, and that he could associate with those kinds of friends. He was such a competent liar that even she, his own mother, had given up trying to catch him out. On top of that he was a thief. She'd caught him stealing money from her purse and there were things like CDs and games that appeared in his bedroom overnight, for which he had no explanation other than that he had 'swapped' for them.

Sometimes he liked to torment the children.

When she confronted him over his thieving his lack of shame was astonishing. That one time she had caught him red-handed lifting a ten-quid note from her purse, after she'd smacked him about a bit he told her simply that he needed it.

He never said sorry.

He never swore not to do it again, and if he had she wouldn't have believed him.

His looks were beguiling. His shaggy fringe and his bold black eyes with their sweeping lashes combined with that sparkly white smile would melt the sternest heart. He was also a perfect shape for his age. Not too tall, not too fat, not too lanky and with silken skin like a girl's. Sometimes she thought he'd pass as a rent boy. Yes, Joey could get away with . . .

Murder?

No way.

No child of hers.

Another place her mind wanted to go (and she fought to prevent it) was to the house of Holly Coates and her mother, her father, her uncles, her aunts. Shelley firmly believed that if anything like that happened to her she would have to top herself for the grief.

To see a child of yours die before you.

And in such a terrible way.

Little Holly with her two months of life . . . They must have had so many hopes and dreams.

She thought about Julie, her precious girl, and

how she might feel if some yobs came along and set her alight.

Shelley retched, gasped for breath, stood up and floundered around the room, blinded by tears. She had to bend double, the pain was so great. How can mental pain clog the brain and take away sight, balance, hearing and speech? No, Joey could never do that, her son could never do something like that. The loss would be the same as bereavement: each day would be a day to endure if she ever thought Joey might have done that.

The squash of car tyres against the kerb, headlights screaming across the ceiling and the sudden loud slamming of doors shot her fast out of her sad reverie. She jumped and drew her cardigan round her, suddenly cold, so cold. She rushed to the window but before she could get there the urgent knocking on her door pulled her to an instant halt.

'Mrs Tremayne, will you open this door immediately, please.'

Shelley had no option. If she didn't obey they would crash their way through. She pulled it open and was pushed back against the wall by a gang of louts who rushed straight upstairs.

'*But you can't*—' she began, terrified they would wake the little ones with their violence. 'Let me show you which room—' There was nobody left to listen to her except WPC Hollis, the last person in the world she wanted around at a time like this, and Shelley saw satisfaction underneath the woman's bland stare.

'Joey Tremayne,' the front man called out while leading the way into the bedroom. 'Get up, get dressed . . .'

'*He's a child*,' shouted Shelley. 'He's a little boy, he's only eleven. I have to come up and sort his stuff out.'

She tried to climb the stairs but WPC Hollis blocked her way with folded arms. 'For God's sake let me up there,' she called. 'I've got to check the others . . .'

'You just stay where you are. We'll be all done here in a minute.'

'*I have to go with him*,' she pleaded before this po-faced cow. 'He can't be allowed to go with you on his own.'

'That'll be fine,' said Hollis. She'd obviously done this before and enjoyed it. 'I'm here to sit with the kids. I'll call you if there's any problem.'

But Hollis didn't even like children. This lunchtime she'd ignored them and Julie, Casey and Jason would bawl their heads off if they came downstairs and found this hostile, frozen stranger sitting in their mother's familiar chair.

Jeans, trainers and a Man United sweatshirt. Joey looked such a sleepy baby.

Ten minutes later, as they left the house in a motley procession towards the cars, Shelley was astonished to see a little gathering of onlookers forming. They had come from out of the dark, out of nowhere, like gremlins, as if all their lives they had been waiting . . .

FIVE

They arrived like the stars of a Royal Command Performance, what with their escorts and flashing blue lights, and the railings across the pavement to prevent the public from getting too close.

There was no-one around. It was past midnight.

As they were rushed past the desk downstairs towards the lift at the end of the corridor, Shelley caught a glimpse of a dishevelled Bob Lessing dragging on a quick cigarette in a corner. So they'd picked up Marcus and Shane as well. She assumed that Darren and Connor were also somewhere in the building. Let her just get her hands on them . . . the scum. Maybe at the end of this dreadful night something positive would come out.

From the lift their little party was ushered into an interview room. The glass on the window was meshed.

'You stay in here with my young PC, Joey, while I have a quick word with Mum next door.' The speaker was a bald-headed, heavily built man with a kindly face and rolled-up shirtsleeves. 'Mrs Tremayne' – he gestured – 'after you' – following her out.

She turned back and said to Joey, 'Don't speak to anyone, mind.'

'Please don't worry,' said her escort, seating himself beside her in a way that suggested he was no threat. He had a friendly smile. 'My name is Hudson, Christopher, Detective Inspector in charge of this case, and my colleague DI William Boyce will be joining us in a moment. Is that OK with you, Mrs Tremayne? You're not uncomfortable with that?' And then he nodded. 'Please smoke if you want to.' And pushed a foil ashtray towards her across the metal table.

This unexpected kindness was such a bloody relief. At last she would have a chance to talk to someone who might understand. At last she could relax and feel that someone was on her side. There were people here who genuinely only wanted the truth. Well, Shelley wouldn't give them that, but she'd do her best to help them. She took up his offer and got out her cigs, crossed her legs and leaned back, as comfortable as was possible on such a hard moulded chair.

She could handle this.

She could cope.

'Now I just want to put you in the picture,' said DI Christopher Hudson, his hand resting lightly on a buff-coloured file. He was quite straightforward and down-to-earth. There was no messing about. 'At the moment we've got five lads in here including your Joey,' he began. 'We have two sound witnesses who saw the incident in the precinct yesterday afternoon and reckon they can identify one or more members of the group.'

'Joey wasn't even there,' Shelley butted in with a shake of the head.

'We'll come to that later,' said Hudson benignly. 'Before we bring in the witnesses we'd like to get the kids' own versions, straight from the horses' mouths as it were.'

'If they say Joey was there they'll be lying,' Shelley insisted, feeling quite safe. This man could be trusted.

'When we go in to interview Joey anything he says will be of his own free will and you must understand that. Part of the reason we brought these lads in was to protect them from rumours. There will be no pressure while I'm in charge. And we're not going to read him his rights, we're not ready to charge anyone, this is just a preliminary session to see how these versions match up.'

'I understand,' said Shelley, looking up as Inspector Boyce came in. A much younger man, he too looked pleasant with an open, ruddy face which suggested a sport like rugby and a preference for the open-air life.

After the introductions, during which the sandy-haired Boyce said little, Hudson finished off by reminding Shelley, 'We need your help here, Mrs Tremayne. The last thing we want is for Joey to feel intimidated. We would like you to reassure him that we're not out to get him, we're not his enemies; all we want to do is help to clear this mess up and let him go home as quickly as possible. Now before we start, would you like a word with him on your own?'

'Would that be OK? Would that look bad?'

'Not at all, I'd encourage it.' Hudson smiled. 'We'll leave you and Joey for five minutes and then we'll join you for a little chat. How's that?'

'Fine,' said Shelley, smiling back and stubbing her fag out with a new vigour.

Things were going to work out fine.

She had a feeling.

She was no longer alone.

'There'll be wires,' sobbed Joey, 'all round, and hidden cameras.'

'Listen,' Shelley urged him, 'we stick to what we said. We don't get riled, we don't lose our tempers, and we don't budge from what we agreed.'

'*Shuddup*,' Joey spat. '*Why don't you just shuddup?*'

'I don't want you to be frightened.'

'Frightened? Jesus, I'm shitting bricks.'

'Joey, you've got to remember, *you did nothing wrong*. You were there, that's all, but they can't prove that.'

'It might be better if I said I was there . . .'

Shelley's voice had a rasp to it. 'We stick to what we said.'

'I wish I knew what the others were saying.'

'The Lessings are saying they weren't there either. So they can't be blaming you, can they?'

'They're both thick as shit.'

Shelley shook her head hopelessly. 'Trust me, Joey, you'll be OK.'

'You know nothing,' he hissed.

* * *

The first ten minutes were like going to hospital. They took down the details: names, ages, addresses, siblings, family history, schools, illnesses, drugs. Joey answered all the questions with a scowl on his face but the officers seemed not to notice; certainly they kept their patience where she might have yelled at him by now if he had been at home.

The moron.

They led him around gently to the 'afternoon in question'.

'Why haven't I got my own brief?' Joey protested childishly. Too much TV, too much dreaming.

'Because we haven't charged you yet,' said DI Boyce with a patient shrug.

'Run us through what happened,' DI Hudson encouraged the boy, 'in your own words. Don't rush.'

Joey threw his mother a glance. She nodded and tried to smile. She failed.

'I went home,' he said. 'I was ill.'

'You went home before lunch, or after?'

'Before lunch. I didn't have lunch.'

'So you didn't spend two pounds in McDonald's on a Big Mac with fries at . . .' and he looked at his notes, 'between five and a quarter past one?'

Joey glanced at Shelley again. This time she looked abruptly away. 'No, I told you, I was ill. I was nowhere near McDonald's. McDonald's is in the precinct. I didn't go near the precinct.'

'And when you got home who let you in?'

'My mum.'

'And then?'

'I went upstairs. I had to lie down.'

'Were you feeling sick? Did you have the runs? Was it a sore throat? Was it a headache?'

Joey faltered just for a moment and Shelley filled in for him quickly. 'He felt sick.'

'Was it something you'd eaten?'

'How should I know?' Joey growled.

His reactions were too defensive. She wished he would make more of an effort. He wasn't lying with his usual aplomb.

Shelley was growing anxious.

They nagged at Joey.

He hated nagging.

They wouldn't leave the details alone. It was all about timing and who he had seen on his way back from school that lunchtime. She watched his frustration growing. He was tired; he'd had little sleep, if any.

The inquisitors stayed friendly. Almost too casual in their reactions. 'So what would you say to us, Joey, if someone suggested the lighter which was used to ignite the substance was yours? That several people had seen you using it as long ago as Tuesday last week?'

'I'd say they were bloody liars.'

'Could somebody have stolen it from you and maybe you hadn't noticed?'

'They could've.'

'*So it was yours?*'

'I never said that.'

Hudson paused here and made some brief notes.

'And what if cameras in a particular store had pictures of you with a can of inflammable liquid walking calmly out of the shop?'

Shelley listened carefully. Joey had told her that the Lessings had nicked the paraffin from B&Q because their mother was decorating their house. On her visit to their scruffy home the smell of paint had not been distinguishable. He had explained to his mother how Darren Long, larking about, had then snatched the can and thrown the contents over Holly's pram.

'I wasn't there,' Joey repeated, kicking the table leg with his trainers. 'So they can't have pictures, can they?'

'Joey always wears a blue jacket,' Shelley put in hopefully. 'He never goes out without it. I never saw any blue jacket on those pictures they showed on telly.'

Hudson turned to Joey. 'Could that be because Darren borrowed the jacket and left it on the car-park wall? Could it be that you picked it up later, as you hurried away from the precinct?'

'I dunno what you're on about,' muttered Joey.

Round and round the questioning went.

They were never unpleasant.

They were calm as you like.

But this was no casual chat.

This was no seeking after the truth.

This was taking the lies that Connor and Darren were telling and trying to catch Joey out with them.

Eventually Shelley said, 'Joey's tired. He's had enough of this, can't you see? He needs to go home to his bed. He can't tell you any more than the truth and I don't like the way you're handling this, to be honest.'

DI Hudson sat back looking serious, more serious than she had seen him yet. 'I take your point. We've gone as far as we can tonight, but I'm afraid we can't let Joey go home. For his own protection we must keep him here until we can finish this line of enquiry.'

'That can't be legal,' Shelley argued, 'not for a kid his age, for God's sake. He's done nothing, he can't stay here . . .'

'It can either be here for the next few hours or in a special unit,' said DI Hudson with a grimace, 'and that might be some distance away and more tiring. It's really up to you, but I'd recommend we keep him until you can come back in the morning.'

'What – *me leave him*?' Shelley spluttered.

'The other kids, you've got them to cope with.' As if she needed reminding.

'Then I'll have to bring them here with me. I'll be buggered if I'll abandon Joey like that. This can't be legal,' she said again. 'What are you trying to do here, screw us up?'

'Please don't get upset, Mrs Tremayne,' said DI Boyce, taking over. 'If you go home tonight and we keep Joey here that gives us time to arrange for alternative care for your kids—'

'Where?'

'I was going to add, that's if you've no friends

or family who might take them in for a few days?'

'No, I haven't,' she said, feeling hopeless. The last thing she wanted was to look pathetic in front of these power-driven men. She imagined they both had families, nice wives who shopped at Monsoon and were probably nurses or hospital administrators, gardens in which they grew vegetables, kids who took music and dance.

'Then it would have to be foster carers . . .'

'Foster carers my arse.'

But her father's family were as unknown to Shelley as her mother's. She had the vaguest memories of being among Chinese people who were chattering away incomprehensibly. Silk jackets with sequins featured somewhere, and a screen with a mountain tipped with snow, and embossed wallpaper in watery green. She remembered her father reading her books and tucking her into bed at night. She remembered him bringing toys off the ferry . . . but then all that suddenly stopped and her mother refused to speak of him.

At this point DI Hudson intervened. 'Could I just mention that it might be easier for them, and for you, if your children were not at home, for the next few days at any rate.'

'Why's that?' she demanded, but she already knew; she just wanted the copper to say it.

'In these sorts of unfortunate cases,' he explained to her carefully, 'the public can sometimes be rather a nuisance. And no matter how discreet we are, word gets around, especially in this internet age. People get angry. It might even be wise at this stage to remove Kez – is it Kez? – from school for a few weeks.'

'Shit through the door, broken windows, is that how the innocent are treated in this country today just because you lot are bungling fools who listen to gossip and arrest the wrong people?'

Her outburst was ignored. Instead the ruddy-faced Boyce said quietly, 'Tomorrow you will have representation, Joey's immediate future will be decided and some long-term measures can be taken regarding your own personal set-up.'

She caught her breath. 'That means you'll charge him?'

'I can't say anything else right now, but I do want to assure you that it would be better if you went home tonight and came back in the morning when we can sort some of these problems out.'

'*I don't believe this is happening.*'

'It must be hard,' said DI Hudson, obviously keen to end the session.

Joey sat back with his eyes closed, the picture of unconcerned innocence.

'Joey,' said Shelley, 'they say I'm to go.'

'Go then,' was all he replied.

'Will you be OK? Have you got everything? How about money?'

'Just go, Mum,' he said sharply, not even opening his eyes.

'I'll stay if you want. You know I will.'

He shook his head and kept tapping the table leg with his shoe.

'I'm not at all happy with this,' she said.

'It would be for the best,' said Hudson tiredly,

rising from his chair and beginning to gather up his papers. Boyce followed his example. 'Joey will be fine. There's people around all the time to look after him. Whatever he needs will be given to him. Please don't worry, Mrs Tremayne. And in a few hours you'll be back.'

Riding home in the back of the law car, Shelley was happy the policewoman driver didn't seem inclined to speak.

If only she had money.

If only she could go off abroad, or to a bolt-hole, a second home, somewhere buried deep in the country. If she had money she could probably influence the behaviour of the police.

If only she had a larger family on whom she could rely. There must be a granny somewhere living in the wilds of Cornwall, one of the Tremaynes of Bodmin Moor whom she had never met and of whom her mother had rarely spoken. She had kept no photographs of her past. But what a shock for the Tremayne relations to discover that their black sheep had given birth to a girl who, in turn, had given birth to a child-killer. They would hardly welcome her and the kids with open arms. More likely they would deny the connection, or else they would point out how right they had been to ostracize the child who had so foolishly broken ranks and married an out-sider. No good will come of it ... bad blood ... It was like an echo Shelley could hear over the sound of the cruising engine.

Man-mad. Oh yes, even after her own sad

experiences, Iris, her mother, had bristled disapproval once Shelley shed her cocoon of
ugliness, the specs came off and she rose and flew
like a butterfly maddened by all the new scents.
Iris was probably very afraid that Shelley's future
might mirror her own. They were both women
alone in the world. Men were anathema to her,
and Shelley's perceived promiscuity threatened
her.

In fact Shelley was no more promiscuous than
most of the girls in her group.

But what was the point in wishing?

As the car climbed the rise and levelled off on
the road to her house, Shelley leaned forward,
stretching to see.

What was this?

Who were all those people?

The peace was broken by excited jabbering on
the driver's walkie-talkie. She slowed down, they
passed the house, and when Shelley shouted,
'Stop here! Stop! Stop!' the policewoman
answered, 'My orders are to carry on. If we pull
over we'll make matters worse.'

'But what's going on? *My kids are in there . . .*'

'My colleagues are in the process of moving
your children right now,' came the answer.

'Why? Who are all those people? Let me out! I
have to be with them, for Christ's sake. Let me
out of here, what's the matter with you, *are you
mad*?'

'Please calm down, Mrs Tremayne. It will
enrage the crowd further if they see you. Just let
my colleagues carry out their orders and no doubt

74

in a few hours from now you will be with your children in a place of safety.'

'*Are they hurt?*' shouted Shelley. 'Did those bastards break in?'

'I don't know the details as yet,' said the driver, still travelling at an irritating fifteen miles an hour. Even so, Shelley's house was long out of sight. 'I don't even know where we're headed. They're unlikely to announce anything over my radio. What I'll have to do now is find a quiet lay-by and contact control on my mobile.'

'But they're going to be terrified out of their lives! They don't know anyone, they won't know what's happening. Dear God, I can't believe this, *this can't be happening to me.*'

As they passed the house Shelley's impression had been of a circle of dark-clad people, blue lights flashing, large dogs barking. Strips of Day-Glo on cops' uniforms. The lights were on, the curtains pulled back as if her house had been stripped of its clothing and exposed to a slobbering, filthy-minded audience, but of her children she saw no sign. The driver must stop. She must reverse.

'*They need me, don't you understand?*'

To this cry from the heart there was no answer.

SIX

It was almost dawn before Shelley followed WPC Molly Lamb up the back stairs to the place of safety that was waiting for her and her kids.

A three-bedroom flat above a launderette on the outskirts of Buckfastleigh, a manky, thin-carpeted flat done out all over in white paint which over the years, uncared for, had faded to a peeling and stained magnolia. The chipboard doors were badly scarred, and half the round metal knobs were missing. The amount of utility furniture was just about adequate. It all dated from about the same time, so when first acquired by the police authority it must all have been neat and new. Pathetically, in the children's bedrooms, which were fitted with bunks for maximum accommodation, half-torn bits of posters of animals and pop groups showed that Shelley's kids were not the first in this area to be forced into hiding.

Waiting anxiously for her children's arrival, Shelley touched the sheets. They were clean but smelled damp. Casey and Julie were still in cots. There was no sign here of any cots.

The street lights were still on. A pre-dawn February fog swirled around them like shreds of angel hair. She looked out of the smaller back-bedroom window to see a narrow street of tatty shops not successful enough for the more prestigious and expensively rated high-street positions – a newsagent, a bookie, a dingy hairdresser and a hardware store. Most of them had flats above with curtains drawn against the night. A light went on suddenly and Shelley instantly ducked back out of sight. She imagined this would be a transient community with high rates of commercial failure, people either on their way down or aiming for something better.

She shivered.

She bet none of them was on such a downward spiral as she and poor Joey were right now.

She needed answers to a hundred questions. 'How will I get into Plymouth from here?' Buses from the suburbs meandered their way into the city via every hamlet and back road and the trip thus took on the aspect of an expedition, almost requiring sandwiches.

'Don't worry,' said Molly Lamb, the only member of the force to allow her to use her first name so far. 'We'll make sure you get transport whenever you need it.'

'The thing is,' said Shelley, desperately tired and worried about so many things she felt sick and giddy, and the air hummed in her ears, 'I'm never going to cope without our stuff.'

'If you just make a list . . .'

'No, you don't understand, *everything, I need everything.*'

'We will do our best to make sure you get it.'

'But how long will it take? The children'll be here in a minute. Look.' She gestured around the kitchen, which smelled of damp wooden draining boards. The cooker was an ancient upright, gas, with a grill protected by tinfoil which wobbled over the top. The kettle was a cheap jug affair without an obvious lid and the flex was padded with sticky tape in patches along its length. But the most depressing room was the lounge with its limp and damp-stained curtains, its forlorn brown-covered furniture, its standard two-bar electric fire with the moth-eaten rug in front of it and those institutional prints on the walls of stark plants with hairy stems.

Children, more so than adults, need their familiar possessions around them, and in this bleak, joyless flat with no garden, not even a yard, their toys and games would be essential. That's if the maddened, baying crowd of last night had been prevented from destroying every item back home.

How soon could somebody bring them tea? Or milk? Or juice? Or biscuits? When the kids arrived she'd need nappies. The least she needed was bread and jam. Instead of these things Molly gave her a mobile along with a list of useful numbers.

Two cars drew up in the street outside as Shelley was searching the kitchen cupboards. She wanted to be at the door to meet her traumatized children and as soon as Julie was unloaded she grabbed her from the policewoman's arms. The child was sound asleep. She felt cold. Shelley laid her on the sofa and covered her with her jacket. The others were pale and drawn, with rings under their eyes and tear smudges on their cheeks. Molly turned the fire on while Shelley removed their coats and cuddled them. The police escort, including that hard-faced WPC Hollis, shambled in behind them rubbing cold hands and looking anxious.

Thank God, thank God for Molly Lamb. 'Tea bags,' the policewoman said. 'If anyone wants a cup of tea we have to go to the all-night garage, and there's a whole list of stuff which we're going to need here before we leave.'

Grumbling, the two male drivers who must have been involved in holding the crowd back at Eastwood turned and, with Molly in tow, drove off for the necessary supplies. To Shelley's relief the hostile Hollis took this opportunity to get a lift home.

The other female escort carried Casey to the sofa and laid him down gently before covering him with her shaggy coat. His nappy, like Julie's, was soaking and she prayed that Molly would remember Pampers. Jason, Saul and Kez stood there pale and shaking with cold, bewildered, like refugees.

'I'm Alex from social services. I thought this night would never end,' groaned the owner of the shaggy coat. 'I thought we'd never arrive. All that waiting while someone decided . . .'

Shelley, now on her knees rubbing small arms and legs, each child in turn, frantically needed to know, '*What happened?* What went on at the house?'

Alex tried to make light of it so Shelley had to remind her that she had caught a glimpse of the crowd and knew how potentially dangerous the whole episode had been.

Alex held out her hands to grab as much warmth from the two mean bars as she could. 'You always get these cretins. The last time we saw this behaviour was during the paedophile exposure a couple of years ago. Kids dragged along in pushchairs, misspelt posters, a baying mob who stay quiet until there's a victim who they feel is deserving of their sick attentions.'

That this young girl was an experienced social worker was hard for Shelley to believe. Although she'd had help from the state in the form of material benefits she had never, so far, had to deal with this side of the system. She supposed this girl had been bleeped from home to deal with this emergency, but she was still surprised at her appearance: long blue fingernails covered in stars, tattoos on the backs of her hands and a nose stud. Hardly the kind of image to reassure a small, frightened child.

'It's the same kind of morons who turn out each time,' Alex continued. 'They are society's victims, losers mostly, and so they relish the chance to condemn someone else – it makes them feel almost righteous. For them it is a kind of success. For once in their sad lives it's not them copping communal disapproval.'

Shelley had the kids sitting round her now, her

inadequate arms trying to shield each one. There were bits on the rug, old crumbs, bits of biscuit. She kept whispering, 'It's OK, you're all right now, I'm here.' She looked up at Alex, needing to know. 'Was it just us they targeted? How did they find out?'

'From what I've heard it wasn't just you and your family,' Alex reported. 'There were others involved but I haven't a clue who they all are. I was on duty last night so when we got the call from the police I just jumped into the car . . . You must have driven by only minutes later. According to the officer at the house, the mob had begun to throw stones at the windows. She didn't hang around to find out what their intentions were – Hollis just knew she must get the kids out.'

Shelley ran her hand through hair that hadn't been touched for twenty-four hours. She must look a sight, but she had ceased to care. She squeezed Jason so hard that he protested. There was a sob in her voice when she said, 'They must have been so terrified . . .'

'They were too tired to realize what was going on. Really. We just got them dressed and straight to the cars outside. They probably thought they were dreaming but then we just drove and drove waiting to hear where we were headed. It was such a relief to get out of that car.'

The thought of having to cope tomorrow with Joey, solicitors and maybe court after so little sleep and so much stress, and on top of that, sort this place out so it halfway resembled a home made Shelley weepy. And while she was at the cop shop who would take care of the others?

Alex reassured her. 'They're looking for a foster mother who lives locally,' she explained. 'As soon as that has been sorted the children will be taken there.'

Shelley despaired. 'So my kids will be in care?'

'Not officially. For that we'd need a court order and there's no grounds for us to go for one of those. No, this will be done on a voluntary basis. You mustn't worry; I promise you, most foster mothers are brilliant people. Every night they'll come back here. Their lives are being disrupted, I know, but we work to keep that disruption down to the absolute minimum.'

It was easy for Alex to talk this way but Shelley was stuck with the knowledge that 'inadequate mother' was the first weapon her critics would throw at her. And if they found Joey guilty of even being with that group at the precinct, what defence would she have against that accusation?

She was inadequate, she had to face it.

She had six kids with three fathers.

Joey had serious behavioural problems.

She'd had four close relationships and countless casual ones during Joey's lifetime. The last man she took up with, Julie's dad Dave, was now in Exeter prison doing a five-year stretch for burglary. There was a chance, and she knew this, that her kids would be taken away. When this thought crossed her mind a hard stab of resentment inside her turned itself on Joey.

How could he do this to her, how could he?

It was hard to fathom out how the mob had discovered the identities and addresses of the lads involved so quickly. If Joey's story was believed and he was released, as he should be, tomorrow, would the press and the public leave him alone? Would there be any law to protect him or did this mean that whatever happened the family would have to move house?

Start again?

Because there's no smoke without fire and everyone knew that Joey was a mess?

And what about compensation? If the police made such a colossal mistake surely Shelley could sue?

She would have to find a lawyer.

She would have to fight to clear Joey's name. At eleven years old, to live with such a repulsive reputation would be too damaging for a kid like Joey. It would destroy him. It might also destroy his whole family.

Alex said, 'Hell, I could kill for a cup of tea.'

But Joey was supposed to have killed a baby for kicks.

'Why don't you try and get some sleep for a couple of hours?' Alex suggested and got no response from Shelley, a thousand miles away. 'You really are going to need it. And we ought to get these children to bed.'

Shelley looked at the sleeping babies. 'There aren't any cots.'

'They could stay here on the sofa tonight. I'll

be with them and the others will soon be back with the goodies.'

With hardly an ounce of energy left and her body now aching all over, Shelley made one last effort. 'Kez,' she asked gently, 'how would you feel about sleeping in a top bunk tonight?'

'With a ladder?' He blinked himself out of his snooze.

'I think so. We'll try and find one. Come on, let's go.'

She shepherded the little ones up the stairs. They were too worn out to complain. There would be no cleaning of teeth tonight, no changing into fleecy pyjamas, no Wibbly Pig or Pooh Bear to act as comforters, and she was right, the sheets were damp.

The last thought that came to Shelley, before she crawled into the double bed fully dressed and too weary to bother with curtains, was that she hoped the policewoman driver would remember to buy a baby bottle.

She dreamed of nothing at all.

Breakfast news showed pictures of crowds besieging the Lessings' house.

Shelley awoke to find tea in the pot and toast getting cold on the Formica table. Someone had brought jelly marmalade, cornflakes, Utterly Butterly and Heinz fruit and custard for Julie. Several used mugs by the sink and the coffee-coated spoon in the sugar suggested that the last few hours had been busy.

Julie and Casey were awake and clean,

although still in yesterday's clothes. This morning Alex looked more extreme with her pink shaggy coat and her spiky hair. 'I'm about to be relieved,' she said, pouring a mug of tea for Shelley, 'and after the kids have had breakfast my colleagues will take them to Mrs Bolton's. Sugar? Two? Don't worry, she's lovely.'

In the fluorescent morning light the kitchen had lost none of its Dettox-and-damp-cloth aura, but the smell of toast did give it some crusty life.

It was slightly warmer down here this morning. They must have kept the fire on all night and Shelley supposed the night-storage heaters were beginning to do their job.

Cries from upstairs interrupted Shelley's first fag. Kez, Saul and Jason tumbled down the stairs, fretful after such a disturbed night. She hauled them into three kitchen chairs, heated some milk, poured three bowls of cornflakes . . .

'I hate cornflakes. I want Coco Pops.'

'I don't want milk. I want Ribena.'

In the midst of their cross fumblings it was almost inevitable that the milk bottle, half full, would go over. With her fag dangling from her lips and her eyes smarting from the spiral of smoke, Shelley used a J cloth to wipe the liquid off the floor.

This was Saul's fault; she whopped him one.

He screamed.

Alex started forward, about to protest, but retreated after second thoughts. Shelley's irritation grew. What did this little punk know about kids? How dare she criticize her methods?

No doubt she would now go about calling Shelley a child-abuser.

She would write a report.

She would inform her superiors.

And this foster mother, this Mrs Bolton. She would take one look at the state of the kids and assume they were routinely neglected.

How vulnerable Shelley was, suddenly so dependent on other people's opinions.

Alex assured her that somebody from the social services department would collect a vanload of stuff from home and have it delivered to the flat by tonight.

Shelley did her best to smarten the children. She combed their hair to loud protestations, she wiped faces and hands with a clean J cloth and a dab of Persil Liquid. She gave Julie a quick wash in the sink so at least the baby smelt fresh and clean although her jumper was soggy with dribble and her leggings were sticky with marmalade. They were ready just in time to be collected by Alex's colleagues, a man and a woman both closer to her own age, she was relieved to see. To any curious onlookers they might look like normal, harassed parents trying to bring order to a riotous family.

The children fussed and protested.

There were tears and tantrums.

Why should they go with these strangers?

Why wasn't Mummy coming too?

They went off noisily in a people-carrier. It seemed to take hours to strap them all in. This was a government department. They could take no short cuts with the law.

'Will I see you again?' Shelley asked Alex, feeling oddly abandoned, almost hurt, forgetting for a moment that this young girl was merely doing her job. Easygoing and capable, she'd begun to feel quite like a friend.

'I don't know, maybe,' said Alex with a yawn. 'That all depends what happens from here.' Shelley and her family were now just clients – interesting clients perhaps, in such a high-profile case. Alex would probably entertain her friends and family on many an evening describing how she spent the night with the mother of one of those 'evil monsters'.

'You should have seen how she whacked that poor little kiddy. He didn't spill the milk on purpose. Some people shouldn't be allowed to breed.'

They came for her dead on nine o'clock.

She hadn't been able to do much for the children, and without a change of clothes herself, without make-up, not knowing what sort of hell she was facing, Shelley felt low and lifeless. She repeatedly tried to convince herself that today they might let Joey go. She must not assume the worst.

By now the police might have dragged the truth out of those two liars, Darren and Connor. The Lessings, supposedly visiting their gran when the crime had been committed, would be too concerned with their own alibi to bother about implicating Joey. Their reputation said they were thick but surely they were street-wise enough to stick to their story, which would be supported by the rest of their family? And as far as identification went, that was notoriously dodgy and nobody could be convicted on the strength of that alone.

Dear God, she hoped that Joey had managed to sleep and that they'd been kind to him, and gentle. Today her son would need all the courage and cunning that he possessed. To survive this they must support one another, so no matter how she felt Shelley must appear upbeat and positive. It was with those resolutions freshly in mind that she spied with alarm the ominous little gathering around the police station entrance.

The car slowed to a halt and waited.

Shelley sat back, afraid to be seen.

'*Get down*,' barked the driver while the indistinct crackles of the walkie-talkie told her that her escorts were in discussion with officers inside the building. They must have suspected this might happen. Shouldn't they have taken some other route? Perhaps this was part of their plan, to wear their witnesses down before the questioning began in earnest. After what seemed to Shelley like hours, the car suddenly leaped into life with a roar and a scream of sirens. She felt every powerful vibration as it shot through the gates, protected on both sides by the law holding batons and shields to press the spectators back.

The obscenities travelled like missiles.

Every one of them struck their target.

The sickness she had felt as a child settled under her heart. '*Specky Four-Eyes.*'

At one point there was a crash on the roof. She felt vicious eyes peering through the smoky glass windows. Then just like she had seen on the news, Shelley was handed a blanket. She used it automatically to cover her head and, with one of the cops holding her arm, she was helped, blind, from the car and into the safety of the building.

The same procedure they adopted for every despised and at-risk prisoner.

SEVEN

Deceptively, they'd arranged the room so it looked almost intimate. Since first stepping into the building with that stagnant blanket over her head Shelley had sensed the electric atmosphere, seen averted gazes or pointed looks, heard low-voiced conversations. Some potent drama was about to be staged and she was part of the cast. Her entrance was now required. She wished somebody would hand her the script.

This interview room was larger than the one she remembered being in last night. The desk had been shoved against the wall, and bottled water and plastic cups suggested an extended session. A circle of chairs had been prepared, each one bearing a pen and paper as if this was some salesmen's convention. Someone had even thought to put a cheery rug on the floor but on the small coffee table above it a tape recorder and speakers reminded the guests that this was no party.

The room was empty.

Where was Joey?

Before she was able to choose a seat an energetic guy in a bright blue shirt was rushing across the room like a train holding out a firm hand for shaking. His straight blond hair touched his collar, his overlong fringe flopped over his eyes and his voice was posh as he said, 'Martin Chandler, glad to meet you, but hardly in these circumstances.'

'I'm sorry, I don't . . .?'

'From Grant and Wilson. My firm has been appointed to act for Joey,' he told her, noting her pale, intense face and the way her small, bony shoulders seemed to sag with the weight of this latest news. He might have called her stunning with that glossy black hair and those almond eyes, had it not been for her smallness and the whiff of poverty she carried with her like some cheap Woolworths scent. There was a lack of charisma about her; she was used to not being noticed. She wore thin blue jeans and an overwashed, bobbly black sweatshirt. Her trainers were old, badly scuffed. In this confrontational situation her efforts to blend into the background were not, unfortunately, going to work.

'So what does this mean?' Shelley forced herself to ask. 'What's been happening that I don't know about?'

'Chris Hudson, the officer in charge of the Holly Coates murder investigation, has been comparing initial interviews. He and his team have been working on the accounts which the five suspects and the numerous witnesses gave them yesterday. The fingerprint results came through an hour ago and there has been time to check them with the fingerprints of the five boys this morning.'

Shelley was uneasy with Martin's invasion of her space. These super-confident classy types were back in vogue, she had read. He had chosen a chair right next to hers and she wanted to shove her own chair back, away from him and his unwelcome news. She asked him warily, 'Jesus, what are you telling me?'

Martin Chandler was a professional and so, Shelley supposed, he would be unmoved by the situation. Still, it was with a surprising lack of emotion that he carried on with his onerous task. 'They've decided to charge Joseph with the murder of Holly Coates, and the other four boys with aiding and abetting.'

Anger, terror and repulsion came together in Shelley's loud protest. '*This can't be true.*'

Martin nodded firmly. 'That's where we're at, I'm afraid.'

Shelley began to cry, defeated and suddenly desperately cold. The very thought of what she faced, her and Joey together, caused her to moan in agonized protest. She pleaded with terrified eyes, 'But he didn't, he might have been there, *but I swear he didn't . . .*'

'You, me and Joseph will meet together later to talk, but now they are going to charge your son and ask him some questions. I realize this must be terribly upsetting but I advise you to say nothing at this stage and leave the talking to me. I've already had a brief chat with Joseph—'

'Oh, call him Joey for God's sake, please.' She couldn't recognize this stranger, Joseph. She had to keep reminding herself that this was her son

92

they were talking about. She was not some out-
sider looking in on the scene, like watching TV
cuddled up in her lounge. She was here, the time
was now, and this nightmare was the reality.

'It was a mistake for you to go round and visit
the Lessings last night. After you left they sussed
that the game was more or less up for them, so
the parents decided that to lie over their sons'
whereabouts would land them in worse trouble.
From what Connor and Darren were saying they
weren't involved in any of the action, and they all
say that everything happened so fast there was no
way they could have stopped Joey . . .'

No! No! Shelley pressed her hands to her ears.
'They're all in collusion, they're lying to protect
one another. Why hasn't anyone listened to Joey?
Why have you all turned against him like this?'

'This afternoon the police are bringing in the
witnesses for a formal identification. Joey will
have to face them, I'm afraid, but if these
witnesses fail to pick him, that's one small but
important success. And we need all those we can
get.'

'But if they do pick him out?'

'We'll take that risk.'

'What's Joey saying about this? Poor Joey, he
must be terrified.'

'He seems to be taking it in his stride,' said
Martin. 'He's denying the charge, of course.
Against all the odds he is still swearing he wasn't
there at the time of the crime, that he was home
with you. Apparently' – here Martin quickly
checked his notes – 'that was your storyline, too.

For his own sake your son has got to start telling the truth. I don't think he quite realizes the serious situation he's in.'

But Shelley couldn't take any more. She chose a rigid, fearful silence, lest she said anything that might harm Joey. She never should have suggested they told that lie. She was his mother, she of all people should have insisted on the truth from the start. Who knows what that mistake might have cost him? What with that lie and her visit to the Lessings, so far she had done Joey nothing but damage.

'Before we start this interview, Shelley,' Martin Chandler went on, 'I would like you to know that the detectives handling this investigation have obtained advice from psychologists involved with similarly sensitive cases, and officers from other forces with experience of dealing with children faced with such serious charges. They are absolutely determined that these interviews should be conducted in a highly sensitive manner. There's been worldwide criticism over the latest cases and it is accepted that these kids need to be handled with expert care.'

So what should Shelley say to that? One look round this stark room with its threatening circle of chairs was enough. It was not only Joey who'd be out of his depth; she wasn't feeling too confident either.

'One more quick question before they arrive.' Martin flipped open his file and thumbed through to the front. She noticed his heavy gold wrist-watch. What had she in common with this man?

Joey had never met anyone remotely like him in his life. How were either of them to relate to this public-school Hooray Henry, however well meaning he might be? 'Joey's father, Kenneth Hill? I believe you never married and that he no longer lives with you. Does he still have contact with his son?'

How the hell did they find out this personal stuff? 'Off and on. When he feels like it. Why?'

'He should be informed of the situation.'

'Some help he'll be,' tutted Shelley.

When they finally led him into the room she leaped up and unthinkingly tried to fold Joey in her protective arms. She hadn't considered his likely reaction, it just felt the natural thing to do, and so when he hissed, 'Gedoff,' and pushed her, the shock came like a slap in the face. But of course he was doing his macho bit, trying for a swagger, face screwed in a scowl. He might fool the law but not his own mother and underneath that bravado she saw a small and frightened eleven-year-old who was up to his neck in something too unimaginable to comprehend.

Joey was a beautiful boy.

They had always called him beautiful, from a newborn baby onwards. All sorts of people would stop and admire him, not just grannies. Although all Shelley's kids were dark, he was the only one who had inherited Liu Qi's neat shape and facial features, the white teeth, the sweetest smile and the natural ability to hide his feelings.

It was understandable, him being the firstborn,

that he should resent his four brothers and his sister. After all, he'd been five when Kez was born and the fact that Kenny moved in after that, another contender for his mother's affections, must have been hard for little Joey to bear. No wonder he did those small, cruel things.

She understood.

He loved them really.

'Sit down then, Joey,' said DI Hudson, offering his hand to Shelley.

She turned away.

She refused it.

This man had deceived her; she had trusted him when all the while, in spite of his comfortable manner and friendliness, he was the snake in the grass. The younger man, Boyce, merely nodded, but he had been equally calm and courteous during their discussions last night. Shelley was a fool to have fallen for that softly-softly approach, the oldest trick in the book. She should know the pigs better than that, particularly after her sojourn with Dave.

'Coffee before we begin?'

Everyone shook their heads.

'Coke for you, Joey? Lemonade?'

Joey ignored the offer and stared intently at the ceiling.

DI Hudson took over the interview, starting by turning on the tape and listing the people in the room.

First off he turned to Shelley. 'I presume you have had a chance to have a short chat with Mr Chandler to put you in the picture? If either you or Joey are unhappy with this legal team then it is perfectly acceptable for you to change it.'

'This is a joke,' Shelley replied. 'You are making such a bloody mistake. You'll be sorry, I swear you'll be sorry.'

Then came the charge and the formal warning. Immediately Martin Chandler asked Joey if he understood what that meant and went on to explain, in plain, patient English, exactly what the warning was for.

Justice?

Rubbish.

This had to seem threatening to Joey – to be confronted by three large men, all strangers to him, in a police interview room, two of them determined to trip him up on some false charge because he was more naive than the others and easier to intimidate.

The public were screaming for blood.

The police needed a sacrifice and Joey had been chosen.

DI Boyce began the interrogation. He went through Joey's original story, asking Joey to nod or shake his head because he was plainly refusing to speak.

Joey did neither.

'Perhaps, Shelley, you could explain to Joey how important it is that he takes part in this, for his own sake,' put in DI Hudson.

'I'm saying nothing,' said Shelley firmly. 'You carry on. You'll get nowhere. You'll see.'

This was going over old ground which Shelley knew off by heart. For an instant her concentration wavered and she was home with Kez as a baby and Kenny back on his ship, all of six years ago. That was a contented year with her still marvelling over the joy of a permanent home after her gypsy lifestyle. At this stage of her life she was even considering marrying Kenny and settling down. She could do worse. She was luckier than most with two bright little boys and regular money coming in and with Kenny away so much of the time she could please herself.

She never knew what took her upstairs. In hindsight it felt like one of those forebodings of horror. She'd left little Joey in the bath; at five he was quite safe to be left playing with his boats while she cooked up his favourite fish fingers. She would only be downstairs for five minutes.

But something in the aura disturbed her. She rushed into the bathroom to find Joey holding Kez, completely naked, under the bathwater, the baby blowing bubbles from his nose like a squeezed rubber doll. She plunged her arms in and whipped Kez out, wrapped him in a warm towel and held him upside down while he coughed and spluttered and sicked and gasped . . . He was only four months old. She sat up with that baby all night, watching his breathing. And listening.

'I was trying to get him clean,' was Joey's laughing explanation.

She'd never told anyone else about that, not even his dad.

What made her think of that now? She was a traitor of the highest order.

DI Hudson put a see-through package on the

coffee table. 'Take a look at that for me, Joey,' he said, telling the tape what the item was, 'and tell me if this is your lighter.'

Joey, losing interest in the ceiling, was now rocking backwards and forwards moronically on his chair. He threw an angry glance at the detective before he returned to the rocking. His hands were out of sight, clasped rigidly behind him. His hands, his fingers, were traitors, they had given him away.

'It has your prints on it, Joey. It has your prints and nobody else's. Unless he was cute enough to wear gloves, Connor Mason could not have used it.'

Still no response. 'Peter Higgins and Lloyd Nosworthy are both pupils in your class at school. Can you confirm that for me, Joey?'

It was a waste of time Hudson asking.

'Because both those boys swear they saw you using that Zippo early last week. They remember the lion engraving on the side. They also remember that you bragged to them about nicking it from the shoe-mender's when you went there to get a key cut for your mum. That would be, let me see, last Tuesday. The owner remembers you in there.'

'*So he nicked a lighter for God's sake . . .*'

'If you don't mind, Ms Tremayne.'

Joey showed no emotion at all, he just kept up his maddening rocking. What the hell must they think of her barmy son? He looked as if he was under hypnosis.

'And then there's the paraffin.' DI Hudson

moved on to the next piece of evidence, relaying the obvious for the tape. 'I am showing the accused the bottle of paraffin, item two on the list . . . Would you look at this for me please, Joey?'

'*Joey?*' said Martin Chandler, flicking his shiny blond fringe as he spoke. 'This attitude is really not helping.'

Surely they weren't about to make out that Joey had thrown the paraffin?

'This bottle is covered with your prints, Joey, and we have a surveillance video which shows you and your mates in the store, and as you pass the display you can be clearly seen picking up this item.'

'If that's the case,' argued Shelley, 'why wasn't he nicked at the time?'

'Because, unfortunately, the manager and his assistants don't have the time to run through the tapes until after the store is closed.'

'I don't believe you,' stated Shelley. 'I want proof. I demand to see this with my own eyes.'

'And you will, in time,' said Hudson patiently. 'For the moment I just want Joey to know that his movements were recorded. You were not at home on the afternoon of Wednesday the sixth of February. You were in the precinct larking about with Darren Long, Connor Mason and Marcus and Shane Lessing. And you all called in at McDonald's for a Big Mac and chips between one and a quarter past. We have witnesses who can testify to that, witnesses who are coming in later this afternoon.'

Was this true? Or was it a trick devised to lower

her son's defences? During the time she had Dave as a lodger she'd learned more about the police than she'd ever learned in her life, let alone off the telly. Dave, Julie's dad, now banged up in Exeter, told stories of police sleaze and deception that would make your hair stand on end. Some stop at nothing to get a conviction, he said; others run drug rings, protection rackets, control the city's toms – turn up anything seedy round here and there'll be a bleeding copper behind it. Shelley had no reason to disbelieve him, he'd had enough experience after all.

She turned in frustration to Martin Chandler. 'I thought you told me that these interviews would be conducted with special sensitivity. Look at the kid. Just look at Joey.' Shelley's voice rose far higher than she had intended. 'He's in a right state. You should stop this now, you're driving him mental with your daft questions. If you'd just leave me alone with him for a moment I could get more of the facts out of him than you lot ever will.'

'What about your dad, Joey?' Chris Hudson tried an alternative tack. 'Would you feel more comfortable if your dad was here with you? We could find him if that's what you want. Come on, Joey, give us a chance.'

Shelley sighed loudly. She'd already told them that his dad was a wanker too wrapped up in himself to give a toss about his three sons and only hanging about in the hopes of a grope if Shelley was pissed. But at this suggestion from Hudson, which didn't affect Joey in the slightest,

101

Boyce caught his colleague's arm and gestured for him to step outside. 'A word,' was all he said. First they had to go through the silly rigmarole of telling the tape what was happening.

During their absence Shelley got up and moved over to Joey. She wanted to stroke his head. She wished he would stop that babyish rocking; he used to do it in his cot when she left him to cry for too long. 'Joey,' she whispered to him gently, not sure if she was getting through, 'Joey, it's OK, it's going to be all right, my chick. They've just made an awful mistake, that's all, and it might take some time to sort out.'

He paused in his rocking for long enough to glare at his mother with the kind of hatred she had never seen in her son's eyes before. They were blaming, burning, accusing . . . but what had she done that he saw as so wicked? All she was here for was to protect him.

That was her role; there was no other.

Boyce opened the door and called Martin Chandler outside to join them. What the hell was going on secretly outside that door? More conspiracies? More devious traps?

There were now just her and Joey in the room. 'I don't blame you for being angry, I do understand how you must be feeling, but just remember, Joey, I love you, whatever happens I will always love you, and nothing you have ever done could make me change how I feel. This shit will soon be over, I promise—'

In came DI Hudson. 'We're stopping the interview here,' he said, seeming vaguely preoccupied.

'PC Frey here will take Joey back to his room while we have a quick discussion.'

Shelley got up to leave. She wasn't about to let Joey go, not in the troubled state he was in. She wouldn't let the kid out of her sight whatever they tried to do to her.

'Please, Shelley,' said her young brief, with such a look in his eyes that she paused and took notice. 'Just for a moment,' he continued. 'You can be with Joey again in a minute but there's something important you should know.'

Shelley sat back down, gripping the useless notepad in one hand, flicking the ballpoint nib in and out while she waited for the three men to be seated. Expectantly she glanced at all three to see who was going to speak. The atmosphere was charged; it was clear that nobody relished this job.

'It's Kenny Hill, Joey's dad,' DI Hudson began with that kindly look of sympathy which Shelley could no longer trust. 'He's in Derriford Hospital in the intensive care unit. Last night, apparently, he went drinking and some louts in the pub worked out who he was and gave him the treatment . . .'

'*Oh my God, no.*'

'He has only just been identified. He was found this morning behind some containers down by the docks. They left him there to die like a dog.'

EIGHT

She did get some time alone with Joey.

It was considered by all concerned to be wiser if Joey was not told about the attack on his father, so it was doubly hard for Shelley to cultivate the upbeat attitude she needed to pass on to her son.

A call to the hospital confirmed there was no change in Kenny's condition. It didn't matter that she had stopped caring, it was unimportant that she found Kenny a loudmouth, a bore and a liability; the knowledge that he had been beaten up disturbed her more than she would have thought possible. Kenny was probably, she realized with sadness, the best friend she had ever had.

Sitting in the discomfort of the unlocked cell with Joey, Shelley was very aware of how alone in the world she was; more alone than most, she suspected, not without pain. There was nobody she could call on in an emergency such as this, no sisters or brothers, no parents left – but worse than this, no friends. Had she deliberately shunned overtures by neighbours and other mums she had met? She had to admit she was not a woman to go actively seeking friendship and this she blamed on her childhood, the innate distrust of others caused by those years of bullying. She knew how quickly a friend could turn and woundingly betray a confidence just for a quick laugh.

Men Shelley found more honest and she preferred their company, but it had always been the laddish, pissed kind of camaraderie she found at pubs and clubs where the music was mostly too loud to allow any meaningful communication.

The other kind of relationship Shelley knew well was the sexual one, and this, too, she had found superficial, all grunts and thrusts and few words. The sort of crazy home life she'd had with three small children needing constant attention had meant that, after Kenny, the men in her life had been turned into instant child-minding assistants.

Caring and sharing.

All except Dave who was never there. Don't fence me in, he'd say. She wondered how he was coping with life confined to a cheerless box.

Dave. How safe was Dave stuck there in jail surrounded by brainless louts and psychos? Once they knew who he was? The fact he was no relation wouldn't count . . . he'd had sex with the monster's mother, hadn't he? Together they had created a child. And he had actually lived for a year in the den where the eleven-year-old fiend was bred and fed.

They might as well have locked Joey's cell door because he was certainly a prisoner with a copper standing outside like a guard, waiting on his every command.

They brought in tuna and cucumber rolls.

They brought in chocolate cupcakes.

Joey had a choice of fizzy drinks, and there were comics and felt pens in a pile on his bed. After lunch they'd be going to court. They needn't worry, they need say nothing, Joey must only give his name and plead not guilty to the charges.

News of the recent arrest of the culprits had been released to a ravenous media and DI Hudson fed their appetites by reading out statements on lunchtime radio and TV.

This was like feeding mice to lions.

An agitated nation was waiting with bated breath for more detailed information. Not again, the pundits cried with one voice. How could this kind of tragedy happen again? It defied the comprehension of normal people. An anguished and bewildered world wept out loud for the baby. This manifestation of the inhumanity present in the human race left the door wide open for the worst kinds of parents to feel self-righteous and the reactionary forces of law and order to paint their bloodthirsty agendas in red.

Hanging was too good.

Bring back the birch for kids like these.

Get the stocks back on the village greens.

Grave examples, the mothers and fathers of murdered children were dragged from their grief and put on the screen to give their awful testimonies.

Throughout the land the peasants were revolting and some sort of appeasement must be thrown their way in the form of meaty revenge.

The twenty-first century's answer to the Roman circus.

Shelley and Joey, in their sheltered refuge, knew nothing of this.

'If they know we were lying about me being sick, they won't believe us over anything else,' Joey reasoned.

Alone together and at last Shelley had persuaded Joey to speak. Instead of rocking on his seat he now paced the floor, fists clenched at his sides. *'What are they going to do to me, Mum?'*

Jesus, what answer could she give him?

'Why won't they believe me?'

'Because the others have ganged up together,' Shelley said. 'It'll all come out in the end, you'll see. They can't keep these lies up for ever. But Joey, that lighter, was it yours? Why did you tell me it was Connor's?'

'I never said that,' muttered Joey morosely. 'I said he threw it, that's all. And he did.'

Another fact that worried her was the film of Joey nicking the paraffin. They seemed so sure about that. But she didn't feel she should push her child too hard at this stage. He needed to know that his mother believed in him, that was the message she must get across. There'd be time for the details later.

'What will they do to me?' he asked again. *'Will I be coming home?'*

107

For the second time since this nightmare began she was filled with an unexpected antagonism towards him. All this pain was his bloody fault. He had put her in this hopeless position and now he was asking her impossible questions; the ignorance behind them was breaking her heart.

At the back of her mind was the nagging concern for the safety of her younger children. Joey was OK, he hadn't a clue about Kenny's terrible injuries or how quickly the righteous had pounced on the evil in their community.

Poor Kenny, pissed and mouthing off, she could just picture him on the stool at the bar putting back lager like there's no tomorrow, and then the pack who crept up on him, sensing blood. News of the arrests on the Eastwood Estate must have travelled like the wind and some prick-head must have recognized Kenny . . . Was there the slightest chance that her kids, with the kindly Mrs Bolton, would also be recognized and punished for being who they were?

This sulky, frightened, stubborn little sod had put them all in danger.

'From now on we have to tell the truth, that's the only way we'll get out of this,' she told her son, only half believing. So far the liars were winning the day . . . Just let her get her hands on those bloody Lessings; these days the law was too bleeding soft.

Ugh, her coffee was cold. With a cautious glance at the copper by the door Shelley turned her back to him and lit another cigarette. She would ignore that no-smoking sign. She would have to use the packet as an ashtray. She wished she could change before going to court: impressions must make a difference. And a bath, how she longed for a bath; she had done some sweating in the last few black hours and Joey himself looked like some scruffy oik.

She couldn't help it, she smiled openly.

'What's so funny?' demanded Joey. 'If you cared about me you wouldn't be smiling.'

It would be unkind to tell him she had just remembered the hours she spent after Joey was born just staring at him in his white Babygro and marvelling, while round and round in her head went her dreams for him . . . Not so much greatness but more that he would find love and laughter, and maybe excel at music or team sport, a talent which would involve other people so he need never be lonely.

But if he had excelled they would never have known it. At the luckless schools Joey attended, sport and music were off the curriculum and how could Shelley ever have paid for him to have private lessons? She had, at times, considered him gifted, just because he was so peculiar and she'd read somewhere that gifted children were often the most difficult.

She was seriously surprised when the only reports that came home from school said 'poor'.

Anxious, in the luxury of the silver-blue Volvo with Joey between her and his brief, Shelley dreaded how she would feel when she saw his smug mates at the hearing.

Some friends.

She couldn't count the number of times she'd warned Joey to stay clear of that lot, mouthy vicious little morons, and Joey was easily influenced especially when he was bored.

At some point before their kids were nicked last night, the Lessings must have contacted the Masons and the Longs and concocted this tissue of lies between them.

In spite of Dave's reservations, Shelley had enough faith in the British justice system to believe that their deceit would come out. All would be revealed in the end. But up until then what would happen to Joey?

'We would normally ask for bail,' said Martin Chandler. 'It would be refused, but we'd ask. But under the present circumstances Joey would be far safer in custody.'

Shelley's voice rose. '*How long for?*'

The brief shook his head. 'We will have to see how it goes.'

'So I'm not going home?' said Joey flatly.

'I'm afraid not, Joey, not this time,' said Chandler.

'Where then?' he demanded.

'They'll find somewhere local if they can, but with five of you involved it's going to be hard to accommodate you all in separate units. There's such a shortage of places for kids.'

'But I don't wanna go,' said Joey.

Childishly he still failed to realize the enormity of the charges against him. That, Shelley thought, was because he was innocent and just could not understand that bad things could happen to an innocent person.

'It won't be for long,' Shelley put in.

'You don't know that,' he said angrily. '*Why do you say that when you don't know?*'

'Your mum's only trying to help, Joey.'

'She should keep well out of it,' was the answer.

In his trauma poor Joey had to be angry at someone, and that someone would have to be her. It was up to Shelley to understand this and not react aggressively.

Nothing had prepared either of them for the crowds outside the Magistrates' Court. What do they do, for God's sake, put up posters to advertise every movement of every poor jerk in this sodding country? But contrary to everyone's expectations the Volvo swept round at the last minute and entered the yard through a side gate which swung open, then clanged tight against the mob.

Joey's face was white with tension. His small hands were clenched tightly on his knee. She noticed there was green felt pen on his thumb. He had been colouring earlier on, *colouring*, didn't that say it all? Shelley had already experienced something of this communal anger, but never with her child at her side. '*Specky Four-Eyes*' sounded pathetic compared to the one shrill voice that managed to reach her over the throng, '*You evil bastard, you devil's spawn.*'

She had no control over her crying. It no longer distressed her, even for Joey's sake. It had nothing to do with grief or fear; it was a physical manifestation as involuntary as a hiccup but silent and almost consoling, an interminable stream.

Joey was staring at her. Her breakdown at this point was not helping. And Shelley saw that his eyes, fixed on hers, were as wounded as her own.

The four fellow accused must be here already, but carefully Joey and Shelley were shown to a waiting room under the courthouse from where they could hear or see no-one else. All the boys were being dealt with individually, Joey's being the most serious charge.

'So you mean we're not going to see them at all today?' a thwarted Shelley asked Martin Chandler.

'Hopefully not,' he replied.

'I have things I need to ask them,' Shelley said with tight control.

'Now is not the time,' he told her.

'If not now, when?' she demanded.

'Counsel will be asking the questions when we meet them in court at the trial.'

'But how long till then?'

'That depends on how long it takes to prepare the cases,' he said.

'What? You mean months? Is that what you're saying?'

'It could be months, yes.'

Joey had never been away from home before. He'd not even stayed with a friend and the one chance he had to go to France with the school he had chickened out of at the last minute for fear of feeling homesick. She'd had to tell them he was ill or he'd have lost face in front of his friends. He was frightened of the dark. She always left a night light on in his and Julie's room.

How could Chandler think of admitting these horrors with such a casual arrogance? Like you'd say if you took two sugars in your coffee. Joey, listening to this conversation from his corner of the room, looked away. She probably shouldn't press on with this in Joey's hearing but she had to know the truth. They both needed to know.

Better now than later.

'So what sort of place will they take him to?' She dreaded hearing the answer.

'To a young offenders' institution.'

'*But they're awful places,*' she pleaded.

'Not all of them. The ones you hear about are invariably the bad apples. Some are run extremely well, with quite encouraging results, I believe.'

'But Joey will be on remand. He's not guilty. He's done nothing wrong.'

'Yes, and naturally that will be taken into account.'

'And how about the other four? Will they be given bail today?'

'I doubt that. For their own safety it would be wiser if their whereabouts were unknown.'

'If they send me away I'll escape,' said Joey darkly. Shelley heard a choke in his voice but when he spoke again the tone was harder. 'There's no way they can keep me inside.'

'There's no need to take this so badly, Joey. Your family will come to see you regularly.' Chandler imagined he was being reassuring. 'And of course your schooling will be resumed. You'll find all kinds of boys like yourself you will be able to make friends with.'

God, this sounded like Enid Blyton. *The Wishing Well. The Faraway Tree.* Once upon a time and all that. Shelley wished the solicitor would keep his daft ideas to himself. With every word he was making things worse and Joey was kicking against the wall, his looks now thunderous.

Chandler checked his watch. 'They'll come for us in a minute. This waiting is often the hardest part.' So cool. So controlled. They could be at the sodding dentist.

'I'm not going anywhere,' Joey growled.

'What d'you mean?' Shelley asked in alarm.

'I'm bloody well staying here.'

'That attitude won't get you far,' said Chandler with a frown. 'Now is the time to cooperate, not start behaving like a bloody fool.'

'He's right,' Shelley began nervously. 'Come on, Joey, don't start—'

'*Fuck off.*'

Come on, come on . . .

She longed for a fag. She looked at her watch for the tenth time; how long this was taking, and with every extra second the tension in this claustrophobic little room was growing. The other lads must be in court now, she guessed. They would leave Joey till last. But what was the point of bringing him in early if they knew he would have to wait for so long? He wasn't an adult, he was a child. Well, they weren't bothering to take that into account, in her view. And dammit, she would tell them so.

Finally, after a period of silence so thick and breathless it was like a grey blanket squashed and tucked in over the windowless room, the copper called them out. Chandler took one step towards Joey, a fatal move with Joey in the mood he was in. He kicked out at Chandler Kung Fu-style and caught him hard on the shin.

Chandler cursed.

'*I said fuck off*,' Joey shouted. His black eyes were flashing pure venom as he crouched in the corner of the room.

Chandler called to the copper outside. These dramatics were quite uncalled for and a waste of time in the circumstances. Had these people never dealt with kids Joey's age before? Had they no idea? Or did they enjoy the drama, the conflict?

Was that how they got their kicks?

The burly officer never paused to find out what was happening, or to ask questions. There was no time to calm Joey down. 'Come on, you nasty little git. We can't have the beaks upstairs kept waiting.' With two quick movements he dragged Joey out of his corner, pinned his arms behind his back and marshalled him down the corridor and up the steep steps to the dock.

Shelley hurried after them both while the limping Chandler brought up the rear.

NINE

'Come down to the front here please, Joseph, so that we can see you properly.'

Suddenly, as Joey appeared, there was a rush of frenzied activity followed by an almost religious hush. But before anybody could act on the magistrate's invitation, the copper raised his spare hand – with the other he still pinned Joey's small wrists – and indicated his need to speak to the clerk of the court. The elderly man shuffled over, the grim reaper without the hood, and a whispered conversation ensued. Urgent information about Joey's state of mind was quickly relayed to the bench and all six eyebrows were raised in interest as their gazes focused directly on the top of the accused's head.

'Well, in that case you better stay where you are,' said the chairman, a ruddy-faced local man with cauliflower ears and a soft West Country burr to his voice. 'Give him a stool please. But I must say this news is very disappointing.'

The contrast between the waiting cell and this airy, spacious room was immediate and striking. It was wood panelled and wooden floored, with bright square lights built into the ceiling. A plush upright chair with a seat of maroon leather was placed beside the dock so that Shelley could be by her son.

She did not sit down.

She stood rigid beside him.

His head was only just visible over the top of the dock. She was reminded of being forced into church by Iris when she was little. Martin Chandler, still limping – it can't have been that bad, thought Shelley, Joey was only wearing trainers – took his place at the front of the court where his spectacled clerk was waiting. The young man seemed worried; in view of the importance of this case he had been expecting Chandler to arrive earlier.

The hearing proceeded as Chandler had told them it would. The charges were read by the ancient clerk, dwarfed by his gown and twisted like a Rackham tree, his thin hands blotched with liver spots, and mumbling. Chandler answered on his behalf when Joey was asked his name and how he was pleading – predictably Joey refused to cooperate.

The three magistrates on the bench then went into a legal wrangle with the prosecution and the defence, something to do with tabloids and Sundays asking for the anonymity rule to be lifted bearing in mind the vast interest in this case and the enormity of the crime.

Shelley, unable to fathom out much, did catch the words 'in the public interest'.

This couldn't possibly be happening. Life had

been unbearable enough before his name was made public; the repercussions of Joey being headline news all over the land would be absolutely horrific.

At last that brute who had manhandled her son up the stairs and into the courtroom released his arms.

About time too.

She glanced to the side and saw Joey's stricken face, his features distorted by fear. He was fighting for control but his small body was shaking in his efforts to appear nonchalant. How she longed to abandon this outmoded formality and hold him close and comfort him. These people, his accusers, did not see a child; their hawk-like eyes saw four foot five of evil incarnate. The repellent crime of which her son was accused had turned him repellent in the eyes of the world. Unlike some notorious previous cases, this time there was no prolonged argument about Joey being too young to know right from wrong.

There were precedents now.

They were using them.

'This is going to take some time, I'm afraid,' said Chandler's assistant, bothering to get up and bring Shelley some welcome answers.

'They won't let Joey's name be printed? They won't let that happen, will they?'

'No way,' he said firmly. 'But they have to try. I would sit down if I were you, take the weight off your feet while we're waiting. Martin will have a chance to ask for bail in a moment.' And the young man returned to his place.

Why raise her hopes at this stage? Martin had already explained that bail would be denied. Maybe the young man with the spots and the glasses had been observing in the courtroom during the appearance of the four fellow accused. Maybe they had not been remanded. Perhaps Martin was ignorant of this. Was there a chance, after all, that Joey could come home tonight and be with his brothers and sister? *Oh dear God, she hoped so.*

Oh Joey . . .

If he broke down in the dock it would help.

'Joey,' she whispered, aware of the attention this small movement caused. 'OK?'

He continued to stare defiantly in front of him. Only she could see his thin legs crossed tightly as he balanced on that wretched stool.

'You can sit down if you like,' the ugly copper muttered to Shelley. He was still poised behind Joey like a hunched-up bear.

Joey ignored him. He seemed in a world of his own.

The last time Shelley was in court it was for Dave's trial. They had waited six months for that day, from the time he was first charged to the time he was banged up, and in those six months which he spent at home on bail the tension between them became unendurable, especially when Shelley knew he was up to his bad old tricks again.

Julie, his child, was born in September and six weeks later her dad was in jail. Some start for a kid.

That relationship had begun ridiculous and ended up the same. They had sung 'Seasons in the Sun' together down at the Las Vegas Club on karaoke night, when the booze had given her confidence to get up and make a prat of herself. They'd both been so carried away by the brilliance of their harmony they spent the rest of the evening together, he came home with her for the night, and that was how it had started. Shelley had been on her own since Malc pissed off the Christmas before ... and that, the end of her shortest relationship ever, had been on account of Joey.

Stinking of drink, the first action she'd had to take the night she came home with Dave was to lift Joey out of her bed and dump him back in his own.

And he hadn't been too happy with that. Can you blame him? But she was so tired of being alone ... She needed some light relief, some fun.

She wondered how it would be for Joey in the Crown Court. She prayed it would not come to that. She had heard that in juvenile cases the lawyers left off their wigs and gowns in an attempt at informality. What a laugh.

The day of Dave's court case Shelley had been a nervous wreck while Dave, the nerd, took it all in his stride.

He knew he would go down.

He was what they called a persistent offender.

She was a witness for the defence. They tore her to shreds. All done up in the way Dave liked, she had stood there in the witness box exposed as a liar, described as a tart. If she answered a question they shouted at her. If she stopped to think for a moment they jeered. Shelley came out of there feeling like some cretinous arsehole. She had sworn she would never do it again and now this . . . She would have no option.

Dave had moved in on a permanent basis and they went through the inevitable tantrums from Joey, whose disappearances from the house became more frequent. To be fair, Dave did his best but being home all day didn't help; he reckoned no-one would take him on because of his criminal record. He'd given up trying for a respectable job and relied on information passed to him by his shifty mates to bring in a fluctuating income . . . Sometimes he had hundreds to spend, sometimes he borrowed off her.

Not a great example to the kids, Shelley had to admit, but he was a laugh, good to have around. She knew looks weren't important but the way Dave looked did make a difference and she could tell other women were envious when they saw her and Dave out and about. Without that small paunch he would look like Beckham when he had his hair long, blue-eyed, blond-haired and square-jawed. Amazing.

She missed him.

She missed him now.

Having another adult around . . .

Dave swore Joey was a serious nutcase, but that was his OCD. She'd discussed it with the clinic nurse, who had told her not to worry, lots of kids were obsessive like that. Obsessive compulsive disorder. Even the Queen had it when she was young. She had to line up her wooden horses in perfect lines before she could sleep. It was just an age thing. Most children came through it. Dave teased Joey about the compulsive arrangement of his possessions – his pillows must be exactly aligned, his CD games and tapes had to be perfectly stacked and his sweatshirts on their shelf must resemble a Jumpers window before he'd begin to try to sleep.

And then came the mantra which he must go through before he let Shelley go ... He'd been much worse when he was little; at least now it was only:

'Night, Mum.'

She'd have to reply, 'Night, Joey, sleep well.'

'I'll try,' was the next line of the script, followed by Shelley's 'See you in the morning.'

'See you in the morning,' Joey would finish, but any slight interruption, like the phone or one of the little ones calling, meant they had to start again before she would be allowed to leave him and go back downstairs.

'Don't pander to the little sod,' Dave used to reprove her. 'Same with the night light. The boy's a wimp. Just shut his door and ignore him.'

'I've tried it,' said Shelley. 'It doesn't work.'

'He needs a shrink,' Dave declared.

Sometimes watching Joey obsessively packing his lunch-box for school was so exasperating you could scream. But to suggest any help or try to take over was to provoke a tantrum. Everything had to be just right. But if she was such a terrible

122

mother how come her other kids were all normal? Or as near normal as kids can be.

He had grown out of it in the end. But had something worse replaced it?

Dave, bored to death at home all day, would sometimes deliberately provoke the boy. He'd do disgusting things like spit into Joey's glass – and Joey could not tolerate the idea of other people's saliva. Joey kept his toothbrush quite separate from those of the rest of the family. He wiped clean glasses and cups obsessively before he would deign to use them. Shelley would scream at Dave to leave Joey alone, it wasn't bloody funny. The time Joey smashed the glass and went for Dave with the jagged edge was the last time Dave tried that one.

'Dave's just got a warped sense of humour,' Shelley said, trying to smooth the waters. 'He thinks you enjoy these stupid jokes, he loves to see you riled. I just wish you'd try and relax. Dave doesn't mean any harm, not really.'

'The little bugger's jealous,' Dave said. 'Someone else in Mummy's bed, someone else to share his chips with.'

Shelley defended her son to the last. 'Well, it can't be easy for him,' she said, 'never able to get into the loo with you sitting there with the door wide open. You're in his face all the time, Dave. And there's no need to walk around starkers. The sight of you naked'd drive anyone over the edge. He's a kid, you're a man, he might see you as a threat.'

'I'll stick my arse in his face, see how he likes

123

that.' Dave laughed. So laid back himself, Dave found their constant sparring amusing; he never sussed the hurt he was causing. He was not the most sensitive of men.

'Why d'you stay with that piss-pot, Mum?'

'Because we care about each other. You'll understand when you're older. And he cares about you, Joey, he's very fond of you really.'

And Dave did care, in his own way. He tried and failed to involve Joey in the junior football league. He went out and bought him all the gear and dragged him out every Sunday morning. Dave taught Joey to swim and Joey was ecstatic when Dave took him off to the moor for the day on his mate's powerful Harley. Dave was the one who gave Joey his most precious possession – that expensive digital Konica. It was a great shame the law removed it when they conducted their first search of the house, but Dave swore he'd replace it one day with a model from less dubious sources.

And Shelley couldn't help but feel that it might be good for Joey to experience the kind of rough-and-tumble that only a man in the family could provide. It was time he got used to jokes, slight teasing, without resorting to childish tantrums. Basically Dave meant no harm.

Two o'clock came and went and the polish smell in the courtroom was overtaken by the dry smell of stale breath.

Dave could never have dreamed he'd be proved so right about Joey's mental condition. Soon there would be psychiatric reports, medical reports, school reports and home reports. Experts on every aspect of life would swarm over Joey, her and the kids, tweaking their past apart and muddling it up like unwound knitting. OK, there were bad times, but they'd had the rainbow times, too. Just like anyone else.

But they were no longer like anyone else, they were the despised Tremayne family.

Was it Shelley's fault that Joey seemed to have no close, regular friends? Could it be because she was stand-offish and he had learned to emulate her? Or was it more the case that, among those yobbos on the Eastwood Estate, not one was worth knowing in Shelley's opinion? Everyone Joey hung out with had a reputation for truancy and vandalism. How could she, as his mother, encourage friendships which she knew would damage her son? He had ignored her advice, and now look.

The application for bail was denied. That was the only straightforward part of this whole shocking court experience and the procedure was over in seconds.

No debate.

No argument.

Nobody gunning for Joey as far as Shelley could see.

Where would they take him tonight? Would she be able to go with him, and what about her other kids? They must be so confused and frightened. Should she abandon them, leave them to the tender mercies of their foster mother and cause them more disruption? The thought of returning to that Buckfastleigh flat with its damp sheets and its brown Formica atmosphere was depressing, but she knew her kids would rather be with their mum anywhere than stuck with a stranger.

And what was happening back at home now? Back at the place she had made her own, where Shelley and her children felt safe in their refuge from the world?

Would the windows be boarded up?

Would barriers be erected to keep the growling hordes at bay?

Would a permanent police patrol be stationed there, on guard?

Perhaps this was the best moment to say farewell to Joey, with the promise that she would see him tomorrow? Perhaps this terrible trauma, if it all worked out OK in the end, would teach him what she never could . . . to cut out the truancy, keep his distance from the dregs of humanity, appreciate his home, aim for something higher than the life of a drifter and a loser? If Joey didn't shape up now, God knows what sort of future he'd have. He should have learned something from knowing Dave. Dave was going nowhere fast.

Whatever happened in that precinct, Joey should not have been there. He was with a group of kids so sick they would set fire to a baby. Because of Joey and his loutish mates a little family had had their hearts broken. A few nights in a special unit might actually knock some sense into him and when all was said and done the staff would be trained, they wouldn't hurt him, they'd know how to respond. She could tell them he hated the dark . . .

'*Don't send him away, please, he's only eleven . . .*'

She was ignored.

Like she wasn't there.

The magistrates stood up, gave her three stern glances and drifted out in a dignified fashion. Behind them they left a cold, empty space and the overhead lights glowed more brightly.

The ignorant copper who had manhandled Joey put a heavy hand on her shoulder. She could feel the sympathy in the grip of it, and in his tone. 'Come on, love, that won't help. They know what they're doing. It's over now. Calm down, love, come with me.'

TEN

'You've never visited Dave,' Joey accused his tearful mother as they sat endlessly waiting again in the room underneath the court. Why did everything take so long? 'So why would you visit me? Just don't bother. I don't wanna see you, I don't wanna see anyone, *right*?'

How long could Joey keep up this façade? But if using aggression was his chosen way of dealing with this series of crushing shocks then what right had she to break down his defences with motherly cuddles and tears?

'You know damn well why I didn't visit Dave,' she said, shredding a matchstick with nervous fingers. 'Me and Dave decided it was best that we went our separate ways. And part of that was because of you, Joey, and you know that as well as I do. Dave wasn't going to change and I didn't want any of you lot to be influenced by his lawless attitude to life.' But she missed him, oh yes, she still missed him.

My God, she could do with a friend right now. If Iris was living she would recommend God.

* * *

Because of the suddenness of the arrests it was proving difficult for the authorities to find five suitable places where the Eastwood Estate boys could be held. They had to be parted, that much was obvious. The custody officials had been busy on the phones most of last night, fully expecting this outcome.

By the time the sun went down this evening Joey's name would be common knowledge. Joseph Tremayne would have gained notoriety – guilty or not – throughout the land. The internet was buzzing with life, tongues were wagging on telephone lines, groups of vigilantes held meetings, families shared the awful gossip with neighbours and friends with delighted horror. So it was essential that knowledge of the boys' destinations be kept under closest wraps. But for Joey, accused of murder, the secure unit near the village of Lister was by far the most suitable choice. Dudley Park, a boot camp established under the last Tory government, had since been converted into a unit for youths convicted of serious crimes but still too young for the mainstream system. It now described itself as a centre for care and rehabilitation.

It was just unfortunate that recently it had received such negative publicity because of the two fifteen-year-old boys who had hanged themselves on the premises in the space of six months. The latest inspector's report was far from encouraging. So Dudley Park, fifty miles from Plymouth, compared in the local collective consciousness with the worst mental asylums of fifty years ago.

Well aware of the effect this knowledge would

have on Shelley, and bearing in mind her outburst in court, Martin Chandler had decided it was best that he kept this news to himself. Joey and Shelley were waiting for transport back to police headquarters. There, later today, Joey would face the witnesses to the crime and after that Martin would try to persuade Shelley to leave.

Joey was a hard nut and well able to play on his mother's emotions. Wherever he went he would survive, but as for her . . .

That was another question.

If Martin could be honest, and his job meant that was impossible, his advice to Shelley would be to go back to her kids and leave that little scumbag to his fate.

He, too, had a baby daughter slightly older than Holly Coates. His wife Jessica had not slept properly since the news of that little girl's murder came out and Jessica was not happy that Martin should be part of the team dealing with Joey's defence.

That little bastard was guilty as sin.

All the facts pointed to it.

How much more would it take before his mother began to question her precious son's role in this most grotesque business? If Joey was identified by witnesses this afternoon, surely then Shelley Tremayne would begin the ordeal of facing up to the harsh reality.

There had been times during today when Martin had been sorely tempted to break that child-demon's neck. Talk about attitude . . .

that yob was laughing at everyone. Smarmy little bastard. Relishing all this attention. Convinced that he had only to flutter those eyelashes at the judge and he'd get away with anything. Dudley Park should sort him out, he wouldn't come out of there so cocky. Just let some of the scrotes in there get a sniff of what the angelic Tremayne was in for.

Martin could so easily understand the vengeful attitude of Holly's relations. If anything so abominable ever happened to his little sweetheart, Martin knew he would lose his mind.

How eleven-year-old Joseph Tremayne, who looked as if butter wouldn't melt in his mouth, had turned into such a devil did not concern his solicitor. Poor parenting; low expectations; the yob culture; sink schools, drugs or booze?

No way.

Not this.

For this abomination there could be no excuses.

Evil had many guises. Often it disguised itself in the most unlikely forms.

Their transport had arrived.

Martin went down to inform his clients. Joey would be perfectly safe in the van's closed-in back, no press cameras could capture him there and two minutes ago a decoy car with a small, female admin worker huddled in the back had left the court premises to confuse the waiting hacks.

Shelley pressed her hands to her ears as they

drove through the waiting crowd. She just couldn't take any more abuse.

This time, thank God, nobody reached the vehicle. There were no crashing sounds on the roof, no thudding fists on the side, but the driver was forced to hold up his hand to protect his eyes from the flashbulbs. The diversion tactic had achieved some success but, she was told, the more wily members of the public would never be so easily fooled.

They were forced to run the gauntlet again at the other end of their short, fast journey.

Joey displayed no emotion whatever. He merely sat there on the opposite bench, his empty eyes staring straight ahead. The mucky clenched fists on his knees were so close to her own hands that Shelley yearned to take them and stroke them. The tuft of black hair that refused to lie down stood up childishly on his crown. In normal circumstances she would smile and smooth it and he would shrug her off and say cheekily, 'Leave it, Mum. Geddoff.' But now . . . how could she reach him?

'It won't be so bad, you know, Joey,' she started. She had to break this heavy silence. 'And what you've got to remember is, this will pass, everything does. You'll be home in no time once they find out the truth . . .'

'What d'you mean?' asked Joey, snarling. 'That one day we'll forget? Don't be so bloody wet. The others, stuck with aiding and abetting, are they going home tonight? Are they? No way.'

'Well, you might get lumbered with aiding and abetting but they'll certainly drop the murder charge, and those sods who did it and lied will cop it worse in the end, you see.'

'I'll still be banged up till the trial.'

'They don't bang kids up, Joey. You've been listening to Dave too much. The reason they're keeping you in is because they want to make sure you're safe.'

'They want to get into my head.'

'Well, they might want to talk to you, doctors, lawyers, social workers, of course they will. And you have to tell them the truth. You mustn't be rude. You should try to be helpful. If we want to get out of this mess we'll both have to start by explaining to Hudson why we gave you that false alibi. We were scared. We didn't think. We even suspected the others would lie and we wanted to protect you, and how right we were when you think about it.'

Within the safety of the police-station yard the driver got out and slid back the doors. Shelley looked up, preparing to climb down the three small steps of the van. There, parked right next to them, was a navy people-carrier, and although it didn't say Dudley Park in glaring letters along the side, there it was, printed on the windscreen next to the tax disc.

She knew now where Joey was going.

To a young offenders' institution with a reputation for bullying and drugs.

Where two teenage kids had died of despair.

Shelley's insides cramped up with fear. The powerlessness of her position was now overwhelming. There would be no point in expending

133

energy trying to fight this appalling decision and, anyway, what the hell had she expected? Some cosy Norland nanny retreat where Joey would be coddled, cooed over and called a beautiful boy? No, but some kind of hospital where expert carers would look out for him would be more acceptable than Dudley Park.

She glanced at him; he was dawdling behind her, he hadn't seen the transparent sign, it was possible that he hadn't heard the rumours about that local hellhole either. Immediately she made her decision: she would not accompany him to that place. Apart from the horrors of clinging farewells, she knew Joey would cope with the trauma far better if she wasn't there to play up to. She would have to visit him, she knew that, but let him settle in first.

Would they strip him and search him and delouse his hair?

Would they shut him up in a cell all alone? And if he was allowed a companion what sort of scum would share his small space?

Look what had happened to Kenny . . . By now Joey's dad might be dead.

As far as Shelley knew, Joey had avoided the city drug scene up to now. Constantly on the lookout for the well-known signs of dope or worse – they peddled the stuff quite openly in the street and Dave was a regular user of Es – she assumed that Joey had tried smoking pot as most kids did these days. That was as natural as hop-scotch in the playgrounds. And it was possible that, unknown to her, he had run messages for the pushers; he'd do most things for a couple of quid. What kid wouldn't? But at Dudley Park there'd be serious users of crack cocaine and heroin. How long would it take those bastards to turn Joey into a dopehead like them? He'd do anything to be big, to be known as one of the gang. And tough.

He was young, he was pretty, would he be gang-raped, torn in half . . . ? There was Aids . . . no, no . . . She winced and closed her eyes.

When they took Joey away to face the witnesses, Shelley sat chain-smoking in an interview room with the door tightly closed 'in case anyone comes by and recognizes you', said William Boyce, the younger detective with the fresh, open-air face.

'But everyone must know we're here,' said Shelley.

'Probably, but that's different. Somebody seeing you in the flesh could result in a serious disturbance.'

'You mean they would attack me? Here, in the cop shop, with you lot around?'

'We have to prepare for the worst, just in case.'

Shelley sat and prayed that the witnesses – the assistant at B&Q, the manager of McDonald's, the man who got his hands burned and two shoppers who reckoned they'd seen the incident – would fail to recognize Joey. She knew she would make a hopeless witness; Dave said that was because she was too self-absorbed. But he was wrong – the reason she failed to notice anything around her was that she was too damn concerned about watching the kids.

Joey had admitted he had gone into B&Q, so the assistant who saw him in there could well identify him . . . So what? That proved nothing.

The manager at McDonald's was likely to recognize him, too, and soon she and Joey would admit he was not at home sick that afternoon – he was at the precinct – so that proved nothing either.

The two women shoppers and the man with the burned hands who had tried to save Holly were a different kettle of fish. If they swore that Joey had thrown the paraffin and the lighter they would either be lying through their teeth, or dangerously mistaken. There was no suggestion in Shelley's mind that these innocent passers-by would be colluding with Joey's four young accusers. Why should they? Even she wasn't that paranoid. And it was unlikely, she reassured herself, that all three of them would make a mistake.

No. The outcome of this could only be good.

Joey had nothing to fear.

Apart from his stay at Dudley Park.

She checked her watch, and sighed. Three thirty already.

What would her kids be doing now? Was the foster mother aware of the danger they were in? Was she patient with Casey going through his terrible twos? Did she know that Saul hated milk? He would never say, he would just spit it out. Kez would be playing big brother, trying to help and spilling things, and Jason might have an accident if she didn't keep asking if he needed the potty. Shelley would have to make arrangements for them to be collected from Mrs Bolton's and delivered back to the Buckfastleigh flat. No question, they would all be ratty, cross with her for abandoning them and ready to wreak their little revenge.

She was already exhausted, at the end of her tether. What she would give for one night off, time to gather her wits and catch up in her head with all that was happening. A night alone with nothing to do but lie and cuddle herself somewhere warm. But maybe keeping busy was the answer . . . Too much time to think might drive her mad.

After an hour or so Joey returned. 'They knew me because of my T-shirt.'

'*Who knew you?*'

'The McDonald's guy, that prat from B&Q and those two slags who reckon they saw me.'

'The women? The shoppers?'

'That's what I said.' As Joey slumped in his chair he tugged at his Man United T-shirt, the scrap of cloth that had betrayed him.

'I don't understand.' A heavy ache settled under her heart. All this was too huge a weight to carry. 'How can they say they saw you do it, how can they say that when you didn't? Where's Hudson gone? *I must speak to someone . . .*'

'Leave it, Mum. They've stitched me up.'

'*Shut up, Joey, for God's sake.*' Shelley got up and paced the room. His surly attitude was driving her mad. She would have opened the door and rushed out but she remembered Boyce's earlier warning: someone might see her, they might flip at the sight, they might do her over and cause a 'disturbance'. Boiling with frustration she banged her fist into her hand. 'Those women, they must be forced to explain, they must be questioned, no-one should be allowed to go round making that sort of bloody mistake . . .'

'It's OK, Shelley, *it's OK*.'

When Hudson opened the door Shelley threw herself at him before he was able to step inside. 'No, it's not OK. *What's going on?* I'm pissed off with being treated like some pitiful jerk and fobbed off all the time. Something sleazy is happening here and I want to know, *who were those sodding women*?'

Hudson held up his palms like buffers. His voice was calm and controlled. 'I don't think this sort of wild talk is sensible, not in front of Joey.'

'I'll be the judge of that, I'm his mother. Are they in your pay? Are they snouts of yours? Is it true what they say about this force, you're so damn corrupt you'll stoop to anything?'

'I think they are waiting for Joey downstairs.' Hudson held out a pathetic bagful of comics, puzzle books and felt pens.

Shelley swallowed hard.

Somebody had thought to collect them.

How would he sleep tonight without Wally Wolf? He didn't have it in bed with him but he insisted on seeing the toy on the dresser . . . just one lingering part of his old nightly rituals. The grey fur of the beloved creature was worn so thin she daren't wash it again for fear it would just fluff away.

She wanted to let fly at the copper; she longed to scratch that comfortable face. She knew where they were taking her son, and comics, puzzle books and felt pens were hardly the fashion at Dudley Park.

'Shelley,' said Hudson reasonably, 'we'll talk later. I promise. Now is honestly not a good time.'

For Joey's sake she must keep her cool. 'I won't come down with you,' said Shelley in a strained voice which sounded ridiculously casual. 'We'll say goodbye here, shall we, and I'm coming to see you tomorrow.' She was about to ask if there was anything he needed from home, as if he was off to hospital, but remembered just in time that home was way off limits, maybe wrecked and all her son's special things ruined.

She stood still in front of him for a moment in case he might want to kiss her goodbye but hoping selfishly that he wouldn't. She didn't know if she could bear that, the familiar feel of the small of his back, the smell of his hair, the brush of his lashes and the trembling inside that no-one could see.

She had the awful, ludicrous sensation that this was the last time she'd see her son.

Tentatively she put out a hand and patted him briefly on the arm and that was enough to set off her tears. She fought back the burning feeling. Her lips were twisted and pressed hard together. She must look as if she was gurning.

Just go, she screamed inside silently.

Just go, Joey love, and don't look back.

ELEVEN

So here was Shelley, waiting again, and in no fit condition to be left all alone with dangerous time to think. Tomorrow she would meet the legal team from Grant and Wilson (because it would be such a high-profile case they wanted the experts brought in early) and they would plot their strategy. Tomorrow she would admit to them that she and Joey had lied. Joey was innocent of this heinous crime . . . But what if he really was guilty? How awkward it must be for lawyers to defend the indefensible.

Since Joey had been taken away she'd been sitting in the same room smoking like a chimney, drinking sour machine coffee and waiting for someone to give her a lift to Buckfastleigh in an unmarked car. In her situation taxis and public transport were out of the question. Simple normalities like these were no longer options for her. The names of the defendants had been held back by law, but they might as well have been splashed all over the newspapers, so fast did the information travel.

Supermarkets would be out of bounds;

someone might recognize her. Shelley would be taking a risk if she popped into a small newsagent for a paper and a packet of fags. It was lucky Kenny had stocked her up with his smuggled supplies ... how long ago? Could it really have been only yesterday that she'd taken the kids to the centre as usual, that she'd been just an ordinary mum flogging her way down the street with her pushchair?

For her a black and endless night had begun when she saw that ten o'clock news on Wednesday.

A tap on the door and Shelley defiantly held on to her fag. A no-smoking area – hah. She was well past the point of caring about such mindless trivia. In walked the shorn-haired Alex, large in her pink fluffy coat and with her nose stud winking. The young social worker, after a hug Shelley found embarrassing, dropped into one of the room's uncomfortable chairs and asked with oozing sympathy, 'Shelley, how you doing?'

'Like shit,' she replied. But she couldn't help being glad to see Alex.

'I know.' Alex shed her coat like a skin and immediately transformed herself from chubby to waif-like.

'How are the kids?'

'Well,' Alex began, 'that's really why I'm here. They're all fine, don't worry, but there is concern about them being moved back to Buckfastleigh tonight, in view of public reaction. I've just come from a meeting where it was decided they should stay at the Boltons' for the time being for their own protection.'

It took a while for that to sink in. 'So where does that leave me?' Shelley asked.

'It means you have a choice. You can go back to the flat if you'd rather spend some time on your own tonight. Or I can take you to Mrs Bolton's – she says there's a bed to spare which you could have if you wanted.'

Shelley asked, 'So they think that we would be unsafe if we all went to the flat?'

'They think that one person going in and out would be worth the risk. You, after all, are able to disguise yourself just by pulling up your hood so your face isn't seen. But a large carload of kids coming and going, strangers to the area, might well attract attention and people might start asking questions.'

'I imagined,' said Shelley naively, 'that we might have police protection.'

'That was discussed,' said Alex, 'but in these sensitive cases events can be sparked off and inflamed with such alarming suddenness, the alternative plan was considered to be the best option.'

Oh God. The idea of sleeping, like a guest, in some stranger's house was depressing. There would be no privacy, no time to pace and think and plan. No space for all the tears. Probably no smoking. Instead there would be enforced politeness and a circling round the issue. And while Mrs Bolton might be prepared to forgive Joey's siblings for being related to the baby-killer, what would her true feelings be towards the mother who spawned him?

On the other hand there was the flat and a

night all alone in that dank place without the diversion of the children. If anyone was verging on breakdown, a few nights in a dump like that would surely send them over the top. Was she confident enough of her sanity to risk a night alone in a place that was regarded as too dangerous for her children to visit?

'Where do the Boltons live?' As if this could decide her. She was merely playing for time.

'They live at Two Bridges.'

'Out near the prison?' That stone monument to misery.

'Only half an hour's drive from here. The brilliant thing about their farm is that it is so tucked away. We have found Mrs Bolton terribly useful for children with severe behaviour disorders, particularly teenagers. She gets them working, she's firm but fair, and it's not easy for them to find transport to get back into sin city. Once they're out there they're virtually stranded.'

So. Not only would Shelley be opting for a spare bed in a disapproving stranger's house – she imagined Mrs Bolton as an upright, hard-working, no-nonsense Devonian with an Aga – but once there she would be stuck.

Much as she longed to check out her kids and hug them, Shelley wasn't ready for such stress, not tonight, not so soon. Alex was assuring her that they were well and happy; for now she would have to take that as read. Tomorrow, after a decent night's sleep, she could move to Mrs Bolton's. Tonight she would have to face Buckfastleigh alone.

* * *

And Shelley was completely alone. Alone for the first time since this darkness descended. The flat greeted her with the same dishcloth aura; when the lights were turned on, the shabbiness blinked.

She wandered from room to room in a silence broken only by the sporadic movement of traffic on the road outside. She drew all the curtains and left all the lights on and all the doors wide open. Alex had thought to buy her an M&S Cumberland pie and a trifle. It was years since Shelley had bought any food from M&S. Too pricey. Although she wasn't hungry after the day's overdose of caffeine and nicotine, she was determined to eat what she could and then she would pop a Valium. Her handbag was never without a bottle; sometimes, when Julie played up, she gave her baby daughter half a tablet just to get a decent night's kip.

The washing-up from last night and this morning still littered the kitchen. Shelley had yet to discover a way to heat the water. If she forced herself to tackle the task, and put off the longed-for moment of slumping down with her head in her hands and curling up over her misery, perhaps her mind would stay clearer. Not only was there no hot water, but someone had taken the washing-up liquid, tea towels and soap, so the next ten minutes were spent dipping her hands in freezing cold water, wiping the stains and grime with her fingers and stacking unsatisfactory mugs, plates and bowls in the rotting wooden rack.

She turned the TV on for company and also to wait for the six o'clock news.

If only some major tragedy would happen to replace the murder story as lead. She didn't wish the horror on anyone, but tragedies do happen, and now would be such excellent timing.

Her children's belongings were still in boxes, mainly untouched save for the cuddly toys she had taken out, one for each child. Forcing herself to fill the time between now and the main news bulletin, she raised the lid of the first. The police had had to move quickly to salvage anything from the mob.

Clothes were stacked in untidy bundles, and talc, toothbrushes and baby wipes were muddled up with the cot sheets. Toys came in a separate box filled to overflowing. You could buy them so cheap these days. Shelley's kids never missed out at Christmas. There was a load of dirty washing. She discovered her make-up and underwear at the bottom of a box full of games. She dragged this out; one day she might need make-up again, although just now she couldn't imagine going to the trouble. She repacked the rest of the stuff. They would need all this at Mrs Bolton's.

Darkness had descended early, a combination of the night and dark storm clouds which carried cold rain. Now, in the street, it was pissing down. Pedestrians scurried, vehicles slushed, but the rain on the windows was comforting; it brought with it a feeling of safety. The rain could not get in, no matter how hard it battered and rattled. When she pulled back the curtains to look quickly outside,

145

her reflection was wavy with rain tears. The feeble electric bars were doing their best in the lounge although, with the dust, they stank of singeing. Shelley made coffee and sat beside them, crouched on the filthy rug.

Five thirty.

Half an hour to go.

And to think only three days ago she would huddle like this, with a very different anticipation, to watch *EastEnders*.

Shelley cowered.

She forced herself to concentrate. She had no video here, so there was only one chance to take this in.

'*Earlier today at Plymouth Magistrates' Court an eleven-year-old boy was charged with the murder of baby Holly Coates on Wednesday 6 February.*' Even with the silence around her Shelley could hear the outraged nation's intake of breath.

Not again.

Not again.

Then came the surveillance tapes, with a blurred circle round Joey's head to blot out his identity, as the deadpan newsreader went on to explain that four of the accused's friends had been charged with the lesser crime of aiding and abetting.

The fact they all came from the same school (unnamed) and lived on the same estate (kept secret) appeared to be a source of fascination for the news team who gave the report. The impression given of the local schools was one of dire failure, of dens of iniquity where the truancy rates were high, standards of education were scandalous and the difficulties in recruiting good staff spoke for themselves. The high walls topped with razor wire that surrounded one anonymous building were hardly reassuring.

At this stage, apparently, one local headmaster, Mr Ronald Cutting, was not prepared to comment. That sour-faced bastard. They'd dug him out fast. At least he was keeping his nasty gob shut. She'd had some right scraps with him.

The scene of the murder was the next port of call, although, as the precinct was closed, there was nothing much to see. Just a few huddled shop workers with carrier bags making their way home in the rain. One woman did stop when approached by a microphone: 'Bring back hanging,' she said, before rushing on. The camera paused at the sacred place where the baby had burned, and already, as if brought by angels, bouquets of flowers and single roses had mounted up on the pavement.

The police had arranged them sensibly so that pedestrians could still get by.

And there they were, the local estates. Shelley had been waiting for this. She saw her old home as the cameras daringly crept past. She took in every detail in the seconds available. Yes, the windows were boarded up, and the door was re-inforced with a thick metal slab. It was dark and wet, but the street light outside allowed her to see that the tiny front garden had not been touched although the gate was nowhere in sight; it must have been torn from its hinges.

A little crowd of neighbours was gathered across the road, watching. Old enemies not on speaking terms had come together tonight. How they must be relishing this – and right on their own doorsteps. Most would probably miss the night's soap if this outside entertainment continued. And especially as it was Joey Tremayne: got his comeuppance at last, the sod. Everyone would be agreeing that they could have predicted something like this if nothing was done to restrain him. Few of the people in that audience had not knocked on Shelley's door in the past, ranting on about Joey's behaviour.

Most of the court proceedings had been conducted in camera, so nothing worth reporting there other than the accused's demeanour. They chose the words 'small and tense'. Shelley was grateful for that. She was sure that tomorrow's tabloids would not be so kind.

Could society be blamed, again, for this unimaginable tragedy?

What had it done, or failed to do?

What could be done to ensure that this was the last of these horrors? The clampdown on truancy had not prevented this nightmare, nor had the millions poured into failing schools, the basic wage, or the determination of governments to condemn single mothers, eliminate illiteracy and provide jobs and futures for an escalating underclass.

There would be an hour-long programme at

eight o'clock tomorrow night to discuss the nation's reaction, with experts taking part. Naturally.

Huh. Would she be one of these so-called experts? Even if the law allowed? Would they consider that the mother of the reviled one might want to put in her tuppence worth? Because in Shelley's mind none of the reasons they put forward applied to her little family.

They weren't desperately poor.

They didn't do without much.

The school was improving. Her other kids weren't displaying any particularly worrying behaviour; they were worlds away from the troubled toddler Joey had been. If Shelley had to blame something or someone for her predicament tonight, she would point the finger at Joey's mates.

Scumbags, the lot of them.

And products of inadequate parents who didn't give a toss about their kids – too busy boozing or using.

Her own mother, Iris, had firmly disapproved of the way Shelley brought up Joey, dragging him round wherever she went, fatherless most of the time, with no routine, no secure home environment. And yet he was 'spoilt', according to Mum. How could he have been both spoilt and neglected, for God's sake? True, she fed him on demand instead of using a sensible routine; true, she rarely put him down in his pram; true, she pandered to his every need. 'You're making a rod for your own back there,' Iris would declare.

She had been less attentive with the other five, not because of Iris's advice but because there wasn't the time or the energy.

Even when Shelley was faced with homelessness or a germ-ridden hostel, she refused to go home to her mother's spotless flat and her mother's mean-minded rules and beliefs. Joey would have been infected by the same rigid discipline Shelley had endured as a child. He would have grown up meek and frightened, believing himself to be less worthy, warned against fighting back. It was something to do with spiritual suffering.

At least Joey had spirit . . .

It had taken Shelley twelve years to find the confidence to fight back, and it happened because of her sudden and startling transformation. As a child she looked like a wounded bird, long, leggy and out of proportion, with specs and plaits and a stammer. After the glasses came off Shelley saved to have her long hair cut into a shaggy, impish style. It wasn't just the mirror that told her she was now one of the best-looking kids in her class, it was the reaction of her classmates, boys and girls. She was popular for the first time in her life and Iris, who was concerned that her daughter would end up a slag, accused the excited Shelley of basking in every second of it.

But when Iris died so young, so suddenly, never knowing her other grandchildren, how Shelley wished she had forced her to speak of her own spartan childhood and, worse than that, the family's cruel abandonment when she fell in love with Liu Qi. Maybe, if she'd understood more, Shelley could have been more of a friend . . . ?

At Iris's funeral there had been her, Joey, the undertaker and the verger. But thousands of people must have met Iris. She had spent her entire working life in the electrical department at Dingles, yet nobody from there had bothered to turn up.

Shelley looked questioningly at her steaming Cumberland pie. Could she even be bothered to scrape it out of its carton on to one of those unpleasant plates? No. She found a tray, left the TV on for company and dug into the foil with a fork. Same with the trifle. Straight from the plastic. She downed as much as she could. Tomorrow would be a whirl of activity: she must see her kids, visit Joey and meet with his legal team.

She would need energy. And eating gave her something to do.

She longed for sleep but dreaded a long night deprived of it. She took two Valium before she went up at eleven. She washed in cold water at a stained, veined basin and dried her face and hands on a blanket. Fully clothed and shivering with cold, she slipped under the thin covers which she had supplemented with four other blankets off the empty beds. Shelley lay listening to the rain, as tightly curled up as she could get.

What was Joey doing now in that notorious prison? She prayed that he was warm, and sleeping. Did they have a shrink in residence perhaps, or a matron, a chaplain, somebody kind? Or did they employ only stubble-chinned screws with ugly biceps and a down on the helpless?

In the unfamiliar flat she lay and listened to its creakings, knowing that she, in the eyes of the nation, was despised so much she might come to harm.

She focused on every sound.

She heard doors squeak open, floorboards crack; she heard sinister taps on the windows and footsteps on the stairs.

The darkness massed in ghostly ways to create shadows and moving shapes. *Was that a pane of glass breaking?* They would come and get her if they knew where she was, faceless thugs in black balaclavas. Folk she would nod to on her way to the shops back in her normal lifetime. Might she have been part of the lynch mob before this happened to Joey? She loathed the crime as much as they did; it would be hard not to seek revenge if only to help with the hurting . . .

Few people would mourn her death – just her kids. Many would think that justice had been done . . . If you bring up a kid to burn newborn babies as they sleep contentedly in their prams, what reaction do you expect?

Holly Coates would be pure and eight weeks old for ever.

Never run or laugh or play; never sing or learn or love or have her own babies . . .

Jesus bids us shine with a pure clear light
Like a little candle burning in the night . . .

At three in the morning Shelley slept.

TWELVE

Two men and two women were waiting for Shelley in a room that reminded her, in its ornateness, of the setting for an official statement from the Houses of Parliament. Heavily embossed fleur-de-lis wallpaper, which must have cost an arm and a leg, overwhelmed the oil paintings of tall ships leaving Plymouth Sound. The massive oval table was cluttered with papers at one end, and only four chairs were in use. The table must seat at least twenty and one immense chandelier blazed above it. This Saturday meeting of such legal giants proved just how massive this case was to be.

If this had been Shelley's room she would have lit a log fire in that chasm of a marble fireplace, not just filled it with a pulsing electric imitation.

For the first time Shelley was introduced to her son's barrister, king in his chambers, a jowly, pompous man with flabby hands, in a pinstriped suit. This stereotypical image pleased her. She assumed the more belligerent the man, the more likely he would be to succeed. Jonathan Formby-Hart was the last word in courtesy. He stood up as she entered, pulled out a chair and at once introduced his elegant and haute-coutured pupil as Miranda Smallwood.

The other male at the table, pouring coffee from a silver jug, was solicitor Martin Chandler, and next to him sat Maggie Dowson, a severe, middle-aged, black-suited person who, as clerk, seemed to be the general dogsbody, note-taker and beaver of the group.

Where the hell should she put her bag? If she rested it on the table it not only blocked her view of Chandler but the plastic material and broken clip lowered the tone. She ended up leaving it on the floor, pressing its bulging sides together to prevent anyone seeing the mess inside. She had come straight from Buckfastleigh; she had slept in the clothes she was wearing and washed hastily in cold water, and she was painfully aware of the unkempt image she must present.

Chandler said, 'I've put Jonathan in the picture. He is confident we have a good chance . . . and now what we need to do is see where you can help Joey's case.'

'A good chance? *Just a chance?*'

'Nobody can ever be surer than that, Shelley.'

'But Joey can't go down for something he didn't do. *He's eleven.*'

'Joey's innocence is precisely what we have to prove to the jury,' said Jonathan Formby-Hart in a deep and resonant voice. Shelley bet his dining room at home was every bit as opulent as this.

'And you're not helping your son,' reproved

Chandler, 'by backing up alibis that are palpably fraudulent.'

Shelley jumped. She reddened, like a child caught stealing. She smiled round weakly; no-one smiled back. 'I was going to tell you . . .'

'From now on you must be completely frank with us,' chided Chandler. 'It puts us at a grave disadvantage if you and Joey don't cooperate.'

From there they moved on to the day in question and Shelley admitted that, yes, Joey was at the precinct with the others when the crime was committed. However, she held out over the question of whether he had stolen the paraffin, and she denied his ownership of that lighter. 'I'd never seen it before,' she insisted, 'and anyway Joey is not a thief.' This last, rather risky remark was made without a flinch.

They listened to her description of Joey's early life. It took her an hour to talk them through that, his troubles at school and his damning reputation on the estate, which she dismissed as neighbours' spite. She dwelt on his reliability, his help around the house and with the kids, his sense of humour, his quick wits . . .

'Allow me to stop you there for one moment,' interrupted Formby-Hart, who had appeared to be dozing. 'You seem to be describing the sort of boy that I for one have never met. Who is this lad, this little darling who is constantly misrepresented by teachers and neighbours? Even his friends find some of his actions alarming.'

Jesus Christ. Here we go.

These people were meant to be on Joey's side,

so why were they so eager to hear only negative stuff about him? Why weren't they concerned with his real character: his sweet and often generous nature, his energy and fun, his shyness, his insecurity, his struggles with his temper, his determination to do better?

'Shelley,' put in the perfectly groomed Miranda Smallwood with a questioning smile that belied the brittleness of her tone. Her little silver earrings sparkled and every tooth was pearl white. 'Why do you think two boys in Joey's class would swear blind that they had seen him with that lighter one week before the incident?'

'For attention,' said Shelley swiftly. 'If you had boys of Joey's age you'd know how they jump on any bandwagon if they are given a chance. It's because they're bored.'

'I see,' said Miranda, leaning back, tapping the table and regarding Shelley like she was some specimen in a jar. 'And what would have driven the Lessings, Connor Mason and Darren Long to testify that it was Joey who committed the offence? Don't forget,' she continued in her lilting voice, 'that they stuck to their guns in spite of some pretty intensive questioning by the police.'

'If you can't work that out then God help your career,' Shelley snapped back before she could stop herself. 'Of course they're not going to admit to what really happened that afternoon. What d'you take them for? They might be thick but they're not bloody cretins.'

The lovely Miranda was not to be thwarted. 'There was no communication between the

156

Lessing brothers and the two other boys after they were arrested. And yet they all told the same story.'

And then Shelley was forced to confess that she had visited the Lessings' house on the night Darren and Connor were arrested. 'I know it was stupid but I needed to know,' she pleaded before the audience of stern eyes. 'And what I heard there suggested to me that the four of them had already agreed to lie through their teeth. At that point the Lessings were trying to make out they had been to their gran's that afternoon. After I left I'm sure they realized that that story wouldn't wash so they'd better go back to their original plan. And they did, the bastards. All four of them.'

'Why would they all decide to use Joey in particular as a scapegoat?'

'Because of his reputation,' said Shelley. 'Because they knew that if anyone was going to be believed, it wouldn't be poor Joey. He was the obvious victim.'

'A reputation which, according to you, was false in all respects?' asked solicitor Chandler.

'I'm not saying that Joey wasn't into all kinds of mischief. And he could be filthy-mouthed at times and that upset the older residents, the ones who write in to the telly to complain if they hear the word damn in a play. I'm not saying he was an angel, he got up to all sorts of antics. What I am saying is that what Joey got up to was the same as any lad his age. Childish naughtiness. There is no real wickedness in him and I should know, I'm his mum.'

She felt like a witness being torn to pieces, same as the time she defended Dave. She was still upset by the news she'd received earlier that Kenny was still in a coma. If she wasn't in such a terrible state she would visit him, sit by him and try to help with his recovery in any way she could. She'd had little sleep last night, haunted by fear and overwhelmed by the monstrous events of the last twenty-four hours. These people ought to be gentle with her, knowing what Shelley had already been through.

They ought not to be treating her like this. Damn them, damn them. She was going to ask if she could smoke.

'Please do,' said the portly Formby-Hart, nodding to his subordinate, frumpy Maggie Dowson. It seemed a sin to spoil the gleam of that beautiful, heavy glass ashtray but she couldn't go on without a smoke, not under all this pressure. She turned away when she lit her fag, trying to avoid the disapproval of the others.

She wished she could have had a bath, washed her hair and changed her clothes. These jumped-up gits considered her and her kind inadequate. She didn't always look so bedraggled, she wanted to tell them.

While she was up, Maggie Dowson poured more of the strong black coffee into bone china cups so small you could hardly get your finger through the delicate handles. For a second time a mortified Shelley was forced to ask for the milk; nobody else seemed to take it.

But her fag was doing her good. She felt a

158

slight return of confidence. She was the reason they were all here. Her son was their client. Without her and poor Joey they wouldn't have what was probably a very good little earner, not to mention the kudos of such a high-profile case.

She must stand her ground here.

She must fight for Joey.

The police driver that morning had informed her that Joey was fine. Well, he would say that, wouldn't he? Not for a moment did Shelley believe it, but after this meeting the legal team were bound for Dudley Park and a first interview with their client. Naturally Shelley would be accompanying them, and she was promised time alone with her son. She would soon know the truth of how her vulnerable child was being treated.

After seeing Joey, Formby-Hart's team were planning to have lunch out at a nearby pub. If it wasn't for the security risk, would they have invited her and happily sat in the village local drinking beer with an alleged murderer's mother?

Martin Chandler stared at his client: the fact that she was just short of beautiful brought a fascination of its own. Given more fortunate circumstances this hopeless woman could have been a model, but, as it was, life's natural damage was too great ever to be repaired.

He couldn't fathom this riddle out. She wasn't brain-dead, she wasn't a fool, so how could she go on like this denying the blindingly obvious – that Joey Tremayne was a vile piece of work who'd be better off banged up for life?

He and his doctor wife, Jessica, had had quite a ding-dong last night and in the end she'd had to admit that in her profession she would treat anyone, no matter what hideous wrongs they had done. So snap, they were equal.

But he would rather have his job than hers. At least he was not required to undress the criminal classes, although it was inside their heads that they were mostly a diseased and pretty repulsive lot.

'That child will never be any good to man or beast, Martin,' Jessica had said. 'The damage has been done. He's a drain on the state. That's sad for the boy, maybe not his fault, but no amount of money, education, care or counselling will ever reach his soul . . .'

'*Soul?* That's a new one for you.'

'I can't think of anything that fits what I mean so exactly.'

'So what should happen to him, in your expert opinion?'

'I suppose they will have to feed and keep him somewhere safe until he grows up, although if I was Holly Coates's mother I'd never give up the search. No doubt he'll find himself living the life of Riley, with far more comforts than his peer group. Maybe he'll pass some exams – although what for I can't imagine. Who would give someone like that a job? Who would want a relationship with someone who once set fire to a baby?' She came back to her original point: 'And I just don't understand how you can bring yourself to go near him.'

160

And that, Martin decided, as he listened to Shelley Tremayne waffling on daftly about innocence, was what most people were thinking.

The legal team had talked privately before Shelley arrived this morning. The unanimous opinion was that Joey was guilty. All the evidence pointed to that; there was no getting away from it. The competent digging of Maggie Dowson, done in the space of one afternoon, had revealed more about Joey Tremayne than even his mother seemed to know.

The boy was notorious: a hood, a gangster, cold and calculating, certainly a pusher of soft drugs. No follower – not someone easily influenced, as his mother was making out – but a bullying leader from whom most decent kids fled in fear.

But while he protested his innocence, and Martin knew that nothing would break him, his defence team would give their all.

It was going to be an uphill struggle.

The psychiatrist's report might prove to be their answer but that stupid woman was even denying there was anything wrong with his head.

Incredibly, Shelley sincerely believed she was giving her kids a normal childhood. What Shelley found acceptable was anathema to her listeners. What kind of role model was she?

Foul language. These days everyone used it to some extent, but most right-thinking people tried to avoid it in front of their children.

Take booze as another example. From what Shelley said, there had been numerous occasions when she'd rolled home so pissed she couldn't climb the stairs. Indeed, where going out was concerned, getting rat-arsed seemed to be her only objective.

Men – pulls, more like – she'd bring home and carry on with as if her kids weren't in the house.

And then there was her attitude. She lacked all respect. The law was the filth, teachers were arse-holes, the bleeding neighbours were all out to get her. Where did this aggro come from? But what made all this so extraordinary was the openness with which losers like Shelley described their shit lifestyles.

Assuming that everyone was the same.

Depressingly, as far as Martin could see, this was the way society was moving. He was so relieved that he and Jessica had the means to put down their little daughter's name for a good public school at birth. He was also thankful that they had a nice house far removed from the dregs of the city.

He watched as Shelley stubbed out her third fag. There was ash ground into her cheap T-shirt. What must once have been perfect teeth were stained a dirty yellow, as was her middle finger. She might at least have made an effort to smarten herself up before arriving at Formby-Hart's chambers this morning.

When at last they called a halt to the meeting Shelley felt drained and bruised.

A message had been received from the police: Malcolm Yelland had been in touch, trying to trace his former lover and wanting her to contact him in case he could be of any help. He had heard about the mess she was in and wondered if there was anything he could do. The police passed on his number in case Shelley was interested, along with the warning that she must not give him her mobile number or any clue as to her whereabouts.

Shelley had never imagined she would hear from that dickhead again. Of the four main men in her life, Malc had been with her the shortest time. She couldn't help but be moved that he had made contact and actually wanted to help her now, especially bearing in mind that Joey was the cause of this shit. Shelley, seeing her son's distress and fearing further disruption, had not felt able to stand up to him, and Joey's difficult behaviour had forced Malc out in the end.

Malc. What a clown. Did he still work on the docks? But someone out there in an unforgiving world had the courage to be on her side. That was touching. But that Malc should be the one surprised her.

They were off to Dudley Park in style. All these signals of success, the swishy chambers, the fancy Audi with its leather interior that took the five of them in comfort, reassured Shelley that her legal team must be the best. As the client's mother, she sat in the front next to Formby-Hart. He wore driving gloves that squeaked.

Malc had a car, a wreck, a silver Capri with the rust falling off it. Flashy like Malc himself, no style. And Malc drove like a maniac whereas

Formby-Hart didn't need to do that. They went at a steady sixty; it felt as if they were crawling. She was slightly put out that they chose to listen to Radio Four instead of making conversation.

As they drew nearer to Dudley Park, Shelley's whole being tensed up. Until now she had been trying to dismiss this dreaded visit from her mind and the day's crowded itinerary had made her efforts easier. She just wasn't used to all this intensity.

Being home all day with the kids meant that, apart from getting Joey and Kez to school, her time was her own. The kind of problems she faced ranged from chickenpox to the phone bill and from finding a cheap plumber to getting the curtains to stay on the rail. She wasn't used to using her head. She wasn't familiar with this sort of company and she'd flick from channel to channel to avoid serious discussion on telly.

She supposed that one day she might go back to work, but not in a shop, not in a wine bar. She'd had enough of being treated like dirt by ignorant customers showing off. She fancied the thought of retraining but only for the higher wages. Daytime TV saw her through the day, that and magazines she could flip through. The last time she had read a real book was back at school – Judy Blume. She had loved it but she just didn't have the time any more, not with the constant interruptions.

A safari-park-style fence marked out the boundaries. Through the diamond mesh was a long, squat wall of red brick without windows.

The sight was just as forbidding as a first view of Dartmoor prison. It yelled at approaching miscreants: abandon hope, all ye who enter here. *Poor Joey, oh poor Joey*. As the luxurious car purred up to the gates, Shelley's heart kicked like a foetus. The fearsome sign, *Dudley Park*, stood out firmly, nailed to the spikes. Maggie, the dogsbody, got out and pressed a button beside a speaker.

They knew what to do. They had been here before.

She was relieved that the others were with her so she wouldn't have to face Joey alone.

THIRTEEN

The automatic gates slid open to let the car move along a short driveway flanked by spindly leafless trees. Freezing rain obscured any worthwhile view. Puddles lined their path, the car sploshing snootily through them. The wipers whispered a soft hypnosis and this, combined with the heat inside, gave the Audi the feeling of a cocoon. Shelley was loath to leave it. The wall of brick she had seen through the fence bore an arrow with the word *Reception* above it.

It was only when they were halted at the second checkpoint and their business here confirmed by a hooded man in a waxed jacket with a clipboard that Shelley got her first view of the courtyard within the four walls. If this place had a chimney it would be an almost perfect copy of the crematorium where Iris's funeral had been held.

The building was just a basic one-storey square surrounding an open space large enough to incorporate a basketball court, a car park and a skateboarding area. In the very centre of the yard one gnarled old oak tree tried hard to create whatever atmosphere it could. Through the sleet all it did was loom, a fuzzy, sinister shape. Maybe, in the summer when the leaves were out, the place would look less dismal.

At least there were windows on this side of the unit and the bars weren't too overpowering. When the second security gate was closed behind them it was hard to see how any poor bastard could possibly escape from here because the flat roofs of this bungalow jail were fenced off by a powerful electric current. There were multiple warnings of this fact – the usual live electricity sign displayed beside pylons, power stations and roadworks, and red lightning warnings everywhere.

They represented Shelley's mood.

In a gentlemanly manner Formby-Hart took her arm and they headed for the swing door, still following the relevant arrows.

Carpet tiles. A potted yucca. Soothing colours on the walls and calming watercolours to match. Neat beige seating. A scatter of magazines. Shelley didn't know what she'd expected but this, so far, was heartening stuff.

They had only just seated themselves when through an inner door came a young man with a face the shade of brick wearing tracksuit and trainers, a white towel round his neck. Shelley, nerves already stretched to the limit, almost laughed out loud. Jesus Christ. This could be a gym or a country club. Talk about getting lucky! Joey had struck gold here.

'Dominic Brownlow,' announced the young man, puffing and shaking hands with each of the team in turn. 'Joey's on his way. We've put you in the green room. You ought to be comfortable there.'

His first night away from home and, dear God, it had to be here.

Joey was clean. He wore new clothes: blue denims, a red sweatshirt and a pair of glaring white trainers which made his feet look enormous. He took one look at his mother and flung himself into her arms.

Shelley broke down and wept. 'Oh Joey, oh Joey, I've been so worried, I've never stopped thinking about you. Are you OK? Tell me what's happened.' She wanted to push him away to look at him, but he clung to her so tightly there was no chance of that, not yet.

She was full of questions but her son said nothing, just hid his face and hung on for dear life. She stroked his hair. She patted his back. She cooed over her child. She kissed the top of his head over and over again savouring his taste and his freshly washed smell. 'Come on, matey . . . I'm here now, love. You're OK, you're OK.'

Pointedly Formby-Hart looked at his watch. Gold and heavy. 'When you're ready, Shelley . . .'

Dominic watched the reunion without any sign of emotion. The only one in the room who might have been moved was that sour biddy Maggie Dowson. She unfolded a man's white handkerchief, polished her spectacle lenses and stared stonily out of the steamy window.

It was up to Shelley to act, she knew that. They couldn't stand here for ever. 'Today we've got our first real meeting with the people who are going to help us,' she told her son. 'So come on, love, let's make a start. Let's get you out of here – that's why we've come.'

Reluctantly he released her and fondly she pushed back his fringe and pecked him on the end of his nose. 'That's it, cheer up, things aren't as black as you think. We've got a lot of work to do so the sooner we get started the better.'

They followed Dominic through the swing doors and entered another world. The highly polished floors with rooms leading off on either side were covered in a worn red linoleum. The walls which should have been white had splodges of added paint here and there, presumably where the screws had tried to cover graffiti. They had not entirely succeeded. Here and there an obscene word or a crude daubing put the artists ahead in the race. During a school trip to London a tube journey had taken Shelley and her classmates down a white-tiled corridor like a public bog which at the time had seemed endless. A foul smell of feet and old farts reminded her of that now, when the same hollow feeling of enclosure hit her like a hammer.

So this was the reality. The true face of Dudley Park.

They didn't go far, and thank God for that, before Dominic unlocked a handleless metal door and showed them inside the green room. Lime green, badly smudged, obviously the work of uninterested inmates. He left the door unlocked when he went, leaving them to their own devices.

Perhaps she could ask to see Joey's room when this meeting was over. Perhaps they could go there and be more private and, she hoped, more comfortable than here. Efforts at informality had been made in the form of a plastic sofa and armchairs coloured a dull moss. Sticking plaster had been used to camouflage the rips. All this was garishly lit by fluorescent lights built into the ceiling. Ghosts of pictures left squares on the walls and the smell was of old fag ash.

Shelley settled down on the sofa with Joey beside her grasping her hand. The legal team pushed up the armchairs so they made an ugly half-circle, the furniture bumping over a badly frayed carpet that had once been green.

Chandler introduced the three strangers to Joey. No effort was made to shake hands with him or even establish eye contact, which was just as well because, throughout, Joey stared stolidly at the ground.

'The first thing we have to do this morning is find out exactly what happened,' said Chandler. 'And this time, Joey, no lies or evasions or bending of the truth. Now, are we all together on this one?'

Oh no, Shelley thought, don't say Joey has decided to be at his most obstructive again, at his most unappealing. How could she convince him that these four people were all that stood between him and a lifetime buried in holes like this? It was so important that they liked him.

As if reading her thoughts, Chandler tried a firmer line. 'D'you really want to stay in this dump for ever, Joey? It seems to me like you do. It's time you grew up and realized that in order for us to help you we must have your full co-operation. We're trying to be patient here. Your QC's time is expensive and all you're achieving at the moment is to dig yourself further in.'

'Shit,' sneered Joey.

Shelley smacked him hard over the head.

He yelped and hit her back.

'*That's enough*,' shouted Formby-Hart in a voice stern enough to quiet the most rampant lunatic. To Shelley's amazement this sudden shock had the required effect. Joey started to cry and began to cuddle into his mum once again.

Any port in a storm.

They concentrated on the paraffin, finally getting Joey to admit that, yes, he had nicked the can from B&Q. Not an enormous leap, as Formby-Hart observed, when you consider he was filmed in the act, but a welcome totter towards cooperation. Then they turned their attention to the lighter, and by the end of an emotional hour which left Joey storming in tears, he had also admitted to the theft of that item from Foresters' newsagents one week before the precinct murder.

His classmates at school had not been lying. It began to seem to Shelley that the only person spinning a web of deceit round here was her bloody beloved son.

Joey then had to explain to the team how that lighter got into the hands of Connor Mason, who he swore had thrown it. And at what point in the morning's rampage had Darren Long snatched the paraffin? He spoke in gulping bursts of denial with Shelley encouraging him, and a recorder on Maggie Dowson's lap took in every word.

'Joey.' Now Miranda addressed him in her familiar brisk manner. 'Between now and your trial you are going to be asked some pretty direct questions about exactly what happened. Your version of the events is going to clash head on with the statements of your four companions. Tears and storms of emotion like we have seen this morning aren't going to help you one iota when you get into that court. If there's anything more you need to tell us – if you want to change your story – then believe me, now is the time you must do it.' And she stared at him, her blue eyes coldly challenging.

'Hang on, love,' said Shelley, her dislike of the woman spurring her on. 'You can see what sort of state he's in. If you and your lot aren't careful you are going to end up persuading Joey to admit to the murder charge just to get you off his back. Hectoring, that's what you've been doing. And that's not right.' Joey was shaking beside her, taking in great gasps of air. His face was smeared with tears. He'd been through a good half-box of mansize Kleenex.

'I hope you realize the kind of pressure that Joey is going to be under, and most of that time we won't be around to make sure the game is played fairly,' said Chandler rather too crisply. 'He's got to get used to this, I'm afraid, and for his sake the sooner the better. You really are not helping him, Shelley, by too much of this protective nonsense. This is the real world. The real world at its worst, if you like. But that's life when you're dealing with crimes like this.'

'M-m-make them go away, Mum.' Joey sniffed and snuffled his way under her arm. 'I want to come home, w-w-with you . . .'

Formby-Hart sighed and uncrossed one tubby leg from the other. 'You've done very well today, Joey,' he said, 'and we're pleased with the progress we've made. We've a good way to go yet, but time enough to get there provided you keep telling us the truth and begin to trust us. We're on your side, you know.' And he moved his polished face closer to Joey's. Joey retreated further underneath Shelley's arm.

A mixture of pity and annoyance made it confusing for Shelley to respond. She wanted to shake Joey out of his uncomfortable refuge; he was being so silly, so unhelpful at the very time when he ought to be sensible. She would have a real go at him later, no doubt about that. But he had been through a hellish ordeal, bearing in mind he was only eleven and had spent last night in God-knows-what conditions, all alone. No wonder he was afraid and didn't know what to say for the best. It was a long while since she had seen her son so hysterical as this shower had made him this morning.

Enough was enough.

After the team drove off for their pub lunch it appeared that nobody knew that Shelley had planned to stick around.

'I did wonder,' she told an older screw in the uniform tracksuit of navy blue with a stripe, 'if me and Joey could talk in his room. Just for an hour. More private.'

'No problem,' said the screw with the Hitler moustache. Why did their wives not tell these men how revolting these nail brushes were, bristling out under their noses? A beard was more acceptable, but not those little tufts. If you must grow hair on your face, you might as well let it all hang out. Same with men who stink of BO and fat women in tight pedal-pushers. Why don't their families tell them?

Even if they had both been blind they could have followed the screw. His clanking keys and squeaky trainers advertised his noisy presence. With Joey determinedly holding her hand, something he had not done since he was three or four years old, they made their way through the tube-like corridors and Shelley caught fleeting glimpses of a large gymnasium, an art room, a recreation room and a canteen area which reeked of onion and beefburgers.

Eventually the three of them reached the accommodation wing. 'They all have their own rooms here,' said the screw. 'We don't like them sharing, for obvious reasons. Not if we can help it. There have been times when we've had to double up, of course.'

'Will there be any chance for me to meet the governor before I go?' Shelley interrupted while watching him select a key and stop in front of room number eight. 'Only I really need to know what special arrangements have been made for Joey, him being so young and only on remand . . .'

'Have you made an appointment?' he asked, pushing open the door to reveal a clean, bright little room with a window onto the courtyard.

'Well, no, I assumed the governor might want to speak to me.'

The man shook his head. 'I've been told nothing,' he said. 'But then who is around here?'

'Well, in that case can you ask if I could see him before I go?' She was pleading now.

This wasn't on. Of course she had to know that someone was looking out for Joey. He was far below the average age for Dudley Park. Sixteen, they'd told her. And what about companionship? Surely he wouldn't be mixing with the dregs and pushers and violent thugs who dominated hell-holes like this? And then there was his education, though she wasn't too frantic about that. No, it was his well-being that weighed so heavily on her mind. Were the social services concerned with any of this? Did they make regular visits? What was Joey expected to do with himself all day?

She had to see someone. Jesus Christ, she couldn't just piss off and leave these essential questions unanswered.

'I will enquire and get back to you,' said the screw, locking them in. 'Ring the bell if you need me.' She wasn't sure how to respond to his wink.

'*Oh Joey love,*' she cried, but this time he pushed her off. Where had her little boy gone, the one who had sobbed his heart out all morning? 'How is it? How's it been?'

The footie magazine, *Score*, always Joey's favourite, was flopped open on the bed. The room, with its colour TV on a stand attached to the wall, wasn't half as bad as she had imagined. Someone had tried to make it child-friendly. The tartan duvet matched the curtains.

She sat on the bed. The mattress gave nicely; this was no cheap foam job. A bottle of fizzy Dr Pepper stood on his bedside table. Christ, this was a damn sight better than conditions at home.

On the strength of this she decided to try to ignore his sudden thunderous change of attitude. Joey could be a user, and he was using her now all right. Manipulative little sod. She understood; she knew her son. She supposed he blamed her for all the hardships that had come tumbling so rapidly into his young life.

She said, 'Tell me what you did last night, after you left me at the cop shop. Did they give you supper? Did you see anyone when you got here? Were they nice to you? Did you get any sleep? I know I didn't.'

Joey turned his back on her.

'Well, how about this morning then? Did you meet any of the others? Are they all older than you? Are you allowed to wander around? They don't keep you locked in here all the time, do they?'

His back, straight and tense, said it all. Suddenly Shelley flipped. She'd been meaning to have a go at him anyway after his dumb performance this morning. 'You little bastard,' she said, standing up and turning him round by force. 'You think you're the only one going through shit just now? Well, let me tell you, you selfish, spoilt, brain-dead git, how d'you bloody well think your brothers and sister are feeling right now, stuck away in some stranger's house, can't go home any more, see their mates, play out? And how about me, you toss-head? Don't you think I'm feeling it all for you? Do you think I'm enjoying traipsing all over the countryside trying to get it together, knowing that most of the wankers I see would give a week's wages to see me sorted? And you! *Just look at you!* Standing there as if butter wouldn't melt, lying your head off, gallivanting about with scum that would stop at nothing for a laugh. And you've got the nerve to turn on the act the minute it suits you: oh poor Joey crying his eyes out, let's give Joey a gentle ride, he's only little . . . *little, my arse.* You're pissing me off, you really are. And I'm warning you for the last time . . .'

By putting her hands each side of his head she forced him to look at her.

'If you're not going to speak to me, Joey, and if you treat me this way, then I'm off. You understand? I'm just not putting up with this. I've bloody well had it up to here—'

'Don't go, Mum.'

She released him.

Her eyes gentled as she met his sadness.

'Next time you come, can you bring Wally Wolf?'

177

FOURTEEN

Joey's haunting screams after he was wrenched from her arms and dragged off down the corridor rendered Shelley incoherent during the first moments of her interview with David Barker, the young governor of Dudley Park.

He did not leave his seat to comfort her as she might have expected, as she sat distraught in the visitor's chair across from his formal desk. Instead, to her disquiet, he sat and watched her, his elbows resting between organized trays, his fingers linked together. She supposed that, to be fair, there was little point in communication at this stage, what with her being out of her head. She couldn't have taken anything in. If Mr Barker had tried kindness it would probably have finished her. He was the only member of staff she'd seen wearing a suit, and a posh one at that. You see suits like that worn by men in the City.

At one point, while she blubbed, doubled over with grief, someone brought in coffee, one for her and one for him, and retreated quietly without a word. He didn't touch his either.

When Shelley was all cried out, a shuddering

wreck reduced to shredding tissues between sticky fingers, he leaned towards her further and said, 'Please take your time, Mrs Tremayne. I just can't imagine what this whole experience must be doing to you and your family. I admire you tremendously for your bravery, and for your support of Joey.'

She hadn't expected this. She looked up at him as if to check that in her hysteria she hadn't started hallucinating. But no, along with the genuine words of sympathy his kindly face spoke volumes. A good-looking bloke around thirty-five at a guess, he wore his dark hair neatly cut, his skin was smooth, his mouth generous and his eyes a sincere and gentle brown. How could a man like him work in a shithole like this? She guessed he was a trouble-shooter, one of those high-flyers the government call in if there's a mega-problem. He was probably only pausing here on his way to the top of the ladder.

'I haven't even had a bath,' she said, 'or a hairwash.'

'No, I don't expect you've had time,' said Mr Barker understandingly.

'You must have heard Joey just now?' Her voice was far from controlled.

'Everyone in the vicinity must have heard him,' he said with a wry smile, 'and suspected blue murder.'

'What will they do with him now?'

Barker wasn't a fudger. He went straight into his answer. 'Well, one of his personal officers, Dominic, who you met when you first arrived, will stay with him until he calms down. After that he'll go to the canteen for lunch. Mealtimes are the only times when Joey will mix with the older prisoners, but there is one thirteen-year-old and one fourteen-year-old being held on remand here at the moment and we are allowing Joey to socialize with them, under constant supervision of course.'

'Are they OK, these two?' They must be pretty dodgy to have been sent here in the first place.

'They shouldn't be here,' said Mr Barker, 'and neither should Joey. We all know that. We can only regret that this country doesn't provide enough suitable accommodation for youngsters needing to be kept secure. Those few units which do exist are full to overflowing. Joey's companions are not the ideal, I'm not pretending they are, but with the correct supervision and sensitivity, better them than no-one at all.'

'So he is allowed out of his cell?'

'He's not in his cell for longer than any of us can help. We've put aside one recreation room for the use of these three young lads. There's table football, videos, a computer with suitable games, a CD player, and a teacher comes in each weekday from nine until three. There's one hour of compulsory PE every day in the gym. Apart from that there's frequent visits from social workers, counsellors and families of course. We do try to make their time here productive, if not exactly happy. But we can't overcome the major obstacle that these boys are prisoners here and away from their own homes.'

'Was Joey OK when he came in yesterday?' She'd been haunted by visions of the kind of hell she wouldn't put an animal through.

'He was naturally upset. And then we have to follow the rules, but the strip search was done—'

'*Strip search?*'

Barker didn't raise his voice. 'The strip search was done by the nurse during the required general medical check-up. Then he was bathed, given new clothes and some tea which I'm told he ate. After that I visited him to see if there were any special problems, and Dominic took him to the recreation room where he was given his sweet pack. He watched some TV with the others before going to bed at nine thirty. He then watched some more TV until that was switched off at ten.'

Shelley breathed out, so much relief. 'He refused to tell me anything. He clammed up completely. You'd think I was the enemy from the way he was.'

'He's a very angry little boy. Wouldn't you be, given the last few days?'

'But the way he screamed . . .'

'Some of our hardened nineteen-year-olds cry when their families leave. This is all very new and frightening for Joey. The staff here are aware of that. Every day, in Joey's case, we will meet to discuss his treatment, and tailor it to his personal needs. We're not here to punish your son; our job is to keep him as happy and safe as is possible until the courts make their decisions.'

'I can't tell you how relieved I am . . . I had imagined . . .'

He didn't beat about the bush. 'And you'd probably have imagined right if it wasn't for Joey's age and special treatment. Life for lots of kids in custody is nothing short of barbarous, with mental illness rife and overcrowding levels intolerable.' Barker sat back and frowned. 'Here we're trying to turn things round. It's an almost hopeless task. But there are some people in this Dickensian system who do care, you know. They may be constantly shouted down, the struggle is enormous, but some of us won't stop fighting until things get better.'

'Joey did mention something about being forced to repeat nursery rhymes. I didn't follow what he meant.'

'Ah yes, the Dudley Park night chorus. The window warriors calling and pipe-banging at night,' said Barker, sighing. 'We try to stop it but it's impossible. Some of our more disturbed residents take it upon themselves to bully the younger, more vulnerable newcomers. Part of this involves forcing them to recite nursery rhymes over and over under the threat of a beating if they stop before they're told. Joey's going to have to get used to this. Threats. Abuse. You name it. But remember, Mrs Tremayne, that in Joey's case none of these lads are going to get within yards of him.'

'But what's all this shit going to do to his head?'

'That depends on Joey,' said Barker, spreading his hands in a helpless gesture. 'There's only so much we can do to protect him.'

They both drank their coffee, still talking. When Shelley left they shook hands.

She was picked up by her legal team after their pub lunch. They were buoyed up by alcohol, Shelley by Barker's reassurances. She was sure she smelled whisky on Formby-Hart's breath as he drove them back into the city, dropping Shelley at police headquarters. Ridiculously this dump was beginning to feel like a second home. She was stalked by the constant fear of being recognized, and never failed to pull up her hood when in possible public view. She would have loved to visit Kenny, his condition was never far from her mind, but she feared some nutter might well be waiting, skulking in the hospital corridors.

Some time during the day the overstretched social services were having to cart the Tremaynes' few battered boxes from the Buckfastleigh flat to Mrs Bolton's farm at Two Bridges. Shelley had decided she could not spend one more night alone in that depressing place. And she missed her children so much it was worth putting up with a strange household and people who might despise her. It wasn't as if this was for life; a few months at most. Surely, with all this horror around her, a few months of community living wouldn't kill her, or her children?

But that wasn't to say she didn't dread the ordeal.

As she passed through the cop shop on her way to that small, familiar room where DI Hudson was waiting for a word, she was well aware that everyone knew her and made disparaging remarks when she'd gone.

This hurt.

But how could she blame them? In their eyes she had bred and brought up a kid so badly he had set fire to an innocent baby, the kind of unspeakable crime that didn't bear thinking about. She was to blame. The responsibility for the child's death was hers.

Her solicitor, Martin Chandler, had warned her that the pundits were discussing the case every night on TV. Everyone seemed to know the accused had five brothers and sisters. There was pressure for her five other kids to be taken into care and adopted. She was unfit to be a mother.

David Barker, Dudley Park's governor, had reassured her that Joey's viewing was being strictly monitored. Nobody was allowed to watch the news at Dudley Park. All the TVs on the premises went off at such sensitive times, and the evening's schedules were carefully vetted.

She would never trust this detective again. This man who, at first, had looked and behaved like a friendly uncle had revealed his true lights and turned out to be Joey's enemy number one, bringing undue pressure to bear, tripping her son up at every turn, assuming his guilt in his questioning and bribing witnesses to lie for him.

So Shelley did not respond to DI Hudson's enquiry, 'How is Joey?'

He ignored her closed expression and her refusal to sit down beside him. 'We've had a

Malcolm Yelland in here looking for you today. Constable Frey spoke to him and tells me this particular friend of yours is eager to contact you. I believe you have already been given his number.'

Where was this leading? Another trick to catch her out? Shelley listened warily.

'I just wanted to warn you, Shelley,' went on the inspector in his chatty, benevolent way as if quite unaware of her stiffness, 'if you are thinking of making contact, be careful not to give this man any ideas as to your family's whereabouts. Or Joey's for that matter.'

'Malcolm is an old friend of mine . . .'

'I'm sure he is.'

'. . . who only wants to help . . .'

'That may well be.'

'. . . and we're not all two-faced gits so freaked out by power that we'd piss on our own grand-mothers for a pat on the head from some superior.'

'Shelley.' Christopher Hudson stopped her with a pained frown. 'I say this for your good, not mine.' He scratched his head and stared at her as if searching for a way in through the barrier. 'I know nothing at all about this Malcolm Yelland apart from the few mentions you made of him when we last talked. It's just that at times like these you will find all sorts of nasty characters creeping out from the woodwork, for all manner of seedy reasons, from wanting to be part of the action to making money from the tabloids. All I'm saying, m'dear, is be careful.'

The thought of Malcolm in either role made her

laugh out loud. She was glad she could laugh that way in front of Inspector Hudson. It made her feel bigger; it made him seem small and mean. Shelley had not made plans to contact Malcolm before this conversation, but now she was determined to prove to this arsehole that she did have friends, *actually*, and that they were decent people.

Damn Hudson.

For her own good, my arse. It was easy to see where his warnings came from. The more alone and vulnerable Shelley and her family were, the easier it was to step up the pressure and bring her and Joey to their jack-booted heels.

And so it was from the back of the car along the A386 to the moor that Shelley used her mobile to speak to Malcolm Yelland for the first time in over a year.

'Shell! How you doing?' The nerd still sounded half out of it like the oldest hippy in town.

'Not so great, Malc.'

'So what about Joey?'

'Same. It's shit.'

'Tell me about it, Shell,' he rambled. 'Nobody's talking about anything else.'

'They're not keen on me, is what I've heard.'

'I wouldn't say you were one of the most popular faces around right now. It looks pretty bad from where I am. I went to your house but . . .'

'I know.'

'Where are you now?'

'I'm in a cop car. I can't say where.'

'So how will I find you?'

She imagined his long blond hair tied back with a black shoelace, his half-bald head with the precious threads so carefully placed to cover the dome. Did he still look the same? Did he still work down the docks? 'You won't,' said Shelley. 'If we want to meet, we'll have to think of somewhere. Somewhere they won't know who I am.' Malc must have forgiven Joey for the wicked behaviour that caused his departure, the time her son rang Childline and informed the anxious listener that he was being abused. They sent someone round . . . They would have taken Malc away, except Joey said if he pissed off of his own accord he'd confess that he'd been lying.

So Malc went.

And that was that.

They did tests on Joey. That shut him up. That put the fear of God up him as well as the sodding rubber glove. It served the little shit right. He came out of it worse than anyone. It took Shelley a while to forgive him.

'Have you still got your car then, Malc?'

'A new one,' he said. 'Got shot of the Capri. Would've cost an arm and a leg to get the old girl through the MOT. No, got an old MG Midget. Racing green. Wicked. Done a lot of work on it. Goes like new.'

'What about a pub then?' she asked him, peering out at the landscape, which was becoming wilder and bleaker as the car climbed the hills and paused to rumble over a cattle grid. The sheep sheltered from the lashing rain, huddled behind broken stone walls. A few early lambs looked shyly out from underneath their mothers' mud-ragged coats.

'Somewhere out of town. How about on the A38? The Moorland. You don't get your locals in there, it's mostly passing trade and they have those cubicles.'

'OK, Malc.' She hadn't a clue how she would get there. The police and social services would not be at her disposal for ever but she could ring Malc and cancel if transport proved impossible. It was Saturday today. 'How about Monday lunchtime? I'll have to fit it in between visits to Joey.'

'Fine,' drawled Malc. 'See you there. We could go for a drive on the moor if we wanted.'

'Malc?'

'Yep?'

'Thanks,' said Shelley.

The prison loomed greyly out of the landscape from which it was cut. The myriads of little barred windows were black burns in the thick material and the skirts of the jail were winter bleak, battered grasses and dead fern.

Dartmoor prison.

An unhappy legend. Surely first in the league for the most forbidding building constructed on this earth. Smoke, not from homely fires but from some archaic heating system, twisted like dead men's fingers through the menacing cold to clutch at a darkening sky.

Shelley was unfamiliar with this moor which had sat on her childhood doorstep, just as she was unfamiliar with the beaches and coves and cliff walks and other natural attractions which brought visitors here in their hordes. An occasional visit with the school was the limit of her experience, and that had been more to do with finding somewhere to hide and smoke well away from the teachers than a lesson in flora and fauna.

That people could actually live out here on this raw-boned frame of the earth, *could choose this place as a home*, was incomprehensible to her. How could anyone normal survive or scrape a living with the temperature frequently a frigid ten degrees lower than that in the valley, with no shops in reach, no clubs, no pubs, no transport, no neighbours . . . nothing but a few scrubby trees and towering, frowning tors to break such a desolate, endless landscape?

People out here must go for weeks without seeing a soul.

At the crest of a hill topped by a stand of dark firs, the car slowed down and nosed carefully between high stone walls into a steep valley, and then Shelley saw the farm. The longhouse itself was of thatch and granite; mottled with lichen, it seemed to be scooped from a basin of sky. It pushed outwards with pails and cans, a woodpile, modern barns, tractors and stacked machinery.

Four slinking collie dogs came out of the yard, barking frantically, and Shelley could only worry about how frightened Kez and Saul were of dogs after their painful experiences with the two German shepherds who lived next door on the Eastwood Estate.

Why the hell didn't someone come out and control them?

What was this weird set-up anyway? Surely a most unsuitable place of safety for her children?

FIFTEEN

Eunice Bolton had a man's moustache and skin the colour of cooked swede. This was the second shock for Shelley before she'd even left the car – the first being six-year-old Kez calling the dogs off with a shrill command. The light from the opened back door pooled on a section of cobbles in the darkening afternoon, and illuminated the farmer's wife with Julie under one arm and Casey hanging on to her hand.

Kez, Saul and Jason rushed out shrieking to meet her.

After dumping her stuff in the porch, the police driver drove off into the curtain of sleet.

God, it was cold. It was freezing. With teeth already chattering, with kiddies climbing all over her, Shelley dived out of the wet and into the safety of the porch, her anxious eyes already scanning for displays of dislike on her hostess's face.

'We've been waiting for this moment all day,' boomed Eunice Bolton in grubby slippers and a pink home-knitted woolly. Her plaid skirt was none too clean and short enough to display eight

fat inches of veined, bare legs before they disappeared into golfing socks. Her red hair was
sparse and over-permed. When she took Shelley's
arm her strength was astonishing. 'Come on,
kiddies, make room for your poor old mum.'

Shelley was commanded to a ladderback chair
next to a cream Aga. A mug of strong tea was
placed beside her and Julie was dumped on her
knee. There was absolutely no sign of censorious-
ness in Eunice's expressions or actions, just relief
that her visitor was out of the cold and safe now
in her capable hands.

The excited children danced round the outsized
refectory table which, scratched and woodwormed
from years of use, dominated the room and over
which hung a rail of drying washing. From a giant
pan on the Aga came the sweet, tempting smell of
ham cooking. A selection of home-made pickles
and jams were already arranged on the table,
along with a loaf that, because of its shape, could
only be home baked.

Shelley made to put Julie down, but saw that
the floor was stone flagged. She hesitated.

'She's fine, she won't hurt,' said Eunice. 'The
back door's closed, she can't get out, and if she
does one of the dogs'll round her up.'

Was the woman being serious? Too bewildered
to argue, Shelley let the baby go and wrapped her
cold hands round the steaming mug. '*How have
they been?*' She longed to know. They looked fine.
They seemed happy. But the poor little mites must
have missed her . . .

'They're lovely,' enthused Eunice. 'No trouble

192

at all. Been helping me round the house and out in the yard, haven't you?'

The children beamed back at her.

'Not too many tears then?' Shelley asked.

'Oh, we had a few at first,' said Eunice, now bustling around in the dresser cupboards and delivering plates to the table with the ease of a gambler dealing cards. 'But we had a few cuddles and we had a few squeezes and that was soon over, I'm glad to say. No, they're grand kids, every one of them. You can be proud of yourself, m'dear.'

Shelley's insides froze when it suddenly struck her that Eunice Bolton might not know why these kids were here. Maybe it was not thought necessary for social workers to tell foster mothers the background situation, as long as it didn't directly apply to the children themselves?

'And how's that other littie tyke of yours? Joey's his name, isn't it?'

Ah, so she knew that much. Shelley must proceed with caution. 'Not too bad, homesick of course.'

'Well, he will be in one of those places. Should be razed to the ground. The thought of all those poor young boys stuck behind bars like that, and all what goes on ... Dear Lord, it's enough to make you weep.'

'You know what they're saying?' Shelley asked. 'You know what they're saying he did?'

'Oh, I know well enough.' Eunice sniffed. 'But he's still a little lad when all's said and done.'

'He didn't do it,' Shelley told her.

'No, I'm sure he didn't, m'dear,' said Eunice comfortingly. 'But now I want you to try and relax and forget about what's going on in that world out there. For your little lad's sake you must keep your health. Make this your home while you need somewhere and don't feel you have to behave like a guest.'

Shelley had to bite her lip hard to stop the tears overflowing. This reception was extraordinary. She found it hard to accept the reality after the last grim few days. Mrs Bolton was so loving and friendly and the children so contented, even if grimy and only half dressed. They wouldn't be boisterous like this if they were in awe of Eunice, which, because of her appearance alone, it would be quite possible to be.

'Now why don't you let the kids show you their bedrooms? Pop them in the bath if they need it while I get the tea. Some boxes of yours came today. I had Oliver and Edward take them upstairs. Maybe you'd like to sort through them. Get a bit organized like.' She then thrust a warmed bottle into Shelley's hand. 'Julie can have this now, stop her whining while you're busy.'

So organized.

So capable.

Kez and Saul led the way. Up a back staircase and over uneven floorboards they went, turning left and right at so many intersections Shelley was amazed they remembered the route. There were two beds in one of the rooms, bunks in another and a cot and a sofa bed in the third. Eunice had already explained that Shelley could either sleep with the baby or on her own beside the fire in the farmhouse lounge. She would far rather sleep with Julie and have some privacy. OK, Eunice was lovely, but Eunice had a family: she'd already mentioned Oliver and Edward, so how many more of them were there? She didn't fancy hanging around until the family went to bed before she could get her head down on the sofa.

With the kids in the large iron bath that took three at a time, Shelley got some feedback as to what life had been like for her children without her. They were bursting with excitement, falling over themselves to tell her. She took this opportunity to light up while she could, not sure about Eunice's views on fags and terrified of upsetting her. She used the soap dish as an ashtray.

'Eunie lets us feed the hens . . .'

'I picked up some eggs . . .'

'There was this baby goat . . .'

'Jason stirred some cheese with this huge spoon . . .'

'Mum?'

'Yes, Kez?'

'I'm not scared of dogs any more.'

'When we go home can I have a puppy?'

'What about Mr Bolton?' Shelley asked eventually. 'Eunice's husband. Is he nice?'

'He drives the tractor.'

'He feeds the calves and, Mum, we saw a lamb born.'

'But what's his name? What do you call him?'

'John's his name. He's big.' And Saul stretched

to prove how large John Bolton seemed to him, slipped and hit his head on the bath.

After the screaming died down, Shelley fed Julie her bottle followed by a bowl of warm apples and custard sent up by Eunice for 'when she's ready'. The cot was clean, the blankets rough but there were plenty of them to keep Julie warm. This country air must suit the child. Her eyes were closed before Shelley left the room.

Then followed the unloading of boxes and the spreading out of familiar clothes and objects around the three rooms that were theirs. The chests of drawers were so ample they would have taken three times as much stuff. Favourite toys were stacked on the shelves and the general mess was sorted. By the time they were finished the rooms looked homely and welcoming. The boys wore their own pyjamas again. Sweaters on top and a pair of thick socks kept out the cold. There was no central heating. Sleet which had formed a fudge on the windows slipped down in chunks when too heavy to hold.

Shelley looked at her children and frowned. Yes, this was home, they would settle here – but for how long?

Would they be forced to move from the area if Joey was found guilty?

Would somebody sell her house for her, and what would she get for it daubed with graffiti and boarded up and with a notorious reputation?

What would happen to the mortgage payments if Kenny didn't survive? And the maintenance he paid, would that stop too?

With a name like Tremayne, wherever they went they would stand out a mile. Did this mean they would have to change their identities? And what about Kez's schooling? Joey's was being continued, but how the hell could Kez go to school without someone finding out who he was? And Saul was due to start in September.

There were so many questions Shelley needed to ask but nobody with the answers.

Downstairs with her well-scrubbed tribe babbling and hungry, Shelley's fears for their personal safety went soaring out of the window with the first sight of Eunice's menfolk in their places at the table. Mr Bolton was at the head, a wiry-haired, stringy man with steely blue eyes and a grizzled chin. He must be well over six foot. His grin displayed strong white teeth and the steel in his eyes softened slightly at the sight of the kids. His sons, Oliver and Edward, sat each side of their father, sleeves rolled up as if ready for work even at this time of rest. Both were dark like their father and had the same infectious grins. Nobody with vengeance in mind would consider taking on this team who were probably as strong as the bullocks they farmed, well built and mega-healthy.

And no wonder, when you looked at the spread Eunice had laid on the table.

Shelley thought such meals existed only in wistful books.

They worked their way through baked potatoes, ham, home-grown beetroot, cauliflower cheese and a massive apple crumble with cream straight from their milking cow. This was followed by roughly hewn chunks of bread, and jams, as if anyone had room left. But it seemed that they did. None of the kids moaned on about wanting Coke to drink, not milk, or having their spuds mashed up for them, or cauliflower stinks, or there's fat in the meat.

Shelley was staggered at this revolution which had taken place so quickly. Maybe it was seeing the men tuck in with such ferocity. Food was there to be enjoyed, not complained over or fussed about. She was surprised at the amount she put away; she hadn't known she was hungry until she was tempted by all this lovely nosh.

Did the men know as much of the truth as Eunice?

And did they share her compassionate views?

They had taken in some hard nuts in their time, Alex had told her that. And Alex had also mentioned the high rates of success achieved by the yobs who had stayed here and worked on the farm. It seemed peculiar that this family, so self-contained and cut off from the world, would take on the hazardous job of nurturing some of society's worst dregs. Eunice was a natural mother, there was no doubt about that, but after bringing up two boys of her own – and more kids might have left home already – and reaching her mid-fifties, you would think she'd like to take life more easily.

It would seem not. Throughout the meal she tended to the children with no fuss, no raised voice, no panic. Shelley could hardly remember such a harmonious atmosphere at her own kitchen table. Someone was always playing up – Joey was moody or Julie was screaming . . . She rarely ate her own food without suffering from chronic indigestion after. Some people, Shelley thought, were just naturally good, born that way most probably, with a need to help others.

Well, she wasn't complaining. This was all just too good to be true.

During her brief exploration of the longhouse, Shelley discovered no sign of a telly. This was unfortunate to say the least. The kids needed telly. Shelley needed telly. They needed telly to calm them down and to shut them up. But now, more than ever, Shelley needed to be aware of the news reports and discussions going on about her and her unnamed son.

When she asked about this Eunice said, 'We listen to the wireless. There's a news programme at ten. We've never had television up here and what you don't have you don't tend to miss. We'd never have the time anyway. Always something to be getting on with.'

Was there? Not in Shelley's experience there wasn't.

In that past life of hers which now seemed as lost as a Jurassic world, once the kids were in bed Shelley enjoyed nothing more than sitting down for the rest of the evening and watching anything that came on. She wasn't picky. She could have cleaned the house, she supposed, or done some more washing or ironing. But why would you want to, once the house was quiet and peaceful?

199

There was something in Eunice's routine that echoed what Iris used to say. Maybe it was that age group. The way they were brought up in those days.

But where cleanliness was concerned Iris and Eunice were poles apart. There was no sign of sterility here, quite the opposite; their lifestyle made such fetishes impossible. Uncovered buckets of leftovers stood on the table beside the sink, ready for the pigs' breakfast. Old potato peelings for the chickens did a rolling boil on a hotplate. And Shelley had to wonder how Eunice had told the difference between the bottle she had sent up for Julie and those standing on the side of the sink waiting for the motherless lambs. Muddy Barbours and boots littered the porch where a couple of dead rabbits were slung on a hook with string, their nostrils crusted with blood.

Underneath the family banter the respect in which the two sons held their parents was very clear to see. This was a time warp compared to the ways of the world outside. They deferred to their father in all things. He carved the joint. His plate and his cider glass were the first to be filled, and he was the one who got the best chair when they finally retired to the lounge.

But Eunice, who served them all, was not excluded from their concerns. Her menfolk were protective of her in a hundred subtle ways. Everything she did was praised; offers of help were made, though refused – but why did none of her loving family tell Eunice to shave her moustache? Maybe they were so used to it they just

200

didn't notice any more. It became obvious that, after the meal, Shelley was expected to wash up.

They couldn't have heard that Janet and John books had been updated since their first editions.

'Bed, you lot,' declared Eunice, after the table had been cleared with help from the older children. Shelley prepared herself for a racket. Kez and Saul, at six and four, had later bedtimes than Jason and Casey and back at home this rule had often been a bone of contention. Not here, apparently.

Shelley smiled as she led them upstairs. What sort of drug had Eunice used to render her children so compliant? Whatever it was she wanted it. They were tired, that was true, from a day spent outdoors in cold weather. They had wolfed their tea like lions at a kill and maybe the novelty of their bedrooms was still a major attraction. So far there had been no complaints at the lack of the addictive TV. Incredibly, they hadn't seemed to notice.

There were books laid out on the bedside table in the elder boys' bedroom. *Thomas the Tank Engine*, two short stories. Shelley looked at them, mildly surprised. They had been picked from the shelf where she had propped them, and deliberately left where they couldn't be missed.

Was Eunice trying to tell her something?

Was she suggesting that Shelley needed reminding that her kids should have a bedtime story?

Or was Shelley being paranoid, tired, confused and over-emotional? Knowing Eunice, she was trying to be helpful. How kind of her to consider such details but Shelley would have preferred to let the boys choose the books themselves.

In the rumpus of bedtime she soon forgot these silly, negative thoughts. She read them the Thomas books – always favourites. She wasn't in too much of a hurry to go down and join the Boltons for an evening in their lounge. She wasn't quite certain what was expected of her. Would they rather she kept to herself once the children were out of the way? The last thing she wanted was to be over-intrusive and in any way upset the wonderful apple-cart which seemed to be working so well.

She missed the telly already.

She desperately wanted to watch the news, and didn't feel happy with the idea of listening to the latest reports on the baby murder surrounded by strangers, however sympathetic, on what they called their wireless. But she could hardly go to bed, although the sofa bed looked tempting now it was made up with sheets and blankets. No duvets in this household. If she went to bed they might imagine there was something wrong. It might look rude, unappreciative – the last thing she wanted.

Eventually she wandered downstairs and found the washing-up stacked and ready. This chore had been left for her to finish. A job for women, not men. The water was hot. It didn't take long, and Shelley made her way into the lounge, a long, thin, smoky room with a fireplace that took up most of one wall.

'Oh there you are, m'dear,' called Eunice, busily

knitting in a charcoal-grey wool. She patted the lumpy sofa. 'Come and sit alongside me.' Edward and Oliver were playing draughts, a game Shelley thought had long been extinct. John was smoking a pipe and flicking through the *Farmers Weekly*. There was a pile of old, well-thumbed magazines on the table beside his chair.

The pipe gave Shelley the courage to ask, 'By the way, would it be OK if I had a fag?'

'I don't think so, m'dear, do you? Not really the kind of thing a nice young woman like you should be doing.'

John glanced over his paper, his eyes more steely than Shelley remembered. She put this down to the acrid smoke drifting out into the room from the logs, and the fact that all of them were frowning slightly. His two sons said nothing, but Shelley was aware of a look which she could not interpret passing over the draughtboard between them.

SIXTEEN

If you included the waiting time, Sunday was taken up almost entirely with visiting Joey.

Shelley was not too fazed by this. There was something about her stifling welcome which, although everyone had been kind, was unsettling.

Severe withdrawal symptoms kicked in after an evening spent sitting next to Eunice, with only one cup of cocoa to drink before she went to bed, so Shelley had hurried upstairs at ten thirty to find her hidden packet of Silk Cut which she urgently needed after tense hours of abstinence. She could open the small lattice window just wide enough to blow out the smoke. But however hard she searched through her newly arranged chest of drawers, of the wretched packet there was no sign. She had either forgotten where she had hidden it, which was highly unlikely owing to her twenty-a-day addiction, or someone had removed it. One of the kids. She'd find out in the morning and give them hell. The sods.

Last night she'd been surprised at the genuine interest Eunice had showed in her guest. With her homely, chatty manner, it was easy to forget that this was a woman Shelley hardly knew. While Eunice knitted a sock on four needles without the benefit of a pattern, she showed such fascination in Shelley's past life, her family and her partners, that Shelley, thinking back, might have been over-enthusiastic, might well have bored her listeners stiff with tales about the children's little exploits, the funny habits of Keith (Jason and Casey's father), and Malc's lazy ways. Oh dear. Stuff that could surely interest nobody but family, like having to flick through other people's holiday snaps. But this was one more sign of how capable this homely, hairy woman was, that she could make her guests feel so relaxed and so intriguing so quickly.

Shelley had never seen herself as an interesting person before.

But last night Eunice had been fascinated to hear about Iris Tremayne's Cornish background, her marriage to Shelley's father, Liu Qi, and her subsequent banishment from the family. 'Can you believe it?' said Eunice. 'Some of those funny old Cornish parties are still fanatical about their religions . . . There's pockets of them to this day, I hear, mostly around Bodmin moor. Won't work on a Sunday, won't even milk their beasts or bring in hay before it's spoiled. Hold these Bible meetings in barns where everyone shouts allelluia and confesses their sins to the rooftops, real Godfearers, forever on watch for the devil and his ways.' The way she described these moorland time warps, with the firelight flickering on her hairy face and the glow of the low lamps in the lounge, she made these people sound sinister. 'Can't read, can't write, most of them. Tie up their trousers with baling twine and sign their names with an X. Your mum did well to get out when she did. Showed some courage, too.'

Shelley had to confess that she'd never met her relatives and that Iris had rarely spoken about her childhood on the moor.

During that entire evening, the three men of the house hardly spoke. Edward and Oliver did exchange the occasional word and every so often one of them rose to add another few logs to the fire. John tapped his pipe, grunted, and flicked back and forth through his pages. But they didn't miss much of the conversation, Shelley was sure of that.

At five to ten precisely, in a ritualistic fashion, John Bolton stretched across and turned on the wireless, a shiny walnut cabinet which, in its base, held ancient records in brown paper cases, thirty-threes and seventy-eights, ready for the news. Shelley felt the tension rising, not only through her own body but filling the room, acrid and eye-watering as the smoke. She just prayed that some major world event would dominate the news tonight, that the baby-burning would be relegated further down the line of importance. What more, after all, could be said? How she wished she was listening alone, not with these four strangers, no matter how compassionate, no matter how supportive.

The announcer's grave and proper BBC voice

launched the country immediately into the heart-breaking subject that still overwhelmed the minds of the listeners. Today baby Holly Coates had been buried in a private ceremony at her local church. Shelley stared blankly into the fire, watching the red ashes turn white and fall. Holly, Eunice had told her earlier in the evening, the wood of the holly tree up the drive; John had cut it back earlier in the year. It burned well. It smelled nice. Apple was best but they tended to keep that specially for Christmas. Their Yule Log was mostly apple, but holly was a good solid wood which lasted longer than most.

Shelley watched, her heart aching, as the sweet boughs burned through to nothing.

She was glad she hadn't seen this on telly; those images would have torn her to pieces. But the commentator's emotive description was almost more heart-rending and came with the awful awareness that these events were becoming familiar . . . little white coffin, teddy bear wreath, vicar with arms spread wide like the wings of a welcoming Christmas-tree angel, the useless wealth of fluffy toys donated by an anguished public, 'All Things Bright And Beautiful', Eric Clapton's 'Tears In Heaven'. And, of course, any such event would not be complete without the morbid, weeping crowds carrying bored and restless children who crammed into every nook and cranny to get a shufti at the mourners.

Was it always the same crowd?

Did they travel in coaches together?

Were they on the internet so they could liaise

with each other and make arrangements, like travellers or ravers?

Or did the crowd vary from tragedy to tragedy?

Of Joey and crew there was no mention on this solemn and most innocent occasion.

Nobody spoke, not even Eunice, and then Shelley realized that this, too, was ritual, and that all the news had to be heard, followed by that all-important weather forecast. It was only after that was over that John Bolton leaned across again and switched off the wireless.

Eunice said, 'How dreadful.'

Shelley nodded, so heavy with responsibility that it wasn't possible to raise her head.

'Dreadful times,' John muttered, 'a dreadful world. But what can one do? The damage is done.'

He did not expand on that remark and Shelley was way beyond listening anyway. All her thoughts were of the parents of Holly Coates. Their grief was beyond the understanding of any-one who hadn't been in their place, and Shelley's own grief at the loss of her son felt selfish beyond all measure. At least he was alive – she could see him. She could hold him. At least he had some kind of future.

Before the final cocoa was served the menfolk heaved themselves from their chairs and went out to check on the lambing sheds and close up the barns for the night. This was the signal for the women of the house to prepare the hot drinks and tidy the kitchen.

And this, it would seem, was their strict routine.

208

* * *

At least, last night, she had managed a bath and a hairwash.

At least she now wore a clean pair of jeans and a heavy sweater to keep out the appalling cold which permeated all the rooms of the house save for the lounge and its eternal fire, and the kitchen with its Aga.

By the time Shelley woke up at about eight, Julie was out of her cot, changed, downstairs, had been given breakfast and was playing happily with pans, dough and a wooden spoon. Not only that, but the other kids had all finished breakfast and were busy about their morning tasks; even Casey was helping to feed the hens and collect the few eggs from those still laying.

'I let you sleep in, m'dear,' said Eunice, bringing bacon and eggs from the slow oven and browning fresh toast on top of the Aga. 'I knew you'd need as much as you could get under the circumstances.' She slapped down a saucer filled with almost white home-made butter.

'What time were you up?' asked Shelley, impressed.

'Oh, we farming folk can't get out of the old habits of rising with the dawn light and sleeping at dusk, if you like.'

'But you didn't sleep with the dusk last night.'

'No, that's just me being foolish, m'dear. But the men have got work to be going to ... we can't stay in our beds when there's beasts to be fed.'

Shelley was relieved by the thought of a few

hours out of this, even if it meant the dubious refuge of Dudley Park and Joey.

That morning there had been frost on the inside of the windows. Attached to gutters and thatch outside, icicles grew to monstrous lengths. The kids plucked them off and sucked them with glee, not caring what germs might be on them.

She had worried about the children being out there in that filthy yard in sub-zero temperatures, not so much Kez and Saul but Jason and particularly Casey, only a toddler, with his trousers trailing in the muck, clumsily falling into every straw-filled, poisonous-looking puddle. His fascination with the ducks and the hens proved more like a serious obsession as he lumped his way after the clucking birds, hurling pieces of toast at them. The ducks seemed threatening. Shelley watched worriedly. One of those sharp-beaked, aggressive creatures could have his eye out in seconds. She traipsed round after him, but after half an hour she couldn't stand the cold and tried to carry him in. The little sod caused such a rumpus she had to let him go.

Although the children were in their element messing about with the animals out in the cold and the Boltons went out of their way to make her feel comfortable, there was an uneasiness in their presence which Shelley decided stemmed from her own shortcomings. Sometimes, compared to the competent Boltons, she felt glaringly inadequate.

Not her fault, of course, that she had not been able to provide this kind of perfect, hearty childhood for her brood but everything that happened around here was beginning to make her feel an inferiority that, up until Joey's arrest, had not seriously crossed her mind.

Of course she would feel vulnerable when faced with Julie's preference for being spoonfed by the older woman, when two-year-old Casey pushed her away when she tried to help him feed the chickens, when Kez and Saul went off with the Bolton brothers, in trainers that were quite inappropriate, to some far-off pasture without even a kiss goodbye.

Eunice, in a striped bobble hat, watched and smiled broadly, taking her stiff moustache halfway across her face.

When Shelley discovered her lost cigarettes hidden underneath the clean washing – she was searching for dry socks for Casey – she knew that her kids wouldn't take a joke this far. If they had hidden the fags it would have been somewhere in the bedroom, somewhere obvious. Late down for breakfast, she hadn't had a chance to question them. Now she stood, with the packet in her hand, bewildered by the knowledge that one of the Bolton family had been rooting through her belongings some time last night after she had unpacked.

Why would anyone do this?

Disapproval of smoking was one thing ... deliberately searching for and hiding the fags was something far more peculiar. There was no way she was going to question Eunice on this one and face a confrontation. She began to wonder whether there was any way the packet could have dropped out of her pocket and ended up in the basket during the previous evening.

No. That was ludicrous.

So her uneasiness grew.

She had been told she'd be fetched around lunchtime. It being Sunday, the police were stretched for manpower, but they'd get someone there as soon as they could. Shelley had told Eunice she wouldn't be staying for Sunday lunch, which, going by Eunice's shocked response, seemed quite an event at the farm.

So she stood to one side when, cooking done, Eunice lined the kids up and wiped their hands and faces hard with a rough dishcloth.

Julie was lifted into a chair piled high with empty eggboxes and tied to the back with a scarf, no messing. A seed tray acted as a high-chair table, a seed tray that had not been cleaned. At one point in the exercise, Jason, aged three, began to play up. Eunice lowered her face to his and gave him such a menacing glare he shut up his fussing immediately and went like a lamb to his chair. Disconcerted by this though she was, Shelley had no room to complain. She would have belted his legs but somehow she found Eunice's tactics more disturbing, although, to be fair, they worked like a dream.

If Shelley had known the police would be late she'd have loved to stay and taste that joint. It was their own, as John pointed out, reared on the farm and slaughtered on the farm, but Shelley erased that fact from her mind. She only ever bought meat, cleaned and wrapped, straight from supermarket shelves; she couldn't stand the stench in a butcher's, or the blood, or the pigs' heads. Disgusting.

In her whole life Shelley had not seen a joint of beef the size of this, nor roast potatoes so succulently done, nor Yorkshire puddings so perfectly risen. And yet all this was accomplished with no cursing or rushing or crashing of pans.

Once again Shelley was forced to review her own pathetic efforts in the kitchen. She tended to cook the kids' favourites to avoid a hassle at the table and this meant chicken pie or beans or fish fingers, almost always frozen peas and chips if she hadn't the time to do spuds. Unless there was tomato sauce the kids wouldn't touch their food, particularly Joey. His likes and dislikes were paramount; if there were scenes his would be the worst. His would last and affect the others. Even Casey, aged two, copied Joey. For convenience sake she pandered to him – surely that was what most mothers did? Why put yourself through the shit?

How would the streetwise Joey have responded to a childhood spent running free like this? What if Joey had been given a positive role in a hard-working family set-up right from Casey's tender age? Mixing with nature and animals. A childhood ranging over purple moorland so vast it stretched to every horizon. Never bored. Never imprisoned by weather, or fear of lurking strangers. And how unlikely it would be

213

in this little corner of the world that he would meet, or be influenced by, the likes of those bloody deviants the Lessings, Darren or Connor.

You only had to look at Oliver and Edward Bolton to know that their mother would never have shed a hopeless tear, or stayed awake nights wondering what the hell to do with the buggers. Shelley wished she could bring Joey here – but would it already be too late? Wouldn't he scoff at the spartan conditions, wouldn't he rebel without his telly, wouldn't he skive off the heavy work and hitch a quick ride back to the city?

Unfortunately that hard-faced copper Juliet Hollis, the one who had been so insensitive during Joey's arrest and so superior in her treatment of Shelley, was to drive her to Lister today.

Still, beggars couldn't be choosers. The policewoman with the aquiline nose did not deign to muck up her shoes by stepping out of the car; instead she sounded the horn to tell Shelley her lift had arrived.

Under Eunice's expert direction the kids had all made potato-print cards for Joey; even Julie's bore a smudged blue hand-print. There were no tears during this exercise, no squabbling, no cheek.

Shelley had searched for Wally Wolf when first unpacking the boxes, but there was no sign of that well-worn toy. He must be back in the house somewhere, and she must remember to ask DI Hudson if he could arrange for someone to go back and find him. Shelley, like a mother out of some fairy tale, also carried a basket containing home-made toffee, two gingerbread men and half a dozen apples. Eunice's contribution.

Shelley feared that twenty fags would be more appreciated. And talking of fags, she must persuade the haughty Hollis to stop at the first newsagent so she could stock up on her own supplies. Typically, she had left Kenny's newly delivered illegal supply back at home, hidden in the biscuit tin.

Once Shelley was in the car, Juliet Hollis didn't need to speak to make it clear that she found this chauffeuring business an unnecessary bore, not a proper part of her job. The message came across crisp and clear in the stiffness of her back and her pointed lack of greeting. Shelley leaned forward and asked politely if a stop at a shop would be possible.

'I would've thought you'd be more concerned with the plight of one of your many exes.'

'Which one?'

Hollis was sneering, Shelley saw in the mirror. 'Kenneth Hill, Joey's father allegedly.'

This was so unfair. Shelley would have asked about his condition at once but she hadn't thought the stiff-haired Hollis would know. 'He's dead . . .' She faltered, feeling sick.

There was a deliberate pause before Hollis said, 'No, I've been told to tell you he's out of his coma and has been moved to a public ward.'

'*Oh, thank God, thank God for that.*'

'I doubt God had much to do with it,'

commented Hollis sharply. 'If God had his way he'd be a goner. And he wouldn't be alone either.'

These were Juliet Hollis's views, and the views of the vast majority of the British public. Shelley had better get used to them. To answer back would be pointless.

'Anyway,' Hollis continued, going back to Shelley's original request, 'there's nowhere open round here on a Sunday.'

There would be once they got off the moor, but Shelley couldn't be bothered to argue. They crept through lanes still shining with ice; at least Hollis was a competent driver. When at last they reached the short stretch of motorway Shelley was surprised and gratified when Hollis pulled up at a service station. 'Only because I need petrol. But you might as well get what you want. Don't be longer than five minutes. I haven't got all day, even if you have.'

After the warmth and kindness that surrounded her at the Boltons', Hollis's attitude came as a shock and a wake-up call to reality. Back there on the moor in that hidden valley the fears that confronted her out here in the real world seemed like flashes of passing nightmare. She kept her hood well up while going round the services shop, looking for something that might please Joey. She ended up with a CD of his favourite group, the Chemical Brothers, and two hundred fags for herself.

The Sunday papers – it was once such a treat to cuddle up in bed with toast, tea and the *Mirror* – shrieked out at her as she passed the display on her way to the cash till.

The little white coffin was centre page, with its teddy bear wreaths and its single rose. But up in one corner in a bold square box, overlooking the baby, was Joey's blanked-out image, surely looking far more menacing than any real-life picture would do.

They needed no face to know him. Or to represent what he stood for.

This, then, Shelley knew, was the picture the press would always use as the image of the monster who had committed, allegedly, this most heinous, this most unforgivable of crimes.

She paid for her items and fled.

SEVENTEEN

The stitches above Joey's eye puckered the two-inch gash into a series of black spidery tracks.

'I leave my son here for one night and when I come back I find he's been knifed only inches from his right eye and nobody round here seems to know a bloody thing about it even after all your reassurances yesterday that he would have twenty-four-hour attention and special treatment because of his age. How can I ever trust you again? How d'you think I'm going to feel leaving my child here with you for one minute longer . . .'

'I know,' said governor David Barker, in his neat suit and his navy and white striped shirt with tiny silver cars to hold back his cuffs. He held both hands up, like a terrorist planting a bomb suddenly come upon by sharpshooters. 'And I just can't apologize enough, but I really must emphasize how certain I am that this unhappy circumstance will never happen again.'

'Jesus,' shrilled Shelley, *'pull the other one.* Just wait until your superiors hear about this "unhappy circumstance". Wait till the press get hold of it. This scandal will outrage the nation.

Here's a little boy being held in a most unsuitable institution, a little boy so far not even convicted of doing anything wrong. And what happens? In this bedlam full of psychos and freaks twice his age, some bastard comes along in broad daylight and tries to gouge out his fucking eye. *My God . . . my God . . .*' Shelley caught her breath and stopped pacing the room for a second to bend over and fight for air. 'If Joey could have been held in the medical block, which you now have the nerve to tell me is safe, why the fuck wasn't he put there in the first place?'

'I explained all that to you earlier, Mrs Tremayne,' consoled Mr Barker, at his wits' end. 'We didn't want Joey to be held in isolation. We believed that it would be detrimental for him to spend time away from his peer group, so we decided to socialize him with the two lads just a few years his senior. We made a serious miscalculation. We know that now and we are doing everything in our power to make sure Joey's stay with us here is safe.'

Shelley stared at him in astonishment. '*You really believe they will make him stay here after this assault?* Are you seriously telling me that "doing everything in your power", which has proved so bloody feeble up till now, is all you can promise me? "Your power" – my arse.

'I want to speak to somebody in authority round here. You just won't do, with your smarmy wheedling ways and lies. You're nothing but a spin doctor covering up for this shithole – how can you do this job and go home and sleep nights?

You tell me that, Mr bleeding Barker. It's you should be behind these bars, not Joey, you and scumbags like you.'

David Barker studied his hands. He laid them out on the desk as if for inspection. They were clean and white and had obviously never done a hard day's work. She compared his hands to the Bolton men's hands, so rough, calloused and somehow honest, whereas this tosser had lifted nothing heavier than a pen in the whole of his miserable goddamn life.

Shelley would never get over her arrival at Dudley Park this afternoon, not half an hour ago.

Still smarting over the shock of the front pages of the Sundays, fresh from her uncomfortable journey under the withering scrutiny of Juliet Hollis, she had been taken straight to Joey's room to find him sobbing on the bed with Dominic Brownlow gathering his pathetic supply of belongings and stuffing them into a laundry bag.

The first sight of his wound took her breath right away.

Some accident?

A fight perhaps? A scuffle which got out of hand?

Against Joey's perfect complexion the gash stood out like a scarlet horror, its untidy black sutures only adding more shudders to the hideous sight.

'*What the hell . . . ?*'

'They cut me,' cried Joey, smearing his tears across his face.

220

You would think they might have covered the scar. You would think they might be so ashamed they would want to plaster it up and conceal it. This was so unbelievable Shelley almost smiled. 'Who cut you?'

'That cunt Smith.'

'Smith?' Shelley turned to the fitness freak in the tracksuit. 'Who's this Smith, for God's sake? What sort of crap is all this?'

Dominic Brownlow dumped his load and sat on the bed beside Joey. 'The governor wants to see you,' he said. 'I'm afraid that last night Joey, Smith and Hawkins, the two boys nearest his age, were having their tea in the canteen, supervised by my colleague Paul Francis, when quite out of the blue and before anyone knew what was happening Smith produced a razor blade and went for Joey across the table. Luckily the staff were onto the problem almost immediately, else Joey's injuries could have been much worse.'

'*Are you serious?* Joey, is this right – what he's saying?'

Gently she touched the skin round the wound. She screwed up her eyes and winced at the ugliness of the thing. It was raw. It must be painful. She held Joey tightly. 'Oh Joey, oh Joey, my poor love, this is just terrible, this is horrible, it must be *so sore . . .* '

'Actually, it's pretty superficial according to—'

Shelley whizzed round to face Dominic who stood up quickly and took two paces backwards.

'*It needed bloody stitches,*' she screamed. 'How the hell can you call this superficial? *What sort of*

221

animal are you? Where were you when this was going on?'

'I was off duty,' he seemed relieved to inform her.

The basket she'd brought, full of childish treats, sneered at her from its place on the floor. Gingerbread men and home-made toffee – how laughable this was. She glared around the small room, gasping for breath, waving her arms like a drowning swimmer. 'He can't stay here, he can't stay here, not one moment longer.'

'We're moving him to the medical block.'

'And what's that supposed to mean?'

'It's a separate unit in the grounds where Joey will be perfectly safe.'

'Don't make me fucking laugh.'

'It's all we can do, I'm afraid. We're all upset by this, Mrs Tremayne. The morale of the staff here was at its lowest ebb before this incident occurred – you can only imagine what it's like now.'

'That's nothing to do with me! Sod your morale, your morale is your own bloody business. The welfare of my child is mine, and it seems to be mine alone. And anyway, how come it's public knowledge in here who Joey is and what he's supposed to have done? I thought you were into protection.' She turned to the shivering Joey. 'Don't you worry about any of this. I'm going to speak to Mr Barker and get this sorted out. You'll be out of here, kid, before you can recite your own name. Trust me, Joey. This is serious. This has to be dealt with right now.'

'Don't go, Mum.'

'I'll be back. Believe me.'

'So what has happened to this person, Smith, who almost blinded my eldest son?'

The governor shook his head. 'Smith is in the special block doing forty-eight hours' solitary and denied all privileges for two weeks.'

'My heart bleeds, it really does. And what is this turd Smith in here for?'

'We can't divulge that information, I'm afraid,' said Barker apologetically.

'Was he acting out his own little thuggery, or were there others behind this attack?'

'We will know more when we have finished our internal inquiry.'

'So the police have not been called in? This Smith will not be charged with causing grievous bodily harm, is that what you are saying? You are pushing this shite right under the carpet?'

'Attacks like this happen in units like ours every day,' said Barker sadly. 'If we called in the police every time there was a violent incident we'd have to employ an officer in residence. Next week Joey will have his own counsellor, somebody from outside who he can talk to and trust . . .'

'I've promised Joey he'll be out of here. My boy is scared shitless. Nobody in their right mind could expect him to remain here and stay sane after this.'

'That was a foolish promise to make, I'm afraid,' said Barker with a sigh. 'There are no plans for moving Joey. The only option we have is to segregate him in the medical block, an option which we had hoped we wouldn't need to use. But the charges against Joey are so high profile right now, there's no way of shielding him. Everyone knows what he's here for, so we have no sensible alternative.'

'Pity that never occurred to you professionals in the first bloody place.'

'I agree with you absolutely, Mrs Tremayne, please believe me, I honestly do.'

'You really are quite powerless, aren't you?' This realization came as a shock and the thought and the question arrived as one. 'You can give me no guarantees about the safety of my son. That's the bottom line, isn't it, Mr Barker?'

He infuriated her with his shrug and his inability to answer. He just stared at her with questioning eyes. What was Shelley supposed to suggest? She reckoned that this sleek go-getter with the perfect manners was at a total loss for words for the first time in his ambitious life.

'I'll tell you what I'm gonna do, Mr Barker. If I don't get a guarantee that Joey will be moved out of here to somewhere safe today, somewhere that I feel happy about, I'm going straight from this building to the NSPCC, and if they fail me, to the press.'

Again his shrug was annoying, and he now took a sympathetic tone as if she was a stupid child who needed to be mollified. 'I hate to say this to you,' he began, 'but that would be a huge mistake.'

'Oh yeah? Worse than yours?'

He ignored her shrill interruption. 'Once you

explained who Joey was, and the circumstances of his case, I fear you would lose all sympathy. The only thing you would achieve if you took either of those actions would be to stoke up more negative publicity and direct the public to your son.' Barker paused as if he was wondering whether to add the last sentence. 'Serve Joey right would be the general response, I'm afraid.'

It took Shelley only a moment to realize this was the truth. Nobody in the world would support Joey now. Even if he'd been thoroughly done over and needed hospital treatment, there wouldn't be many folks out there rooting for him.

But what about his legal team? They should know what had happened. They must have some muscle round here.

And the social services – surely it was their duty to look out for Joey's welfare?

Barker said she could use his phone, but she didn't trust anyone here any more. She stood in the courtyard freezing to death and dialled her solicitor's number. No reply, of course, it being Sunday. She tried directory enquiries but she didn't have Chandler's home address so they more or less told her to piss off.

Eventually she got through to the social services weekend emergency cover and managed to speak to some useless bloke who said it was not department policy to contact workers on their days off. He refused to give her Alex's number. He said they could do nothing till Monday as Joey was in Home Office care and procedures would have to be gone through.

'Up yours,' shouted Shelley. But dammit, you can't bang a mobile down.

She stood in the courtyard and gazed at the sky, and how the whiteness of it filtered through the branches of the great oak tree like cold splinters. She cried silent tears which were no bloody use; she was helpless and so was Joey. How was she going to go back to his cell and admit to him that nothing had changed, that his mother, who had protected him, fed him and kept him warm through all the eleven years of his life, was of no more use to him now than that tree?

She supposed she would have to go back inside. She supposed she would have to face him.

Dead man walking.

They went in line. Dominic Brownlow led the way, then Joey with his bag of belongings, followed by Shelley with her fairy-tale basket. It was like the last time he was excluded from school – there was that same sense of shame and fear of being stared at – but this time Joey had done nothing wrong. This time he was the victim.

Wasn't he?

But hadn't she always seen him this way? Never the perpetrator of the sins the head, Ronald Cutting, accused him of: the theft of games equipment from the gym, namely two footballs and one set of knee pads; the bullying of poor Graham Lewis who had now developed a complex and might never attend classes again; the attack on a teacher, an overreaction to a blackboard rubber being misdirected; the fire in the caretaker's basement which could have developed into an inferno; the weeks of non-attendance; the disregard of school property in general and the refusal to bother with homework.

A thoroughly disruptive pupil whose academic performance was poor.

Countless times Shelley had defended him in that old fogey's office and as soon as Jocy was legally identified she was sure that Cutting would wreak his revenge by distributing pictures right and left. And no doubt that old fart would have plenty to say if the trial went wrong and the press approached him for comments.

OK, he was a handful. Joey had never been easy. But treat him with the right attitude and he wasn't a bad boy at heart. Joey needed more attention than a ratio of thirty to one could provide; he needed a slower pace, he needed to be reasoned with rather than ordered about by harassed staff who hardly knew him.

Well, now he would get all that, and more.

Two staff to one inmate was the ratio here but even that was not enough to stop the kids from cutting each other.

The medical block was an uninspired brick square, self-contained in case of infections which could run riot in a closed community.

There were two small dormitories each with four beds, and four private rooms with en suite bathrooms. Joey got one of these with a view over fields through the bars. A fat male nurse all in whites greeted them with keys at the door and no word of welcome. 'Eric's had to come in on his off-duty day,' Dominic explained, 'so he's not a happy bunny.'

'There's nobody else in here then?'

'Nobody permanent right now. But every day the lads who sign sick are marched over here for their treatment ... But don't worry,' he added, seeing Shelley's shattered expression, 'they will have no access to Joey. The treatment room is through those double doors which are kept locked at all times.'

Joey had clearly decided to punish his mother for letting him down by lapsing into total silence. Nothing she tried could raise a response. She assured him that tomorrow she would inform his legal team of the assault, and she would get Alex on the phone and make sure she knew the score.

No reaction.

Warily she showed him the contents of the farmhouse basket. He took one look and turned away.

Even the CD was rejected.

She was his mum, she understood: how else could the poor little sod let her know how utterly despairing he was without losing face and breaking down and surrendering what fragile control he still had? His slim little back was so straight, so tense, his face tight, without expression, and the wound stood out like the scream for help he would have liked to make. His fists were curled into small, hard balls as he struggled inside this punitive world which was way beyond his understanding.

'I tried to find Wally,' she said, deliberately quietly so only he could hear. 'But he must have been left at home. I'm going to ask Inspector Hudson to go and get him for you.'

Oh Jesus Christ. She shouldn't have said that. When Joey turned round, his questioning face asked her why this would be necessary.

Why wasn't she living at home? Why couldn't she fetch Wally Wolf herself?

It was with anguish that Shelley watched the comprehension dawn. The only sign he gave was a swallow and she thought tears might have touched his eyes but he blinked and turned away so quickly she couldn't be certain of that.

She arranged the cards the kids had made on top of his small bedside table, the same as those in hospital wards. The bed was the same, a hard waterproof mattress with an iron rail for a headboard. There was no token rug on the floor, no curtains at the windows. Joey would have no company save for the flabby Eric and who knew what Eric's preferences were.

No creature comforts in here.

Joey took no notice of his family's artistic potato-print efforts, but she knew that when he was alone he would sit on his bed and study them all and perhaps, Shelley prayed, he would realize that he was a little-boy-loved in spite of the walls of hatred that were closing in so relentlessly around him.

Later, on her return to the farm, she was scooped up in Eunice's comforting strong arms, where she sobbed out her story, her terrible fears for Joey's life. A welcoming brandy was put before her but – 'Where are the kids?'

'Julie's having a kip and the others are out in the playbarn being supervised by Oliver,' said Eunice. 'Nothing for you to worry about.'

So all was well.

It was strange that they hadn't greeted the car but, to be honest, sitting in the warmth with Eunice and being reassured by her endless platitudes – 'You can't do a thing until tomorrow and tomorrow may never come' – was just about all Shelley could cope with.

EIGHTEEN

Only a dried-up, wrinkled old prune would have been totally immune to the physical proximity of brawny Edward Bolton, the macho driver of the Land Rover, Shelley's voluntary lift into town the following day. She was sure he would not have put himself out had she not come upon him at four in the morning when, in spite of her exhaustion, she had been unable to sleep.

How could she possibly sleep with Joey's safety so terrifyingly precarious?

How could she let her mind go blank with all the plans she was forced to make to guarantee his future protection?

She tossed and turned for hours and then, afraid her thrashings might wake Julie, and cold despite the pink hot-water bottle provided so thoughtfully by Eunice, she dragged on her jacket and a thick pair of socks and crept down the stairs to the kitchen, in search of a fag and a cup of tea.

She was surprised that the kitchen light was on, but glad in case she had difficulty in locating the switch. The kettle, always hot where it stood on the edge of the Aga, took under a minute to boil once she moved it to the hotplate. She sat in the cushioned ladderback chair, the warming tea beside her and a comforting cigarette in her mouth, but still her thoughts raged on. She knew the folly of thinking at night when the brain was at its most weary, but yesterday's attack on Joey and Barker's casual response to it were just too unimaginable to take in. There was nobody else to do anything but her. She wondered, as she felt the warmth flow from her hands to her frozen feet, how much more of this she could stand and stay sane. There was only so much a body could take; if God was after laughs he'd be rolling around on the floor by now.

She stood up and began to pace, rubbing a patch of steamed-up window to see if the forecasted snow had started to fall already. She hoped not. She couldn't afford to be stranded here, she had her meeting with Malc tomorrow, as well as her lone campaign to get Joey moved. She was intrigued to see the light shining through the stable door of the large stone barn that bordered the courtyard.

As she watched, as the light moved around, Shelley became more curious. Someone out there had a lantern. She was warmer now, but the thought of bed and that thrashing half-sleep appalled her. She would stay awake until morning if need be rather than endure those long dark hours alone and at the mercy of her own nightmares.

She slung on one of the various waterproofs

that hung muddily in the porch, pushed her feet into boots too large, lifted the latch and ventured outside. The wind cut through her as she floundered towards the light, determined to do anything that might divert her from her own thoughts. The farmhouse walls were surprisingly thick; no matter how cold it was indoors, the temperature out here was far lower.

Edward or Oliver?

It wasn't John; he was tall but more slightly built than both his sons. The navy Barbour hat was pulled down so the rim disappeared inside the raised collar of the coat. Waterproof trousers completed the outfit. The figure was bent inside a stall containing a struggling ewe; one ungloved hand was inside the creature.

Shelley moved silently forward, fascinated by this biblical scene made gentle by the lantern light. She stopped at the crude wooden partition, unable to take her eyes off a sight so familiar and yet so alien to her.

Edward saw Shelley when he stood to remove the lantern from the hook above the stall to place it beside him on the straw.

'Hi there,' he said. 'Feel like helping?'

'Is she OK?'

'She'll be fine in a second. If you could just hold this light . . .' and he showed her.

She watched the birth of the lamb. She couldn't help it, she was near to tears when its black nose poked out between its feet. Edward's natural skill along with his patience and gentleness left her marvelling that such strong hands could turn so effortlessly to healing. Shelley helped him clean the lamb off with straw, watched it struggle to its feet, and saw the exhausted ewe take on an entirely new lease of life as she nudged and licked her wobbly offspring.

'Another one down, fifty to go,' said Edward, easing his back with a rub as he stood aside to view the age-old scene. The stalls down the length of this long barn were heaving with sheep, some with lambs already at foot, some due to lamb any time.

She asked him, 'How long have you been out here?'

'An hour, maybe longer. There's not much sleep for any of us at this time of year.' He shrugged. 'You get used to it in the end.' He took off his hat and banged it free of straw against the partition. 'How about you?' He smiled, the first time he had smiled directly at her, and she thought how completely natural he was – his looks, his movements, the way he stood, how his dark hair suited his solemn green eyes ... 'What brought you out here at this time of night?'

She hugged herself. 'Worried sick. Couldn't sleep for thoughts. You know ...' She trailed off.

'It must be hard. When you're on your own.'

'Sometimes I just don't know ...'

'You'll cope,' he said, 'you will.'

'Yeah, I suppose.'

There was a tranquillity about him. Shelley suddenly yearned to be not on her own any more, to be part of a loving family like this one, so secure in the knowledge that come hell or high

234

water she would be surrounded by love and support. Brought up as an only child with a mother preoccupied by work, money worries and keeping face, she'd never known this. Maybe that was part of the reason she had recklessly produced six kids of her own, so that wherever they went and whatever happened somebody would always be there for them.

But it wasn't turning out like that, was it?

Back in the kitchen Edward made two mugs of hot chocolate topped with fresh cream, and opened a tin full of home-made shortbread biscuits. With someone who seemed so laconic, Shelley was surprised at how easily they talked . . . about everything. Perhaps it was the night, the cosiness of the kitchen contrasted with the wildness outside . . . and the drama of a birth, of course. She felt an unexpected closeness to this serious and sensitive man who had the same skills as his mother when it came to putting people at ease.

In the same way in which she had opened up to Eunice, she found herself talking to Edward about Joey, the trouble she'd had with him and the fears for his future that now tormented her. They sat side by side like a couple of crumblies, dunking their biscuits and despairing of life.

'You're so lucky,' Shelley said unexpectedly and it came out as an accusation: it was so unjust, *so unfair*. The pathway had been so easy for this farmer's son and his younger brother, apart, of course, from the constant worries he had already moaned on about – the weather, market prices, ridiculous hours, puny profits. But compared to her horrendous concerns, these matters seemed trivial.

'Our lives would have been very different if we hadn't both been adopted,' he confided.

How strange. They looked so similar to their father she could have sworn they were his natural sons.

'No,' said Edward. 'They couldn't have children of their own. They adopted Oliver and me when we were three and four.'

'Why not babies, I wonder?' Shelley asked.

'They knew that babies had no trouble finding decent homes. They wanted to offer a happy home to kids who weren't so easily placed.'

'They're nice,' said Shelley, smiling. 'They've been lovely to me.'

'They're genuine,' Edward agreed. 'And they've helped so many hopeless kids in trouble over the years. We tell them it's time they eased up, but they don't listen. They like what they do. And all sorts of dodgy types seem to settle around them. Like they've got some kind of magic about them.'

'I know what you mean. They're amazing,' said Shelley. Was she one of the dodgy types to whom he was referring? 'God knows where we would have ended up without them.'

Edward told her how one renowned villain named Dillon Dukes, a fourteen-year-old tearaway the courts had long despaired of, stayed with the Boltons for over a year when the probation service recommended, instead of a custodial sentence, a period of fostering with the couple. There had been a public outcry – Shelley remembered that. Why should this little prat be given so many chances? Dukes was a scourge of society, a long-term loser, a natural jailbird.

'I wasn't around when Dukes stayed here,' Edward told her and she saw how carefully his blue Guernsey sweater had been patched and darned. Families like this didn't chuck stuff out and replace it with cheap tat like she did. 'I was doing my second year at Seale-Hayne, the agricultural college, and Oliver had just started. Looking back now it was probably best we weren't around ... Dukes was a right little bastard. Neither of us would have had the patience, or put up with hearing him effing and blinding in front of Mother and Father.'

'What happened?' Shelley couldn't help comparing the fortunate Dukes with Joey.

'He's an animal-welfare worker at a local charity now. Drives the ambulance, takes care of the lost dogs and cats, takes parties of kids round. You name it. They used to call Dukes "Catspaw".'

'I read about that,' said Shelley. 'He could get in any window, they reckoned.'

'Well, they sorted him out all right,' said Edward. 'And then there was Shane Duffy, another yob everyone had given up on. He stuck around for eighteen months. He's married now with a kiddy and driving buses in Plymouth. Mother and Father still see them both, keep up the contact. They're here if they need them.'

Maybe, if Joey was found not guilty, Shelley could suggest to the social services that they give him a chance up here? God, how fantastic that would be for that mixed-up kid. If it worked for those two wicked little gits, it could be the answer for Joey.

Sitting alongside Edward this morning in the fumy, bouncing Land Rover with a sheep in the back on its way to the vet, Shelley was more relaxed than she'd felt since this gloom first descended.

She was determined to get Joey moved.

She had made a friend in Edward.

She was on her way to see Malc and what a relief it would be to talk to someone who knew her and Joey and was not a stranger full of assumptions. OK, she and Malc split up more than a year ago, but they'd had some good times together and if it hadn't been for the scheming Joey and his phone call to Childline they might still be partners. At the time it had seemed incredible how the experts had jumped on Joey's ludicrous lies and taken that sordid nonsense as read.

Malc had interfered with him, Joey said. Well, how do you prove otherwise? Especially when faced with Joey's cunning and expertise. Shelley threatened him with his life; she'd never gone for him that viciously before. Still he wouldn't budge, wouldn't change his story – not unless Malc left the house and swore he'd never come back.

And then he went round accusing his own mother of child abuse.

It was unbelievable. The whole thing escalated and they were threatened with court proceedings. Malc kept on at her, 'This little bleeder is going to manipulate you for the rest of your bloody life if you don't stand up to him now.' And, he pointed out rightly, if he did give in to Joey and leave, there'd be such a stain on his character – no smoke without fire – he'd carry that smear around for ever.

In the end the thought of court and the repercussions of that had made Malc so jumpy he'd just pissed off. Only then did Joey confess that his accusations had been downright lies. It took a while for the pigs to believe him. They did some intimate tests. Joey hated that. They were furious when they saw they'd been had; they hauled him up to the station and made him apologize.

Malc never risked coming back. 'It's just too hairy for me, you dunno what that prick's planning next.'

Jesus Christ – the shit that kid was capable of . . .

But those lies had been part of a game he was playing.

This time he was telling the truth. She knew her son. She could tell.

When they reached the Moorland pub, a brick building made bizarre with Tudor-style beams inside and out, Edward dropped her and set off to the vet. He would pick her up in a couple of hours. Then she would get her lift to Lister, where Alex, Joey's social worker, had promised to arrange a meeting to deal with his brutal attack.

* * *

Malc was sitting in one of the red-curtained cubicles suggestive of a seventeenth-century coffee house, in his same old donkey jacket and with his lustreless hair tied back in that familiar lank ponytail.

He got up and hugged her. 'You look like shit.'

'Is that any wonder?' she asked him.

Halfway through a pint already, he got her a rum and black. They pulled the cubicle curtains across. Shelley was adamant about that.

'It's that bad then?' he asked.

'Worse, believe me,' she said, relieved to be able to smoke at last and be her old self again.

'Where are you living?'

She must be careful. Even with Malc she mustn't blab. But she'd have loved to be able to describe the time warp she'd found herself in, the outlandish couple who'd befriended her. You've never seen anything like that moustache, she'd say ... the spartan conditions ... the strict routines ... God, Malc would laugh. Instead she said bleakly, 'Some flat on the main road in Buckfastleigh.'

'Grim,' he said understandingly. 'And the kids?'

'Yep, the kids are all there with me but they go to a foster mother in the day.'

'And Joey, poor sod. Where have they stuck him?'

'In some special unit, I'm not allowed to say where.'

'But you can visit him?' Malc persisted.

'Yes, they give me lifts.'

240

'Chauffeured around?'

'Like a proper lady.' And then she launched into the horror of Joey's assault, how he wasn't safe, they were all out to get him, 'and him not even found guilty'.

'But he did it, didn't he?' asked Malc insensitively.

Malc knew Joey. So how could he think this way? *Course he didn't do it, jerk.* 'He was there, but he never took part. Those other four wankers have got him stitched up. It'll all come out at the trial; before, most likely. Once they start getting their evidence.'

'Come on, Shell. What's the bottom line here? He's got to plead not guilty, but they'll get him on something in the end. You must know he's up to his neck in it. He must have told you by now.'

'Give up, Malc. What's the matter with you? This is Joey we're talking about. He's no angel but he's no monster either, not like they're painting him to be. Just give over. Leave it out, will you? I didn't come here to hear this crap.'

He could see how edgy she was. He started to check out the menu. It was warm in here, too warm. Shelley slipped out of her jacket. It crossed her mind that Malc must be hot; under that donkey jacket he was wearing a thick woollen sweater. She changed the tricky subject of Joey and tried to move him on. She asked how work was going. Did he have a new bird? Was he living in the same digs? Did he still go down the Las Vegas on a Saturday?

But he seemed to want to talk about Joey. He said he wanted to help.

'There's nothing anyone else can do,' Shelley insisted wearily.

'I can't visit him then?'

She was amazed he could be so dim. 'No-one can,' she explained, annoyed. 'No-one's supposed to know where he is.'

'I can't write to him then?'

'Why would you write to him?' This was odd. 'Why the hell would you want to do that?'

'I could give you a letter, some chocolate, some games. I don't suppose he's allowed fags in there?'

'He's got all he needs, Malc, OK?'

Why would Joey want to hear from Malc? The last person in the world, most likely. He'd always hated Malc and he wouldn't have suddenly changed his mind.

Malc chose the gammon and chips, Shelley stuck to the ploughman's. She wasn't hungry, she was more disconcerted. This meeting was not proving to be the stress-free exchange she had hoped. She wished she hadn't agreed to come and started agonizing over the next hassle she faced . . . removing Joey from Dudley Park.

She picked at her food. Malc wolfed his, getting tomato sauce on his jacket which he still kept on in spite of the heat, in spite of the sweat on his forehead which leaked back into his sparse hairline. She'd forgotten the reason why she had come. She supposed she'd hoped for sympathy, for someone to tell her they understood, they had seen her mothering efforts close up and knew she was not completely inadequate.

She did her best. What more could she do?

He insisted on buying her more drinks than she wanted. She repeatedly checked her watch, uneasy, and when the two-hour session was up she was the first to slide out of the cubicle and make for the welcome door. As Shelley stepped out of the gloom and into the crisp white afternoon, she fell back in shock as her eyes took the onslaught of the flash of a close-up camera.

'This way – look at me, darling . . . Just turn round here, just one more shot . . . Come on, Shelley, just pull down the hood . . .'

The slob in the duffle jumped about madly like a pig on a prickle. His camera never left his eye as he followed her, crouching, round the car park.

She rounded on Malc. 'What the hell . . .?' Malc shrugged, but he didn't protect her. He kept a careful few paces back. 'Malc, for God's sake, *what's bloody going on*?'

Malc stood aside, without any answer.

'This arsehole won't leave me alone. Look, *look at him*. How did this maniac know . . .?'

This was a set-up.

Malc rigged this up.

Suddenly it struck home. What did Malc have in his donkey jacket – a hidden mike? Had he expected some grisly confessions straight from the mouth of the mother of the most notorious child-killer in the land? Was that why he had got in touch with her? Nothing to do with wanting to help?

She felt like she'd had a kick in the stomach.

She searched frantically for his car, a green MG from what he had told her. But that wouldn't work ... She backtracked, heading desperately for the pub and the safety of the dimness behind the Elizabethan nail-studded door.

A shriek of tyres and a blasting horn stopped everyone dead in their tracks. Edward Bolton leaped out of the Land Rover while it appeared still to be moving. With no apparent effort, he ripped the camera from her tormentor's hands and smashed it down on the tarmac. He grabbed Shelley's arm, bundled her into the cab without a word, slammed the rickety door behind her and roared off onto the motorway.

She sat, slumped and sobbing beside him, cursing herself for her naivety, shaking from the sudden shock of what felt like a physical attack. Every bone in her body was aching with the kind of tension that felt like bruising. But worse than this was the confirmation that she had no friends any longer. From now on everyone she met would have their own agenda, would be scheming out ways in which to use this loathsome mother for their own ends.

NINETEEN

Having assured Edward that she had not shouted her mouth off or said anything to alert the sickos to her whereabouts, Shelley was dropped off at Crown Hill nick. From there she had to take yet another discreet lift from the city to Dudley Park.

She hadn't seen Molly Lamb since that first hellish night at Buckfastleigh but Shelley hadn't forgotten how helpful and considerate the policewoman had been when she had badly needed someone to be on her side. Shelley sat in the passenger seat of the unmarked cop car as Molly, in plain clothes, pulled away. 'I've never stopped thinking about you and those little kids,' said Molly. 'How's it going? How's Joey?'

Shelley launched into an immediate summary of the dire situation at Dudley Park and her need to get Joey moved to a specialized unit which dealt with kids of his own age.

Molly's reaction was not encouraging. 'Part of the reason they chose Dudley Park was because it was local, bearing in mind your family circumstances,' she said. 'If they move Joey miles away it would mean you all uprooting and going God knows where.'

Shelley realized what she was doing and stopped herself chewing her nails to pieces. 'Just when the kids are so settled,' she said. 'I couldn't think of moving them now – not again – not in the middle of all this shit.'

Molly, fresh-faced, freckled and definitely a country girl, sympathized wholeheartedly. 'But the only alternative would be for you to go and be with Joey and leave the children at the farm.' She glanced across at Shelley, noting how pale and tired she looked. 'They'd be fine without you,' Molly continued hopefully. 'There's nobody more well thought of round here than Eunice Bolton.'

'I hear the Boltons are miracle workers. Did you know those two sons were adopted?'

'They hit the jackpot then,' said Molly wryly, 'when you think of the wonders the Boltons performed on Duffy and Dukes. Those kids were before my time but their transformation is still part of the folklore round here.'

'I wish they could have a go at Joey,' said Shelley longingly, and she looked for Molly's reaction when she expressed her greatest hope: 'If he's found innocent d'you think there would be any chance of that?'

Molly stalled for time, concentrating on her driving and carefully checking the mirror before she confronted Shelley directly. 'So you still think Joey may get off?'

'Don't you?'

'There's so much evidence against him now, Shelley.'

'But it's faked, it's a fix. Even the witnesses Hudson brought in – they're lying through their back teeth.'

'Why would they do that?'

'God knows, there's so many reasons ... maybe in a pact to get off a charge?'

'We don't work like that,' said Molly, sensing that the tension between them was growing. 'Particularly DI Hudson. He's a really straight kind of bloke.'

Shelley bit the bullet. 'So you believe that my Joey deliberately set fire to that baby?'

'I'm trying to be realistic,' said Molly, attempting to backtrack, but what was the point of Shelley hiding behind these rose-coloured spectacles? Someone had to warn her that soon she was going to have to face it. 'Those boys probably had no idea there was a baby in that pram when they were larking about with fire last Wednesday. What does seem certain is that they were determined to set something alight in order to cause a stir.'

'Why would they want to?'

'Why does anyone commit arson? You tell me.'

They travelled on towards Lister wrapped in an uneasy silence.

Was Shelley the only one who still believed in Joey's innocence?

Eunice Bolton appeared to be the most un-condemning person she'd bumped into so far. But then the dumpy farmer's wife had such faith in the basic goodness of kids – not a theory, going from experience, that Shelley would support.

Yes, her children would be fine if she abandoned them to the Boltons, and if they were older then perhaps Shelley would have considered that option. But not at the ages they were, from six down to six months. They would miss their mum far too much and God only knew how long she would be away if she went. There was still no date for Joey's trial.

Who depended most on Shelley's support right now?

Shouldn't she be backing Joey with everything at her disposal, bearing in mind the mess he was in? Her other kids would survive, but would he? Again those treacherous, unwanted feelings washed through her: how dare he throw his family into such desperate straits just because he couldn't be fagged to stick around school for one afternoon? Just because he chose to ignore her warnings about those four brain-dead rejects . . . Jesus Christ, she could slaughter him. He did deserve to be punished, and languishing behind bars in Dudley Park seemed like a just reward when she was feeling like this.

But not for too long.

Not getting bashed up.

Not with everyone choosing to reject his side of the story – even the placid Molly Lamb.

'You've just got to face the facts, unfortunate as they are,' said Molly, breaking the silence.

'Wherever they put Joey now they'd have to watch him day and night in case some jerk took it into his head to make a name for himself by giving him a going-over.'

'But that's so disgusting.' Shelley groaned. 'He's in their care, it's their duty to protect him whatever they think he's done.'

'And they will,' said Molly. 'They'll not let their guard down again, Shelley, you can be sure of that.'

'They let it down once.'

'You think that was deliberate?'

'I'm not saying that, but you do hear of screws leaving doors unlocked . . .'

'Not at Dudley Park,' stated Molly.

'How can you defend that place? Its name stinks round here.'

'Not since David Barker took over.'

'He hasn't got eyes in the back of his head.'

'He's all about staff training.'

Huh. How naive this young woman must be – but then she hadn't got a child at the mercy of a system that, no matter how much it might deny it and rant on about rehabilitation and training, was all to do with punishment.

Punishment of eleven-year-olds who hadn't the nous to stay in school.

She was taken straight through to the medical block, where the doors were unlocked by the unlovely Eric. She would spend some time with Joey before joining the meeting with social services in the governor's office.

The gash on his forehead still looked raw and painful. Since she had left him yesterday the private room he had been given had acquired a CD player and a small colour telly. Alex had spent most of the morning talking to Joey, and afterwards with David Barker. Not only Alex; Martin Chandler must have got Shelley's message because he had spent some time in here first thing this morning. Something must be decided . . . her child could not be left at risk.

She noticed that the potato-print cards which he had ignored yesterday were now arranged neatly on his window sill, and the Chemical Brothers CD was in the player. Joey's attitude was less defensive; he allowed her to give him a kiss and a friendly cuff round the head.

'What have you been doing with yourself?' At once she wished she hadn't asked that – in his confined circumstances there was hardly a range of activities he could ramble through and list.

'Nothing much. It's dead boring here.'

Shelley put more verve in her voice. 'You had some visitors this morning?'

He showed her a packet of charcoal and a pad of expensive sketching paper. 'Alex gave me this.'

'Have you done any, Joey?'

Reluctantly he allowed her to take the pad from his bed. On the first page was a picture of her with 'Mum' and kiss-crosses scrawled underneath it. Shelley swallowed hard. The second showed a childlike hill with vague cows and sheep round the base. 'That's where we went with Dave, when the ham was off. Remember?' he asked her.

'That awful picnic.' Shelley laughed.

'I dammed the stream.'

'You got bloody soaked.'

'Jason was sick.'

'Jason's always sick,' said Shelley fondly.

'I'd like to be there now,' said Joey.

He had never said he'd enjoyed that day. From his sulky behaviour anyone would think it had been a drag. Shelley fought down so many emotions. 'Not in this weather, you wouldn't.'

She began to tell him about the farm. He didn't even pretend any interest. 'I was thinking how good it would be if we could all spend some time there together,' she told him.

'What for?' Joey asked. 'I'd rather go to Disneyland.'

'Some chance.'

'We'll win the lottery.'

'Pigs might fly.'

'When I get out of here I'm not hanging around.'

'When you get out of here you're going back to school. Not the same school perhaps, but school, and things are going to be different.'

'Too right.'

Shelley said, 'There's stuff you and I need to talk about. Seriously talk, I mean.'

'*I am going to get out, aren't I, Mum?*'

'They don't lock innocent people away.'

'But they'll do me for something, won't they?'

This was such stressful stuff. If only Shelley had all the answers. There was no point in reassuring Joey with worn-out platitudes now. She had to be as honest as possible. 'You shouldn't have been there, Joey. You shouldn't have nicked the lighter, you shouldn't have nicked the paraffin. And as a consequence of what you did one little girl is dead.'

'That Chandler bloke was telling me we might have to plead guilty to manslaughter.'

Shelley was shocked. *What was this?* Some new development she knew nothing about? 'Well, only if you did it,' she said, confused.

'What if I did do it, Mum?'

'Shut up, Joey, I'm not listening to this.' Shit. This was just what she had feared might happen. Put kids this age under pressure, remove them from their familiar surroundings, have them knocked about a bit and they're going to crack up, big time. Shelley firmly changed the subject. 'What about Eric?' she asked Joey. 'What's he like? Is he here all the time? Do you still see that nice Dominic?'

'Eric's a ponce,' said Joey.

'How d'you mean, a ponce?'

'He's a sodding fudge packer.'

'He's not!'

'Course he is. You can tell. And there's kids come in here at night, he lets them in through . . .'

This was typical Joey. In some ways she found his lies reassuring. He was trying to blacken his situation, attempting to wound her further. In spite of his clever talk, in some ways he was so transparent.

'He tried it on with me,' he began.

'Joey . . .'

'I sorted that fat freak out.'

'*Joey.*'

'He dishes out spunkies to the arse bandits in here.'

She had to stop this crap going any further. Couldn't Joey see how concerned she was about his safety and his welfare? He really did not need to lay it on as thick as this. 'Leave it out, Joey.'

His face darkened immediately. 'You don't give a shit about me.'

'Stop it, Joey. Please.'

'You're glad I'm in here.'

'You know that's not true.'

'*You think I did it, don't you?*'

Shelley answered him wearily. 'I'm your mum, I'm on your side and I always will be. Whatever you say. Whatever you do.'

He never asked about his brothers and the baby sister he was so fond of. He expressed no interest in the farm, in her struggles, in her little gifts. All Joey seemed to want to do was stir up conflict between them. They were starting on their psychiatric reports tomorrow. Would they find some flaw, some inability to love? She wondered what line Joey would take, how far he could manipulate the shrinks until they sussed what he was up to. He would be bound to spin his new line about Eric the bent male nurse. Fleetingly she felt some sympathy for the flabby man with the fat lips. Maybe she ought to warn them . . .?

Good God no, whose side was she on?

Joey said he couldn't care less whether they moved him from Dudley Park or not.

When Shelley told him the difficulties of visiting long distance, he merely shrugged and gave a small smile.

'Of course I could come and stay somewhere near, but that would mean leaving the others.' He should damn well know about this dilemma. Joey should be made to realize how hard things were for the rest of his family.

'Up to you,' he said, dismissing the problem with characteristic flippancy.

She felt she had to press for an answer. 'You don't feel in danger now?'

'Wherever I was I'd be in the shit.'

'But you're not frightened, Joey? Not like you were?'

'No.'

'And you're sure?'

'Yep.'

'So you don't want me to press to get you moved?'

'I said already, that's up to you.'

Jesus, he was such a pain. What more should she do? Her main concern now was his isolation, but from what she had been told it seemed wherever he went he'd be segregated for his own safety. He would have no contact with other kids, but what effect that might have on a developing eleven-year-old was something Shelley knew nothing about. He would still have his lessons, his time in the gym, his personal officers, his visits, his videos. All in all it seemed to her it might be better if he stayed where he was. At least that wouldn't mean she would have to abandon the others for what might be months at a time.

And it was convenient.

And it was familiar.

And the governor was friendly.

When she left him he turned his back and she could tell that Joey was crying.

Everyone reassured her that she need not worry about making a fuss, this meeting was not a waste of time, and she had been perfectly within her rights to request a move to another unit.

Once again she raised the subject of the possibility that, one day, Joey might be given a second chance at the Boltons'.

'You don't seem to realize,' said the shorn-headed Alex, whose nail polish of the day was green with scarlet fishes, 'that the lads who went to the Boltons were not accused of murder, or even manslaughter. Joey's in quite a different category to the Duffys and Dukes of this world. And while I do agree with you, the Boltons are extraordinary with kids with severe behaviour difficulties and they might well have a beneficial effect on Joey, it really is very unlikely that the courts would permit a course like that.'

'It just might be possible later, when we see how Joey is progressing, for a visit to be arranged,' said David Barker, keen, Shelley thought, to make amends for the unforgivable assault on her son while in his care.

A visit? What earthly good would a visit be? The whole point of her idea was that Joey should spend time on the farm learning how to work, and relate, and appreciate those wild surroundings. That she and her five younger children would no longer be with the Boltons after Joey's fate was decided did not occur to Shelley. How could she focus on the future when the present was so bewildering? Thoughts of going back to her old life – alone all day except for the kids, with brief, manic outings to the family centre and the supermarket, superficial relationships with men who were prepared to betray her and nights watching mindless TV – were more than Shelley could cope with.

TWENTY

Was Edward Bolton in the courtyard to meet her, or had he merely been crossing it on his way to one of the barns? But the most curious question must be: why was Shelley so hopeful that he had heard the car and come out here specially?

He looked great in the dull afternoon in his mucky overalls and waterproofs, his wide smile of welcome like balm to a woman in her flaky state. She ceased to feel like a refugee pursued by society's most violent troops, and instead felt more like a person coming home to people who actually liked her. She knew that his brother was engaged to a girl who worked for the tourist board; she marvelled that it was possible for a man like Edward to reach thirty without being snapped up.

Eunice's familiar bear hug confirmed the warmth of the welcome. Julie was having her tea in the makeshift high chair with the seed-tray table ... a soft-boiled egg with soldiers followed by mashed pears and custard. Eunice didn't approve of ready-made food for babies. Not when there was home-grown grub bottled, jarred or salted in her enormous walk-in larder.

'You can sit in that chair and give her a bottle before I put her down,' said Eunice, 'and tell me about that dreadful man who tricked you outside the pub. What a blessing Edward turned up, else Lord knows what could have happened.'

Already, after a two-day stay, Shelley knew better than to ask where her tribe had gone. She could hear baby laughter coming from the play-barn, which was attached to the wing of the house where the stock had been kept before it was converted. The barn was in its original stone state, with cold slabbed floors and the odd rug slapped down over the dampest bits. In there were laundry baskets of toys dating back to God knows when, and how typical it was of the kids to ignore their own modern versions and prefer these old relics. Many wouldn't stand a chance of passing a safety test; probably all were lead-painted. She'd already spotted some sharp tin edges. From the kitchen chair beside the Aga she identified the voice of Casey, and was that John in the background acting as babysitter? The older boys would be out 'working' until the last possible moment. They were fully occupied and having a great time, but it still hurt some place inside her that they hadn't come rushing to meet her.

They must have heard the car.

They couldn't possibly have missed Eunice's hearty greeting.

Where was three-year-old Jason?

'How did you come to get mixed up with a common-looking man like that? Edward told me about him – ponytail, earrings and a working jacket mostly in holes. Fancy you going to meet a person of that sort.'

'Malcolm works on the docks . . .'

'It makes no difference where he works, a man of his age with a ponytail – huh.'

Shelley felt oddly ashamed to admit her close relationship with the man who so disgusted Eunice. When she confessed to having lived with Malc, if only for a few months, she saw Eunice's quick intake of breath. 'How awful for the children,' she muttered. Shelley decided to keep Malc's ignominious departure, the result of Joey's loathing, strictly to herself.

'Nothing more destructive for children than life with a series of transient men.'

If anyone else had expressed this view Shelley would have given as good as she got, but as it was Eunice she bit her tongue. She asked instead, 'Where's Jason?'

'Jason's in bed,' stated Eunice, readying the table for supper. 'Jason deliberately broke the Harrods delivery van by wrenching off its wheels. John went to mend it but it was irreparable.'

'*Jason's ill?*' Why hadn't Eunice told her this immediately?

'There's nothing wrong with the little lad that a bit of discipline won't cure. No, he's in bed and he'll go without any supper. He's a little upset, understandably, but it's never too early for children to learn the value of things.'

How the hell should Shelley deal with this? In her eyes punishments for small misdemeanours should be immediate and soon over – a good slap did the trick. And sweets and kisses and cuddles afterwards. This kind of banishment was reminiscent of Iris's outmoded system of discipline, but here she was in Eunice's house dependent on Eunice's charity, and poor little Jason, only three, was stuck upstairs in all sorts of distress.

'I'll go and see him,' said Shelley, winding Julie.

Eunice paused in her vigorous preparations. She confronted Shelley, stood right in front of her. There were beads of sweat on her rust-coloured moustache. 'I'd rather you didn't do that, m'dear.' It was a threat. It was an order.

'*But I have to go to him . . .*'

'Nonsense. Jason understands perfectly well why he is being punished. He also knows that tomorrow he will get up with the others and his bad behaviour will not be mentioned. If you go upstairs interfering, the messages he gets will be crossed. I think you will find,' Eunice went on, a determined expression on her swede-coloured face, 'that Jason will take more care of other people's belongings in future.'

'He's just not used to—'

'Precisely,' said Eunice firmly. 'So let's leave it there, shall we?'

One broken toy.

When Shelley thought of the overfilled toy cupboard at home with almost every item missing a wheel, a leg hanging off, a wing dangling, she caught her breath at the unfairness of it. Jason had no idea that he might be punished for breaking a toy, an event that happened daily, usually to tears and squabbles and promises of a new one. The most remarkable part of it all was that the kids had been here three days and this was the first breakage – or the first one Eunice knew about. She would have to warn them quickly to prevent this misunderstanding becoming a regular feature of their life with the Boltons.

And it was strangely contradictory how loving and caring the Boltons were towards the kids, but how strict they were over trivial matters. Table manners were forever being pushed. No slurping, no elbows, no getting down in the midst of a meal, and pleases and thank yous were compulsory. If they had sweets, they chose one from a packet or just one piece from a bar of chocolate, when at home they would have expected the lot. Amazingly, so far the kids had happily acquiesced, and one stern look from John normally quashed any attempt at rebellion.

But now Shelley's dilemma was unavoidable.

'Jason'll be starving,' she said with a hopeless, forced laugh, attempting to break the tension. 'You know what a pig that kid is.'

'All the more likely for the learning experience to bear fruit,' Eunice replied, satisfied enough to turn away and carry on peeling the spuds.

'I'll go and give Julie a bath and then put her down,' said Shelley, knowing full well this was a chance to check up on Jason. But Eunice wasn't so easily conned.

'If you are thinking of disturbing that boy then think again,' she said, shocking Shelley into sudden stillness with the fervour of her command.

'*I won't have it, Shelley*, I just won't have this kind of slackness in my house.'

Shelley, gobsmacked, backed straight down.

What else had been going on during her daily absences? What other punitive measures had been taken against her kids without Shelley knowing? But then again, none of her children showed any signs of fear or unhappiness, quite the contrary, and she was sure they would have told her if anything untoward had gone on. This confrontation with Eunice was the last thing she needed right now. Everyone said the woman was a walking marvel, the sun shone out of her arse where the social services were concerned and even the hard-nosed cops were awed by her unlikely successes. But Shelley had been directly accused of being 'slack', whatever that meant.

A slack disciplinarian? Hardly – she'd never have thought so. She was forever on at the kids. Joey called her a sad old nag and Dave used to tell her to leave them alone when she lost her temper and laid into them.

But Eunice's ways were different.

'Don't worry,' she decided to say. 'I'll just sort Julie out, she's ready for sleep.'

'She's had a busy day.' Eunice smiled, bustling again as if the last few minutes had never happened. 'Say goodnight to Eunice, sweetheart.' And she bestowed on the baby a great hairy kiss.

Shelley had no time to talk to Edward before supper and the children's bedtimes, all strictly adhered to no matter how many pleas were received. All she planned to do was bring up this difference of attitude towards the children's handling, see what Edward said, see if he thought it mattered, see if he couldn't influence Eunice to take some small, tentative steps into the twenty-first century.

As usual certain books had been laid out on the boys' beds, as if Shelley wasn't up to choosing the type of story they liked best. This time Eunice had picked Enid Blyton's *The Faraway Tree*, a magical book, Shelley admitted, although it smacked of a different age and dwelled on old-fashioned values.

'There's a phone call for you,' yelled John, just when she'd finally tucked her boys in and kissed them goodnight. She had crept around the bedroom, taking care not to wake poor Jason who had stayed sound asleep throughout. By now it was after nine and Shelley was eager to get back downstairs and finish the washing-up before the wireless went on. 'Take it in the hall.'

It was Alex from social services. 'Terrible news, I'm afraid,' she began, 'and I wanted to tell you before you saw it on TV.'

'*It's Kenny,*' gasped Shelley, '*he's dead, isn't he?*'

'Not so bad as that, but still pretty awful: the Buckfastleigh flat has been gutted by fire, even though four fire engines spent two hours fighting the blaze. It's just so lucky you weren't in there, and when I think of the children . . . oh God. Either somebody found out where you were or it's just an awful coincidence.'

'*Malcolm,*' Shelley said instantly, wishing there

was a convenient chair; her legs would hardly hold her. 'It was no coincidence. It was him.'

'Malcolm Yelland, your ex?'

Her voice was so weak and trembly it seemed to come from some distant place like the back of a cave or a hole in the ground. 'The only one of my old partners who wasn't the father of one of my kids.'

'Surely that's too far-fetched? Why would someone so close to you ...?'

'We weren't close. We'd split up. And today he set me up.'

'Does he have some grudge against you?'

'I didn't think so, not until now.' The only real grudge Malcolm might have was over Joey's abuse accusations, but although Malcolm had gone berserk at the time, he wasn't the violent sort. He was wet. Shelley couldn't imagine that he'd do an atrocious thing like this. But then he wouldn't have had to, would he? All he would have needed to do was tell someone the secret of the Tremaynes' whereabouts. There were plenty of maniacs out there happy to do the rest. She didn't care about herself, but the thought that groups of human beings were prepared to see her children burn ...

Just as Joey had burned little Holly.

Perhaps these psychos would call that justice.

'The fire was too well established by the time the firemen arrived,' said Alex, so upset and breathless she kept stumbling over the nightmare words. 'Already they know it was arson. There was no attempt to camouflage that fact.'

Shelley was shivering now as if she was outside naked. *'What if they find out that we're here? What can we do? Where can we go?'* She began to sob like a child. Eunice heard and came to her rescue, surrounding her with one burly arm and seeming to take her weight. Shelley's tears flowed more fiercely. 'Surely the Boltons are in danger? It's not just us any more. *Alex, Alex, what the hell can I do?'*

'Stay put, don't venture out, warn the Boltons, keep the kids indoors . . .'

'We'd be safer locked up with Joey.'

Shelley forced her mind to return to the conversation she'd had with the treacherous Malc. She could not remember any mention of the Dartmoor farm or the Boltons. *Thank God for that, thank God.* 'What about police protection? Surely they'll give my kids protection?'

Eunice pushed in, saying, 'Give me that phone.'

Shelley, too weak to argue, let the older woman take over. There were long silences while Eunice listened to the details of the Buckfastleigh fire which the flustered Alex seemed keen to repeat, to get it out of her system.

At this point Shelley almost collapsed.

She pictured how it would be. They'd be out of here by tonight and travelling where, for what, for how long? Was there anywhere in this country where the public weren't out for revenge? Some remote croft on a Scottish island? Or perhaps it would be decided that the family should split up, the kids going to separate homes, no contact allowed between them?

Jesus wept. If anything could get worse than this, Shelley would like to know how.

She finally managed to calm down long enough to hear what Eunice was saying. 'That's pure nonsense,' she said, at her most strident, her free hand on her rolling hip. 'We've men here, we've dogs, we've fought off gyppos and we've fought off travellers and we've fought off foot and mouth, so no mean posse of ne'er-do-wells is going to mess with us.'

A short silence. Eunice listened.

'I don't care what anyone says, we demand to be left alone. We've two-twos and twelve bores, powerful tractors with bale-spikes, and diggers, but most important we've got common sense, which is more than can be said for some. Panicking like this. God help you young ones if there was a war.'

My God, here was Shelley listening to a half-mad old woman turning away police protection and doing nothing to prevent her. Whose decision was this to make? Would they take Eunice's protestations seriously or would they do what they thought was best and get a cop car out here right now? Were they all safe at the Boltons' farm, or were they sitting ducks?

When Edward came in, covered in straw, he immediately saw the state she was in and led her by the hand to the kitchen.

'What is it?'

She told him. 'Your mother is still on the phone out there.'

'She'll sort it out. Don't worry.'

Shelley burst out, '*Oh, how can you say that?* They burned that flat to the ground. They believed we were in there. They wanted us dead, not just me but my children.'

His grip on her hand turned gentle. He sat her down in the ladderback chair and squatted beside her, his eyes on hers. 'Do you trust me, Shelley?'

She shook her head. 'I dunno any more.'

'Do you think I would allow anyone to hurt you?'

She shook her head childishly, brushing away stray tears.

'There's me, there's Oliver, there's Father, there's Mother, and on the end of the phone there's the Dawsons down the valley with four strong young farmhands just raring for a fight . . .'

'But what would be wrong with police protection? Why is Eunice so against the idea?'

'She's an independent woman.' He smiled wryly. 'She's had some fights with the law in her time, mostly over the lost sheep she likes to take in to prove them wrong.'

'Duffy and Dukes?'

'Oh, not only them. I can remember when we were small, there was hardly ever a time when there weren't strange children in the house being rescued from somewhere.'

'That must have been hard for you, having to share her?'

Edward shook his head. 'Not really. Me and Oliver, we were the lucky ones.' His green eyes unlocked themselves from hers and he slowly withdrew his hand, but not without it touching

267

her arm and briefly resting on her shoulder. 'If Mother and Father feel they can handle this without help,' he said quietly, 'it means that they can, and they want to. What you've got to do is stay calm and take care of your little family. OK?'

Any ideas Shelley might have had of questioning him about Jason's treatment seemed so unimportant now they were not worth the effort. Eunice, like so many of her generation, was old-fashioned, revered the Queen, stood for family values and probably voted Tory. And if Shelley couldn't stomach that in view of all the help she was getting, then she should be ashamed of herself.

Her children would come to no harm from all these new experiences; some good might well come out of them. The benefits of the Boltons' system were already apparent. Mealtimes were comparatively peaceful, their play was less fractious than usual, the freedom and the cold fresh air were doing them nothing but good, they were sleeping better and eating better . . .

The World Tonight led on the story of the unruly mob who had razed the Tremaynes' flat to the ground, believing the family to be in residence.

At least this behaviour was frowned on.

Critics came out of the woodwork for the first time since the murder, and the news of the hospitalization of the accused child's father added fuel to their argument. Nothing, however, was said about the attack on Joey himself – Shelley wondered if this omission was deliberate. Maybe the general public were not ready for such contentious news? A majority might firmly believe that such behaviour was justified, whereas Joey's siblings and his father were a different kettle of fish. Where would his mother feature in this weird equation, Shelley mused.

Throughout the programme (which cleverly succeeded in protecting identities and which everyone listened to in respectful silence), Shelley was aware of Edward's glances. At one point their eyes met and held for longer than necessary. She was deeply ashamed to feel those hot old stirrings of excitement. How could she react to a man, no matter how sensual and powerful he was, in the middle of all this mayhem? What sort of woman did that make her, when her children's lives were in danger, her son accused of such a vile crime it was hard to take it in, and she herself was homeless, penniless and reviled? What sort of loathsome creature was she?

But Shelley returned his look. She would love to feel his strong arms around her, keeping her safe from this dark, eerie pit. They exchanged soft smiles of understanding which brought some longed-for warmth back into her lonely heart.

TWENTY-ONE

'I would be very surprised,' said Tim Lee, the child psychiatrist employed by the firm of Grant and Wilson for Joey's defence, 'if Joseph Tremayne was innocent.'

'And so say all of us,' replied Martin Chandler, cradling the phone between shoulder and cheek as he poured the first of his morning coffees while he listened to this first unofficial report – or chat, more like.

'I saw Joseph yesterday afternoon after his mother had visited,' Lee continued, 'and after an hour of aggressive stuff there were the usual tears and recriminations. As you know, we never label kids Joseph's age psychopathic, but going on this brief encounter I would have to say he meets most of the criteria for an adult diagnosis.'

'*Hell*,' Chandler replied. 'And you can come to that conclusion after just one session?'

'I'm sticking my neck out on this,' said Lee, 'and whatever you do don't quote me, but another point of concern is Joseph's fascination with fire. I did wonder if he and his mates had any history of fire-raising which didn't get mentioned in the notes?'

'No.' Chandler shuddered at the thought. 'And the last thing we want is to probe that issue. Not now. But it could well be that those five kids went about incinerating the area; everyone knows that the fire chaps here have a hefty problem with petty arson.'

'I say this because I feel fairly certain that the theft of the paraffin took place before they had formed any specific idea of committing a crime.'

Chandler thoughtfully sipped his coffee. 'Are you saying the theft was routine stuff? Are you saying they went round whipping accelerants on a regular basis?'

'I'm saying that I wouldn't be surprised. My guess is they were on their way to some predetermined destination when they happened upon the pram.'

'*Bastards*,' spat Chandler, spinning round in his swivel chair.

'And,' Lee went on, 'I suggest that if we direct our questioning of Joseph with that idea in mind, we might get the boy to open up.'

'Confess?'

'If you like.'

'Maybe we'd rather not know,' Chandler said. 'It would change the nature of the case. We would have to go with a guilty plea to manslaughter. We would have to convince the DPP.'

'So it would be beneficial to us,' Lee continued in that carefully unemotional voice of his which irritated Chandler no end, 'if we could ascertain that these children had, in fact, been starting fires in the area with no set intention of putting human

271

life in danger. When Joseph says they did not know that child was in the pram, there would then be a pretty good argument for believing him.'

Hell, this shrink was meant to be impartial. It was beginning to look like he was taking over the defence of this damn case. 'And yet you say this kid could be an up-and-coming psychopath?'

'That is my judgement, yes. But these are early days.'

Chandler asked, 'Between you and me, in your opinion, is this kid dangerous?'

'In my opinion, could be,' said Lee.

These wretched woolly liberals spend their whole lives watching their backs, never coming down firmly on one side or the other, Chandler thought. In his opinion, if the Tremayne boy was dangerous, they should stick with the murder charge and get the nutter off the streets. Get him labelled insane if necessary, anything in order to protect innocent little kids from being fried alive ever again. Given what Chandler knew of Joey, his future was already ordained and stretched out down a lethal pathway of muggings and rapes, drug trafficking, paedophilia *et al.*, before finally leading, once again and inevitably, to murder most foul.

However, he and his firm were acting for Joey and he would certainly pass on the psychiatrist's initial opinions to Formby-Hart and his team.

The condition of Chandler's wife, Jessica, sedated and suffering seriously from post-natal depression, meant that life at home was not what it had been. Chandler firmly believed that her worrying mental state had been aggravated by the attention given to this atrocity, not helped by the fact that he was involved. In vain he tried to reassure her that their little one was safe and yes, she could take her out, although to leave her outside a shop in a pram had never been a great idea, even before the Holly Coates case.

'But while I'm at home all day fighting the demons,' whined the grey-faced and stragglyhaired Jessica, 'you are out there trying to make sure this devil is back on the streets.'

'That's not strictly true, darling.' Last night he had had to get his own supper and their lovely house was beginning to resemble that of a problem family. 'You know very well that I share your feelings on this and that this case is the most traumatic one I have ever had to deal with.'

'Surely, Martin, somebody else could . . .?'

'We've been through this over and over, Jessie. I can't just back off from work that isn't pleasant. I've defended all sorts of sickos in the past, from rapists to child abusers, and you haven't reacted like this before.'

'I haven't had a baby before,' Jessica replied, bleak-eyed. 'I haven't known what it was like to have someone so dear and so small to protect.'

In her fear she was backing away from her child; it looked as if she was afraid to love her in case her baby was taken away. Chandler had spent two exhausting hours last night trying to get his daughter to take a bottle, and him with a heavy workload in front of him. During that hellish session of screamings, pacings and endless repetitions of 'Baa baa black sheep', Jessica had not stirred from her bed. The tranquillizers were working well. Chandler felt he had been through a wringer but the very worst of this was that Jessica's mother was threatening to come down and take over.

Thoughts of the mob and the burning flat had taken their toll.

The only way Shelley had managed to sleep a wink last night was by taking one of her precious Valium. She would have preferred not to do this, first because they were so precious and she never knew when she might need them more desperately, and secondly because they left her so woozy the following day. This morning she felt she was seeing the world with her head submerged under tepid bathwater.

Jason was clingy this morning, not to her but to Eunice, as if he was keen to make amends for yesterday's naughty behaviour, and Eunice was as loving as always, so you would think the incident had never happened. Shelley wished the kids would concentrate on their own boxes of toys and leave the Boltons' laundry-basket collection strictly alone. Such a fuss over one model van.

What if they broke a cup or a plate?

On edge, Shelley followed them round with warnings.

With Julie well wrapped up in her pushchair, Shelley ventured outside to find a cold, crisp, sunny morning and Edward and Oliver forking hay bales from the top of one of the vast stone barns. She took them tea. Although, in her former life, the temperature out here would have kept her inside with the central heating on full, the Bolton men were stripped to their vests and sweating from their heavy work. They sat on a mounting block and basked in a sharp dart of sun; Julie was red-faced from the cold and dozing. With her close proximity to Edward, Shelley didn't need much sun to send a warm glow rushing through her. He was strong and muscled, without a spare inch of flesh on his body. In a light-hearted fashion she brought up yesterday's unsettling treatment of Jason.

As Shelley suspected they would, Eunice's sons took the matter lightly.

'Traditional family values,' said Oliver.

Shelley persisted. This was important. She had to understand. 'But what have they got to do with sending a three-year-old child to bed all alone without his supper?'

'Mother is convinced that her way of bringing up children is the right one,' said Edward. He smelled of sweet silage and summer grass. 'And who knows, maybe she's right? She's had enough experience.'

'What other methods does she use to bring kiddies to heel? Is there a strap somewhere in the house? Or a wooden spoon? Or a dark little room used for solitary confinement?'

Their easy laughter put her at ease. They drank their tea companionably, the steam frosting in the air around them. Theirs was a joky relationship. They went through the jobs they faced that morning, the state of a bullock they were worried about, the number of ewes that were due to give birth, and then the conversation turned to the animal sanctuary where Dillon Dukes worked. One load of hay was due to be delivered there that afternoon.

'Mother thinks she knows best,' said Oliver. 'And she can upset folk with her outspokenness. Apparently Dillon's mother visited here just one time while he was staying, and that was enough. She quit. She abandoned the lad after that; he tried to trace her but no luck. Now in Mother's opinion that woman's departure was the best thing that could have happened to Dillon. A tramp, she called her. A mother from hell. And it does look as if she was right.'

'Eunice blamed Dillon's mother for his behaviour?' Shelley asked.

'Oh yes,' said Oliver casually. 'She never blames the kids.'

'I wonder what she thinks of me,' Shelley mused.

'You love your kids, that's obvious,' said Edward. 'You're very different. Mother wanted you and your tribe. She felt she could help, you see. We heard about the case on the radio and she contacted social services and volunteered. Strictly she is too old now to be on their regular list of foster carers. You were chosen. You were special. So you can't make comparisons between you and Dillon's mum.'

'Did you know her?' Shelley asked. 'Did you meet her?'

'We were away at college while all that was going on,' said Edward, returning his cup and folding her hand around it, holding on for a fraction too long, long enough for Shelley to flush. 'But Dillon's turned out a real decent guy. Maybe he *is* better off without her.'

When Eunice called her indoors, Shelley thought she was probably imagining the concerned look on her face. What would Eunice's attitude be if she and Edward got something going – an event that looked quite possible from the way the electricity was flashing between them?

Although Edward, to Shelley's delight, volunteered to take her on her visit to Lister this afternoon, these casual arrangements were soon ruled out. Eunice quickly pointed out that, apart from the fact that Shelley needed a police escort in order to enter Dudley Park and to minimize the risk of being seen, what about the farmwork, intense at this time of year?

The thought of Edward, in the middle of this cold, black period of Shelley's life, was like a distant beacon shining, beckoning her back to a normal world which held not just bad things but good too. She had no preconceived ideas about where their relationship would go, if anywhere. It might be that he was merely a warm friend being protective in a time of trouble, and that nothing more would come of it. Although she would be disappointed if this was the only outcome, it certainly gave her the energy to get out of bed in the morning. He was a far stronger and more thoughtful, more charismatic man than Shelley had ever attracted before.

Oliver's fiancée was not a born-and-bred country girl and yet the Bolton family seemed fond of her, and approved of that match. But the girl had a career, no chequered past, no kids, so obviously she was more suitable than someone like Shelley would ever be. How much would Edward be influenced by his parents' opinions, Shelley wondered. He was thirty years old, for God's sake, he had been away to college – if only over the hill – but both sons appeared to treat Mother and Father with a special concern, almost reverence.

They hung around home at nights, they never went clubbing or pubbing. They put up with life without a TV, and computers didn't interest them.

Was this natural?

How would Shelley know?

And when Oliver married his English Tourist Board lover, would they live here on the home farm, or would they lead independent lives?

All this was playing on Shelley's mind when her lift arrived. The driver was a stranger, thank God; an hour with the waspish WPC Hollis would have been the last bloody straw. She opened the carrier bag in the back and gasped at the sight of Wally Wolf: so DI Hudson had kept his word, he had sent somebody round to see if the hapless animal had survived. She clasped him to her in pleased satisfaction, attempting to fluff up his dead grey

278

fur. This would make a difference to Joey; throughout his early childhood Wally Wolf had been a constant companion.

Joey was finishing his lunch when Shelley arrived with her carrier bag. Baked potatoes, ham and beans, and he hadn't left much on his plate. The ice-cream pudding stayed abandoned on his tray and she guessed it was because she'd arrived that he'd decided not to eat it. Attention-seeking, as ever.

He sneered when he saw what she'd brought for him.

'Come on, Mum, get real.'

'But you asked for Wally,' she said, astonished.

'I was joking,' Joey snarled.

'So you want me to take him home again, is that it?'

'Burn him, if you like. I don't give a toss.'

She didn't think Joey associated these thoughtless instructions with the fate of Holly Coates. She put Wally Wolf back in his bag and handed over the parcel of CDs that he had requested, several favourite computer games and a giant Toblerone.

'I saw the shrink,' he said. 'He told me to call him Tim. He was a right arsehole.'

'But you cooperated, I hope.'

'I told him what he wanted to hear.'

'That sort of attitude's not going to get us anywhere, Joey.'

'He said that whoever burned Holly Coates probably didn't mean to.'

'Well,' Shelley began, unsure of her ground, 'he is probably right.'

'He said it was a terrible mistake which would haunt us for the rest of our lives.'

'Us?' Shelley questioned him. 'He meant all five of you?'

'He didn't seem bothered by who done it.'

Eric came by and offered Shelley a cup of tea. 'How's Joey doing?' she asked the flabby male nurse with the chubby lips and the baby face. She tried to fathom out if he was a raging queer as Joey had suggested. There was a sway about his walk, and a feminine lilt to his voice, but nothing she could be certain of. If he was an arse bandit he'd certainly be in his element here. She wondered if Joey had told the shrink about Eric's come-ons that first night and if Joey's friend 'Tim' had believed him.

Eric said, 'He wants to go home. He's not settling in. He's in tears half the night. He shouldn't be in here, he's a baby.'

'Is that right, Joey?' Shelley asked with a sinking heart as Eric moved fatly off.

'That git talks crap.'

'I'm in tears half the night too,' said Shelley, wishing he would open up and cut out this macho shit. 'I think about you all the time. Hey, when you get out of here we'll celebrate. What shall we do on the day you're free? You choose. You think what you'd like best.'

Joey gave Shelley a contemptuous smile. 'I'm not getting out of here and you know it. Why do you pretend, Mum? Why can't you take the fucking truth?'

'I can't accept what you say, Joey, because I

280

know that you didn't do it.'

'*You know fuck all.*'

'Well, tell me then. Tell me,' Shelley insisted in despair. 'Look, I'm here and I'm listening.'

'I didn't know about the kid.'

Shelley wasn't sure what he'd said. 'You mean Holly?'

'I thought the pram was empty,' said Joey, turned away from her so she couldn't see his expression. 'I thought we could start the fire in the pram and it might spread into the shop . . .'

'*Hang on, Joey,*' said Shelley, heart pounding, '*who's been telling you to say this?* This Tim you saw yesterday? Did he put this crap into your head?'

Joey turned to face her again and the anger on his face was shocking. 'Oh, forget it, Mum,' he said. 'Just you go home and feed bloody Julie. Go and have a few halves down the club. Go and listen to Queen and have a cry for me.'

By now Shelley was shaking with fury. '*That's enough from you,*' she screamed, smacking him over the head so he cringed. '*Don't you dare patronize me.* As if there isn't enough of that crap going on around here at the moment. We're all in the shit because of you – Kez, Saul, Jason, Casey and even little Julie. And Kenny's half dead, beaten to a pulp. God knows how Dave's surviving. You little bastard, if you knew what trouble you've caused with your disgusting ideas of fun, with your twisted mates and your warped behaviour. *Joey, you are seriously sick.*' She stabbed him on the forehead. 'You make me want to puke with your whingeing ways – "*It's not fair, it's not fair.*" Fuck that. Fuck you. D'you think I enjoy coming up here every day listening to your bloody moanings? Well, I don't. And I wish I didn't have to come. But more often than that I sodding well wish that you had never been born, *you fucking little freak.*'

This was the second time she had lost it with him.

She picked up the bag holding Wally Wolf and stalked out of the room, the drama of her exit spoiled only by her need to ask fat Eric for the keys.

On her way home Shelley's heart broke.

TWENTY-TWO

'Pop him in the laundry basket. Some other child will love him.'

Shelley was crying when she placed Wally Wolf on top of the pile of discarded toys used not just by Edward and Oliver, but by countless children who had come to the farm for tender loving care and gone on to face some unknown future.

Normally so understanding and supportive, Eunice had reacted to her furious outburst at Joey this afternoon in a surprising way. Eunice wouldn't have it that Shelley had lost her cool and 'just cracked' and that all the tension and underlying emotions of the last few days had erupted with such lethal lava. 'You are an adult,' said Eunice, her moustache bristling and her orange colour up. 'You have no right to lose your temper when it comes to dealing with children. Who knows what damage you've done. That poor little boy of yours will be breaking his heart as we speak.'

Shelley, guilt-ridden, went into an immediate attack. 'So in all your years of dealing with kids are you telling me you never lost it?'

'I got angry, of course I did, but I swallowed it. I took a deep breath, and I never said or did anything I knew I would come to regret.'

'*Well, good on you,*' Shelley retorted, her face reddening, her voice breaking.

'Children are like animals, Shelley,' Eunice persisted, ignoring Shelley's distress. 'They will never respond to temper, which only leaves them cowering and unable to use their own brains, however tiny. Take our four dogs, for instance. D'you really think they'd be any use if they hadn't been trained with patience and kindness? Well, don't you think it's up to you to give your children that same respect?'

If Eunice hadn't been who she was, Shelley would have yelled, fuck off, you know-it-all bitch.

'You should phone Dudley Park right now,' Eunice insisted, 'and reassure poor Joey that everything's all right.' And she went off muttering, but loud enough to be heard, 'Trust and respect. Bless me, that's not much to ask for.'

And yet, only ten minutes before, to Shelley's dismay, Kez had had his Eskimo action man binned for nicking cake from Eunice's plentiful larder. His pathetic tears and pleas for forgiveness went unheard. At home the kids were used to dipping their hands in the biscuit tin or helping themselves to crisps whenever they felt the need. Here Eunice's policy of not eating in between meals was adhered to like a bloody commandment. Kez had looked to Shelley for help but she could only look away; this was not her house.

She did ring Dudley Park, to be told that Joey

was unavailable. She left a message. She told him, 'I love you.' Although Eunice's theories would make sense to a saint or some child fanatic, Shelley couldn't agree that extreme emotion should play no part between a mum and her kids. Surely they ought to know that their mother was only human, they should see her cry and understand why, they should feel her anger and recognize it to be the same as theirs. There was something eerily cold about Eunice's methods when it came to her clinical punishments, like the state demanding a life for a life and stamping the decision on a document.

But dammit, it seemed to work. Kez was himself in a matter of minutes and overeager to please. This did remind Shelley of the sheepdogs, of their belly-crawling, rolling-eyed dependency. It was true, though, she had never seen a kick aimed in their direction or anything other than kindness bestowed with pats and frequent strokes – although they were never allowed in the house and lived in basic conditions in an unheated shed, once an outside toilet, with straw on the floor. And their food was not much better than the pigs'.

It was the presence of the dogs that made life at the farm feel so safe. Long before the human ear could hear the approach of a vehicle, all four started up a manic barking which did not cease till one of the Boltons arrived to calm them. Eunice had been right when she'd refused to consider police protection. All that would have done would have been to set the dogs off each time a copper closed a car door, or changed shifts, or approached the farm gate. And the collection of family guns was always close at hand ... dangerously so, Shelley considered, when there were so many kids around.

She said to Eunice when they washed up after supper, 'How many kids d'you think you and John have fostered over the years?'

Eunice, sleeves up to reveal her burly, hairy arms, sniffed over the washing-up water. 'Countless.'

'Even when Edward and Oliver were small?'

'The more the merrier is my opinion.'

'But they weren't all kids with problems?'

'They all had the same problem, m'dear. Their parents, or the lack of them.'

'D'you still see some of them?'

'Not the younger ones, no, although I do get Christmas cards from four or five. They never forget.'

'But you're still in touch with Dillon Dukes and Shane Duffy?'

Eunice swung round. '*Who told you that?*'

'Edward or Oliver,' Shelley explained. 'Why? Shouldn't I know?'

'No matter,' said Eunice coldly, returning to her work.

Eunice was disdainful of counsellors and shrinks and the like. So when Shelley was informed by phone next morning that Tim Lee would like to see her and was suggesting coming over, she made her feelings plain.

'They mess up people's heads. They do more ruddy harm than good.'

'But he's on Joey's side,' said Shelley, 'so I've got no option really. I had to agree. I've got to cooperate.'

'Well, you can't see him in my kitchen. It'll have to be the lounge,' said Eunice. 'And I'm not making tea.' She added a further warning: 'Watch what you say. Mind your back.'

Shelley fully intended to. She shared Eunice's views. She had struggled all his life to keep Joey away from the educational psychologist who was forever being used as a threat by that mealy-mouthed headmaster Ronald Cutting. The most the school had been able to do was force Joey to spend one term in a special needs class where the pseudo-shrink made occasional visits.

Joey told him to piss off. Hah.

But this Tim Lee was different, an expert and much respected, apparently, in his field, and paid a fortune by Formby-Hart to take on Joey's case. His reason for seeing her at the farm was that he preferred to meet Joey's mum 'on safe ground'. Whatever that meant.

The shrink arrived early, driving a posh convertible Saab which the dogs immediately pissed all over. He wore deceptively informal clothes, cord pants, Hush Puppy boots and a grey and blue Fair Isle sweater which Shelley would have liked. He topped all this with a sheepskin coat and matching hat, perfect for the weather although he did look a bit of a poof. His hair was manic, uncut and curly – part of his desire to suggest he was unbalanced himself and therefore no threat to his clients.

Eunice was a silent, glowering presence in the kitchen so Shelley quickly made coffee and took it through to the lounge, where the fire was smoking particularly badly. 'You have to sit right down in your chair,' she explained before his eyes could begin to sting. 'The lower you sit, the better.'

'Nice for you to have the freedom and know your children are being looked after,' was his first observation.

Should Shelley oblige him by admitting she wanted to rid herself of her kids at the slightest opportunity? She proceeded warily. 'With this thing with Joey going on, worrying about the state of the others would be too bloody much at the moment,' she told him. 'Every part of me is focused on Joey.'

Lee nodded understandingly. 'Terrible for you,' he agreed. He took out a small tape recorder and placed it on the coffee table. 'Would you mind?' he asked her. 'Needless to say, whatever we discuss will remain strictly confidential.'

'I don't mind,' said Shelley. But she did. She detested the sound of her own voice almost as much as she loathed seeing herself on photographs.

Shelley took Lee back through her past; she'd known he would want to delve into that. But other than her acute lack of confidence due partly to Iris and partly to the bullying, there was nothing much there for Lee to latch onto.

Her childhood was a lonely, old-fashioned one,

her mother a cold fish who worked full time in Dingles' basement. Shelley was brought up with no family connections. *But so what?* It worked out OK in the end.

She would have preferred to get married, she supposed, if the right man had come along, but these days that hardly mattered. She was a damn sight better off with the benefits paid to single mothers.

She described her life with the Boltons: all positive stuff; she certainly didn't bother him with her worries about Eunice's unfashionable methods or the way she felt undermined sometimes because of Eunice's vast experience. She managed to get in her wish that one day Joey might come to the farm, bearing in mind the Boltons' successes with other difficult children. She also told him about her fears that Joey was being intimidated by methods subtle and cunning into admitting that he was the instigator of the Holly Coates murder.

'When he wasn't,' she insisted. 'I know when Joey is lying or not. He is being ground down.'

'I met with Joseph yesterday,' said Lee, 'and we started to talk about fire.'

'*Fire?*' Shelley was nonplussed.

'We started to talk about the possibility that he and his friends were regular fire-raisers,' said Lee, looking hard at her.

'So what did Joey say about that?' Shelley was intrigued.

'Not much,' said Lee. 'But I left him to think about what I had said.'

'I don't know anything about Joey and fire.'

'I think you do,' said Lee, to Shelley's annoyance. 'And I'd like you to take your mind back. I know there was one incident at the school when Joey and some friends were accused of starting a fire in the caretaker's basement. Can you enlighten me about that?'

'They couldn't touch him. There was no proof,' Shelley blustered.

'Did Joey ever confide in you about that?'

'Why would he?'

'Have you ever had cause to remove matches from Joey's possession?' asked Lee carefully.

Shelley paused. '*What's he told you?*'

'As I said before, he said nothing to me about fire.'

'Joey carries matches around because he's a secret smoker,' said Shelley. 'Most kids do.'

'Do they?' asked Lee in a meaningful way.

'At his age they experiment with all that crap,' said Shelley, wishing she could light up right now. She took the chance. Eunice wasn't around and not likely to butt in here, and the smell of woodsmoke was so strong in this room that traces of the odd fag wouldn't pose any problem. Lee watched her with unnecessary interest, she thought.

'And then he got himself a lighter?' said Lee, staring at hers, a cheap green disposable.

'That's what they say,' said Shelley, puffing hard.

'And you think that was because of his smoking habits?'

'Probably. Why?'

290

'Shelley,' said Tim Lee confidentially, donning a pair of gold-rimmed, intellectual half-glasses, 'have you ever heard of a condition called pyromania?'

She was pleased with the sarcasm in her voice. 'Could it be something to do with fire?'

'It is an illness where the sufferer is impelled to go round starting fires.'

Shelley was on her guard. 'So? What are you getting at?'

'If we could show to the court that Joseph fitted into this category then I think we could also suggest that he couldn't help what he did, and that his intention was never to murder Holly Coates. Far from it.'

She was scared to dare to hope. 'It would *help* him? Is that what you're saying?'

'Definitely. Please, trust me. I am on your side, you know.'

Yes, thought Shelley. Who wouldn't be, charging your fees? 'What d'you want me to say?'

'I don't want to put words in your mouth. I am not your defence counsel and I have a reputation to protect, but I want to ask you again, do you remember any of Joey's activities that concerned you at the time, any activities related to fire? Please think carefully before you answer.'

Shelley thought desperately. 'He could tell you more than I could.'

'Yes, and that is precisely why I want you to concentrate on this subject next time you visit. He's extremely defensive at the moment and I need Joseph to trust me and you are the only one who can convince him to do that.'

Shelley listened in total confusion. She got up, crossed the room and stubbed her fag out on a smoking log. 'What made you think he was a bloody fire freak?'

Lee looked at her disapprovingly. 'We must steer clear of the word freak. The Lessing brothers and Mason and Long all talked about other fires in their statements. But certain attitudes Joseph displayed when I saw him, hints, the school report on the caretaker's quarters – Joseph is a textbook case of a child who might well resort to this type of behaviour. Bright, bored, attention-seeking, a lover of drama . . .'

'If the courts knew that, he'd be behind bars for ever.'

'Far from it. There are treatments for this condition,' said Lee.

'So what would he get if we went down that road? Time in an asylum with dribbling old men and rapists?'

Tim Lee dragged himself further back in his chair to avoid the eye-scorching smoke. 'Joseph would plead guilty to manslaughter and ask that his condition be taken into account.'

'*No way,*' Shelley exploded.

'It's either that or a childhood locked in a young offenders' institution, an institution that will destroy him,' said Lee.

'There are places . . .' Shelley began.

'You read about places,' said Lee with a cynical smile. 'You hear about them on the TV but in reality they don't exist. Delinquent kids are not vote catchers. There's nothing in them for the powers that be. They start up special units when faced with unpleasant statistics but before you can turn around they're pandering to a medieval public baying for blood. No,' said Lee, 'Joseph would be far safer given specialized medical care.'

'*But Joey's as sane as you or me.*'

Tim Lee ignored her. She imagined he looked uncomfortable. 'It's all down to you,' he said, spreading long, thin, pen-pushing fingers in a gesture of relinquishing a burden he no longer felt able to carry.

Finally Shelley admitted, 'He's always been attracted to matches.' She looked at her own hands, gripped whitely on her knees. 'I had to hide them away,' she said, 'because of the times I came downstairs and found him fooling about with waste-paper baskets and the other kids sleeping . . .'

'Were you ever forced to call for help?'

'Only once,' Shelley said, thinking back. 'He and his sodding mates had been smoking in the garden. Not much of a garden . . . I kept a sunbed and an umbrella in an old coal bunker which was put in before the houses were centrally heated.'

She paused.

She remembered.

The few times she had managed to lie out in the sun, the sunbed and the umbrella had been tinged with green mould. 'This day I saw the smoke billowing out of the bunker and ran out. There was this stench of petrol fumes. Joey and his mates were long gone but the flames were spreading towards the fence. It's a wooden fence and there's a shed next door full of garden implements. I thought – that's going to catch light, the whole estate could go up in flames. I dialled nine nine nine. When they came I told them I was to blame. I said there must have been a fault with the plug which went into the mower.'

'How long ago was that?' asked Lee.

'Joey must have been eight, maybe nine.'

Lee persisted. 'And the incident at the school? Can you tell me any more about that?'

There was no point in lying any longer. For Joey's sake she had to come clean. 'That day Joey came home with the soles of his trainers scorched. I was livid. I'd put myself in hock for those, the payments were falling behind and the bugger had the nerve to come home with the soles charred and flapping off.'

'So what was his excuse?'

'Joey told me some kid had nicked them while he was at gym.'

'And . . . ?'

'He said this kid had a grudge against him. He said this kid torched them in the waste bin in the playground. He said he only just reached them before they went up in flames.'

'Soon after that you must have been told about the basement fire,' said Lee. 'What was your reaction to that?'

'I resented the fact that they blamed Joey.'

'So you went up to the school and raised merry hell?'

Shelley nodded. 'They were always blaming Joey,' she said. 'I was bloody fed up with the whole shitting mess. Ronald Cutting, the head . . .'

'I have spoken to him.'

'Well, that arsehole's got a down on Joey. Ever since Cutting came he's been trying to nail him.'

Lee stared at Shelley with a sad expression she found hard to interpret. She didn't like it. She felt like a prick. This, too, was Joey's fault. 'What makes you think an intelligent man with a life-time's experience of children would pick out Joseph for special treatment?'

'I can see whose side you are on,' she said crossly. 'Paranoid, is that what I am?'

'And now – now that you're wiser, do you think that Joseph was possibly involved in the fire in the caretaker's basement?'

'I know he was,' said Shelley. 'I knew he was then. I just couldn't face it.'

'That's perfectly understandable,' said Lee, unconvincingly. 'But from now on, Shelley, if we want the best for Joseph we are going to have to be honest with each other, and persuade him to tell the truth.'

'He didn't mean to kill Holly?'

'No.'

'He and his mates thought that pram was empty?'

'Yes, I've no doubt about that,' said Lee.

'And the court will accept that idea and treat him more gently because of it?'

'If Joey gives me the help I need, yes.'
'Did Joey light the fire that killed Holly?'
'Yes, Shelley,' said Lee gently, 'he did.'

TWENTY-THREE

If calling Joey a pyromaniac was going to make life more bearable for him, then Shelley would go along with that. But the idea that her son was totally responsible for the death of Holly Coates was too grotesque to contemplate. The fact that now the experts were reaching the awful conclusion that Joey was a murderer, albeit by accident, left Shelley tortured, breathless with powerlessness.

Those sodding experts should drag Joey's accomplices down into some subterranean basement and thrash the truth out of them. And Joey, the prat, wasn't helping himself with his stupid squirmings and half-truths.

With the energy of a shot-putter Eunice was preparing a special lunch for today. Alex, the social worker, on a routine visit to check on the kids, was bringing with her Doreen Blennerhasset, a county bigwig and buddy of Eunice's. They had worked together in the good old days when Eunice was fostering kids on a regular basis and Doreen was a foster-care caseworker. Doreen now chaired the special committee which had been set up to monitor the welfare of the Tremaynes, and which included the police and the health and education departments.

Shelley already felt ruffled that so many case conferences had been held in secret, without her. With her knowledge of Joey she could have contributed, couldn't she? Or were they saying such things about her that they would rather keep her at a safe distance?

Leek and potato soup with home-made rolls would be followed by plum crumble, cream and custard. Just the sort of warming meal for a day of gale-blown sleet and dark, threatening skies. Everyone was made aware of the importance of this event by the massive checked cloth that Eunice spread across the table.

Shelley prayed the kids would behave. She felt their behaviour would be watched and assessed. She feared that they might fail some test and be taken away from their hopeless mother.

Eunice had no such qualms. She seemed to have recovered from the unwelcome visit of Tim Lee and Shelley noticed that her carrot-coloured hair appeared less sparse this morning, having been freshly washed. Also, she had changed her apron from the regular butcher's stripes to a cheerful check. 'Doreen is a brick. That woman sacrificed her whole life in order to care for children. Her career is her life and now she's made it to the top and has even sat on parliamentary committees to give the government the benefit of her knowledge.' Eunice drew herself up with pride. 'Doreen and I go back a long way.'

It was no good trying to help her. Eunice turned down any attempts; she wanted to do this Bolton style and in her eyes Shelley was not the most efficient of kitchen assistants.

Today, thank God, it was thought too cold for the children to play out. Anyone lingering out there in this freeze would end up spiked rigid as an icicle. While Julie and Casey had their morning naps Shelley, nervous and in the way, slipped on her jacket and nipped out to collect the cream for the soup from the Boltons' cold room where they pressed their cheeses and shaped their own butter. The cream, Eunice instructed her, would be found in a small metal churn on top of one of the freezers.

Her meeting with Lee filled her head.

Was Joey really addicted to fire?

Was it wise to admit this in a court of law? Surely it would be better to deny all involvement and stick with the fact that he was just an observer, like the other four gits were doing?

Take a chance?

Fly in the face of logic?

Because the lighter was undoubtedly his and it was Joey who nicked the paraffin.

Three witnesses to the crime had picked him out.

He was now suggesting he might have done it, but he thought the pram was empty. Whatever, if the present looked black the future had no colour at all.

'Penny for them?'

Shelley jumped. She'd been so lost in her own thoughts she had missed Edward's entrance. 'Joey,' she said. 'What else can I think about?'

He smelled of milk and beet nuts, and his overalls of Persil. His dark hair stuck to his head and his face was wet, his eyelashes beaded with tiny drops of moisture. 'Come here,' he said and when Shelley approached very slowly as if in a dream, his arms went straight round her. She nestled against his strength and his calm, and when he began to stroke her hair she shuddered and raised her face to his. When he kissed her she knew without any doubt that here was a man with experience; he might spend most nights indoors with his mum, but some time, somewhere, he'd found out how to kiss.

'You're lovely, you know that, don't you?'

She thought about Eunice back in the kitchen. 'Edward, this is crazy, we shouldn't be doing this. What if . . .?'

He stifled her question with his lips, and her nervousness changed into eager responses. His skin was smooth and lightly scented. His stomach was muscled and flat. Drops of rain fell on her from his hair. Where his hands pressed against her back the power in them flooded through her. Shelley, trembling, wanted more. Her face turned scorching hot and her eyes felt heavy and weighted.

When he released her she staggered slightly and he balanced her with his arm.

'Eunice needs some cream,' she stuttered. And

300

then they both laughed so freely, with such pure happiness, that any shred of embarrassment over how sensual and sudden had been their kisses was melted as fast as the sleet on the cobbles.

Doreen Blennerhasset drove a filthy blue Volvo, the square-fronted kind you don't see around much. Her arrival was announced by the dogs and Eunice bowled from the door in her grubby slippers and they greeted each other like the old friends they were. Slaps on backs and gripping hands – certainly not the kissy embrace favoured by friends of today. Behind Doreen, Alex trailed carefully, making her way through the puddles.

'We thought we might not get here, that sky looks pretty menacing,' said Doreen, public-school prim, allowing Eunice to take her sleet-glistening camel coat, shake it and hang it up. As favoured guest she was ushered to the best ladderback chair, the one with the fatter cushions, the one closest to the Aga.

'This is Shelley,' said Alex brightly, dealing with her own curious hand-knitted coat. The number of nose rings and earrings she wore had increased since their last meeting and she had added a streak of pink to her hair. 'Shelley, this is Doreen Blennerhasset. She knows your case very well.'

How was it possible that these two women, Doreen and Eunice, both somewhere in their mid-fifties at a guess, had worked well together? From the sublime to the ridiculous. Doreen's grey hair was pulled strictly back and fixed with no fuss, only grips. Twinset and pearls. Plaid skirt, thick tights and zip-up furry boots, the kind they sell in the Damart catalogue. Her bag was no different from a briefcase and from it she pulled a lacy handkerchief to wipe the cold from her nose. Tall and gauntly thin, Doreen made the rotund Eunice beside her look like Humpty Dumpty, and Alex in her padded pink snowsuit could be a circus clown.

Shelley suddenly knew she ought to have changed out of her jeans and sweater. She ought to have made an effort in view of this important guest. Something in Eunice's expression told her that with no need for words, but the sting was taken out of it – Shelley was still back in the creamery, dreamy in Edward's arms.

Even the dour John had changed for this special occasion. Instead of his moth-eaten Guernsey and workworn trousers, he came downstairs in a crisply fresh shirt and a baggy pair of cords. That he and Doreen were fond friends was obvious in his cheerful greeting as he bent to kiss her papery cheek. Shelley had never seen John making a special effort before.

Oh God, she hoped the kids would shape up.

While the adults chatted and Kez, Saul and Jason built car parks round the kitchen floor, Shelley went up to wake Julie and Casey, freshen them up, brush their hair, find clean bibs and socks.

Her success as a mother was on trial here but Edward's kisses had sent her off balance; she feared she wasn't taking this as seriously as she ought to be. She must be careful. She must be on guard.

The atmosphere round the table was easy. Edward's eyes caught Shelley's and again she felt that rush of excitement and prayed that nobody else could feel it. It was hard to believe that the energy between them wasn't a visible, electric-blue charge.

She was pleased to see her boys sitting waiting politely for the soup to be served, their faces semi-clean. Incredible. They weren't messing with their bread rolls, not like they usually did at home, chucking bits across the table so she had to scream at them from the kitchen with everything getting on top of her and Julie bawling from upstairs. Mind you, John's presence at the head of the table did have a cautionary effect; even Shelley sometimes felt like a child when she caught his disapproving eye, so steely under its matching grey brow.

Everything here was so well organized.

Everything seemed to go to plan.

Doreen Blennerhasset asked her, 'How are you coping with the cold up here?'

'It does take a bit of getting used to,' Shelley admitted, careful not to make it sound like an ungrateful criticism.

'The children don't seem to notice,' said Alex, slurping away down her end of the table.

'The kids have never been fitter,' Shelley agreed, dunking bits of bread for Julie, making sure she didn't stuff her mouth and dribble it out in the way she liked.

'It's such an ideal environment for them,' said Doreen, breaking off bread with delicate fingers

303

which bore no rings, and the nails no polish. 'It must be tempting for you busy mums,' she went on, 'to leave them here with dear Eunice and let her get on with her splendid work unhindered.'

'I'm sorry?' Shelley didn't quite catch her meaning.

'Well.' Doreen paused politely while swallowing a spoonful of the utterly delicious and creamy soup. 'It's been done before.' She smiled, she was joking. The smile cracked through her powdery make-up and split the pale lipstick round her mouth. 'I remember two occasions when the parents of some of our children upped and left, having reasoned, no doubt, that their offspring were better off here.' She turned to her friend Eunice. 'What happened to the Watmo children? There were three of them, weren't there? If I remember rightly they were adopted.'

'By a lovely couple,' said Eunice, handing round the basket of rolls.

'And the Slades? Those terrible twins.' Doreen tapped her forehead to demonstrate the twins' screwed-up mental states. 'Their mother came once and never came back.'

'Disgraceful woman,' said Eunice.

'Every time I come I look round and realize we could easily have lost more parents. If I had been blessed with children I think I'd have been tempted to leave them here with all the benefits of this country life. Good food, fresh air, sunshine, solid family relationships and as much love as they could ask for.'

Shelley asked, 'What happened to the twins?'

Doreen frowned. 'Do you remember, Eunice? It was such a long time ago.'

'They were fostered on a long-term basis by that nice headmaster and his wife . . . came from North Devon. They still pop a note in with their card at Christmas.'

This conversation struck Shelley with the force of a poisonous dart. Yes, it was true, in her dreams she had imagined how it would be if she just upped and fled, leaving Joey to his fate, her children in this perfect environment; the temptation to flee the whole situation and disappear somewhere where she wasn't known had crossed her mind more than once. How often she'd longed for escape from this turmoil. An open door. A train ticket to somewhere. She could well understand the feelings of mothers under unbearable stress who had visited here, seen the transformation of their hellish kids, and taken the enormous step of opting out, calling it a day. Given up the struggle which too often seemed so defeating.

Would they be better off without her?

When Shelley came to move on what would she have to offer her kids? If she was lucky she could sell her house, pay off some of the mortgage and buy a small one up north somewhere where prices were lower and opportunities fewer.

Education would probably be on a par.

Violence and crime would be worse.

In order to survive she would have to find some kind of work, which meant the kids would be farmed out. She would come home nights exhausted, money would be short, the creation of any kind of happy home life would be an uphill struggle.

And Joey?

What difference did it make to Joey having his useless mum hanging around? The experts were in charge of him now and whatever happened it looked as though he was in for a custodial sentence. Would he feel abandoned if she scarpered without a forwarding address? He displayed such anger towards her anyway, what difference would pissing off make?

But although these thoughts had arrived unwanted from time to time, Shelley never seriously imagined she could abandon her kids, not even in paradise. One look at their faces was enough to convince her. They loved her, no matter how useless or inadequate she might be, and she loved them with a love so fierce it was painful, a permanent ache round her heart.

Even when she was screaming at them, belting them round their dirty legs, sneaking out of the house for a half-hour without them, cursing them, smacking them, dragging them squalling round supermarkets, yes, even at those times when she hated them it was a hatred dominated by a ferocious love.

So there must have been something very wrong with those parents who had left their kids here and never returned. Not only those little ones whom Doreen and Eunice remembered so fondly; Dillon Dukes's mother had also disappeared without trace, Edward had told her that. She wondered about that other no-hoper, Shane Duffy, married with a kid. The Boltons had made such progress with him, did his mum stick around?

Was everyone secretly expecting Shelley to throw in the towel?

Just go?

Like the others?

This idea upset her terribly. But then she thought of what Edward had said: 'You can't compare yourself to those mothers. You love your children, that's plain to see.'

After lunch Doreen, Alex and Eunice sat round the table drinking tea.

The men returned to work.

The giant paint set was brought out, newspapers were spread on the table and the children got to work on their art. Shelley would never have put up with this mess in her own house at Eastwood, but Eunice seemed perfectly happy to see little Casey up to his elbows in paint, to see Saul artistically daubing Jason's face green, to watch the jam jar of water topple over and calmly wipe the spill dry with a cloth. At home Shelley insisted on plastic aprons, tiny brushes, a non-spill water container and a paintbox full of calm watercolours.

Here the paints came in squirting tubes and were thick and rich in colour and texture. Eunice sneered at painting books and lopped down sheets of old wallpaper which they tore and messed up. She did draw the line, thank God, at Julie, who played propped up on the floor with a panful of water instead. Washing-up water with bubbles.

Shelley could hardly concentrate when her kids were mucking about like this, her nerves were at screaming pitch. Eunice, however, was chatting unworriedly to her old buddy Doreen, while Alex listened and made the occasional comment.

Shelley felt out of it.

She was the odd one out.

The client.

She was relieved she'd be gone in a minute, off for her daily visit to Lister. That would allow them to chew the fat and say what they really thought.

Write their reports.

Make their plans.

Screw up her life if they wanted.

And Edward?

Was there a future for Shelley and Edward? Or was this a quickie in the dark? Dare she take his attentions seriously or did he see her as an easy lay, so convenient he didn't have to go out? Did he guess that a poor cow like her would be grateful for anything in trousers? They hardly knew each other, after all, but that hadn't stopped Shelley in the past.

What normal bloke would want to take on a woman reviled by all right-thinking people, a mother of six from three different fathers, a woman who liked her fags and a drink and a raucous night out down the Plymouth clubs? A woman who would not recognize the back end of a heifer if she saw one? Edward was the complete opposite of any of the guys she had been with before. Solemn, hard-working, gentle, sensual, he'd be sick if he knew what she really was. Holed up on the farm it was different. Shelley was nothing like her true self.

But oh how she wished she was an innocent little country girl, blue-eyed, freckled and hair the colour of summer corn, starting out on life and love with a newborn lamb tucked under her arm.

She would be proud to go to him then.

She wouldn't be dragging all this shame behind her. The she-devil who had spawned a son in the way of sea fish and toads.

TWENTY-FOUR

Martin Chandler was a broken man.

He sat in Jonathan Formby-Hart's opulent office and forced his eyes to stay open. Last night, he calculated bitterly, he might have managed two hours' sleep. In spite of the wretched drugs prescribed by an overly casual GP, Jessica's mental condition was worsening. Her mother, June, had arrived as threatened, but that self-righteous piece of work didn't reckon on doing night duty. As far as Martin could see, her only contribution had been some useless floral arrangements in unpleasant greens and browns.

Martin's house was no longer his own.

When he poured himself a welcome-home drink he could feel June's eyes boring into him. When he tried to avoid the washing-up she clattered about so violently in the kitchen he was terrified for their precious crystal. He wished, now, he had succumbed to Jessica's pressure for a dishwasher, but he was against such dubious luxuries; everyone knew how they damaged the silver. Same with a microwave oven. While his wife was at home all day she would enjoy preparing a tasty supper for her hard-working husband.

And it had seemed this was right. Before this descent into madness.

The team sat round the walnut table while severe, grim-faced clerk Maggie Dowson filled them in on the unsolved cases of suspected arson in the area during the last twelve months.

With the help of a computer, on which she was an ace, she had managed to link more than half of those fires suspected to have been started by juveniles to the times Joseph Tremayne and his friends had bunked off school. The defence teams dealing with Joseph's fellow conspirators had been quick to cooperate once Maggie pointed out the benefits of concentrating on this angle. Their four clients, accused of the less appalling crime of aiding and abetting, were happy to spill the beans and Maggie produced a list of the dates, times and places those kids remembered starting fires.

It was looking good.

But neither the Lessings nor Long nor Mason had changed their accounts of the crime itself. It was Joseph Tremayne who had thrown the accelerant, it was Joseph Tremayne who had thrown the lighter. When questioned on the essential point of whether their friend had known the pram was occupied, none of them seemed certain.

Joey had been in the lead, Joey had spotted the pram, the act had been committed before they had time to catch up properly. They had been on their way to torch a vandalized reject of a van which was crouching without tyres on a piece of waste ground behind Safeways.

'*In broad daylight?*'

The necessity of this question and its casual answer showed just how impossible it was proving to police the behaviour of louts round here.

'We need a new statement from Joseph,' boomed Formby-Hart from behind his cigar. 'His mother has been advised by Lee to speak to him about these matters and encourage the boy to change his story.'

'His mother's a waste of time,' said Chandler.

Formby-Hart raised Denis Healey eyebrows. 'You're not keen on the woman then, Martin?'

'You should see the rest of her scummy brood.'

'One of those, is she?' asked Miranda, Formby-Hart's elegant pupil, her bracelets tinkling as she raised one delicate wrist. 'I rather liked her. But then I don't know her as well as you do.'

'She's a type,' said Chandler, slurring his words. 'Hitler was bloody well right when he hit on sterilization for those with a non-existent IQ.'

'She didn't strike me as particularly thick,' said pretty Miranda in Shelley's defence, expecting some kind of enlightenment.

'She's a mess,' was the only response Martin could come up with in his weakened, exhausted state. His eyes had a blue-black bruised look around them, his hair flopped untidily over his eyes and Miranda noticed a stain on his shirt. The stain was milky baby-sick, a reminder of his efforts to burp his fractious baby daughter. Jessica's mother, June, had approached him in the hall, carrying a napkin on which she spat copiously in order to erase the stain with a gob of saliva. He had pushed her off in disgust, deciding the stain would have to remain.

'Well, we all know Tim Lee's opinion of Joseph's true mental condition,' said Formby-Hart dourly, 'but we must keep that under our hats. This is not a good time to go bandying the word psycho about. And anyway, psychopath is a label not applicable to children of Joseph's age.'

'That damn mother of his is more than a sandwich short of a picnic,' said Chandler. 'Listen to this. Ms Tremayne has requested, in all seriousness, that Joey should be given an opportunity to reform with a spell on some blasted farm in the care of a foster mother who she feels would be good for him. *I ask you.* As if any judge worth his salt is going to agree to that. Why don't we send the sod to Barbados? Or a safari might be more appropriate. Ms T. seems battily unfazed by the enormity of her son's crime.'

'Self-protection, that's all,' said Miranda sweetly. 'You'd just want to deny it, wouldn't you? If he was yours? Imagine . . .'

But nobody round the table could.

More birdlike than normal in her flat-chested grey sweater, so tight the bones of her arms showed through, Maggie Dowson mused, 'Is she talking about the Boltons by any chance?'

Chandler was sweating now. If he could just find a bed with cool sheets and get his head down on that pillow . . . 'That whole wretched family are staying with the Boltons right now. But I haven't a clue where the farm is. It's all very hush-hush, understandably.'

'We were involved in a case around six years ago when we defended a young client who ended up there,' said Maggie. 'Shane Duffy. Hard as iron. Street-raised and streetwise; only fourteen, I think. The Boltons were recommended highly by the probation department. The court took a risk and sent him there.'

'And?' asked Formby-Hart with impatience, consulting his heavy gold wristwatch. Joseph Tremayne would be lucky if he set foot in green fields for the next ten years. This conversation was irrelevant.

'And,' continued Maggie Dowson, her serious fingers drumming the table, 'and those foster parents wrought a miracle – not for the first time, I'm told.'

'It's the parents who should be punished,' slurred Chandler.

'Making them appear in court beside their luck-less offspring is one step in the right direction,' said Miranda. 'And compulsory parenting classes.'

'Parenting classes my arse,' said Chandler.

'Duffy's mother was fined, I believe,' Maggie Dowson went on, pleased that her memory was still so sharp. 'But they never collected the money because she legged it before the courts could act. Duffy drives buses now; he was driving the number six to Mutley last time I used it. A completely reformed character. He's got his own little family, too.'

314

'God help them,' muttered Chandler out of the depths of his soggy dream.

Shelley was appalled when Joey started listing the times and dates that he and his mates had lit fires during time off school.

His fascination with fire had caused him to burn his own arms. He showed her the old blister scars, cunningly hidden inside so even when he wore T-shirts it would be hard to identify them amid the bruises and general grot. It reminded her of a rap, the rhythmic way he confessed to his idiotic behaviour.

How had she never suspected?

And the fires! Dear God, so many! She would have smelled smoke on his clothes, wouldn't she?

'I always took my jacket off,' he said, seemingly unashamed of the dangerous habits he had developed.

'But the smoke would have got on your sweat-shirts surely?'

'Well, you didn't smell it, did you, *so why are you ranting on about that?*'

It was more than depressing every day fat Eric let her in and she found Joey listlessly passing the time, either lounging across his bed in his private room or out in the larger dormitory where Eric allowed him to skateboard hour after hour.

She worried about the lack of fresh air or proper exercise. Surely the powers that be could organize some time outside, well away from the other inmates? But Joey's private time in the gym was meant to compensate for all that and his brain was certainly being stretched to its limit because of the regular lessons he had, one to one with his teachers. There was no bloody way he could skive off here, or sit at the back drawing porny pictures.

He must have done more schoolwork in the last week than he'd ever done in his life before.

His forehead wound was beginning to dry up a little, and Shelley was pleased to be able to tell him that his dad's condition was stable. Neither of them mentioned her outburst last time she visited but she was keen for Joey to know that she didn't blame him for Kenny's attack, or for his family's homelessness. Both those unfortunate consequences of his disgraceful behaviour were unforeseen and not his fault. Eunice had been mortified to hear that Shelley, in temper, had accused her son of having caused such terrible misfortunes, but in her heart of hearts Shelley knew that Joey would not have been wounded by this in the way most kids would.

Joey had always had the ability to cut himself off from pain. Even as a small child. And he'd always found it difficult to imagine himself in another's shoes. This was the reason why, in spite of pressure from her three eldest sons, she had refused point blank to have pets in her house. Something warned her this would be a mistake.

Nothing to put your finger on, just intuition, that was all.

The only animals her kids knew were the wicked Alsatians who lived next door and they could give as good as they got. That was partly why Shelley found it so wonderful that her kids were involved in farm life. The calves, the lambs, the pigs, the chickens and the four sheepdogs – they loved them all and they had that natural rapport with them that she wasn't at all sure Joey would feel. But under the influence of the Bolton men, maybe Joey's gentleness would flourish.

It had worked for Dukes and Duffy. Dukes had even chosen a career in caring for animals.

So here was Joey, at long last, telling his mother about what happened on 6 February, that fatal Wednesday afternoon. Yes, the five of them had been on their way to start a fire. There was a van behind Safeways they'd had their eye on for some time and they thought it would go up 'wicked like'.

She thought of her own childhood, the time she discovered the Famous Five in a second-hand bookshop and gradually read through them all. Enid Blytons were banned at her school so she was even keener to read them. She hid them under the covers at night the same as she hid *The Story of O*. She wasn't sure which book Iris would be more angry about if she caught her reading by torchlight. Shelley used to dream, in her loneliness, that she was part of a group like the Famous Five, having adventures, being close.

Joey was part of an Infamous Five. Had the closeness been something to do with it all?

'Was it your idea, Joey?'

'I was the leader of that lot.'

'So it was your idea to bunk off school?'

'I didn't have to force anyone.'

'And that's why you needed the paraffin?'

'Darren wouldn't do it, so I did.'

Shelley slowed down here. She felt herself wincing even before her son could give his answer. 'And then you suddenly saw the pram?'

'It looked empty to me.'

'How could the pram look empty when the hood was up and there were blankets, too?'

'Nobody leaves their kids outside shops. You never do. You lug them inside.'

'*But why, Joey, why?* You'd decided to go for the van. Why change your mind like that? And wasn't there a tiny moment when it might just have sodding occurred to you that there might be a baby inside?'

Joey scowled and irritatingly picked up his Gameboy. He tapped the buttons with urgency so as to avoid Shelley's eyes and then said, 'I don't remember what I thought. I don't know why I changed my mind.'

'Once you said it would be good fun to see a fire in the precinct with so many people about because it might spread to the shops and be a laugh,' Shelley reminded him, longing to snatch that damn game from his fingers. 'But didn't it click that everyone would know who did it? You didn't even bother to hide your face. I just can't understand you being so bloody daft.'

'You!' he spat. '*You never understand.*'

'How can you say that? You can't believe that?' She thought of the hours she had spent trying to reason with him from the time he first started walking.

'*It's always been the others, not me.*'

What a load of childish crap. This accusation was so bloody unjust it left Shelley speechless. If anything, she had abandoned the others in order to minister to Joey first. He had to be the centre of attention. His needs had to be satisfied quickly. He was the eldest and the strongest, the other kids tiptoed around him. He was in charge of the remote control. It never mattered what the others might want. Even she gave in to Joey in order to keep the peace.

She wondered how Eunice would have dealt with this. Would she have snuffed it out from the start?

'So you're going to cooperate with DI Hudson when he visits tomorrow?' She wanted to hear him confirm this promise.

'Yeah, yeah, yeah . . .'

'He's been told that you're going to change your statement and I'll be here to help you.'

'Yeah, yeah.'

'And we're pleading guilty to manslaughter but asking for your condition to be taken into account, and promising that you'll submit to treatment until they reckon you're cured,' she reminded him. 'You do understand all this, Joey, don't you?'

He didn't bother to answer. He was slouched more deeply in his chair, still pressing those bloody buttons.

'A lot of people are trying to help you,' said Shelley, raging with anger inside but determined not to end this visit on the same furious note as the last. 'And with luck Chandler thinks you won't be inside too long,' she added. But she left out the probability that Joey would be confined in a secure hospital. God knows what he'd do if he knew they were saying he was off his head. As it was, he was threatening to abscond at the first opportunity. Her son was on some other planet – either that or refusing to face reality.

Before she left him she risked the question she'd been wanting to ask since this hell began. 'Do you ever think about Holly Coates?'

He moved his quick fingers from the buttons. His lashes came down over his eyes, hiding those windows like soft sweeps of curtain. She saw his small body tense all over and half wished she hadn't asked the question.

'*Yes,*' he whispered, '*I think about her.*'

'Does that make you feel unhappy?'

'Yes.' He chewed on his finger. 'Sometimes it does. Sometimes I talk to her at night, when it's dark.'

'What would you say to Holly, Joey, if you got the chance?'

'I'd say I was sorry and that I wouldn't ever do it again.'

He allowed her to put her arm round his thin, boyish shoulder. 'I wish you could talk to the police like this, or Chandler, or Alex. You see, none of these people understand just how sorry you are. They only see the side of you that makes them think you don't care . . .'

'*Well, I do care, so fuck them . . .*' and those

dark curtain-lashes blinked tears from his wounded eyes.

'Oh Joey. *Joey. Joey.* You can be such a lovely little boy. Why must you pretend . . . ?'

'I want to come home.'

She looked away. At the bars on the windows. 'I know you do, sweetheart.'

'I want to see Julie.'

'She'd like to see you, too.'

'Is she walking yet?'

Shelley swallowed hard. She forced a smile. The smile hurt her heart. 'No, still trying to sit up.'

'She'll be walking when I see her again.'

'Yes, Joey love, I guess she will be.'

TWENTY-FIVE

No, Shelley was not sticking her nose into other people's business as Eunice made out so bluntly.

This is how it came about.

After a boring evening spent in the sitting room pretending to read with Eunice knitting on one side and John flicking through the latest *Farmers Weekly* on the other, Shelley went to bed early, fed up with waiting for Edward. He and Oliver were lambing in the barn and there was no way Shelley could get over there without Eunice knowing, and something told Shelley that the farmer's wife would not be amused if she knew what was going on right under her strawberry nose.

Shelley's plan was to try later when the family were asleep. The thought of his arms holding her again, the sight and the smell and the sound of him were like opiates; already she was an addict. The guilt at having the space inside her for feelings as strong as these when her son was jailed and her children homeless didn't do much for her self-esteem, but Edward's caresses were too powerful to resist. OK, she was weak.

Shelley didn't have to be strong when Edward was around.

She needed another blanket – or two. She should have asked Eunice earlier but she had forgotten. In spite of Eunice's hot-water bottle Shelley had started waking at dawn and lying in bed with her teeth chattering, driven almost mental by a thousand anxieties which stung like red ants. She couldn't even toss and turn because she was so cold she had to stay curled in the same position.

She made her way up the back stairs and onto the second landing of the rambling farmhouse where she'd seen a stout, oak blanket box. This part of the house was used for storage, the rooms unswept, the beds unmade, the mattresses down to their buttons and springs. The wooden floors squeaked and bowed slightly as she moved over them.

Damp or death-watch beetle, most probably.

Shit. No blankets, just a mess of junk ... Not even when she delved underneath could she feel the stout material she was after. But a photograph album balanced on top caught Shelley's eye. Maybe if she took that with her and returned it before anyone knew, she would learn more about Edward as a child and the Boltons in their younger days, and see images of Dartmoor that so far had evaded her owing to the foul weather and the fear of wandering too far from the farm.

There was still the overriding fear that the lynch mob would root out her sanctuary and the pack would descend baying for blood.

The album would give her something to focus on, so that getting to sleep might be less of an ordeal tonight. She was finding books impossible to read, her concentration shot.

Hugging the bottle and the album to her, she scurried back to her room where Julie was well covered up and sleeping soundly. She turned on the small bedside lamp. She left her socks and her sweatshirt on and bundled herself into her dressing gown before sliding between the ice-cold sheets. She could have had a bath – at home that would have been the answer – but by the time you got out of the few inches of hot water the farmhouse geyser provided, dried yourself on a rock-hard towel and slithered around on the broken lino you were back to shivering all over again.

How could anyone live like this? Surely the Boltons weren't short of dosh. Even her room was carpetless, with just a thin rag rug on wooden boards.

When she turned the first page she saw her mother.

She saw her mother as a girl on a swing.

She saw her mother with Eunice Bolton, both in plaits and gym tunics.

Jesus Christ. Was this a dream?

What the shit was going on here?

She left all thoughts of the cold behind and stared at the black and white photographs in shocked disbelief. She had seen old photographs of her mother so this didn't pose a problem, and Eunice could be identified because her whole childhood was here, and in adolescence the similarities to the grown woman were obvious.

But how could this be Iris? This had to be some other child, the spitting image of Iris. There was no way she and Eunice could possibly have known each other, the coincidence was too bloody fantastic. And why hadn't Eunice told Shelley? She'd had enough opportunity. Shelley had rambled on for hours about her own past and Kilmar Hill, the Cornish hamlet where Iris grew up. What little Iris had told her of the place had stuck in Shelley's memory. So Eunice, this Devonshire farmer's wife, had once lived in Cornwall?

Knew her mother?

And by the look of the photographs had been close friends with Iris?

Maybe that was why the Boltons had volunteered to take Shelley's kids when they heard of their plight. Maybe Eunice had made enquiries, discovered that the Tremaynes were related to her old friend Iris and volunteered to take them, payback time or something?

This tattered, neglected photograph album went way back before Edward's birth. It belonged to Eunice. It was a record of her childhood. There were some baby pictures loose in a flap at the front. There was no sign, in those early days, that Eunice was going to turn into the troll-like figure she presented now.

Shelley fought to remember, lying back on her damp-stained pillows and concentrating with all her might.

Had Iris ever mentioned a girlhood friend called Eunice? Sod it, her mother had spoken so little of those unhappy times. Would Eunice know if Shelley's grandparents were still alive in Kilmar Hill, if she had uncles, aunts perhaps, cousins, a whole family she'd never known?

This discovery was breathtaking. If she wanted any sleep tonight the Valium bottle would have to come out.

Over the next few hours Shelley's anxieties multiplied when she tried to puzzle out what reason on earth Eunice Bolton might have for keeping this weird secret to herself. It was right out of the question that Eunice would not have registered the name of the hamlet. And 'Tremayne' might be common in Cornwall, but hardly when linked to Kilmar Hill.

Clearly there must be something Eunice was keen to keep from her.

Not only Eunice, but her husband as well. John had heard Shelley talking about her mother's miserable past.

Did Edward know?

Were they all in on it?

Were they mad?

Shelley pored over the photographs, stroking the images. Were they real?

The friendship of Iris and Eunice appeared to last into their teenage years. There were pictures of them with satchels, in uniform, standing by a windy bus stop, obviously on their way to school. Their home clothes consisted of old-fashioned skirts and blouses which must have been bought from a jumble sale. Even in those days surely fashions weren't that dull? Maybe this was all part of the strict religious code the inhabitants of the hamlet and nearby villages lived by?

No make-up. No high heels. No fancy hair-styles. As they grew older the two girls wore their hair short, pudding-basin style.

But why the hell had Eunice said nothing?

Shelley shivered. It wasn't the cold that affected her now. It was the dangers of time travel, the sight of a place that until now she had only imagined. Her mother never said a good word about it. Now Eunice could finally tell her all she needed to know.

Shelley waited until after breakfast, until the children were occupied and the men were out about the farm.

'Why didn't you tell me you knew my mother?'

Eunice's benign eyes narrowed. 'What are you talking about?'

Shelley produced the photograph album. 'This is what I'm talking about.'

'What a nerve you've got, going nosing and poking about in my private things.'

Shelley calmly explained how she'd come across it, how she'd been intrigued to see more of the Boltons' family life . . .

Eunice bellowed, enraged. 'But you must have realized at once that this was my personal property and nothing to do with so-called family life?'

Eunice's anger was unnerving. This was the

327

anger she'd always sworn she kept under control, particularly when dealing with children. Shelley could see why. She was frightening. She appeared to grow larger, her pale eyes almost disappearing between the folds in her forehead and cheeks. Her lips thinned and she blew out like a toad.

But Shelley could not back down on this one. *'How could I sodding put it down once I'd seen my mum?'*

'Your language is revolting.'

'This is more important than language,' Shelley blasted back. *'Why, Eunice, why did you keep this from me?* And don't tell me you didn't connect our name and the name of the hamlet where you must have grown up alongside Iris.'

'I resent your intrusion into my private life.'

'And I bloody well resent the fact that you have been deceiving me. Jesus Christ, there I was blabbing on about Mum and Cornwall, and you knew all along. Was that why you decided to take us in? I need to know, Eunice. And I'll not give up till I sodding well do.'

Eunice's stare was menacing now. If Shelley hadn't been high on resentment she would have slunk away in defeat. 'I'd rather forget that time in my life,' said Eunice with a growl in her voice.

Shelley knew she was pushing her luck. She almost expected a physical attack. She'd have stood no chance in a spat like that. 'In that case I will have to ask John.'

'I ought to have known there'd be trouble from you,' said Eunice spitefully, her large fists clenched by her sides. 'Like mother, like daughter.'

'I am nothing like my mother,' Shelley defended herself. 'You knew Iris, so you must know that.'

'Your mother was a whore,' Eunice spat. 'And if I were you I would leave it at that.'

'I'm not going to do that,' said Shelley, striving for calm in spite of her thumping heart.

'Your mother was a disgrace to her sex.'

What outdated claptrap was this? 'Whore' and 'disgrace'? Shelley was tempted to laugh, but Eunice's angry, orange face and those mean little eyes prevented her. She slid out a chair and sat down at the table, demonstrating to Eunice that she wasn't prepared to leave until her demands were satisfied.

'OK, she was a disgrace to her sex. So now you've got to tell me why.' The very idea that the strait-laced Iris, the law-abiding, man-hating, flat-heeled Iris who demonstrated kitchen mixers in the basement at Dingles, could ever have been a 'disgrace to her sex' was so bizarre it was laughable. Where was all this shit coming from? It smacked of a sick and bygone age.

As far as Shelley knew, the reason poor Iris had been banned from the hamlet was because she chose to marry Liu Qi and this was because of the nationalistic, small-minded zealotry of her family who believed their wind-blasted paradise should be independent from the rest of the land. She had relayed all this to Eunice, and Eunice had not contradicted her.

In fact, Eunice had had the gall to criticize these pockets of religious intolerance, scornful of their refusal to bring in hay on a Sunday and their love of fanatical alleluia meetings. Now Shelley knew that Eunice had strong Cornish connections, it was easy to identify and compare small burrs and rolls in her accent, the occasional local inflection that Iris used to use. She'd been living in Devon for so many years these clues were only apparent when you knew what you were listening for.

Eventually Eunice sat down beside Shelley, still puffing with fury but resigned to giving some answers. 'Like Iris,' she began, her big hands overlapped round her mug, 'I was born in Kilmar Hill just off Bodmin Moor. God knows it was a backward place in those early years. Poor as church mice, we were; you read about childhoods like ours and you're hard-pushed to believe it. But that was what it was like fifty years back. We worked from four years old on. We were lucky if we went to school but Iris and I, we went. We started the junior school together and went on to the secondary away in Launceston.'

Shelley listened open-mouthed as Eunice recounted some of the many deprivations they suffered, some caused by sheer poverty, others by the Wesleyan chapel where their families worshipped. 'I can understand why Iris rarely spoke about it,' she said. 'Ours wasn't the kind of childhood you want to dwell on with fond memories. But we were best friends, we confided in each other, we trusted each other, we supported each other' – her face turned harder – 'and then that Iris got herself pregnant.'

'*Me?*'

'You. But the slag wasn't married.'

'*But I thought . . .*'

'Well, this is the kind of surprise you get when you go delving into other people's belongings,' declared Eunice, puffed up and gratified.

'So she got pregnant and married my father?' Shelley wasn't too fazed by that. Her children were all bastards, she was a bastard, so what?

Eunice brought her big face closer. Now her eyes were beady, hard as glass. 'You don't have a clue, you young ones, do you? *You have no idea.* You sleep with who you like, you shove two fingers up at authority, you drink till you drop, you take what benefits you can grab, your kids screw up, you rid yourselves of your unborn babies like you'd rid yourself of leeches. Well, it wasn't like that in Kilmar Hill, m'dear, I can tell you. It wasn't remotely like that.' Eunice blustered on in that manic vein, getting herself in a helluva state. In the end Shelley stopped her.

'So it wasn't because of Liu Qi that my mum was hounded out?' Shelley asked. 'It was because she got herself up the duff?'

'Iris had sinned. She was ostracized wherever she went. She was cut off from the church, she was thrown out of her home and left on the street with nothing, not even a small bag of essentials.'

'Where did she go?' Shelley asked.

'I never heard from her again. If I'd kept in touch with that harlot I would have been tainted in the eyes of the whole community. But from what you tell me she went to find Liu Qi and he took her in.' Eunice seemed lost in some dark

331

memory. She finished bitterly, 'After Iris left, the discipline that governed our lives was increased a hundredfold.'

'If you were under such tight control then how did Iris meet Liu Qi in the first place?'

'His father ran a small caravan site near Camelford, a rubbishy place, it didn't survive.' Iris and Eunice had met Liu Qi loitering outside the local shop. 'She picked him up,' said Eunice, 'the hard-faced tart. It was all secrecy and slyness after that. I was sometimes dragged into it, but I never lied for her, I refused.'

The saddest part of this story was surely the way Iris's friend had abandoned her in her time of need and even now looked back on Iris through the eyes of the church she had rejected. Even the language went back to those days. Whore, sinful, harlot. Maybe she was still writhing in anger a good thirty years later because of the stand the church took after Iris's horrible fall from grace. It was possible that the rage of the righteous had fallen on Iris's friend and companion. What Eunice said next confirmed Shelley's guesses.

'I was her friend,' said Eunice bleakly, 'so I was tarred with the same brush. I was an example to any others who might be tempted to the wayward path to hell. I was exorcized in front of the whole congregation. I was held down naked and subjected to extremes of baptism in cold water followed by baths of steam. They chanted over me day and night to drive the devil out of my body. I was kept awake when I longed to sleep. My arms were lashed to my sides so that I couldn't

332

"touch myself". These days I could sue. It was torture.' Eunice's ungainly head fell heavily on her large hands. 'And I don't want to speak of it any more.'

A boulder of silence lay heavily between them.

Was it any wonder that poor Iris had turned into a nervous, neurotic woman who daren't say boo to a goose and yet was so fearful for her own daughter's moral decline? Unlike her friend Eunice, she had not dared to reject the church, not completely. But Iris's church, the church she attended so regularly and pushed the young Shelley into doing the same, was a gentle church, a forgiving church, a world away from those Cornish hellmongers.

But still Shelley's overriding concern remained unanswered. 'You must have known who we were when you volunteered to foster the kids,' she said. 'If you still feel such hatred towards Iris why would you put yourself out for us?'

Eunice's face did a violent manoeuvre directed towards pulling it together. She sniffed. She straightened her humpty back. 'I was talking to Doreen on the telephone when the name Tremayne slipped out. I asked myself . . . I said it can't be. For the rest of my life that name will haunt me. But the reason I rang the social services was nothing to do with that; it was the plight of the kids that convinced me I had to do something to help. I couldn't know you were related until you started to talk about Iris and Kilmar Hill. There must be thousands of Tremaynes dotted around this country. I couldn't know you were

Iris's daughter. Believe me, that came as a shock but by the time I realized who you were it didn't seem all that important. I didn't want to bring all that up. That part of my life is something I still have to struggle hard to forget.'

'And my kids can't be blamed for who they are?'

'The children are never to blame.'

Shelley said, 'But you blamed Iris . . .'

'She was not a child. She was a young woman of seventeen with a sensible head on her shoulders.'

'She used to be your friend. Are you normally so unforgiving?'

Eunice didn't hesitate before coming back with her answer. 'Some behaviour is unforgivable.'

And Shelley didn't need to ask to know which behaviour, in Eunice's eyes. After her hideous, hell-fire-and-damnation experiences it wasn't at all surprising that kindness to children in distress was one of Eunice's most sacred laws and that anyone who broke that law was doomed to roast in eternal flame.

No wonder Eunice was so bloody odd.

TWENTY-SIX

The meeting at Dudley Park went well. Joey, for once, behaved himself and his defence team could now begin to prepare their course of action. Everyone was there, the cops, the social services, the shrink Tim Lee, the governor and Joey's personal officers. To her enormous relief Shelley hardly had to speak. She was just so glad that something was coming together at last even if it might mean a custodial sentence for Joey. A sentence which, she was assured by the shrink, wouldn't be half as long, and would mean care in an appropriate place, once their plea was considered.

Shelley was uneasy, still puzzling over the extra-ordinary coincidence that had brought her family and the Boltons together. When you thought about Iris and Eunice and their shared ordeals in the past, it seemed too weird to be accidental. Fate doesn't work like that, Shelley thought, but Eunice insisted she'd had no idea of the connection when first she volunteered herself as a foster mother to Shelley's kids.

Sadly, but understandably, Eunice had never returned to the hamlet of Kilmar Hill once she'd met John and made her escape across the Tamar. She couldn't enlighten Shelley about her extended family. Eunice didn't even know if her own parents were still living. 'What's more, I don't care,' she said. 'I've got my own little family now, and your lads and little maid to look after. I couldn't be happier.'

It must have been devastating for Eunice when she found that she couldn't have kids of her own. Shelley would have liked to talk about this with her, but Eunice wasn't the type to open up unless forced to do so. The fact that she and John had chosen to adopt three- and four-year-old kids instead of babies proved just how much they cared. Edward and Oliver, from the same dysfunctional family, could have been ready-made toddlers from hell. Eunice and John had taken that gamble and luckily for them it had paid off.

After the meeting Shelley popped in for a few words with the Dudley Park governor, David Barker. 'How did you find Joey this morning?' he asked.

'A little quiet. A bit subdued.'

'I think that at last he's beginning to face up to the reality of his circumstances.' Barker offered her coffee. She refused. They wouldn't be long and her lift was waiting for her outside. 'When this happens to our lads we tend to get problems,' he said calmly.

Shelley leaped to attention. *Oh no, not more shit. What was that bloody kid up to?*

'The boys come in here, it's a shock to the system, their defences are working overtime. They need to adapt to their new surroundings, work out ways to survive, find out where they fit in the hierarchy. Not Joey of course – he's on his own. But the same dilemmas beset them all and in Joey's case he's begun to accept that his future won't be quite so rosy as he might have liked.'

'*So?*' What was this beating about the bush?

'He's depressed. He's stopped eating. He's cut down his activities. He lies on his bed for most of the day, he won't talk to his personal officers.' Barker paused, shaking his head. 'Time goes slowly for the kids in here, and I think Joey's just beginning to realize how long he's got before his trial.'

This was awful. She should have guessed something like this would happen. 'What can we do to help him?'

'Not a lot. We're keeping a special eye on him obviously—'

Shelley broke in, aghast, 'You don't think he might . . . do something? *You don't think he might hurt himself?*'

Barker was quick to reassure her. 'We're a long way from that yet.'

'*How do you know that?*' Shelley demanded. 'You didn't think he'd be beaten up but he was. You're not bloody God, all-seeing, all-knowing . . .'

'Most of our remand boys are allowed out

occasionally, under careful supervision of course. We find that having something to look forward to can work miracles. It's the bleakness of the present, and the future, which tends to defeat them. They're mostly young men with mental problems and low IQs, still children in lots of ways. Badly damaged children.'

'You think Joey could benefit from a trip outside?'

'Or a treat of some kind. I wanted to ask you.'

'But what about his safety? What if the public found out?'

'We're well used to dealing with sensitive issues like this,' said Barker. 'We have our ways and means of making sure nothing leaks out. But if we did decide on a jaunt for Joey I would have to get permission from the Home Office first. So I can't promise you anything yet.'

'What really worries me,' said Shelley, thinking hard, 'is how these kids feel when they're forced to come back. Treat over. Back to square one. Doesn't everything seem more desolate to them after that?'

'In our experience that isn't the case,' Barker reassured her. 'Particularly if their outing reunites them with friends and family. When this policy works they come back more self-assured. They have a place in the outside world, they are still important to somebody, they're not just worthless rejects who society has shunned for ever.'

'You think that would apply to Joey?'

'Joey's one of the few lucky ones who could take advantage of this kind of therapy. So many of our young offenders don't know where their families are, or come straight from care, or come from abusive backgrounds, or have had the door slammed in their faces. Jocy has five younger siblings, I believe?'

'They're very close,' Shelley enthused. 'He's been asking after them lately.'

'In your opinion would a family outing buck Joey up?'

Shelley fought for breath. If she could just get the Boltons to see little Joey at his best, they might be willing to go to court . . . It was obvious they had enormous influence . . . All the authorities praised them to high heaven. Shelley wasn't being ridiculously over-hopeful, she realized how unlikely this was, but, hell, the slimmest chance was worth taking. 'I do think Joey would love to visit the farm where we're all staying,' she said. 'I've talked to him about it and he asked lots of questions,' she lied. Joey, so self-obsessed, had expressed no interest at all.

'We are particularly lucky to have Dartmoor on our doorstep,' said Barker, 'so it's not too difficult to take some of our lads on jaunts up there. We've been camping, we've been swimming, we've been hiking, even horse-riding. Needless to say, in Joey's case the security measures would have to be tight and nobody must know of our plans. Even after the event complete discretion is essential.'

Shelley was still desperately anxious about Joey's sudden black depression. What if he did . . . hurt himself? He'd burned his arms in the past

339

and she, his mother, hadn't known. Was he likely to cut himself like the nutters she'd seen on TV? Or end up hanging on the end of a rope, not discovered until some cold grey morning?

Dear God, how much worse could this get? What kind of sodding justice was this that an eleven-year-old child could be subjected to these sorts of pressures? Could be made to want to die? Could be made so vulnerable, could be tortured to this extent? Joey's treatment defied all reason.

No matter what David Barker said, Shelley wouldn't be reassured. 'I want someone with him all the time,' she insisted. 'He's afraid of the dark, you know that already. Are you sure they leave a light on in there? And how about Eric? I wasn't going to mention this but Joey told me that Eric made sexual passes at him. Is that guy queer? Is that true? Do you know that and do nothing about it?'

'Please, Shelley. Please.' Barker tried to calm her down with his tone of voice and his soothing expression. 'Eric is not gay. And yes, Joey controls his light himself. And while I can't guarantee that one of his personal officers will stay with him twenty-four hours a day, I can assure you that an almost constant watch will be kept over him.'

What more could she do?

Here she was, fighting for Joey's life, and all they could bring out were platitudes.

If anything happened to Joey she would know for the rest of her life that she'd tried to save him but they hadn't let her.

She stood up.

She marched out.

She didn't answer the governor's goodbye.

She was all out of words, and any action was out of bounds.

If Edward hadn't been waiting for her Shelley didn't know what she'd have done. She didn't care if Eunice was watching, she couldn't give a toss if this was unseemly. His Fiat tractor was scraping up slurry round the back of the barns. Unashamedly she went right over. He stopped in his tracks and opened the door. Shelley climbed into the cab behind him and collapsed.

He drove the tractor into the barn where they were out of sight of the house. He dried up her tears with his kisses. He calmed her fears with common sense. He helped her up the steep steps of hay and they sat on the top together, like children, watching the hens peck at grain down below.

The summer colours of the hay and the smell of mown grass were heady. The vast, corrugated barn roof above them straddled so many tons of the stuff it seemed you could disappear in the gold and never be found again. They were birds nesting together, so that when he slid his hand underneath her jacket and cupped her breast and traced its shape, it felt like the most natural thing in the world. He removed her jacket. Shelley wasn't cold; on the contrary she pulsed with fire. Edward's hand moved and pushed up her sweater; he didn't fumble around like Kenny would, pushing up her bra so it cut her in half, but unclipped it from behind and released her breasts to his gaze.

He kissed her forehead, her cheeks, her chin, he nuzzled his face in her hair. He kissed her breasts, he muttered sweet things, he tantalized her with the tracks of his lips and all the while, breathing hard, she placed her hands against his chest just to absorb the power of him.

She lay back against the hay, against the jacket he had thrown behind her. She lifted her breasts for him, she wanted nothing concealed from his eyes, and then raised her arms above her head, her hips moving provocatively.

'You're beautiful,' he said, smiling, staring at her with admiration.

For the very first time in Shelley's life she felt herself incredibly lovely, soft and warm and desirable. This sensation was new and astonishing. It seemed that Edward was transforming her, making her lovable to her own self. Gone for a while was her crippled esteem. He was fantastic in the powers he possessed.

Between her fingers she felt the crispness of the dark curly hairs on his chest. She smelled his breath and tasted his mouth. She felt the hard muscles of his back as he freed her from her clothing, opening her in readiness for him, touching, stroking, feeling.

Edward was in no hurry. He gazed, he admired and he flattered. When she was burning up with desire he pumped his energy into her and every sensation was so intense she was swept by waves of feeling that rushed through her and filled her with a new erotic longing. Then came a welter of vivid sensation as he drove Shelley onwards towards an almost unendurable bliss.

The lunch bell sounded from the kitchen, followed by Eunice's strident cry. *'It's ready. Come and get it.'*

There was a new tension between Shelley and Eunice since their conversation early this morning. Was it that, or had Eunice guessed what had happened five minutes before in the privacy of the barn?

Was now a bad time to bring up the possibility of a visit to the farm from Joey? Or should Shelley broach it with Edward first and let him deal with his awkward mother?

Shelley was so overwhelmed by emotions – the scare about Joey, Edward's lovemaking – that she wished she could get away from people, be alone for a while with her own crazy thoughts. But how would that be possible? Anyone could be out there with a camera or even a carving knife just waiting for Shelley to show her face. She ought to stay here with her kids and give Eunice a well-earned break; she knew she was lumbering Eunice, taking advantage of her willingness to cope. And worse, she had caused her all sorts of grief by bringing up such unhappy memories.

But still Shelley could not understand how she and Eunice had come together without Eunice knowing who she was. And then all that secrecy crap.

It didn't make sense.

It was just too weird.

She was desperate to get out of this house and away from the tensions inside it.

'I wondered,' she began, 'how safe it would be if I took the kids out for a walk?'

This new plan was so opposite to her normally huddled, warmth-loving, anti-outdoor-activity self, and also such a security risk, that Shelley expected outraged objections, and Edward did look concerned. But to her surprise Eunice encouraged her. 'You go,' she said. 'You could do with some time on your own. I know what that feels like, believe me. Get some colour in those cheeks, m'dear. But leave the children here with me, they're perfectly happy pottering round and the younger ones would just be a nuisance.'

Kez and Saul had already planned to help Oliver castrate the calves. Their fascination with this was disgusting. It had not seemed like a good idea but when Shelley had objected she was shouted down. Well, she supposed, whatever else, they had seen life in the raw in the short time they had spent with the Boltons.

There followed a complicated discussion in which everyone took part. Which was the safest route to take? The five hundred acres of land owned by the Boltons stretched widely over the moor; flat, grey granite slabs led on to distant ridges, just visible when the clouds parted. Little bridges spanned brown streams, Shelley had seen that much from here. She wasn't normally a walker – far from it, she avoided walking whenever she could, she couldn't see the point of it –

but needs must, she had to get out and have some precious time to think.

The general consensus was that if she kept away from the lanes and stuck to the left of the huge stone cross that hung on the horizon, she should be OK.

Wicked thoughts kept intruding.

Maybe, if Edward knew where she was going, he might be able to sneak off and meet her? Surely there must be some broken stone barn where they could be together for once without constant fear of interruption?

She caught his eye; he winked, she smiled.

Ought she to be smiling, ought she to be making love when Joey was so lonely and unhappy? What sort of mother was she? And look how her kids showed no concern when she put on some boots and unhooked her jacket. None of them rushed to her side. None of them volunteered to go with her, not even little Jason who used to be so clingy.

There was no need to go very far, she thought. The ground was more marshy than she'd envisaged. The going was quite hard in places, and surprisingly steep. My God, the men who worked this land must be fit. She watched the dark clouds scudding by like a spectator at a show; she heard the rush of them as they fought out their conflicts among the stones along the tops of the distant tors. A few bedraggled ponies scattered and watched her move on with relieved satisfaction.

If Shelley was hoping for some spiritual

enlightenment, she doubted, now, that she'd find it here. All her energies were directed on her breathing and her slipping socks. She was forced to scramble over some low stone walls and to skirt her way round some kind of mire; she should have seen it earlier, slightly more green than the grass around it, with black stalks sticking up from it.

She had gone much further out than she'd planned. She was heading for a copse – that was her new aim, but whether she would make it was a different matter.

She must give up smoking, she was so unfit. She took a cigarette out and lit it, making several attempts as the wind blew the light out before she could pull sufficiently hard. How she would have managed to cope with the kids through this lot was mind-bending. Eunice, as usual, had been right to keep them at home.

Thoughts of Edward refused to leave her. He was there, gigantic on her mind, giving her extra energy to keep going: all that exhilaration, all that luscious, steamy stuff, she'd never had sex like that before. No, nothing like it. If she reached the copse he would come, if she failed he wouldn't. If she reached the copse they had a future, if she failed they had none. Shelley played these games with herself as she staggered on, puffing grimly.

At last Shelley reached the pathetic, scrubby trees – not a copse, more like a sad accident. She would have sat down but the grass was soaking and the mossy boulders were sharp and uneven, and anyway she needed the view. She scanned the landscape from horizon to horizon, looking for signs of a moving tractor or a small figure in a blue Barbour making his way towards her. Her heart pounded now, but not with the effort. It pounded with the expectations of more of Edward's lovemaking to come.

The high-pitched whistle screamed through her hair.

The bullet thwacked, then passed straight through the tree.

Air burst from her lungs and a light exploded inside her head. Shelley threw herself to the ground, hands clamped against her ears. A mixture of grass and mould and soil pressed into her face, blocking her nostrils and her eyes . . .

A small group of indignant birds flapped and squawked their way to safety.

The impact, just inches away from Shelley's head, meant nothing to her – yet. In bewildered chaos she only turned, wiped her eyes and stared at the wizened tree. With two hands she could circle its spindly trunk, she thought. Look at that clean hole bored right through it . . .

She became aware of somebody frantically shouting, '*Shelley? Shelley? Are you all right?*' Edward's voice coming towards her, and there was John in the distance, two dogs at his heels and a .22 rifle over one shoulder, hurrying in her direction.

Shelley stood up and brushed herself down, still so shaky her knees hardly held her. So Edward was coming after all . . . but so was his father, with a face grim and furious.

'What the hell were you doing stood out here like that, stood against the trees?' John turned to a panting Edward. 'I had no way of seeing her in the shadows like that. *What a fool you are, girl, what a bliddy fool . . .*'

'Shelley, thank God,' was all Edward said as he put his arms tightly round her.

TWENTY-SEVEN

Shelley was marched back to the farmhouse. It was hard to match their masculine strides, and John was cursing her under his breath and Edward battering her with questions. The closeness of her brush with death took time to sink in. But why was Edward blaming her for his father's incompetent and dangerous actions when all she had done was go for a walk?

'Why didn't you stick to the route we agreed on?' Edward demanded over and over. 'What made you stop in that spinney? Didn't you know you were almost invisible to someone on the opposite hill?'

Shit, this was so unjust.

How was Shelley to know that John Bolton in his killing mode would be aiming his rifle at anything that moved? Rabbits, for God's sake, small, helpless rabbits. 'I knew I wouldn't make the cross so I just scrambled over this wall and headed for the nearest landmark, which happened to be those trees,' she insisted, hurt by Edward's anger. It sprang from relief, she realized that and loved him more for his concern and his ridiculous disbelief that she was really completely unhurt and untouched by any ricochet that might have grazed some precious part of her.

'I think I'd know if that had happened.'

'Awareness of pain sometimes comes later,' was Edward's silly response.

Eunice flapped like a bat caught in sunlight. She, at least, raged on at her husband for his foolish and near-lethal mistake. Shelley was pushed into the special chair and a large brandy was thrust into her hand. Her mouth was flaked with soil from the desperate way she'd gone down flat on her face, and her clothes were stained green from moss and wet grass.

'You've the luck of the gods on your side, m'dear,' Eunice insisted. 'If you only knew what an expert shot John is . . .' She turned to her angry husband. 'You must be losing your grip in old age,' Eunice mocked him as he stood there, surly, his gimlet eyes avoiding contact, the muscles in his face hard and tense and stubble darkening his cheeks and chin.

Shelley thanked God that Edward had been making his way towards her when the accident happened, otherwise she would have been left to the less than tender mercies of John. If looks could kill she'd be well dead by now.

Then the arguing world fell silent around her.

She was suddenly alone in this room – alone save for her thoughts.

A freezing splinter of fear pierced her heart.

If Edward had not arrived on the scene . . . if

she hadn't caught his suggestive wink when her walk was being discussed ... if John had had the chance of a second shot ... *if, if, if,* would she still be sitting here now being pampered? Without that secret arrangement of theirs, Edward would have been inside the barn helping Oliver with the calves and unable to hear the gunshot. John could not have known that Edward was outside, approaching the area, when he took aim, fired and missed. John was an ace shot. She must have moved her head just a fraction in the millisecond it took ...

She struggled to shake herself free from these fiendish illusions; they could lead to nothing but madness. But the logical thread of events that brought her to this terrifying conclusion could not be interpreted in any other way.

If these suspicions were true, then this murder attempt must have something to do with Eunice's strange refusal to admit she had known who Shelley was, and that she had been friends with Iris.

It must be the trauma of her dance with death that was driving her thoughts in this crazed direction.

The Boltons, a family highly regarded and trusted by all the caring professions, would be the last people in the world to be involved in violence, let alone death. Over the years their credentials must have been thoroughly investigated. Not only had they adopted two orphans which, even thirty years ago, demanded almost unreachable standards, but they had fostered children on a regular basis. Eunice was the perfect mother, even if her ways were outdated, and John was the ideal hard-working provider and gentle head of the household.

Shelley, in shock, had actually begun to believe that this man had aimed a gun at her head with the intention of blowing her brains out. If Edward hadn't announced his presence, Shelley was in danger of convincing herself, a second shot would have splattered her face all over the trunk of that black, twisted tree.

And then what?

In the distance she heard Eunice say, 'She's in shock. Come on, Shelley, sip some of that brandy.' Like a puppet Shelley obliged before sinking back into the darkness of her warped and nauseating thoughts.

Nobody would have heard.

And if anyone had, they would only imagine that someone was out shooting rabbits or crows.

And if Shelley had failed to return?

Well, Edward would have raised the alarm. But John knew nothing about Shelley's closeness to Edward, and even if Eunice guessed, she couldn't be sure.

Somehow this had to be linked to Eunice's friendship with Iris and her strange desire to keep this fact hidden. Even now, over thirty years on, Eunice despised her old friend and blamed her for the indignities she had suffered after Iris's moral collapse and eviction from church and county.

How safe was she in this house? How safe were her children? Could this be some manic revenge –

could Eunice be avenging the sins of the mother on the dependent daughter? And would John play a part in such screaming madness?

There was now no doubt in Shelley's mind that Eunice knew bloody well who she was when she volunteered her services as foster carer of the Tremaynes.

What if ... what if ... After the second shot did its work John could have picked her up and buried her. With the heavy farm equipment he owned this would have posed no problems. And everyone would have assumed she had done a runner like so many mothers who abandoned their kids when the going got tough, accepting that the Boltons made far better parents than they did.

Eunice had never disguised the fact that she thought Shelley was inadequate. She didn't need words to get her point over. She made it every time the kids sat at the table and ate their meals politely and quietly.

She made it each time they went up to bed without fights and tantrums.

She made it with the freedom she gave them, the way she shoved them outside in the cold and they came in with happy red faces, whenever she competently wiped up their messes, whenever she so lovingly prepared Julie's home-made meals, whenever she ironed their clothes (Shelley never did), whenever she chose those old-fashioned books as opposed to the stories Shelley might read like the Teletubbies or the Tweenies ... *The Water Babies* was last night's choice. It went straight over their heads of course. Far too old and much too sophisticated for kids their age.

The children are innocent.

Mother from hell.

Better off without her.

That was Shelley.

And not only Shelley but most of the other unfortunates who had passed through the Bolton system.

Shelley shivered. She fought for breath as dreadful ideas sowed their seeds in her mind.

'Bed, with a hot-water bottle,' said Eunice. 'See what you've done, you fool,' she said, blaming John. Edward merely sat beside Shelley and stroked her hand and looked anxious.

Numb with fears she could hardly believe, Shelley did not dare let anyone see what she was thinking.

There was just one telephone call she must make before she rejected these outrageous ideas and asked for medical help. But to make the call she must find some privacy.

With a deep breath, and leaning on Edward, she got up from her chair and made her way to her room without speaking, bent and exhausted like an old, old woman.

How could she ever confront Edward Bolton with the malevolence of her thoughts?

She imagined his shock and his pain. He revered his father and mother in the way, she supposed, most countryfolk do, lumbered with their old-fashioned ways. He would reject her out of hand. Never in a million years would he begin to believe such sickening suspicions.

But who would believe Shelley?

Nobody.

She was not in the strongest of positions, not with Joey inside and five kids fostered.

They would lock her up like they had locked up her son.

With hypodermic syringes the experts would chase these demons from her body and her malignant soul.

Thirty minutes later, in her spartan bedroom and clutching the faded pink hot-water bottle, she took out the mobile phone given to her by the police and so far used only in that fateful communication with Malc. This was rather more important but she dreaded its repercussions.

She dialled one nine two. With one eye fixed on the closed door and her hearing attuned to the sound of footsteps in the corridor outside, she asked the operator for the number of the city's main bus depot. The automatic voice came back and Shelley quickly scribbled down the number, thrusting the phone under the covers just like, when a child, she used to thrust her secret reading. Any interruption now might well end in violence – if she was thinking right.

There was a sudden knock at the door. Shelley froze. A shiver of terror travelled up her spine. She whispered, *'Yes?'*

'Just wondered if you were all right?' came Eunice's gruff, manly voice.

'Fine,' was all Shelley could manage.

'You get some sleep now, m'dear,' Eunice told

her. 'Don't you worry about the children.' And her slippered footsteps shushed away.

There she was, half hysterical, trying to get her message through to an impersonal machine of a company dealing with thousands of enquiries a day. She was answered by a recorded message which asked her four inane questions. She was forced to concentrate hard to hit the buttons with quick, jerky movements – the star, the three, then the four – after which a different voice told her that she was in a queue.

The music came on, as she knew it would, a tinny, time-wasting marching tune.

She longed to scream down the phone, '*For God's sake, help me*' – but nobody would have heard, and if they had they would have assumed her to be some kind of sicko joker and cut the connection pretty damn promptly. When, at last, Shelley asked to speak to Shane Duffy she was met with a curt, uninterested 'Who?' She repeated her request. She must not let her constructed calm crumble now and she daren't raise her voice any further; there might well be listeners behind the door.

'He drives your buses,' she tried to explain.

'*Duffy?*'

'Yes, Shane Duffy.'

'How are you spelling that Duffy?'

Shelley's pulse beat at a furious pace as she spelled out the letters without shouting.

A pause, during which she feared she might have been cut off because the music was no longer playing and she had not been advised to hang on.

After an extended lifetime the voice came back, 'Dial this number for a direct line.' And then the phone did go dead.

Shelley's mind now flip-flopped between the desire to dress, creep downstairs and flee for her life, or to make that second essential call. It was thoughts of her children that kept her prisoner in that small, cold, darkening room.

If she was at risk, what about them? There was no previous mention of children disappearing from the Boltons' farm, but that didn't mean they were safe; far from it. If she made that brave bid for freedom, she knew she would be leaving her kids in the care of a couple capable of great evil . . .

Her stomach knotted as once again she picked up the phone which the Boltons could not know she had. Maybe, if she could get through, the result of this call would calm her fears. There was, after all, a bloody good chance these unbelievable ideas of Shelley's sprang from nothing but a natural hysteria caused by the shock of her brush with death.

The door opened suddenly.
Silently.

Shelley just had time to shove the phone down under her covers. Inside her stomach something like terror curled up into a cold, hard ball. She almost retched with the pain of it. Her chest heaved. She knew with an awful certainty that she would not leave this house alive.

Eunice planted herself beside the bed, her heavy

brow furrowed and a vein bulging at her temple. Otherwise her face was a perfect carving in apathy. 'I thought you might be asleep so I just crept in, careful not to wake you.'

'I'm OK,' said Shelley. 'Really I am.'

Eunice stayed where she was for a moment, her hairy arms crossed, her head turning on her thick neck as if there might be something in the room that could give a clue to Shelley's state of mind. However, she seemed satisfied, and said, 'There's been a call from Dudley Park. Someone called Barker says Joey's outing is planned for tomorrow.'

This message from the outside world did more than anything to calm Shelley down. She had completely forgotten to ask Eunice if Joey could come to the farm. Events had overtaken her. She hadn't imagined the visit would be organized so quickly. Now, desperately hoping that Eunice would refuse her request – the last thing she wanted was Joey mixed up in this sodding nightmare – she said, 'I meant to ask . . .'

'That's fine by me,' said Eunice, as if she already knew. 'I shall look forward to meeting him.'

Shelley's stomach lurched.

She listened intently as Eunice closed the door and not until ten minutes later did she attempt her second phone call.

This time she got straight through to the depot canteen.

The voice that answered yelled over the sounds

of clattering crockery, 'Duffy my boy, it's for you.'

One moment later Duffy said, 'Yeah, who is it?'

'I used to be a friend of your mum's,' Shelley started evenly, remembering to keep her voice low and praying the line was a good one. 'I haven't been in touch for some time so I wondered if you could tell me where I could contact her?'

Shelley's heart pounded as she waited for his reply. Everything depended on this, her sanity was at stake here, the safety of her children, *her life* ... Jesus Christ, make him answer before Eunice came creeping back.

'I can't help you there,' said Duffy. 'I haven't seen her for over six years and there's been no news, not that I've heard.'

'I'm so sorry to hear that,' said Shelley, shaking uncontrollably now.

'Don't be, not on my account,' Duffy continued casually. 'I'm much better off without her, and I didn't know she had any friends. She was mostly too high on meths to bother.'

'You stayed with the Boltons for a while?' Shelley ventured, risking five more dangerous minutes to confirm or dismiss her very worst fears.

'Eunice and John, they sorted me out. Mum never really clicked with them.'

'Did she know them well?'

There was a pause while Duffy pondered on who this pushy stranger could be.

'It's OK, I'm a friend of theirs too. I'm staying with them at the moment.'

This explanation of Shelley's seemed like the right button to press. 'Mum stayed with them all the time. Eunice and John were well miffed when she just pissed off without a word.'

'Did anyone try and look for her?'

'What was the point?' said Duffy. 'You knew my mum, once she got on the crack she stayed in shelters or on the streets. She could turn up tomorrow or she could be in clink for all we know.'

'*Or dead?*'

Another pause warned Shelley that maybe she'd gone too far. But then Duffy said, 'No bugger would know.'

'That's what I thought,' said Shelley, pressing the off button on the phone and turning it off to prevent callbacks.

TWENTY-EIGHT

DI Hudson's number was programmed into the mobile. If Shelley couldn't get through to him there were always the emergency services.

Oh God oh God oh God. Shelley had to reach someone for help, someone who would come with the urgency that was desperately needed. The trouble was it was almost time for Julie to come to bed. Eunice would be wandering around solidly after that, getting the other kids sorted, and when the final quiet descended on the household around eight o'clock this evening it would be far too risky to make the call for fear of her voice being overheard.

When Eunice brought Julie in, already half asleep, Shelley pretended she was out for the count. But she gave Eunice ten minutes, waited till Julie stopped fidgeting and then took the child into bed with her, unable, now, to tolerate the few feet of separation. Shelley had never known and never imagined that she would experience this level of fear.

The sounds of the boys being put to bed came to her through the walls. Now and then Eunice's voice broke into the proceedings, always calm, always firm. Shelley shuddered at the sound and dreaded to think how many others like her must have watched and listened and admired Eunice's amazing way with kids. Eunice, who at this very moment was bathing her kids, tucking them in and reading them stories before finishing off with a blessing and a bristly kiss.

Jesus Christ. *How safe were her little ones in the care of this woman?*

Were Edward and Oliver up to their necks in it?

Were they part of this ugly set-up?

When Shelley began to talk to Edward about Eunice's strange reluctance to admit to her friendship with Iris, he had pressed a kiss on her lips and stopped her. Suddenly this, her greatest worry, had been soothed with sweet endearments and after that there had been no chance to confide in him a second time.

Had he deliberately made love to her in order to shut her mouth? Or had it been more the case that, if he had given any thought to the matter, he would have seen it as quite unimportant compared to the closeness of his lover? Most likely, had Edward considered the facts in that commonsense way of his, he would have pronounced his mother peculiar, unable to fathom out sometimes, and left it in the air like that. He wasn't the sort of person to go around looking for sinister motives.

Was Shelley?

Could she trust Edward now?

Was that a risk she dared take?

Hell. Her children's lives might depend on it. Either she was correct in her macabre calculations or she was about to make the biggest arsehole of herself in her life.

Doing nothing except lie awake listening felt like the hardest thing Shelley had ever done. She watched Julie smile in her sleep, she felt her quick baby heartbeat, she saw the happy dreams pass by her butterfly eyelids. At last there was silence from the boys' bedrooms and she imagined that she heard Eunice's footsteps retreating down the back stairs. But if Eunice suspected that Shelley had guessed the nature of her motherly role, she wouldn't be gone for long.

Nobody was a better mother than her, Eunice Bolton.

Unmarried mothers like Shelley created only damaged children. And worse, they bred like rabbits, reproducing their feral brats.

Joey was a good case in point.

The spawn of the devil.

Therefore, in Eunice's twisted mind it figured that the children must be rescued and the mothers dispatched.

Simple as that.

If the negligent authorities were not prepared to deal with these people then she, Eunice, would do the job for them. And the disturbing part of all this was that Eunice's basic but sinister logic was shared by a mass of the British people.

How could Shelley's suspicions be wrong? The fact that so many mothers had conveniently dropped from the picture after being involved

363

with the Boltons was statistically unacceptable. Shelley knew about Duffy and Dukes, and during Doreen Blennerhasset's visit she had learned of the fate of two other families. God knows how many more there might be in the Boltons' long history of fostering. OK, unmarried mothers could be feckless, harassed, depressed, unstable, as could any struggling parent, but few would just abandon their kids and make no future contact. The idea was obscene.

Weighing even heavier for Shelley was the knowledge that Eunice had known who she was, had actively volunteered to take the Tremaynes under her roof while harbouring an unresolved resentment of Iris.

Shelley's future did not look bright.

World-weary, she was no feeble flower dependent on a man for survival. She despised film heroines whose high heels tripped them up, whose screams rent the air, and who ventured into dark cellars at night even when the electric had blown and the stench of putrefaction clogged the nostrils. Shelley was no such drama queen, although her plan did remind her of videos taken out and turned off because of the preposterous plots.

Shelley's plot was simple. Somehow she must get out of this house and telephone for help. The window was too small and the drop too great and, to be honest, that did seem like overreaction. No, there was no alternative but to get down those stairs and out of the kitchen without being detected, knowing full well that if Eunice or John were even slightly edgy they would be keeping careful watch tonight. If that couple were really guilty of the nauseating crimes in Shelley's head, no way would they allow her to escape from here alive.

Shelley's only secret weapon was her precious mobile phone.

She managed to wait until four o'clock.

Although she was exhausted she had not been remotely tempted by sleep. Her nerves were tautened wires, her heart resembled an athlete's about to run an Olympic race. In her agitation she dared not smoke in case that might give Eunice a reason to come knocking and complaining. Instead she panted, in the way she had been taught when giving birth. She was all geared up for furious action but furious action was not what was required.

Shelley gagged with relief to find the kitchen in darkness. From this she could assume that no-one was out there lambing tonight. Fully dressed, she grabbed her jacket and a bunion-shaped pair of Eunice's boots from the porch.

If she had been less single-minded, Shelley might have noticed that the key to the powerful F100 Fiat tractor was missing from the hook on the wall.

An icy wind, which picked up straw, grain and sleet in its twister-type fury, hurled itself against her as she crossed the yard. Leaning into it, eyes screwed up against the freezing needles, she made for the barns and the fields beyond. She could not have checked for pursuit even if she had wanted to – every ounce of concentration was directed towards achieving her goal – but if she had been less intent she might have cast one backward glance and caught sight of a figure at an upstairs window, a squat figure in a candlewick dressing gown of dirty pink, watching her progress through the dark.

All Shelley knew was that if the Boltons were following there was still a chance she might raise the alarm in time. If she could just make that call and find a safe hiding place, she would have achieved her aim.

Muffled to her teeth, Eskimo-style, Shelley rounded the huge stone buildings where the howl of the gale was briefly overpowered by the shriek of tortured corrugated iron and the warning clank of unsecured metal. She staggered on, eager to put a decent distance between herself and the farmhouse, banging her gloved hands together and dislodging clumps of sleet as she did so. Eventually Shelley cowered beneath a low stone wall, removed her gloves with her chattering teeth and retrieved the phone from an inside pocket as if it was made of pure gold.

In the mayhem and the darkness it was hard to pick out the numbers. She was reassured by the small glow and the welcome message from Orange. She held her breath when the phone told her it was searching for a network. She lifted it higher, then checked again. She held it out to one side, then took a risk and stood up and held it above her head.

Still the agonizing message read: '*Searching for network.*'

She moved further up the bank, knowing as she did so that when she got through to Hudson he would be pushed to hear her cry for help. Her voice would be fighting overwhelming decibels. What sort of phones do these people have which function from mountaintops in the world's most desolate places? What make of phone, Shelley asked herself in a terrible mixture of rage and terror, functions in macabre cellars, caves and tunnels of death? Sod the films and the news reports and their bloody false messages. Dear God, if you're there, make this sodding thing work. Her tears of frustration were blown away and joined the flotsam and jetsam reeling with the wind.

No way could Shelley stop now.

She ventured further before giving up and changing direction. She dared to take to the road. She sheltered under a battered hedge and tried again. No change. She went to the end of the lane. She climbed a bank. She stood on a gate, clinging on for dear life in the teeth of the gale.

In this weather it was impossible to suss out the lie of the land. From her trips backwards and forwards by car Shelley knew there was one hotel half a mile away, closed for the winter. But maybe she could reach that hotel, break her way in and phone from there. Over the hill in the opposite direction there was a farm which Edward had mentioned several times. It seemed the Boltons swapped machinery and gave mutual assistance to these neighbours when needed. Dare she wake them at this hour of the night and risk their rejection once they knew who she was? Did they know that the mother of Joseph Tremayne was a guest so close to their home?

But did that matter in these circumstances?

So what if they set the dogs on her?

So what if they barred their doors or went for the nearest axe?

She'd be dead if she did nothing.

But there was a larger deterrent than that which made Shelley think twice before setting off down the road. Her kids were asleep in that house of horror not a hundred yards away. If, by any hellish chance, the Boltons realized that Shelley was missing, might they vent their anger on them as part of their ruthless vengeance campaign?

Nothing, after all, would hurt Shelley more. Against that appalling possibility her own death was unimportant.

Then again, her whirling brain reminded her, this was the day of Joey's visit. He would arrive with either a police escort or an official from Dudley Park, maybe both. Shelley, with her kids around her and with no need to give reasons that might be questioned, could insist on being taken off the farm. There was no law that could stop her doing that. Her children were not wards of court, nor were they on any at-risk register. The authorities had no rights over them.

Only slightly consoled – first she had somehow to get through the night – she retraced her way towards the courtyard and was passing the barn where, yesterday, she and Edward had made love, when she decided on one last attempt to contact the police.

The massive doors gaped open, but further inside the roaring settled down to the tolerable moan of a madwoman's lament. She climbed halfway up the stack, the route she and Edward had taken, and balanced on a solid overhanging bale. With her heart banging from fear and physical exertion, once again she attempted to dial. But whatever sodding buttons she pushed, whichever direction the mobile faced, that hopeless message remained the same.

'*Searching for network.*'

Oh Jesus, Jesus . . .

The roaring outside changed so subtly it was a while before she identified it as the engine of a tractor. Two tracks of light crossed the opening, and the growl of the engine revs picked up.

Please God, please God, make this be Edward.

Make this be Edward fetching hay for some unforeseen emergency.

But this was not Edward.

She ought to have known this sliver of hope was so far-fetched as to be ludicrous. Why would any of the Bolton men use a tractor if they needed just one bale of hay? And why would they need more at this time of night? She was still reasoning this out, the mobile with its feeble green light sitting uselessly in her hand, when the headlamp beams were directed full at her and through her initial blindness she saw that attached to the front of the massive tractor was a fork lift sporting two

369

lethal metal prongs, each one at least four foot long.

It was impossible to identify the driver, who appeared in the cab as a dark and malignant shadow. It was also impossible to mistake that driver's murderous intentions. All her suspicions turned into fact as she watched the orange metal monster begin its lethal advance.

Without the slightest hesitation the tractor, roaring powerfully, plunged forward for its first attack. With seconds to spare Shelley was able to swing herself between the two spikes which pierced the hay either side of her. The headlights were blinding as they retreated and the colossal machine was directed once again towards the skewering of its prey. The driver must know very well that however loud the tractor's engines the tumultuous wind outside the barn would smother the sound. Nobody in the farmhouse could possibly hear the deafening reverberations inside this cavernous barn.

For a second time the machine lurched towards her and once again Shelley side-stepped, but this time the spikes came closer and one almost caught in her hair. One more thrust and the menacing form behind the wheel would have his sights perfectly adjusted.

During the few seconds of the tractor's retreat Shelley began to climb. She climbed and clutched and cried out like a wild beast in the throes of death. If she hadn't come here with Edward she would have assumed that this wall of hay touched the domed barn ceiling and that there was no

370

escape to be had. She would have assumed that the bales were packed, as they were further down, tight like sardines with no spaces between them. The unknown driver must have relied on her ignorance before he began on this savage course.

So therefore it couldn't be Edward.

But there was no room in Shelley's brain for logic. She had to make the top of the stack before she was pierced, removed and buried all in the space of a couple of hours. She was almost out of the lethal reach when the third push grazed an ankle, which she removed in the nick of time. She continued to climb, deranged with terror, her mouth and her eyes now cluttered with chaff and her gloveless hands scratched so badly they bled. If she could just reach the top of this stack, crawl along the roof space and down to the other side of the barn where she knew there was a small door – *if, dear God, it would open.*

Sweat poured down her face, attracting more shreds of the dusty hay. Shelley's movements across the top were frenzied in this new darkness.

Had the tractor withdrawn?

What were the driver's plans now he realized his attack had failed? Would he be waiting for her in the dark as she clambered down the other side?

She didn't have much resistance left. She was a rat in a trap.

Suddenly Shelley's clawing hand caught hold of something solid. After her initial cry and recoil, she slowed and felt for the object again. It was a pitchfork – hardly surprising, and worth more to

Shelley at this perilous moment than a gun, which she would not have known how to load and fire.

This find convinced her to stay where she was at roof level, looking down on her proposed exit. From here she could see the small wooden door and it seemed that there was no hay stacked against it. With this weapon in her hand and a hay retreat behind her, nobody could touch her without suffering serious wounds. And in the mood she was in, she would have no remorse whatever gruesome wounds she inflicted. She would aim for the heart.

Slowly, so slowly, Shelley's breathing eased.

Her heart rate reduced from treble the average beats to double. She was resigned to the fact that she would have to remain on her perch until morning when the men began their early chores. In the light of day, in front of the children, the Boltons, however many of them were involved, were unlikely to make any further attempts on her life and if they, too, were bearing in mind Joey's escorted visit, they wouldn't want the children telling awkward tales.

But what did they imagine Shelley would do, faced with this opportunity for escape?

Were they resigned to letting her go, along with her suspicions?

Or did they plan to keep her some sort of prisoner all day tomorrow – perhaps making the excuse that she had already scarpered, like all the rest, unable to take the flak?

Just another feckless single mother, certainly

nobody worth precious police time or taxpayers' money to keep tabs on or to trace.

To keep her prisoner they must catch her first, so Shelley determined to stay hidden in the barn right up until the moment when Joey arrived with his escort. Only then would she come down and face her would-be killers.

Somebody else, not too far away, was also sleepless on this stormy night, and lying in a bed that felt almost as cold as Shelley's imperfect refuge. Martin Chandler, flat on his back, lay listening to the medicated sleep of his distraught wife. Matters had gone from bad to worse since his involvement in the Tremayne debacle. With hindsight he knew he should never have touched it. Always fragile and with neurotic leanings, Jessica was finding motherhood an almost impossible strain. In spite of his employing an expensive nanny, the baby's constant demands were threatening to wreck their short marriage.

One course of action, and only one, seemed to offer a hope of soothing her troubled mind. Martin must have the snip. Another child would kill her. Covered by BUPA, he was booked in tomorrow. He lay in bed fondling his penis in the same way he had done as a child. It lay limp and vulnerable beneath his fingers. Unresponsive, accusing, as if it knew . . .

When dawn arrived on Dartmoor in the cold quiet after the storm, when the farm cockerel so beloved of Jason gave his first awakening cries,

Shelley was still alert on her perch, hollow-eyed, scarecrow-tattered, her bleeding hands still clutching the pitch-fork to which she owed, if not her life, then undoubtedly what remained of her sanity.

TWENTY-NINE

Shelley spent what was left of the night praying to God to forgive her sins and her previous lack of belief and begging him to guard her children from whatever devilish fate might befall them.

She was so near to them, yet so far.

She guessed that John would be first to emerge from the farmhouse door. From her crouched position on top of the hay, still in total darkness, she couldn't see him but could hear his low whistle to the waiting dogs. She heard him checking the stock, freeing the chickens and the geese and preparing to feed the calves and milk the house cow.

All chores that had to be finished before breakfast.

His sons must be having a lie-in this morning. The time was half-past six. At least Shelley knew that John must be almost as exhausted as she was because he could only have had one hour's sleep. There was no doubt in her mind that John Bolton was the man who had attempted to kill her last night. His younger son, Oliver, was most unlikely to be involved and Edward would have known that she knew about the claustrophobic tunnel between the hay and the roof.

Once again her phone was useless. The weather was working against her. The slightest sound would be magnified on this still, frosty morning. The smallest noise would echo crisply across the yard from building to building and at any time, Shelley knew, Eunice herself might venture out.

After so long in her cramped position Shelley was stiff, aching all over and frozen through to the bone. Fear combined with the cold to freeze her muscles into tortured ropes; these parts of her body felt like fragments separate from her and totally out of her own control. All she could do to bring back some life was to use what energy she had to massage furiously the bits she could reach, praying that this numbness would leave her when she most needed her strength and courage.

Black memories of last night's ordeal came with harrowing regularity and turned her stomach to jelly. She had come so close to a hideous death she found it hard to blot out the image of her body impaled and writhing helplessly on that wickedly sharp spike. Unless she had been lucky and the prong had pierced her heart, she would have taken some time to die.

So they had heard her leaving the house.

They must have been lying in wait.

They must have watched her every movement and only given up when they realized she was not coming out of her hiding place – to reach her in there would have required at least two massively strong and agile people. Eunice was certainly strong, but the idea of her climbing that stack with her humpty back and her bad feet was too far-fetched to believe. Age, apart from her other impediments, would have worked against her.

The Bolton sons were the next to emerge. Shelley heard their voices and because of their bland conversation she knew that her disappearance had not yet been announced. It was agonizing for her to know that Edward was so close but she was not trusting enough to throw herself on his mercy. Her main concern was not being believed, was being labelled as paranoid, the stress of her situation having finally taken its toll. Of only secondary importance was the slight chance that he might be involved. She would have been prepared to risk that – that scenario was so unlikely – but the first concern took precedence.

She could not afford one mistake.

From the farmhouse wafted the smell of frying bacon and mushrooms. It did not even make Shelley's stomach churn. Hunger and thirst played no part in her bodily requirements now. Life and death was all that concerned her. She wished her kids would come out. She longed to see them, to know they were safe.

When the men disappeared for breakfast Shelley risked one more try on her mobile. She had already guessed the result. She was right. It was obvious that from here there was no signal. Her bedroom in the farmhouse roof was higher and less obstructed. *'Searching for network.'* The message mocked her but at least this time it was what she'd expected.

It was just gone nine o'clock, the men were outside and about their work when the collies began to bark. This was the moment Shelley had been waiting for. What would she do if the visitor was a stranger – the man from MAFF or the vet or a salesman? No, she'd already decided she wouldn't risk involving a stranger who would be so taken aback by the extraordinary tale she had to tell that accusations of madness would be bound to follow. She didn't intend to make this easier than it need be for John and Eunice Bolton. She must stick to her original decision and not be forced into action just for the sake of it.

But it wasn't a stranger – *it was Joey*.

The kids came flooding out of the house and surrounded the car with their calls and cheers. As she clambered down the stack, willing her body to obey her commands, Shelley recognized the voice of one of Joey's personal officers, the one she had met on her first visit to Dudley Park, the sporty, tracksuited Dominic Brownlow. But it wasn't until she opened the door, having pressed her whole body against it until it creaked reluctantly open, that she saw to her dismay that the driver of the car was Juliet Hollis, the hard-faced WPC who took no trouble to disguise her disgust for Shelley and her brood.

Julie began to cry.

Otherwise Shelley's appearance caused instant silence as her audience took in her wild hair, her hay-strewn clothes, her smudged face, her torn hands, but worse than this was her anguished expression. The sunlight was almost blinding. She tried to stand upright but could not. But before the Boltons could stop her she rushed towards a perplexed Dominic Brownlow, grabbed him and shouted desperately, '*I need to talk to you, Dominic – RIGHT NOW.*'

Eunice stepped forward.

She took Dominic's arm in a motherly fashion. 'We don't know what to do,' she confided so that everyone could hear. 'The poor thing's been missing all night, we've been out of our minds. Look at the state this woman is in, and the social services expect us, at our age, to cope with this kind of hassle, as if her children aren't enough . . .'

Joey, oblivious, rushed to his mother and flung himself upon her.

Edward turned on Eunice. '*What's this? She's been missing all night?* I never knew. Why didn't you tell me?'

'There's quite a lot we chose not to tell you,' said Eunice cunningly. 'But now, I suppose, you will have to know.'

Edward's puzzlement was almost amusing. '*Know what?*'

'You will have to know the level of paranoia which John and I have been trying to deal with, and which involves ludicrous accusations against your father and me. According to Shelley we're out to kill her . . .'

'*What?*' Edward stepped back, astounded.

'*You can't mean that?* Shelley, this isn't true?'

Eunice intervened. 'Shelley's psychosis is so bad it forced her to run from the house in the middle of the night while we were all asleep, and hide away in the barn. You can see what sort of state she is in – Edward, open your eyes.'

'Don't listen, Edward,' Shelley begged. '*For God's sake, please, don't listen.*'

'*But is it true?*' he was forced to ask her. 'You really believe that Mother and Father want to kill you? Is it?'

'The shooting was no mistake,' Shelley pleaded 'Please think, Edward, don't just take her word. If you hadn't turned up he would have tried again . . .'

'But why would Father want to do something like that?' Edward shook his head in total disbelief 'And what would Mother have to do with it?'

Half of Shelley clung to Joey, she had missed her son so much, and the other half fought to defend herself from an accusation she'd guessed they would use. After her son's initial joy at being reunited with his family, he was now tuned in to the turmoil that was raging above his small dark head. His solemn eyes followed each speaker. He gripped his mother's hand more tightly.

Was this all to do with him?

Was it his fault Mum looked like she did and they were telling her she was mad? Mum was frightened; nobody believed her, a situation Joey could well relate to just now. He couldn't bear to see so many people surrounding her, accusing her being unkind to her . . .

While Dominic Brownlow stayed embarrassed and silent, WPC Hollis added her opinion. 'The social services had no right at all to dump this troublemaker on you,' she said. 'Why should someone like her be cosseted and spoilt up here when so many struggling mums who have managed not to produce a killer in the family have no help, nobody to turn to, work all hours on the minimum wage and go without food themselves so their kiddies can be fed? It's disgusting. It's right out of order.' She sniffed.

'Edward,' Shelley cried. '*Who are you going to believe?* You can't make love to me one minute and the next call me insane and a liar. Have I ever struck you as mad? Have I ever said or done anything—?'

'She is so manipulative,' put in Eunice.

'Oh, they can be,' said Hollis while Edward spun round confused, in a daze.

In a frenzy now Shelley tried to straighten her hair, to pluck the hay from her clothing, to rub her face clean and to adopt a super-sane tone and expression.

'All I am asking,' she said with feigned composure, 'is that my children and I be removed from this place and taken somewhere else right away.'

'Hey, wait just a minute, madam,' said Hollis contemptuously. 'Who d'you think you are to give orders?'

'I want to telephone DI Hudson,' Shelley demanded calmly.

'I don't think so somehow,' said Hollis.

'Are you telling me that you can prevent m from making a private phone call to anyone choose?' asked Shelley, shocked.

'In the state you are in at the moment, yes Hollis replied. 'I shouldn't think anyone in the right mind would welcome a phone call fro you.'

These highly charged exchanges went over th children's heads. Julie had stopped crying and wa now contentedly chewing one of the straps o Eunice's butcher's apron, Kez, Saul and Jaso were feeding their leftover toast to the ducks an Casey had found a puddle in which he was stamp ing hard.

Only Joey still clung, only too well aware of h mother's distress.

Through his childish eyes he saw Edward as th main cause for concern. His mother was needin this man's support and he was refusing to give i He was supposed to be her friend. He was lettin her down, making her cry. Before Shelley kne what was happening he had launched himse from her grasp, kicked Edward fiercely on th shin and was over the courtyard wall like monkey and away.

Dominic Brownlow set off in pursuit.

'*Bloody hell,*' yelled Juliet Hollis.

'Little bugger,' said Eunice.

'Why don't you just leave him?' said Edward 'He'll be back. Poor kid.'

Shelley shouted, '*Joey, don't. Joey, come back Joey, it's OK.*'

The agitated group in the courtyard watche

382

the chase like followers watch hounds. At one point Brownlow appeared to be gaining, but Joey was faster on the slopes, zigzagging like a hunted deer. He was eleven years old and fit and ready to die for his freedom.

'I'll have to phone for assistance,' said Hollis, the wind blown from her superior sails.

'Surely that won't be necessary,' said Eunice with concern, and Shelley remembered how she had refused police protection on the farm when they had feared that the press or an angry public might find them.

'I have to,' said Hollis. 'This is dreadful. All hell is going to break loose here if that little sod gets away.'

Half of Shelley so badly wanted Joey to find his freedom. The other half, the sensible half, knew this was no answer. Her child would be hunted down; the news would somehow get out and whatever happened to Joey now would be worse because of this stupid behaviour. She couldn't bring herself even to look at Eunice and John – they had won as she had feared they would, and after this little drama was over she would still be faced with the urgent problem of getting herself and her kids off this farm. She was now determined to walk, if necessary.

If she wasn't prevented.

Edward moved towards her and put a comforting arm round her neck. 'Talk to me, Shelley,' he said.

She pushed him away in despair.

* * *

They sat, waiting, round the farmhouse table Nobody spoke; nobody dared.

The tension was at fever pitch.

The kids played round them on the floor and Hollis continued to receive scrambled messages on her walkie-talkie.

After two hours, when Dominic returned without Joey, breathless and beetroot-faced, Hollis said, 'They're bringing in the tracker dogs.'

John stayed quiet and glowering. Since this morning Eunice had spoken for them both. John had remained characteristically quiet but Shelley sensed the malignant force behind those steel-grey eyes; the tendons of his stubbly neck, taut as wires, were a giveaway. She tried desperately to avoid him as fear slithered down to the ends of her nerves. How he must be cursing the fact that he had failed in his murderous task last night. With Shelley dead, 'gone missing', the first thing the Boltons would have done was to cancel Joey's visit. All this would have been avoided.

Another wasted hour went past before the dog van arrived with two handlers and two sleek German shepherds.

They didn't waste any time.

They were given the coat that Joey had worn and pointed by Dominic in the right direction. The Bolton men had left the kitchen to catch up on the farm work. Shelley felt Edward's hand on her shoulder as he crossed the room towards the door. She shrugged him off angrily. In her time of desperate need he had failed her.

* * *

It was less than five minutes later that they heard the sound of dogs on the trail. Shelley paled – had he doubled back? She leaped up from the table and rushed outside to be with him. From deep barking to troubled howling and back to hysterical puppy-style yelps, the dogs would not be budged from their scrabblings on the edge of a mossy green peat bog a short distance up the incline of the field nearest the farmhouse. The handlers struggled to urge them on; they had obviously been diverted and should know better than to lapse into this foolish pack behaviour.

Shelley took one look at the bog, where poisonous, oily-black water squelched between hummocks of grass. She staggered. '*Oh no, Joey, oh no . . .*'

Edward was at her side in an instant, unsure whether to speak or touch her. He finally decided just to stay as close as he could.

'Could you take Ms Tremayne away, sir,' shouted one of the handlers.

'*Why?*' screamed Shelley. '*Why?*'

'Please come away,' pleaded Edward, gently taking her arm.

'*Why?*' she screamed at him, tormented now and half mad with grief.

'Just in case.'

She didn't need to ask any more. Joey, frightened, had doubled back, perhaps wanting his mother. *Dear God.* A troubled little boy afraid of the dark had ended his life in a stinking mire, dragged to the surface by a couple of dogs . . .

John Bolton's face as he watched this unfolding

tragedy was a mixture of horror and disbelief Eunice stood silent and humped beside him Oliver was inside with the kids. Shelley, all hope gone, allowed herself to be led away. She didn' care who was with her, she wouldn't have noticed anyway.

Some chemical process in the peat had slowed down the rate of decay and the first two bodies the policemen uncovered were nowhere near as putrefied as their age would otherwise have meant.

Before dusk a task force arrived equipped with spades, cameras and ropes and including a pathologist, a cameraman and a forensic expert The bodies of two young women were followed by one male before one more female was brought out to join them, laid on a gurney and loaded into an unmarked van.

Tomorrow draining equipment would arrive together with a JCB and heavy lifting gear. But for tonight the scene was roped off.

The search for Joey was called off temporarily 'We would have found him by now, if he'd been in there,' Shelley was told by a well-meaning copper. 'He would have been somewhere near the top, floating, what with his small size and that.'

Brief statements were taken before Eunice and John Bolton, with pride on their faces, were charged with the murder of persons as yet unknown and immediately removed from the premises.

No messing.

THIRTY

And so began what was to be the longest night of Shelley's life.

While Edward and Oliver, who knew this land like the backs of their hands, searched the moor with torches calling Joey's name, Shelley stayed in the farmhouse accompanied by a varied assortment of police and their advisers.

Heads would roll after this appalling fiasco.

Questions would be asked in the House.

A public inquiry would be called for.

Resignations would fill the air and flutter down like confetti.

Promising careers would bite the dust.

Not only had Joey's minders lost the most notorious child-killer of the decade, having allowed him what would be a much-criticized day of freedom, but the county's caring services had been sending a procession of needy children and their mothers into the hands of a couple with the moral stability of the Wests. Who knew how many bodies would be hauled up out of that bog by the time they had drained it and raked it?

The courtyard was blazing with light. A watch

was kept over the grave site, silent and macabre. Security guards prowled round the perimeter of the farmyard keeping an eye out for Joey.

There was no way these dramatic events could be concealed. Tomorrow Eunice and John would appear in court. It hadn't helped Edward or Oliver, both in a state of denial and shock, to be told by DI William Boyce that their parents were not only confessing to their crimes but were boasting about the services they had performed in the name of humanity.

Incredulous, their sons could not understand how Eunice and John had committed these crimes under their very noses, or, more worryingly, how they had posed for so long as perfect parents. But the reasons for this were simple. Both boys had been too young to know of the Boltons' earlier enterprises and they had been away at college when the mothers of Duffy and Dukes disappeared, so the only murder they could have detected would have been Shelley's.

Edward would always blame himself for his narrow-minded stupidity. Why hadn't he believed Shelley? Why hadn't he given her his protection? He was overcome with shame – but then it would never have been easy to accept that the two people he admired and trusted most in life had always had a darker, hidden side to their natures.

But Shelley had no space in her heart for sympathy now. Joey's safety was paramount. She dealt with the children, gave them supper, then bed, while fending off their nagging questions

388

'Where's Joey gone?' and 'When will Joey come back?'

When she came downstairs DI Boyce was there to explain to her why, after so many years of abstinence, the Boltons had once again reverted to their murderous habits.

'In the same year as your mother left Kilmar Hill, something terrible happened to Eunice,' he began, making good use of the constant supply of tea or coffee in the warm, busy kitchen. 'Something so traumatic it was to colour the rest of her life. Eunice was raped,' said Boyce gravely, 'in the local churchyard by a gang of fourteen-year-old youths. Because of the church's intolerant attitude towards Iris's pregnancy and the humiliating consequences for Eunice, she didn't dare tell anyone, or go for medical help. Nobody in that rigid community would begin to understand; they would blame her, call her a slut, accuse her of asking for it. The yobs would get away scot-free and Eunice would be hauled before that evil congregation and punished.'

Boyce told his astonished listener of the extraordinarily casual way in which John had related all this to him, believing these ordeals to be quite enough to exonerate Eunice from blame for any future behaviour.

'Eunice and John lost their first child before he was born,' Boyce explained. 'The doctors told her this was because of the damage done during the rape. If she'd gone for help at the time, apparently, they would have been able to sort her out. She and John could have no more children.

Eunice was infertile.' DI Boyce gave Shelley a sympathetic smile. 'Eunice blamed Iris,' he told her. 'She blamed Iris for getting pregnant and bringing all this shit down on her.'

The rest was easy to follow. 'And then she heard our name from Doreen,' Shelley was able to continue. 'I was one of those useless mothers who create the monsters who rape and kill. Not only that, but I was Iris's daughter.' Shelley's eyes filled. She rolled them towards the ceiling. 'Jesus Christ, no wonder she jumped at the chance. My death would have been her final revenge.'

Boyce shrugged. 'The Boltons saw it as their sacred mission to destroy the type of inadequate parent who might produce the kind of scum who raped Eunice in the churchyard all those years ago. They must eliminate the parents while at the same time saving the innocent children.

'Even now' – Boyce's smile was a wry one – 'incredibly they refuse to accept the fact that they have done anything wrong. The really terrible question now is how many poor sods are swimming around in that damn bog?'

Shelley shuddered.

It could so easily have been her.

No wonder Eunice and John saw her as inadequate. Putting Joey aside for a moment, compared to Eunice's mothering skills Shelley was a non-starter. The change in the behaviour of her five kids since they came to live with the Boltons was quite remarkable. They were happier, healthier, livelier. Not once had they whined about missing the telly or the huge assortment of toys they had been forced to leave behind at Eastwood.

So what was Shelley doing so wrong?

Well. Eunice had bags of patience. Eunice never seemed to tire. Eunice was firm but fair. Eunice allowed the kids far more freedom than Shelley would ever have done. But then Eunice was fighting a holy war. She'd acquired the skills of a lifetime of mothering, while Shelley had only just begun. Lob all this together with idyllic childhood conditions, no yobs hanging round in the street outside vandalizing and flogging dope, no pressures from TV, videos or advertising, no long hours of boredom with nothing to do; put this alongside a firm set of values and a safe family unit, and even Shelley could see that Eunice was bound to be ahead in the race.

It was harder being a mother now.

Especially a mother whose son was still missing.

Opinions differed over where Joey was.

He could have reached the road by now and hitched a lift to anywhere. Even if this was the case the chances of catching him were high. Once an enraged public discovered that the focus of all their venom had shoved two fingers up in their faces and scarpered, every canal bank and woodshed, every service station toilet, every abandoned car, every allotment would be scoured by a thousand eyes in the rush to recapture the bastard.

There was the distinct possibility that after the news came out tomorrow lynch mobs would swarm over the moor armed with sticks and stones and worse in case Joey was hiding there.

The chance that he could have been taken in by a sympathetic member of the public was no worthy of a moment's thought. There was no house in the land where Joseph Tremayne would have been made welcome.

Readying themselves for a dawn start, the police searchers had maps laid out and sectioned off on the farmhouse table. So urgent was this high-profile exercise that already official Dartmoor wardens and guides had been put on the alert for tomorrow's huge hunt.

And all this for one frightened child.

Shelley watched these frenzied preparations with a heart that dragged with the pain of it.

Joey was terrified of the dark.

He had gone off without his coat; he'd be frozen.

He wasn't a country boy, he was born and bred in the streets of the city. How awesome and bleak Dartmoor would be, especially Dartmoor at night with the red eyes of animals coming out of the dark and the hidden bogs and the rearing shadows of the moor's giant boulders . . .

She longed to hold him and keep him warm.

She yearned to cradle his head in her lap. But above all she ached for the joy of being able to tell him, 'It's all over, Joey, you're coming home now. This was just a bad dream. There is no dead baby. No broken family. You're safe. You are loved. You are special.'

Edward and Oliver returned empty-handed.

'You should sleep,' Edward told Shelley.

She merely looked up at him with blank eyes. It was early, much too early.

'You should eat,' he tried again, eager to make up somehow for his failure to protect her, his massive betrayal. His concern was so apparent she couldn't help but be moved by his need to help her. 'You shouldn't be here' – he angled his head – 'with all this going on around you. Won't you come and sit by the fire for a while?'

'I can't let go,' she said, her voice broken. 'I have to know the instant anything happens.'

She allowed him to stroke her hands. He tried in vain to relax her tight fists; he massaged her shoulders, which were knotted like ropes. If only she and Edward could have met under different conditions. What future did they have now? He with his parents facing hideous charges of serial killings which would rock the nation, she with her son despised by the world; both lepers now, in their own ways. Unclean. Diseased. Contaminated by evil.

And yet their worlds were miles apart.

'I know you probably can't even hear what I'm saying to you,' said Edward softly, ignoring the busy activity of those around him. 'You're so far away. But I want you to know, whatever happens after this, I would like you and the children to stay here with me until you're ready to make other plans. No matter how much you might loathe this place, it could be a home.' He faltered. 'We could make it safe. We could care for the children. Of course we could never forget what happened and it might be that you can never forgive me ... It might be that you'll want to leave here the instant Joey is found?'

She couldn't answer. She was hearing this, but all her thoughts were of Joey.

'Whatever decision you make, I want you to know I'll support you and help you and be around if you need me ...'

The shout of 'Fire!' first came from the copper stationed outside the farmhouse door.

Instantly the small crowd in the kitchen jumped from lethargy to alert.

The door was flung open and from the darkness beyond the courtyard came glimmers of torchlight as those on the fringes rushed towards the source of the alarm. Long wisps of smoke were snaking out from the double doors through which only last night Shelley had awaited the approach of the deadly tractor.

Immediately help was summoned. The fire brigade was on its way but it had to come from Plymouth and would take some time to arrive.

Shelley didn't need Edward to tell her, as he was busily telling the officer in charge, that this massive barn was packed tight with hay and any conflagration there would mean a fire on a frightening scale. It was essential to get the thing damped down. The temperature in the midst of those bales was probably high anyway – not as hot as when the hay was first packed down but hot enough to cause serious problems.

Edward rigged up hoses.

Half a dozen coppers dragged them into place and directed them as high up the stack as they would reach. But this was a private water supply; it came from a natural spring, sufficient for the daily requirements of a farm – causing anxiety only in drought conditions – but faced with this sudden demand the hoses would not work for long.

'Shall I get the kids up?'

'Not yet,' shouted Boyce as he wrestled with a broken bucket. 'But stick around here, don't leave the house.'

Thank God Shelley had spent last night without a lighter in her pocket or a packet of fags at hand. There was no doubt in her mind that, once she had reached her hiding place, once she sensed the chase was over, she would have passed the time puffing fag after fag in an effort to find some kind of calm. She would have blamed herself for this. You were always reading about cigarettes that burned slowly but surely . . . Fags were the cause of most household fires. She would have hated to be the reason for Edward's losing all this precious feed.

For once she was an innocent party.

And Shelley thanked God for that.

It was turmoil out there. So far, however, there was no sign of flames, just the same relentless trails of black smoke which seemed to be getting no worse.

Shouts.

Crashes.

Curses.

The movement of animals as Edward fought to save his stock. Some – pigs and goats – he let loose in the fields along with the lambs and the sheep. The bullocks, moaning loudly and releasing streams of dung as they went, were herded noisily to safety. Then they began on the heavy machinery, parking it a good distance away in case the fire raged out of control.

Shelley watched nervously from the window.

Fire – baby – Joey . . .

The shocking association of thoughts which exploded so suddenly in her head knocked all the breath out of her body. Could Joey have doubled back here without anyone seeing him? He was cunning enough, slick enough, and one look at the brooding moor might have made up his mind for him pretty damn quickly.

Could Joey have even come to the house in an effort to find her and his brothers and sister? There was only one place where he could have got in without being discovered and that was the children's playbarn with its unlocked stable door. Could he be in there now – having diverted the cops with the fire?

Carefully, so no-one would notice, Shelley slipped from the room and along the old flagged corridor. The cold increased the further she went. This part of the house was not well insulated and half the windows were badly fitted; there were patched-up holes in the ceilings, and cobwebs. This was her children's favourite place. She arrived at the unlit playbarn and yes, the stable doors hung open but this was quite normal. Inside, once her eyes had adjusted, she could make out boxes of Lego bricks, a home-made wooden cooker laden with lurid plastic pans, a tool bench equipped with hammers and screwdrivers and, in the corner, well protected, the laundry basket full of the Bolton kids' rejects.

She held her breath before she whispered into the silence, 'Joey?'

Heart hammering hard, she went further into the room, eyes watchful and expectant. 'Joey, are you here? It's OK, love, I'm on my own. You're quite safe.'

Nothing.

The stench of smoke from the open door caused her eyes to smart and water. She wiped them and continued, hope driving her on. He must be here somewhere, he must be . . .

She bumped into the laundry basket and cursed her clumsiness. She caught hold of the lid to move it back and only slowly realized that something that used to be on the top was missing.

The kids had most probably dragged it out and stuffed it in the bottom when they'd finished. But Shelley couldn't leave it alone. In a frenzy now, she tipped up the basket so that boxed metal toys, clockwork cars, an ancient knitted golliwog and a broken Jack-in-the-box were only part of the tumbling flood that landed on the flagstones.

Wally Wolf was missing.

She fought for breath. She called once more, 'Joey? Joey?'

But she knew it was no use. She backed out of

the room and ran screaming towards the kitchen and out into the courtyard ...

'*He's in there.*' But no sound came.

She found Edward and clawed at his back. 'He's in there, God help him, he's in the barn, he's got Wally Wolf...'

She tore round the groups of fire-fighters, beating at their chests, tugging at their arms ... The brigade had still not arrived but Edward was already running, heading straight into the belching smoke which was mixed with bursts of pure scarlet flame.

Nobody could have stopped him. He was strong, he was determined and he had vowed never in his life to let Shelley down again. There was nothing anybody could do but stand at the entrance to the cavernous place with faces covered against the smoke. The hoses were dry now, the water all run out.

'He's had it,' shouted one of the coppers. 'The arsehole.'

'He'll fry in there,' another agreed.

'Bugger, I've never seen nothing like this.'

But WPC Hollis was crying.

The fire's bellow and ferocious roar defeated all other sound. The flames fought like the limbs of a giant, imprisoned beast. They forced their way through the stone in the walls, they licked up from under the very foundations, they began to claw at the sky and coloured the whole world blood red.

Shelley stood at the farmhouse door. There were

no tears for a moment like this. She only moved, not hurriedly, when Edward came out of the swirling smoke like a contestant from the talent show *Stars in Their Eyes*.

He carried the limp young child as easily as he carried his lambs.

His lambs had no future, not a future with hope, and nor had Shelley's son.

He never had.

Edward stopped in the farmhouse doorway, his small burden light in his arms.

Still in a place that lay way beyond tears, Shelley bent her head and placed a kiss on the little sod's filthy face. She tried to straighten him out. Look at the state of his jeans, she thought. He must have worn those socks for a week; you'd think someone would have made him change them. Trust Joey to end up mucky like this. She pulled at the thin grey tuft of fur that stuck out from under his sweatshirt.

Wally Wolf.

He had found him.

Dear God, oh God, thank you. Joey had not died alone.

'Let's all go home,' said Edward gently. And she followed her little boy into the farmhouse.

THE END

A SELECTED LIST OF CRIME NOVELS
AVAILABLE FROM CORGI BOOKS

14221 2	WYCLIFFE AND THE DUNES MYSTERY	*W.J. Burley*	£4.99
14117 8	WYCLIFFE AND HOW TO KILL A CAT	*W.J. Burley*	£4.99
14115 1	WYCLIFFE AND THE GUILT EDGED ALIBI	*W.J. Burley*	£5.99
14661 7	WYCLIFFE AND THE REDHEAD	*W.J. Burley*	£4.99
14174 7	PERFECTLY PURE AND GOOD	*Frances Fyfield*	£5.99
14512 2	WITHOUT CONSENT	*Frances Fyfield*	£5.99
14525 4	BLIND DATE	*Frances Fyfield*	£5.99
14526 2	STARING AT THE LIGHT	*Frances Fyfield*	£5.99
14225 5	BEYOND RECALL	*Robert Goddard*	£6.99
14597 1	CAUGHT IN THE LIGHT	*Robert Goddard*	£6.99
14601 3	SET IN STONE	*Robert Goddard*	£5.99
14602 1	SEA CHANGE	*Robert Goddard*	£5.99
14623 4	THE RETURN	*Andrea Hart*	£5.99
14985 3	OUTSIDE THE RULES	*Dylan Jones*	£5.99
14986 1	UNTO THE WICKED	*Dylan Jones*	£5.99
14584 X	THE COLD CALLING	*Will Kingdom*	£5.99
14585 8	MEAN SPIRIT	*Will Kingdom*	£5.99
15038 X	THE SLEEPER	*Gillian White*	£5.99
15039 8	UNHALLOWED GROUND	*Gillian White*	£5.99
15040 1	VEIL OF DARKNESS	*Gillian White*	£5.99
15037 1	THE WITCH'S CRADLE	*Gillian White*	£5.99
14766 4	NIGHT VISITOR	*Gillian White*	£5.99
14555 6	A TOUCH OF FROST	*R.D. Wingfield*	£6.99
13981 5	FROST AT CHRISTMAS	*R.D. Wingfield*	£6.99
14558 0	NIGHT FROST	*R.D. Wingfield*	£6.99
14409 6	HARD FROST	*R.D. Wingfield*	£6.99
14778 8	WINTER FROST	*R.D. Wingfield*	£6.99